REJUVENATION

"Sleep," she said aloud. "Sleep."

"Asleep on the sleeping river," the voice was saying. "And above the river, in the pale sky, there are huge white clouds. And as you look at them, you begin to float up towards them. Yes, you begin to float up towards them, and the river now is a river in the air, an invisible river that carries you on, carries you up, higher and higher . . .

"Out of the hot plain," the voice went on, "effortlessly into the freshness of the mountains . . . How fresh the air feels as you breathe it. Fresh, pure, charged with life!"

He breathed deeply and the new life flowed into him.

Will Farnaby, dying of the disease called Civilization, returns to life in paradise . . . Pala—**ISLAND** by Aldous Huxley.

"A mirror for modern man . . . Should be read and reread."

—**Saturday Review**

ISLAND

ALDOUS HUXLEY

A PERENNIAL CLASSIC
Harper & Row, Publishers
New York, Evanston,
San Francisco, London

ISLAND

This book was originally published in hardcover by Harper & Row, Publishers in 1962.

First PERENNIAL CLASSIC edition published 1972.

STANDARD BOOK NUMBER: 06-0831014

83 84 20 19 18 17 16 15 14

To

Laura

In framing an ideal we may assume what we wish, but should avoid impossibilities.

ARISTOTLE

i

"ATTENTION," A VOICE BEGAN TO CALL, AND IT WAS AS though an oboe had suddenly become articulate. "Attention," it repeated in the same high, nasal monotone. "Attention."

Lying there like a corpse in the dead leaves, his hair matted, his face grotesquely smudged and bruised, his clothes in rags and muddy, Will Farnaby awoke with a start. Molly had called him. Time to get up. Time to get dressed. Mustn't be late at the office.

"Thank you, darling," he said and sat up. A sharp pain stabbed at his right knee and there were other kinds of pain in his back, his arms, his forehead.

"Attention," the voice insisted without the slightest change of tone. Leaning on one elbow, Will looked about him and saw with bewilderment, not the gray wallpaper and yellow curtains of his London bedroom, but a glade among trees and the long shadows and slanting lights of early morning in a forest.

"Attention"?

Why did she say, "Attention"?

"Attention. Attention," the voice insisted—how strangely, how senselessly!

"Molly?" he questioned. "Molly?"

The name seemed to open a window inside his head. Suddenly, with that horribly familiar sense of guilt at the pit of the stomach, he smelt formaldehyde, he saw the small brisk nurse hurrying ahead of him along the green corridor, heard the dry creaking of her starched clothes. "Number fifty-five," she was saying, and then halted, opened a white door. He entered and there, on a high white bed, was Molly. Molly with bandages covering half her face and the mouth hanging cavernously open. "Molly," he had called, "Molly . . ." His voice had broken, and he was crying, was imploring now, "My darling!" There was no answer. Through the gaping mouth the quick shallow breaths came noisily, again, again. "My darling, my darling . . ." And then suddenly the hand he was holding came to life for a moment. Then was still again.

"It's me," he said, "it's Will."

Once more the fingers stirred. Slowly, with what was evidently an enormous effort, they closed themselves over his own, pressed them for a moment and then relaxed again into lifelessness.

"Attention," called the inhuman voice. "Attention."

It had been an accident, he hastened to assure himself. The road was wet, the car had skidded across the white line. It was one of those things that happen all the time. The papers are full of them; he had reported them by the dozen. "Mother and three children killed in head-on crash . . ." But that was beside the point. The point was that, when she asked him if it was really the end, he had said yes; the point was that less than an hour after she had walked out from that last shameful interview into the rain, Molly was in the ambulance, dying.

He hadn't looked at her as she turned to go, hadn't dared to look at her. Another glimpse of that pale suffering face might have been too much for him. She had risen from her chair and was moving slowly across the room, moving slowly out of his life. Shouldn't he call her back, ask her forgiveness, tell her that he still loved her? Had he ever loved her?

For the hundredth time the articulate oboe called him to attention.

Yes, had he ever really loved her?

"Good-bye, Will," came her remembered whisper as she turned back on the threshold. And then it was *she* who had said it—in a whisper, from the depths of her heart. "I still love you, Will—in spite of everything."

A moment later the door of the flat closed behind her almost without a sound. The little dry click of the latch, and she was gone.

He had jumped up, had run to the front door and opened it, had listened to the retreating footsteps on the stairs. Like a ghost at cockcrow, a faint familiar perfume lingered vanishingly on the air. He closed the door again, walked into his gray-and-yellow bedroom and looked out the widow. A few seconds passed, then he saw her crossing the pavement and getting into the car. He heard the shrill grinding of the starter, once, twice, and after that the drumming of the motor. Should he open the window? "Wait, Molly, wait," he heard himself shouting in imagination. The window remained unopened; the car began to move, turned the corner and the street was empty. It was too late. Too late, thank God! said a gross derisive voice. Yes, thank God! And yet the guilt was there at the pit of his stomach. The guilt, the gnawing of his remorse—but through the remorse he could feel a horrible rejoicing. Somebody low and lewd and brutal, somebody alien and odious who was yet himself was gleefully thinking that now there was nothing to prevent him from having what he wanted. And what he wanted was a different perfume, was the warmth and resilience of a younger body. "Attention," said the oboe. Yes, attention. Attention to Babs's musky bedroom, with its strawberry-pink alcove and the two windows that looked onto the Charing Cross Road and were looked into, all night long, by the winking glare of the big sky sign for Porter's Gin on the opposite side of the street. Gin in royal crimson—and for ten seconds the alcove was the Sacred Heart, for ten miraculous seconds the flushed face so close to his own glowed like a seraph's, transfigured as though by an inner fire of love. Then came the yet profounder transfiguration of darkness. One, two, three, four . . . Ah God, make it go on forever! But punctually at the count of ten the electric clock would turn on another revelation—but of death, of the Essential Horror; for the lights, this time, were green, and for ten hideous seconds Babs's rosy alcove became a womb of mud and, on the bed, Babs herself was corpse-colored, a cadaver galvanized into posthumous epilepsy. When Porter's Gin proclaimed itself in green, it was hard to forget what had happened and who one was. The only thing to do was to shut one's eyes and plunge, if one could, more deeply into the Other World of sensuality, plunge violently, plunge deliberately into those alienating frenzies to which poor Molly—Molly ("Attention") in her bandages, Molly in her wet grave at Highgate, and Highgate, of course, was why one had to shut one's eyes each time when the green light made a corpse of Babs's nakedness—had always and so utterly been a stranger. And not only Molly. Behind his closed eyelids, Will saw his mother, pale like a cameo, her face spiritualized by accepted suffering, her hands made monstrous and subhuman by arthritis. His mother and, standing behind her wheelchair, already running to fat and quivering like calf's-foot jelly with all the feelings that had never found their proper expression in consummated love, was his sister Maud.

"How can you, Will?"

"Yes, how can you?" Maud echoed tearfully in her vibrating contralto.

There was no answer. No answer, that was to say, in any words that could be uttered in their presence, that, uttered, those two martyrs—the mother to her unhappy marriage, the daughter to filial piety—could possibly understand. No answer except in words of the most obscenely scientific objectivity, the most inadmissible frankness. How could he do it? He could do it, for all practical purposes was compelled to do it, because . . . well, because Babs had certain physical peculiarities which Molly did not possess and behaved at certain moments in ways which Molly would have found unthinkable.

There had been a long silence; but now, abruptly, the strange voice took up its old refrain.

"Attention. Attention."

Attention to Molly, attention to Maud and his mother, attention to Babs. And suddenly another memory emerged from the fog of vagueness and confusion. Babs's strawberry-pink alcove sheltered another guest, and its owner's body was shuddering ecstatically under somebody else's caresses. To the guilt in the stomach was added an anguish about the heart, a constriction of the throat.

"Attention."

The voice had come nearer, was calling from somewhere over there to the right. He turned his head, he tried to raise himself for a better view; but the arm that supported his weight began to tremble, then gave way, and he fell back into the leaves. To tired to go on remembering, he lay there for a long time staring up through half-closed lids at the incomprehensible world around him. Where was he and how on earth had he got here? Not that this was of any importance. At the moment nothing was of any importance except this pain, this annihilating weakness. All the same, just as a matter of scientific interest . . .

This tree, for example, under which (for no known

reason) he found himself lying, this column of gray bark with the groining, high up, of sun-speckled branches, this ought by rights to be a beech tree. But in that case—and Will admired himself for being so lucidly logical—in that case the leavès had no right to be so obviously evergreen. And why would a beech tree send its roots elbowing up like this above the surface of the ground? And those preposterous wooden buttresses, on which the pseudo-beech supported itself—where did *those* fit into the picture? Will remembered suddenly his favorite worst line of poetry. "Who prop, thou ask'st, in these bad days my mind?" Answer: congealed ectoplasm, Early Dali. Which definitely ruled out the Chilterns. So did the butterflies swooping out there in the thick buttery sunshine. Why were they so large, so improbably cerulean or velvet black, so extravagantly eyed and freckled? Purple staring out of chestnut, silver powdered over emerald, over topaz, over sapphire.

"Attention."

"Who's there?" Will Farnaby called in what he intended to be a loud and formidable tone; but all that came out of his mouth was a thin, quavering croak.

There was a long and, it seemed, profoundly menacing silence. From the hollow between two of the tree's wooden buttresses an enormous black centipede emerged for a moment into view, then hurried away on its regiment of crimson legs and vanished into another cleft in the lichen-covered ectoplasm.

"Who's there?" he croaked again.

There was a rustling in the bushes on his left and suddenly, like a cuckoo from a nursery clock, out popped a large black bird, the size of a jackdaw—only, needless to say, it wasn't a jackdaw. It clapped a pair of white-tipped wings and, darting across the intervening space, settled on the lowest branch of a small dead tree, not twenty feet from where Will was lying. Its beak, he noticed, was orange, and it had a bald yellow patch under each eye, with canary-colored wattles that covered the sides and back of its head with a thick wig of naked flesh. The bird cocked its head and looked at him first with the right eye, then with the left. After which it opened its orange bill, whistled ten or twelve notes of a little air in the pentatonic scale, made a noise like somebody having hiccups, and then, in a chanting phrase, *do do sol do,* said, "Here and now, boys; here and now, boys."

The words pressed a trigger, and all of a sudden he remembered everything. Here was Pala, the forbidden island, the place no journalist had ever visited. And now must be the morning after the afternoon when he'd been fool enough to go sailing, alone, outside the harbor of Rendang-Lobo. He remembered it all—the white sail curved by the wind into the likeness of a huge magnolia petal, the water sizzling at the prow, the sparkle of diamonds on every wave crest, the troughs of wrinkled jade. And eastwards, across the Strait, what clouds, what prodigies of sculptured whiteness above the volcanoes of Pala! Sitting there at the tiller, he had caught himself singing—caught himself, incredibly, in the act of feeling unequivocally happy.

"'Three, three for the rivals,'" he had declaimed into the wind.

"'Two, two for the lily-white boys, clothèd all in green-oh; One is one and all alone . . .'"

Yes, all alone. All alone on the enormous jewel of the sea.

"'And ever more shall be so.'"

After which, needless to say, the thing that all the cautious and experienced yachtsmen had warned him against happened. The black squall out of nowhere, the sudden, senseless frenzy of wind and rain and waves . . .

"Here and now, boys," chanted the bird. "Here and now, boys."

The really extraordinary thing was that he should be here, he reflected, under the trees and not out there, at the bottom of the Pala Strait or, worse, smashed to pieces at the foot of the cliffs. For even after he had managed, by sheer miracle, to take his sinking boat through the breakers and run her aground on the only sandy beach in all those miles of Pala's rockbound coast—even then it wasn't over. The cliffs towered above him; but at the head of the cove there was a kind of headlong ravine where a little stream came down in a succession of filmy waterfalls, and there were trees and bushes growing between the walls of gray limestone. Six or seven hundred feet of rock climbing—in tennis shoes, and all the footholes slippery with water. And then, dear God! those snakes. The black one looped over the branch by which he was pulling himself up. And five minutes later, the huge green one coiled there on the ledge, just where he was preparing to step. Terror had been succeeded by a terror infinitely worse. The sight of the snake had made him start, made him violently withdraw his foot, and that sudden unconsidered movement had made him lose his balance. For a long sickening second, in the dreadful knowledge that this was the end, he had swayed on the brink, then fallen. Death, death, death. And then, with the noise of splintering wood in his ears he had found himself clinging to the branches of a small tree, his face scratched, his right knee bruised and bleeding, but alive. Painfully he had resumed his climbing. His knee hurt him excruciatingly; but he climbed on. There was no alternative. And then the light had begun to fail. In the end he was climbing almost in darkness, climbing by faith, climbing by sheer despair.

"Here and now, boys," shouted the bird.

But Will Farnaby was neither here nor now. He was there on the rock face, he was then at the dreadful moment of falling. The dry leaves rustled beneath him; he was trembling. Violently, uncontrollably, he was trembling from head to foot.

ii

SUDDENLY THE BIRD CEASED TO BE ARTICULATE AND started to scream. A small shrill human voice said, "Mynah!" and then added something in a language that Will did not understand. There was a sound of footsteps on dry leaves. Then a little cry of alarm. Then silence. Will opened his eyes and saw two exquisite children looking down at him, their eyes wide with astonishment and a fascinated horror. The smaller of them was a tiny boy of five, perhaps, or six, dressed only in a green loincloth. Beside him, carrying a basket of fruit on her head, stood a little girl some four or five years older. She wore a full crimson skirt that reached almost to her ankles; but above the waist she was naked. In the sunlight her skin glowed like pale copper flushed with rose. Will looked from one child to the other. How beautiful they were, and how faultless, how extraordinarily elegant! Like two little thoroughbreds. A round and sturdy thoroughbred, with a face like a cherub's—that was the boy. And the girl was another kind of thoroughbred, fine-drawn, with a rather long, grave little face framed between braids of dark hair.

There was another burst of screaming. On its perch in the dead tree the bird was turning nervously this way and that; then, with a final screech, it dived into the air. Without taking her eyes from Will's face, the girl held out her hand invitingly. The bird fluttered, settled, flapped wildly, found its balance, then folded its wings and immediately started to hiccup. Will looked on without surprise. Anything was possible now—anything. Even talking birds that would perch on a child's finger. Will tried to smile at them; but his lips were still trembling, and what was meant to be a sign of friendliness must have seemed like a frightening grimace. The little boy took cover behind his sister.

The bird stopped hiccuping and began to repeat a word

that Will did not understand. "Runa"—was that it? No, "*karuna.*" Definitely "*karuna.*"

He raised a trembling hand and pointed at the fruit in the round basket. Mangoes, bananas . . . His dry mouth was watering.

"Hungry," he said. Then, feeling that in these exotic circumstances the child might understand him better if he put on an imitation of a musical-comedy Chinaman, "Me velly hungly," he elaborated.

"Do you want to eat?" the child asked in perfect English.

"Yes—eat," he repeated, "eat."

"Fly away, mynah!" She shook her hand. The bird uttered a protesting squawk and returned to its perch on the dead tree. Lifting her thin little arms in a gesture that was like a dancer's, the child raised the basket from her head, then lowered it to the ground. She selected a banana, peeled it and, torn between fear and compassion, advanced towards the stranger. In his incomprehensible language the little boy uttered a cry of warning and clutched at her skirt. With a reassuring word, the girl halted, well out of danger, and held up the fruit.

"Do you want it?" she asked.

Still trembling, Will Farnaby stretched out his hand. Very cautiously, she edged forward, then halted again and, crouching down, peered at him intently.

"Quick," he said in an agony of impatience.

But the little girl was taking no chances. Eyeing his hand for the least sign of a suspicious movement, she leaned forward, she cautiously extended her arm.

"For God's sake," he implored.

"God?" the child repeated with sudden interest. "Which god?" she asked. "There are such a lot of them."

"Any damned god you like," he answered impatiently.

"I don't really like any of them," she answered. "I like the Compassionate One."

"Then be compassionate to me," he begged. "Give me that banana."

Her expression changed. "I'm sorry," she said apologetically. Rising to her full height, she took a quick step forward and dropped the fruit into his shaking hand.

"There," she said and, like a little animal avoiding a trap, she jumped back, out of reach.

The small boy clapped his hands and laughed aloud.

She turned and said something to him. He nodded his round head, and saying "Okay, boss," trotted away, through a barrage of blue and sulphur butterflies, into the forest shadows on the further side of the glade.

"I told Tom Krishna to go and fetch someone," she explained.

Will finished his banana and asked for another, and then for a third. As the urgency of his hunger diminished, he felt a need to satisfy his curiosity.

"How is it that you speak such good English?" he asked.

"Because everybody speaks English," the child answered.

"Everybody?"

"I mean, when they're not speaking Palanese." Finding the subject uninteresting, she turned, waved a small brown hand and whistled.

"Here and now, boys," the bird repeated yet once more, then fluttered down from its perch on the dead tree and settled on her shoulder. The child peeled another banana, gave two-thirds of it to Will and offered what remained to the mynah.

"Is that your bird?" Will asked.

She shook her head.

"Mynahs are like the electric light," she said. "They don't belong to anybody."

"Why does he say those things?"

"Because somebody taught him," she answered patiently. What an ass! her tone seemed to imply.

"But why did they teach him *those* things? Why 'Attention'? Why 'Here and now'?"

"Well . . ." She searched for the right words in which to explain the self-evident to this strange imbecile. "That's what you always forget, isn't it? I mean, you forget to pay attention to what's happening. And that's the same as not being here and now."

"And the mynahs fly about reminding you—is that it?"

She nodded. That, of course, was it. There was a silence.

"What's your name?" she inquired.

Will introduced himself.

"My name's Mary Sarojini MacPhail."

"MacPhail?" It was too implausible.

"MacPhail," she assured him.

"And your little brother is called Tom Krishna?" She nodded. "Well, I'm damned!"

"Did you come to Pala by the airplane?"

"I came out of the sea."

"Out of the sea? Do you have a boat?"

"I did have one." With his mind's eye Will saw the waves breaking over the stranded hulk, heard with his inner ear the crash of their impact. Under her questioning he told her what had happened. The storm, the beaching of the boat, the long nightmare of the climb, the snakes, the horror of falling . . . He began to tremble again, more violently than ever.

Mary Sarojini listened attentively and without comment. Then, as his voice faltered and finally broke, she stepped forward and, the bird still perched on her shoulder, kneeled down beside him.

"Listen, Will," she said, laying a hand on his forehead. "We've got to get rid of this." Her tone was professional and calmly authoritative.

"I wish I knew how," he said between chattering teeth.

"How?" she repeated. "But in the usual way, of course. Tell me again about those snakes and how you fell down."

He shook his head. "I don't want to."

"Of course you don't want to," she said. "But you've got to. Listen to what the mynah's saying."

"Here and now, boys," the bird was still exhorting. "Here and now, boys."

"You can't be here and now," she went on, "until you've got rid of those snakes. Tell me."

"I don't want to, I don't want to." He was almost in tears.

"Then you'll never get rid of them. They'll be crawling about inside your head forever. And serve you right," Mary Sarojini added severely.

He tried to control the trembling; but his body had ceased to belong to him. Someone else was in charge, someone malevolently determined to humiliate him, to make him suffer.

"Remember what happened when you were a little boy," Mary Sarojini was saying. "What did your mother do when you hurt yourself?"

She had taken him in her arms, had said, "My poor baby, my poor little baby."

"She did *that?*" The child spoke in a tone of shocked amazement. "But that's awful! That's the way to rub it in. 'My poor baby,'" she repeated derisively, "it must have gone on hurting for hours. And you'd never forget it."

Will Farnaby made no comment, but lay there in silence, shaken by irrepressible shudderings.

"Well, if you won't do it yourself, I'll have to do it for you. Listen, Will: there was a snake, a big green snake, and you almost stepped on him. You almost stepped on him, and it gave you such a fright that you lost your balance, you fell. Now say it yourself—say it!"

"I almost stepped on him," he whispered obediently. "And then I . . ." He couldn't say it. "Then I fell," he brought out at last, almost inaudibly.

All the horror of it came back to him—the nausea of fear, the panic start that had made him lose his balance, and then worse fear and the ghastly certainty that it was the end.

"Say it again."

"I almost stepped on him. And then . . ."

He heard himself whimpering.

"That's right, Will. Cry—cry!"

The whimpering became a moaning. Ashamed, he clenched his teeth, and the moaning stopped.

"No, don't do that," she cried. "Let it come out if it wants to. Remember that snake, Will. Remember how you fell."

The moaning broke out again and he began to shudder more violently than ever.

"Now tell me what happened."

"I could see its eyes, I could see its tongue going in and out."

"Yes, you could see his tongue. And what happened then?"

"I lost my balance, I fell."

"Say it again, Will." He was sobbing now. "Say it again," she insisted.

"I fell."

"Again."

It was tearing him to pieces, but he said it. "I fell."

"Again, Will." She was implacable. "Again."

"I fell, I fell. I fell . . ."

Gradually the sobbing died down. The words came more easily and the memories they aroused were less painful.

"I fell," he repeated for the hundredth time.

"But you didn't fall very far," Mary Sarojini now said.

"No, I didn't fall very far," he agreed.

"So what's all the fuss about?" the child inquired.

There was no malice or irony in her tone, not the slightest

implication of blame. She was just asking a simple, straightforward question that called for a simple, straightforward answer. Yes, what *was* all the fuss about? The snake hadn't bitten him; he hadn't broken his neck. And anyhow it had all happened yesterday. Today there were these butterflies, this bird that called one to attention, this strange child who talked to one like a Dutch uncle, looked like an angel out of some unfamiliar mythology and within five degrees of the equator was called, believe it or not, MacPhail. Will Farnaby laughed aloud.

The little girl clapped her hands and laughed too. A moment later the bird on her shoulder joined in with peal upon peal of loud demonic laughter that filled the glade and echoed among the trees, so that the whole universe seemed to be fairly splitting its sides over the enormous joke of existence.

iii

"WELL, I'M GLAD IT'S ALL SO AMUSING," A DEEP VOICE suddenly commented.

Will Farnaby turned and saw, smiling down at him, a small spare man dressed in European clothes and carrying a black bag. A man, he judged, in his late fifties. Under the wide straw hat the hair was thick and white, and what a strange beaky nose! And the eyes—how incongruously blue in the dark face!

"Grandfather!" he heard Mary Sarojini exclaiming.

The stranger turned from Will to the child.

"What was so funny?" he asked.

"Well," Mary Sarojini begun, and paused for a moment to marshal her thoughts. "Well, you see, he was in a boat and there was that storm yesterday and he got wrecked—somewhere down there. So he had to climb up the cliff. And there were some snakes, and he fell down. But luckily there was a tree, so he only had a fright. Which was why he was shivering so hard, so I gave him some bananas and I made him go through it a million times. And then all of a sudden he saw that it wasn't anything to worry about. I mean, it's all over and done with. And that made him laugh. And when he laughed, I laughed. And then the mynah bird laughed."

"Very good," said her grandfather approvingly. "And now," he added, turning back to Will Farnaby, "after the psychological first aid, let's see what can be done for poor old Brother Ass. I'm Dr. Robert MacPhail, by the way. Who are you?"

"His name's Will," said Mary Sarojini before the young man could answer. "And his other name is Far-something."

"Farnaby, to be precise. William Asquith Farnaby. My father, as you might guess, was an ardent Liberal. Even when he was drunk. Especially when he was drunk." He gave vent to a harsh derisive laugh strangely unlike the full-throated merriment which had greeted his discovery that there was really nothing to make a fuss about.

"Didn't you like your father?" Mary Sarojini asked with concern.

"Not as much as I might have," Will answered.

"What he means," Dr. MacPhail explained to the child, "is that he hated his father. A lot of them do," he added parenthetically.

Squatting down on his haunches, he began to undo the straps of his black bag.

"One of our ex-imperialists, I assume," he said over his shoulder to the young man.

"Born in Bloomsbury," Will confirmed.

"Upper class," the doctor diagnosed, "but not a member of the military or county subspecies."

"Correct. My father was a barrister and political journalist. That is, when he wasn't too busy being an alcoholic. My mother, incredible as it may seem, was the daughter of an archdeacon. An *archdeacon*," he repeated, and laughed again as he had laughed over his father's taste for brandy.

Dr. MacPhail looked at him for a moment, then turned his attention once more to the straps.

"When you laugh like that," he remarked in a tone of scientific detachment, "your face becomes curiously ugly."

Taken aback, Will tried to cover his embarrassment with a piece of facetiousness. "It's always ugly," he said.

"On the contrary, in a Baudelairean sort of way it's rather beautiful. Except when you choose to make noises like a hyena. Why do you make those noises?"

"I'm a journalist," Will explained. "Our Special Correspondent, paid to travel about the world and report on the current horrors. What other kind of noise do you expect me to make? Coo-coo? Blah-blah? Marx-Marx?" He laughed again, then brought out one of his well-tried witticisms. "I'm the man who won't take yes for an answer."

"Pretty," said Dr. MacPhail. "Very pretty. But now let's get down to business." Taking a pair of scissors out of his bag, he started to cut away the torn and bloodstained trouser leg that covered Will's injured knee.

Will Farnaby looked up at him and wondered, as he looked, how much of this improbable Highlander was still Scottish and how much Palanese. About the blue eyes and the jutting nose there could be no doubt. But the brown skin, the delicate hands, the grace of movement—these surely came from somewhere considerably south of the Tweed.

"Were you born here?" he asked.

The doctor nodded affirmatively. "At Shivapuram, on the day of Queen Victoria's funeral."

There was a final click of the scissors, and the trouser leg fell away, exposing the knee. "Messy," was Dr. MacPhail's verdict after a first intent scrutiny. "But I don't think there's anything too serious." He turned to his granddaughter. "I'd like you to run back to the station and ask Vijaya to come here with one of the other men. Tell them to pick up a stretcher at the infirmary."

Mary Sarojini nodded and, without a word, rose to her feet and hurried away across the glade.

Will looked after the small figure as it receded—the red skirt swinging from side to side, the smooth skin of the torso glowing rosily golden in the sunlight.

"You have a very remarkable granddaughter," he said to Dr. MacPhail.

"Mary Sarojini's father," said the doctor after a little silence, "was my eldest son. He died four months ago—a mountain-climbing accident."

Will mumbled his sympathy, and there was another silence.

Dr. MacPhail uncorked a bottle of alcohol and swabbed his hands.

"This is going to hurt a bit," he warned. "I'd suggest that you listen to that bird." He waved a hand in the direction of the dead tree, to which, after Mary Sarojini's departure, the mynah had returned.

"Listen to him closely, listen discriminatingly. It'll keep your mind off the discomfort."

Will Farnaby listened. The mynah had gone back to its first theme.

"Attention," the articulate oboe was calling. "Attention."

"Attention to what?" he asked, in the hope of eliciting a more enlightening answer than the one he had received from Mary Sarojini.

"To attention," said Dr. MacPhail.

"Attention to attention?"

"Of course."

"Attention," the mynah chanted in ironical confirmation.

"Do you have many of these talking birds?"

"There must be at least a thousand of them flying about the island. It was the Old Raja's idea. He thought it would do people good. Maybe it does, though it seems rather unfair to the poor mynahs. Fortunately, however, birds don't understand pep talks. Not even St. Francis'. Just imagine," he went on, "preaching sermons to perfectly good thrushes and goldfinches and chiff-chaffs! What presumption! Why couldn't he have kept his mouth shut and let the birds preach to *him*? And now," he added in another tone, "you'd better start listening to our friend in the tree. I'm going to clean this thing up."

"Attention."

"Here goes."

The young man winced and bit his lip.

"Attention. Attention. Attention."

Yes, it was quite true. If you listened intently enough, the pain wasn't so bad.

"Attention. Attention . . ."

"How you ever contrived to get up that cliff," said Dr. MacPhail, as he reached for the bandage, "I cannot conceive."

Will managed to laugh. "Remember the beginning of *Erewhon*," he said. " 'As luck would have it, Providence was on my side.' "

From the further side of the glade came the sound of voices. Will turned his head and saw Mary Sarojini emerging from between the trees, her red skirt swinging as she skipped along. Behind her, naked to the waist and carrying over his shoulder the bamboo poles and rolled-up canvas of a light stretcher, walked a huge bronze statue of a man, and behind the giant came a slender, dark-skinned adolescent in white shorts.

"This is Vijaya Bhattacharya," said Dr. MacPhail as the bronze statue approached. "Vijaya is my assistant."

"In the hospital?"

Dr. MacPhail shook his head. "Except in emergencies," he said, "I don't practice any more. Vijaya and I work together at the Agricultural Experimental Station. And Murugan Mailendra" (he waved his hand in the direction of the dark-skinned boy) "is with us temporarily, studying soil science and plant breeding."

Vijaya stepped aside and, laying a large hand on his companion's shoulder, pushed him forward. Looking up into that beautiful, sulky young face, Will suddenly recognized, with a start of surprise, the elegantly tailored youth he had met, five days before, at Rendang-Lobo, had driven with in Colonel Dipa's white Mercedes all over the island. He smiled, he opened his mouth to speak, then checked himself. Almost imperceptibly but quite unmistakenly, the boy had shaken his head. In his eyes Will saw an expression of anguished pleading. His lips moved soundlessly. "Please," he seemed to be saying, "please . . ." Will readjusted his face.

"How do you do, Mr. Mailendra," he said in a tone of casual formality.

Murugan looked enormously relieved. "How do you do," he said, and made a little bow.

Will looked round to see if the others had noticed what had happened. Mary Sarojini and Vijaya, he saw, were busy with the stretcher and the doctor was repacking his black bag. The little comedy had been played without an audience. Young Murugan evidently had his reasons for not wanting it to be known that he had been in Rendang. Boys will be boys. Boys will even be girls. Colonel Dipa had been more than fatherly towards his young protégé, and towards the Colonel, Murugan had been a good deal more than filial—he had been positively adoring. Was it merely hero worship, merely a schoolboy's admiration for the strong man who had carried out a successful revolution, liquidated the opposition, and installed himself as dictator? Or were other feelings involved? Was Murugan playing Antinoüs to this black-mustached Hadrian? Well, if that was how he felt about middle-aged military gangsters, that was his privilege. And if the gangster liked pretty boys, that was *his*. And perhaps, Will went on to reflect, that was why Colonel Dipa had refrained from making a formal introduction. "This is Muru" was all he had said when the boy was ushered into the presidential office. "My young friend Muru," and he had risen, had put his arm around the boy's shoulders, had led him to the sofa and sat down beside him. "May I drive the Mercedes?" Murugan had asked. The dictator had smiled indulgently and nodded his sleek black head. And that was another reason for thinking that more than mere friendliness was involved in that curious relationship. At the wheel of the Colonel's sports car Murugan was a maniac. Only an infatuated lover would have entrusted himself, not to mention his guest, to such a chauffeur. On the flat between Rendang-Lobo and the oil fields the speedometer had twice touched a hundred and ten; and worse, much worse, was to follow on the mountain road from the oil fields to the copper mines. Chasms yawned, tires screeched round corners, water buffaloes emerged from bamboo thickets a few feet ahead of the car, ten-ton lorries came roaring down on the wrong side of the road. "Aren't you a little nervous?" Will had ventured to ask. But the gangster was pious as well as infatuated. "If one knows that one is doing the will of Allah—and I *do* know it, Mr. Farnaby—there is no excuse for nervousness. In those circumstances, nervousness would be blasphemy." And as Murugan swerved to avoid yet another buffalo, he opened his gold cigarette case and offered Will a Balkan Sobranje.

"Ready," Vijaya called.

Will turned his head and saw the stretcher lying on the ground beside him.

"Good!" said Dr. MacPhail. "Let's lift him onto it. Carefully. Carefully . . ."

A minute later the little procession was winding its way up the narrow path between the trees. Mary Sarojini was in the van, her grandfather brought up the rear and, between them, came Murugan and Vijaya at either end of the stretcher.

From his moving bed Will Farnaby looked up through the green darkness as though from the floor of a living sea. Far overhead, near the surface, there was a rustling among the leaves, a noise of monkeys. And now it was a dozen hornbills hopping, like the figments of a disordered imagination, through a cloud of orchids.

"Are you comfortable?" Vijaya asked, bending solicitously to look into his face.

Will smiled back at him.

"Luxuriously comfortable," he said.

"It isn't far," the other went on reassuringly. "We'll be there in a few minutes."

"Where's 'there'?"

"The Experimental Station. It's like Rothamsted. Did you ever go to Rothamsted when you were in England?"

Will had heard of it, of course, but never seen the place.

"It's been going for more than a hundred years," Vijaya went on.

"A hundred and eighteen, to be precise," said Dr. MacPhail. "Lawes and Gilbert started their work on fertilizers in 1843. One of their pupils came out here in the early fifties to help my grandfather get our station going. Rothamsted in the tropics—that was the idea. *In* the tropics and *for* the tropics."

There was a lightening of the green gloom and a moment later the litter emerged from the forest into the full glare of tropical sunshine. Will raised his head and looked about him. They were not far from the floor of an immense amphitheater. Five hundred feet below stretched a wide plain, checkered with fields, dotted with clumps of trees and clustered houses. In the other direction the slopes climbed up and up, thousands of feet towards a semicircle of mountains. Terrace above green or golden terrace, from the plain to the crenelated wall of peaks, the rice paddies followed the contour lines, emphasizing every swell and recession of the slope with what seemed a deliberate and artful intention. Nature here was no longer merely natural; the landscape had been composed, had been reduced to its geometrical essences, and rendered, by what in a painter would have been a miracle of virtuosity, in terms of these sinuous lines, these streaks of pure bright color.

"What were you doing in Rendang?" Dr. Robert asked, breaking a long silence.

"Collecting materials for a piece on the new regime."

"I wouldn't have thought the Colonel was newsworthy."

"You're mistaken. He's a *military* dictator. That means there's death in the offing. And death is always news. Even the remote smell of death is news." He laughed. "That's why I was told to drop in on my way back from China."

And there had been other reasons which he preferred not to mention. Newspapers were only one of Lord Aldehyde's interests. In another manifestation he was the Southeast Asia Petroleum Company, he was Imperial and Foreign Copper Limited. Officially, Will had come to Rendang to sniff the death in its militarized air; but he had also been commissioned to find out what the dictator felt about foreign capital, what tax rebates he was prepared to offer, what guarantees against nationalization. And how much of the profits would be exportable? How many native technicians and administrators would have to be employed? A whole battery of questions. But Colonel Dipa had been most affable and co-operative. Hence that hair-raising drive, with Murugan at the wheel, to the copper mines. "Primitive, my dear Farnaby, primitive. Urgently in need, as you can see for yourself, of modern equipment." Another meeting had been arranged—arranged, Will now remembered, for this very morning. He visualized the Colonel at his desk. A report from the chief of police. "Mr. Farnaby was last seen sailing a small boat singlehanded into the Pala Strait. Two hours later a storm of great violence . . . Presumed dead . . ." Instead of which, here he was, alive and kicking, on the forbidden island.

"They'll never give you a visa," Joe Aldehyde had said at their last interview. "But perhaps you could sneak ashore in disguise. Wear a burnous or something, like Lawrence of Arabia."

With a straight face, "I'll try," Will had promised.

"Anyhow, if you ever do manage to land in Pala, make a beeline for the palace. The Rani—that's their Queen Mother—is an old friend of mine. Met her for the first time six years ago at Lugano. She was staying there with old Voegeli, the investment banker. His girl friend is interested in spiritualism and they staged a séance for me. A trumpet medium, genuine Direct Voice—only unfortunately it was all in German. Well, after the lights were turned on, I had a long talk with her."

"With the trumpet?"

"No, no. With the Rani. She's a remarkable woman. You know, the Crusade of the Spirit."

"Was that *her* invention?"

"Absolutely. And personally I prefer it to Moral Rearmament. It goes down better in Asia. We had a long talk about it that evening. And after that we talked about oil. Pala's full of oil. Southeast Asia Petroleum has been trying to get in on it for years. So have all the other companies. Nothing doing. No oil concessions to anyone. It's their fixed policy. But the Rani doesn't agree with it. She wants to see the oil doing some good in the world. Financing the Crusade of the Spirit, for example. So, as I say, if ever you get to Pala, make a beeline for the palace. Talk to her. Get the inside story about the men who make the decisions. Find out if there's a pro-oil minority and ask how we could help them to carry on the good work." And he had ended by promising Will a handsome bonus if his efforts should be crowned with success. Enough to give him a full year of freedom. "No more reporting. Nothing but High Art, Art, A-ART." And he had uttered a scatalogical laugh as though the word had an "s" at the end of it and not a "t." Unspeakable creature! But all the same he wrote for the unspeakable creature's vile papers and was ready, for a bribe, to do the vile creature's dirty work. And now, incredibly, here he was on Palanese soil. As luck would have it, Providence had been on his side—for the express purpose, evidently, of perpetrating one of those sinister practical jokes which are Providence's specialty.

He was called back to present reality by the sound of Mary Sarojini's shrill voice. "Here we are!"

Will raised his head again. The little procession had turned off the highway and was passing through an opening in a white stuccoed wall. To the left, on a rising succession of terraces, stood lines of low buildings shaped by peepul trees. Straight ahead an avenue of tall palms sloped down to a lotus pool, on the further side of which sat a huge stone Buddha. Turning to the left, they climbed between flowering trees and through blending perfumes to the first terrace. Behind a fence, motionless except for his ruminating jaws, stood a snow-white humped bull, godlike in his serene and mindless beauty. Europa's lover receded into the past, and here were a brace of Juno's birds trailing their feathers over the grass. Mary Sarojini unlatched the gate of a small garden.

"My bungalow," said Dr. MacPhail, and turning to Murugan, "Let me help you to negotiate the steps."

iv

Tom Krishna and Mary Sarojini had gone to take their siesta with the gardener's children next door. In her darkened living room Susila MacPhail sat alone with her memories of past happiness and the present pain of her bereavement. The clock in the kitchen struck the half hour. It was time for her to go. With a sigh she rose, put on her sandals and walked out into the tremendous glare of the tropical afternoon. She looked up at the sky. Over the volcanoes enormous clouds were climbing towards the zenith. In an hour it would be raining. Moving from one pool of shadow to the next, she made her way along the tree-lined path. With a sudden rattle of quills a flock of pigeons broke out of one of the towering peepul trees. Green-winged and coral-billed, their breasts changing color in the light like mother-of-pearl, they flew off towards the forest. How beautiful they were, how unutterably lovely! Susila was on the point of turning to catch the expression of delight on Dugald's upturned face; then, checking herself, she looked down at the ground. There was no Dugald any more; there was only this pain, like the pain of the phantom limb that goes on haunting the imagination, haunting even the perceptions of those who have undergone an amputation. "Amputation," she whispered to herself, "amputation . . ." Feeling her eyes fill with tears, she broke off. Amputation was no excuse for self-pity and, for all that Dugald was dead, the birds were as beautiful as ever and her children, all the other children, had as much need to be loved and helped and taught. If his absence was so constantly present, that was to remind her that henceforward she must love for two, live for two, take thought for two, must perceive and understand not merely with her own eyes and mind but with the mind and eyes that had been his and, before the catastrophe, hers too in a communion of delight and intelligence.

But here was the doctor's bungalow. She mounted the steps, crossed the veranda and walked into the living room. Her father-in-law was seated near the window, sipping cold tea from an earthenware mug and reading the *Revue de Mycologie*. He looked up as she approached, and gave her a welcoming smile.

"Susila, my dear! I'm so glad you were able to come."

She bent down and kissed his stubbly cheek.

"What's all this I hear from Mary Sarojini?" she asked. "Is it true she found a castaway?"

"From England—but via China, Rendang, and a shipwreck. A journalist."

"What's he like?"

"The physique of a Messiah. But too clever to believe in God or be convinced of his own mission. And too sensitive, even if he were convinced, to carry it out. His muscles would like to act and his feelings would like to believe; but his nerve endings and his cleverness won't allow it."

"So I suppose he's very unhappy."

"So unhappy that he has to laugh like a hyena."

"Does he know he laughs like a hyena?"

"Knows and is rather proud of it. Even makes epigrams about it. 'I'm the man who won't take yes for an answer.'"

"Is he badly hurt?" she asked.

"Not badly. But he's running a temperature. I've started him on antibiotics. Now it's up to you to raise his resistance and give the *vis medicatrix naturae* a chance."

"I'll do my best." Then, after a silence, "I went to see Lakshmi," she said, "on my way back from school."

"How did you find her?"

"About the same. No, perhaps a little weaker than yesterday."

"That's what I felt when I saw her this morning."

"Luckily the pain doesn't seem to get any worse. We can still handle it psychologically. And today we worked on the nausea. She was able to drink something. I don't think there'll be any more need for intravenous fluids."

"Thank goodness!" he said. "Those IV's were a torture. Such enormous courage in the face of every real danger; but whenever it was a question of a hypodermic or a needle in a vein, the most abject and irrational terror."

He thought of the time, in the early days of their marriage, when he had lost his temper and called her a coward for making such a fuss. Lakshmi had cried and, having submitted to her martyrdom, had heaped coals of fire upon his head by begging to be forgiven. "Lakshmi, Lakshmi . . ." And now in a few days she would be dead. After thirty-seven years. "What did you talk about?" he asked aloud.

"Nothing in particular," Susila answered. But the truth was that they had talked about Dugald and that she couldn't bring herself to repeat what had passed between them. "My first baby," the dying woman had whispered. "I didn't know that babies could be so beautiful." In their skull-deep, skull-dark sockets the eyes had brightened, the bloodless lips had smiled. "Such tiny, tiny hands," the faint hoarse voice went on, "such a greedy little mouth!" And an almost fleshless hand tremblingly touched the place where, before last year's operation, her breast had been. "I never knew," she repeated. And, before the event, how could she have known? It had been a revelation, an apocalypse of touch and love. "Do you know what I mean?" And Susila had nodded. Of course she knew—had known it in relation to her own two children, known it, in those other apocalypses of touch and love, with the man that little Dugald of the tiny hands and greedy mouth had grown into. "I used to be afraid for him," the dying woman had whispered. "He was so strong, such a tyrant, he could have hurt and bullied and destroyed. If he'd married another woman . . . I'm so thankful it was you!" From the place where the breast had been the fleshless hand moved out and came to rest on Susila's arm. She had bent her head and kissed it. They were both crying.

Dr. MacPhail sighed, looked up and, like a man who has climbed out of the water, gave himself a little shake. "The castaway's name is Farnaby," he said. "Will Farnaby."

"Will Farnaby," Susila repeated. "Well, I'd better go and see what I can do for him." She turned and walked away.

Dr. MacPhail looked after her, then leaned back in his chair and closed his eyes. He thought of his son, he thought of his wife—of Lakshmi slowly wasting to extinction, of Dugald like a bright fiery flame suddenly snuffed out. Thought of the incomprehensible sequence of changes and chances that make up a life, all the beauties and horrors and absurdities whose conjunctions create the uninterpretable and yet divinely significant pattern of human destiny. "Poor girl," he said to himself, remembering the look on Susila's face when he had told her of what had happened to Dugald, "poor girl!" Meanwhile there was this article on Hallacinogenic mushrooms in the *Revue de Mycologie*. That was another of the irrelevancies that somehow took its place in the pattern. The words of one of the old Raja's queer little poems came to his mind.

> All things, to all things
> perfectly indifferent,
> perfectly work together
> in discord for a Good beyond
> good, for a Being more
> timeless in transience, more
> eternal in its dwindling than
> God there in heaven.

The door creaked, and an instant later Will heard light footsteps and the rustle of skirts. Then a hand was laid on his shoulder and a woman's voice, low-pitched and musical, asked him how he was feeling.

"I'm feeling miserable," he answered without opening his eyes.

There was no self-pity in his tone, no appeal for sympathy—only the angry matter-of-factness of a Stoic who has finally grown sick of the long farce of impassibility and is resentfully blurting out the truth.

"I'm feeling miserable."

The hand touched him again. "I'm Susila MacPhail," said the voice "Mary Sarojini's mother."

Reluctantly Will turned his head and opened his eyes. An adult, darker version of Mary Sarojini was sitting there beside the bed, smiling at him with friendly solicitude. To smile back at her would have cost him too great an effort; he contented himself with saying "How do you do," then pulled the sheet a little higher and closed his eyes again.

Susila looked down at him in silence—at the bony shoulders, at the cage of ribs under a skin whose Nordic pallor made him seem, to her Palanese eyes, so strangely frail and vulnerable, at the sunburnt face, emphatically featured like a carving intended to be seen at a distance—emphatic and yet sensitive, the quivering, more than naked face, she found herself thinking, of a man who has been flayed and left to suffer.

"I hear you're from England," she said at last.

"I don't care where I'm from," Will muttered irritably. "Nor where I'm going. *From* hell *to* hell."

"I was in England just after the war," she went on. "As a student."

He tried not to listen; but ears have no lids; there was no escape from that intruding voice.

"There was a girl in my psychology class," it was saying; "her people lived at Wells. She asked me to stay with them for the first month of the summer vacation. Do you know Wells?"

Of course he knew Wells. Why did she pester him with her silly reminiscences?

"I used to love walking there by the water," Susila went on, "looking across the moat at the cathedral"—and thinking, while she looked at the cathedral, of Dugald under the palm trees on the beach, of Dugald giving her her first lesson in rock climbing. "You're on the rope. You're perfectly safe. You can't possibly fall . . ." Can't possibly fall, she repeated bitterly—and then remembered here and now, remembered that she had a job to do, remembered, as she looked again at the flayed emphatic face, that here was a human being in pain. "How lovely it was," she went on, "and how marvelously peaceful!"

The voice, it seemed to Will Farnaby, had become more musical and in some strange way more remote. Perhaps that was why he no longer resented its intrusion.

"Such an extraordinary sense of peace. *Shanti, shanti, shanti.* The peace that passes understanding."

The voice was almost chanting now—chanting, it seemed, out of some other world.

"I can shut my eyes," it chanted on, "can shut my eyes and see it all so clearly. Can see the church—and it's enormous, much taller than the huge trees round the bishop's palace. Can see the green grass and the water and the golden sunlight on the stones and the slanting shadows between the buttresses. And listen! I can hear the bells. The bells and the jackdaws. The jackdaws in the tower—can you hear the jackdaws?"

Yes, he could hear the jackdaws, could hear them almost as clearly as he now heard those parrots in the trees outside his window. He was here and at the same time he was there —here in this dark, sweltering room near the equator, but also there, outdoors in that cool hollow at the edge of the Mendips, with the jackdaws calling from the cathedral tower and the sound of the bells dying away into the green silence.

"And there are white clouds," the voice was saying, "and the blue sky between them is so pale, so delicate, so exquisitely tender."

Tender, he repeated, the tender blue sky of that April weekend he had spent there, before the disaster of their marriage, with Molly. There were daisies in the grass and dandelions, and across the water towered up the huge church, challenging the wildness of those soft April clouds with its austere geometry. Challenging the wildness, and at the same time complementing it, coming to terms with it in perfect reconciliation. That was how it should have been with himself and Molly—how it had been then.

"And the swans," he now heard the voice dreamily chanting, "the swans . . ."

Yes, the swans. White swans moving across a mirror of jade and jet—a breathing mirror that heaved and trembled, so that their silvery images were forever breaking and coming together again, disintegrating and being made whole.

"Like the inventions of heraldry. Romantic, impossibly beautiful. And yet there they are—real birds in a real place. So near to me now that I can almost touch them—and yet so far away, thousands of miles away. Far away on that smooth water, moving as if by magic, softly, majestically . . ."

Majestically, moving majestically, with the dark water lifting and parting as the curved white breasts advanced—lifting, parting, sliding back in ripples that widened in a gleaming arrowhead behind them. He could see them moving across their dark mirror, could hear the jackdaws in the tower, could catch, through this nearer mingling of disinfectants and gardenias, the cold, flat, weedy smell of that Gothic moat in the faraway green valley.

"Effortlessly floating."

"Effortlessly floating." The words gave him a deep satisfaction.

"I'd sit there," she was saying, "I'd sit there looking and looking, and in a little while *I*'d be floating too. I'd be floating with the swans on that smooth surface between the darkness below and the pale tender sky above. Floating at the same time on that other surface between here and far away, between then and now." And between remembered happiness, she was thinking, and this insistent, excruciating presence of an absence. "Floating," she said aloud, "on the surface between the real and the imagined, between what comes to us from the outside and what comes to us from within, from deep, deep down in here."

She laid her hand on his forehead, and suddenly the words transformed themselves into the things and events for which they stood; the images turned into facts. He actually *was* floating.

"Floating," the voice softly insisted. "Floating like a white bird on the water. Floating on a great river of life—a great smooth silent river that flows so still, so still, you might almost think it was asleep. A sleeping river. But it flows irresistibly.

"Life flowing silently and irresistibly into ever fuller life, into a living peace all the more profound, all the richer and stronger and more complete because it knows all your pain and unhappiness, knows them and takes them into itself and makes them one with its own substance. And it's into that peace that you're floating now, floating on this smooth silent river that sleeps and is yet irresistible, and is irresistible precisely because it's sleeping. And I'm floating with it." She was speaking for the stranger. She was speaking on another level for herself. "Effortlessly floating. Not having to do anything at all. Just letting go, just allowing myself to be carried along, just asking this irresistible sleeping river of life to take me where it's going—and knowing all the time that where it's going is where I want to go, where I have to go: into more life, into living peace. Along the sleeping river, irresistibly, into the wholeness of reconciliation."

Involuntarily, unconsciously, Will Farnaby gave a deep sigh. How silent the world had become! Silent with a deep crystalline silence, even though the parrots were still busy out there beyond the shutters, even though the voice still chanted here beside him! Silence and emptiness and through the silence and the emptiness flowed the river, sleeping and irresistible.

Susila looked down at the face on the pillow. It seemed suddenly very young, childlike in its perfect serenity. The frowning lines across the forehead had disappeared. The lips that had been so tightly closed in pain were parted now, and the breath came slowly, softly, almost imperceptibly. She remembered suddenly the words that had come into her mind as she looked down, one moonlit night, at the transfigured innocence of Dugald's face: "She giveth her beloved sleep."

"Sleep," she said aloud. "Sleep."

The silence seemed to become more absolute, the emptiness more enormous.

"Asleep on the sleeping river," the voice was saying. "And above the river, in the pale sky, there are huge white clouds. And as you look at them, you begin to float up towards them. Yes, you begin to float up towards them, and the river now is a river in the air, an invisible river that carries you on, carries you up, higher and higher."

Upwards, upwards through the silent emptiness. The image was the thing, the words became the experience.

"Out of the hot plain," the voice went on, "effortlessly, into the freshness of the mountains."

Yes, there was the Jungfrau, dazzlingly white against the blue. There was Monte Rosa . . .

"How fresh the air feels as you breathe it. Fresh, pure, charged with life!"

He breathed deeply and the new life flowed into him. And now a little wind came blowing across the snowfields, cool against his skin, deliciously cool. And, as though echoing his thoughts, as though describing his experience, the voice said, "Coolness. Coolness and sleep. Through coolness into more life. Through sleep into reconciliation, into wholeness, into living peace."

Half an hour later Susila re-entered the sitting room.

"Well?" her father-in-law questioned. "Any success?"

She nodded.

"I talked to him about a place in England," she said. "He went off more quickly than I'd expected. After that I gave him some suggestions about his temperature . . ."

"*And* the knee, I hope."

"Of course."

"Direct suggestions?"

"No, indirect. They're always better. I got him to be conscious of his body image. Then I made him imagine it much bigger than in everyday reality—and the knee much smaller.

A miserable little thing in revolt against a huge and splendid thing. There can't be any doubt as to who's going to win." She looked at the clock on the wall. "Goodness, I must hurry. Otherwise I'll be late for my class at school."

V

THE SUN WAS JUST RISING AS DR. ROBERT ENTERED HIS wife's room at the hospital. An orange glow, and against it the jagged silhouette of the mountains. Then suddenly a dazzling sickle of incandescence between two peaks. The sickle became a half circle and the first long shadows, the first shafts of golden light crossed the garden outside the window. And when one looked up again at the mountains there was the whole unbearable glory of the risen sun.

Dr. Robert sat down by the bed, took his wife's hand and kissed it. She smiled at him, then turned again towards the window.

"How quickly the earth turns!" she whispered, and then after a silence, "One of these mornings," she added, "it'll be my last sunrise."

Through the confused chorus of bird cries and insect noises, a mynah was chanting, "*Karuna. Karuna . . .*"

"*Karuna,*" Lakshmi repeated. "Compassion . . ."

"*Karuna. Karuna,*" the oboe voice of Buddha insisted from the garden.

"I shan't be needing it much longer," she went on. "But what about you? Poor Robert, what about you?"

"Somehow or other one finds the necessary strength," he said.

"But will it be the right kind of strength? Or will it be the strength of armor, the strength of shut-offness, the strength of being absorbed in your work and your ideas and not caring a damn for anything else? Remember how I used to come and pull your hair and make you pay attention? Who's going to do that when I'm gone?"

A nurse came in with a glass of sugared water. Dr. Robert slid a hand under his wife's shoulders and lifted her to a sitting position. The nurse held the glass to her lips. Lakshmi drank a little water, swallowed with difficulty, then drank again and yet once more. Turning from the proffered glass, she looked up at Dr. Robert. The wasted face was illumined by a strangely incongruous twinkle of pure mischief.

"'I the Trinity illustrate,'" the faint voice hoarsely quoted, "'sipping watered orange pulp; in three sips the Arian frustrate' . . ." She broke off. "What a ridiculous thing to be remembering. But then I always was pretty ridiculous, wasn't I?"

Dr. Robert did his best to smile back at her. "Pretty ridiculous," he agreed.

"You used to say I was like a flea. Here one moment and then, hop! somewhere else, miles away. No wonder you could never educate me!"

"But *you* educated *me* all right," he assured her. "If it hadn't been for you coming in and pulling my hair and making me look at the world and helping me to understand it, what would I be today? A pedant in blinkers—in spite of all my training. But luckily I had the sense to ask you to marry me, and luckily you had the folly to say yes and then the wisdom and intelligence to make a good job of me. After thirty-seven years of adult education I'm almost human."

"But I'm still a flea." She shook her head. "And yet I did try. I tried very hard. I don't know if you ever realized it, Robert: I was always on tiptoes, always straining up towards the place where you were doing your work and your thinking and your reading. On tiptoes, trying to reach it, trying to get up there beside you. Goodness, how tiring it was! What an endless series of efforts! And all of them quite useless. Because I was just a dumb flea hopping about down here among the people and the flowers and the cats and dogs. Your kind of highbrow world was a place I could never climb up to, much less find my way in. When this thing happened" (she raised her hand again to her absent breast) "I didn't have to try any more. No more school, no more homework. I had a permanent excuse."

There was a long silence.

"What about taking another sip?" said the nurse at last.

"Yes, you ought to drink some more," Dr. Robert agreed.

"And ruin the Trinity?" Lakshmi gave him another of her smiles. Through the mask of age and mortal sickness Dr. Robert suddenly saw the laughing girl with whom, half a lifetime ago, and yet only yesterday, he had fallen in love.

An hour later Dr. Robert was back in his bungalow.

"You're going to be all alone this morning," he announced, after changing the dressing on Will Farnaby's knee. "I have to drive down to Shivapuram for a meeting of the Privy Council. One of our student nurses will come in around twelve to give you your injection and get you something to eat. And in the afternoon, as soon as she's finished her work at the school, Susila will be dropping in again. And now I must be going." Dr. Robert rose and laid his hand for a moment on Will's arm. "Till this evening." Halfway to the door he halted and turned back. "I almost forgot to give you this." From one of the side pockets of his sagging jacket he pulled out a small green booklet. "It's the Old Raja's *Notes on What's What, and on What It Might be Reasonable to Do about What's What.*"

"What an admirable title!" said Will as he took the proffered book.

"And you'll like the contents, too," Dr. Robert assured him. "Just a few pages, that's all. But if you want to know what Pala is all about, there's no better introduction."

"Incidentally," Will asked, "who *is* the Old Raja?"

"Who *was* he, I'm afraid. The Old Raja died in 'thirty-eight—after a reign three years longer than Queen Victoria's. His eldest son died before he did, and he was succeeded by his grandson, who was an ass—but made up for it by being short-lived. The present Raja is his great-grandson."

"And, if I may ask a personal question, how does anybody called MacPhail come into the picture?"

"The first MacPhail of Pala came into it under the Old Raja's grandfather—the Raja of the Reform, we call him. Between them, he and my great-grandfather invented modern Pala. The Old Raja consolidated their work and carried it further. And today we're doing our best to follow in his footsteps."

Will held up the *Notes on What's What.*

"Does this give the history of the reforms?"

Dr. Robert shook his head. "It merely states the underlying principles. Read about those first. When I get back from Shivapuram this evening, I'll give you a taste of the history. You'll have a better understanding of what was actually done if you start by knowing what had to be done—what always and everywhere has to be done by anyone who has a clear idea about what's what. So read it, read it. And don't forget to drink your fruit juice at eleven."

Will watched him go, then opened the little green book and started to read.

I

Nobody needs to go anywhere else. We are all, if we only knew it, already there.

If I only knew who in fact I am, I should cease to behave as what I think I am; and if I stopped behaving as what I think I am, I should know who I am.

What in fact I am, if only the Manichee I think I am would allow me to know it, is the reconciliation of yes and no lived out in total acceptance and the blessed experience of Not-Two.

In religion all words are dirty words. Anybody who gets eloquent about Buddha, or God, or Christ, ought to have his mouth washed out with carbolic soap.

Because his aspiration to perpetuate only the "yes" in every pair of opposites can never, in the nature of things, be realized, the insulated Manichee I think I am condemns himself to endlessly repeated frustration, endlessly repeated conflicts with other aspiring and frustrated Manichees.

Conflicts and frustrations—the theme of all history and almost all biography. "I show you sorrow," said the Buddha realistically. But he also showed the ending of sorrow—self-knowledge, total acceptance, the blessed experience of Not-Two.

II

Knowing who in fact we are results in Good Being, and Good Being results in the most appropriate kind of good doing. But good doing does not of itself result in Good Being. We can be virtuous without knowing who in fact we are. The beings who are merely good are not Good Beings; they are just pillars of society.

Most pillars are their own Samsons. They hold up, but sooner or later they pull down. There has never been a society in which most good doing was the product of Good Being and therefore constantly appropriate. This does not mean that there will never be such a society or that we in Pala are fools for trying to call it into existence.

III

The Yogin and the Stoic—two righteous egos who achieve their very considerable results by pretending, systematically, to be somebody else. But it is not by pretending to be somebody else, even somebody supremely good and wise, that we can pass from insulated Manicheehood to Good Being.

Good Being is knowing who in fact we are; and in order to know who in fact we are, we must first know, moment by moment, who we think we are and what this bad habit of thought compels us to feel and do. A moment of clear and complete knowledge of what we think we are, but in fact are not, puts a stop, for the moment, to the Manichean charade. If we renew, until they become a continuity, these moments of the knowledge of what we are not, we may find ourselves, all of a sudden, knowing who in fact we are.

Concentration, abstract thinking, spiritual exercises—systematic exclusions in the realm of thought. Asceticism and hedonism—systematic exclusions in the realms of sensation, feeling and action. But Good Being is in the knowledge of who in fact one is in relation to *all* experiences. So be aware—aware in every context, at all times and whatever, creditable or discreditable, pleasant or unpleasant, you may be doing or suffering. This is the only genuine yoga, the only spiritual exercise worth practicing.

The more a man knows about individual objects, the more he knows about God. Translating Spinoza's language into ours, we can say: The more a man knows about himself in relation to every kind of experience, the greater his chance of suddenly, one fine morning, realizing who in fact he is—or rather Who (capital W) in Fact (capital F) "he" (between quotation marks Is (capital I).

St. John was right. In a blessedly speechless universe, the Word was not only *with* God; it *was* God. As a something to be believed in. God is a projected symbol, a reified name. God="God."

Faith is something very different from belief. Belief

is the systematic taking of unanalyzed words much too seriously. Paul's words, Mohammed's words, Marx's words, Hitler's words—people take them too seriously, and what happens? What happens is the senseless ambivalence of history—sadism versus duty, or (incomparably worse) sadism *as* duty; devotion counterbalanced by organized paranoia; sisters of charity selflessly tending the victims of their own church's inquisitors and crusaders. Faith, on the contrary, can never be taken too seriously. For Faith is the empirically justified confidence in our capacity to know who in fact we are, to forget the belief-intoxicated Manichee in Good Being. Give us this day our daily Faith, but deliver us, dear God, from Belief.

There was a tap at the door. Will looked up from his book. "Who's there?"

"It's me," said a voice that brought back unpleasant memories of Colonel Dipa and that nightmarish drive in the white Mercedes. Dressed only in white sandals, white shorts, and a platinum wrist watch, Murugan was advancing towards the bed.

"How nice of you to come and see me!"

Another visitor would have asked him how he was feeling; but Murugan was too wholeheartedly concerned with himself to be able even to simulate the slightest interest in anyone else. "I came to the door three-quarters of an hour ago," he said in tones of aggrieved complaint. "But the old man hadn't left, so I had to go home again. And then I had to sit with my mother and the man who's staying with us while they were having their breakfast . . ."

"Why couldn't you come in while Dr. Robert was here?" Will asked. "Is it against the rules for you to talk to me?"

The boy shook his head impatiently. "Of course not. I just didn't want him to know the reason for my coming to see you."

"The reason?" Will smiled. "Visiting the sick is an act of charity—highly commendable."

His irony was lost upon Murugan, who went on steadily thinking about his own affairs. "Thank you for not telling them you'd seen me before," he said abruptly, almost angrily. It was as though he resented having to acknowledge his obligation and were furious with Will for having done him the good turn which demanded this acknowledgment.

"I could see you didn't want me to say anything about it," said Will. "So of course I didn't."

"I wanted to thank you," Murugan muttered between his teeth and in a tone that would have been appropriate to "You dirty swine!"

"Don't mention it," said Will with mock politeness.

What a delicious creature! he was thinking as he looked, with amused curiosity, at that smooth golden torso, that averted face, regular as a statue's but no longer Olympian, no longer classical—a Hellenistic face, mobile and all too human. A vessel of incomparable beauty—but what did it contain? It was a pity, he reflected, that he hadn't asked that question a little more seriously before getting involved with his unspeakable Babs. But then Babs was a female. By the sort of heterosexual he was, the sort of rational question he was now posing was unaskable. As no doubt it would be, by anyone susceptible to boys, in regard to this bad-blooded little demigod sitting at the end of his bed. "Didn't Dr. Robert know you'd gone to Rendang?" he asked.

"Of course he knew. Everybody knew it. I'd gone there to fetch my mother. She was staying there with some of her relations. I went over to bring her back to Pala. It was absolutely official."

"Then why didn't you want me to say that I'd met you over there?"

Murugan hesitated for a moment, then looked up at Will defiantly. "Because I didn't want them to know I'd been seeing Colonel Dipa."

Oh, so *that* was it! "Colonel Dipa's a remarkable man," he said aloud, fishing with sugared bait for confidences.

Surprisingly unsuspicious, the fish rose at once. Murugan's sulky face lit up with enthusiasm and there, suddenly, was Antinoüs in all the fascinating beauty of his ambiguous adolescence. "I think he's wonderful," he said, and for the first time since he had entered the room he seemed to recognize Will's existence and give him the friendliest of smiles. The Colonel's wonderfulness had made him forget his resentment, had made it possible for him, momentarily, to love everybody—even this man to whom he owed a rankling debt of gratitude. "Look at what he's doing for Rendang!"

"He's certainly doing a great deal for Rendang," said Will noncommittally.

A cloud passed across Murugan's radiant face. "They don't think so here," he said, frowning. "They think he's awful."

"Who thinks so?"

"Practically everybody!"

"So they didn't want you to see him?"

With the expression of an urchin who has cocked a snook while the teacher's back is turned, Murugan grinned triumphantly. "They thought I was with my mother all the time."

Will picked up the cue at once. "Did your mother know you were seeing the Colonel?" he asked.

"Of course."

"And had no objection?"

"She was all for it."

And yet, Will felt quite sure, he hadn't been mistaken when he thought of Hadrian and Antinoüs. Was the woman blind? Or didn't she wish to see what was happening?

"But if *she* doesn't mind," he said aloud, "why should Dr. Robert and the rest of them object?" Murugan looked at him suspiciously. Realizing that he had ventured too far into forbidden territory, Will hastily drew a red herring across the trail. "Do they think," he asked with a laugh, "that he might convert you to a belief in military dictatorship?"

The red herring was duly followed, and the boy's face relaxed into a smile. "Not that, exactly," he answered, "but something like it. It's all so stupid," he added with a shrug of the shoulders. "Just idiotic protocol."

"Protocol?" Will was genuinely puzzled.

"Weren't you told anything about me?"

"Only what Dr. Robert said yesterday."

"You mean, about my being a student?" Murugan threw back his head and laughed.

"What's so funny about being a student?"

"Nothing—nothing at all." The boy looked away again. There was a silence. Still averted, "The reason," he said at last, "why I'm not supposed to see Colonel Dipa is that he's the head of a state and *I'm* the head of a state. When we meet, it's international politics."

"What do you mean?"

"I happen to be the Raja of Pala."

"The Raja of Pala?"

"Since fifty-four. That was when my father died."

"And your mother, I take it, is the Rani?"

"My mother is the Rani."

Make a beeline for the palace. But here was the palace making a beeline for him. Providence, evidently, was on the side of Joe Aldehyde and working overtime.

"Were you the eldest son?" he asked.

"The *only* son," Murugan replied. And then, stressing his uniqueness still more emphatically, "The only *child,*" he added.

"So there's no possible doubt," said Will. "My goodness! I ought to be calling you Your Majesty. Or at least Sir." The words were spoken laughingly; but it was with the most perfect seriousness and a sudden assumption of regal dignity that Murugan responded to them.

"You'll have to call me that at the end of next week," he said. "After my birthday. I shall be eighteen. That's when a Raja of Pala comes of age. Till then I'm just Murugan Mailendra. Just a student learning a little bit about everything—including plant breeding," he added contemptuously—"so that, when the time comes, I shall know what I'm doing."

"And when the time comes, what will you be doing?" Between this pretty Antinoüs and his portentous office there was a contrast which Will found richly comic. "How do you propose to act?" he continued on a bantering note. "Off with their heads? *L'état c'est moi?*"

Seriousness and regal dignity hardened into rebuke. "Don't be stupid."

Amused, Will went through the motions of apology. "I just wanted to find out how absolute you were going to be."

"Pala is a constitutional monarchy," Murugan answered gravely.

"In other words, you're just going to be a symbolic figurehead—to reign, like the Queen of England, but not rule."

Forgetting his regal dignity, "No, *no,*" Murugan almost screamed. "*Not* like the Queen of England. The Raja of Pala doesn't just reign; he rules." Too much agitated to sit still, Murugan jumped up and began to walk about the room. "He rules constitutionally; but, by God, he rules, he *rules!*" Murugan walked to the window and looked out. Turning back after a moment of silence, he confronted Will with a face transfigured by its new expression into an emblem, exquisitely molded and colored, of an all too familiar kind of psychological ugliness. "I'll show them who's the boss around here," he said in a phrase and tone which had obviously been borrowed from the hero of some American gangster movie. "These people think they can push me around," he went on, reciting from the dismally commonplace script, "the way they pushed my father around. But they're making a big mistake." He uttered a sinister snigger and wagged his beautiful, odious head. "A big mistake," he repeated.

The words had been spoken between clenched teeth and with scarcely moving lips; the lower jaw had been thrust out so as to look like the jaw of a comic strip criminal; the eyes glared coldly between narrowed lids. At once absurd and horrible. Antinoüs had become the caricature of all the tough guys in all the B-pictures from time immemorial.

"Who's been running the country during your minority?" he now asked.

"Three sets of old fogeys," Murugan answered contemptuously. "The Cabinet, the House of Representatives and then, representing *me*, the Raja, the Privy Council."

"Poor old fogeys!" said Will. "They'll soon be getting the shock of their lives." Entering gaily into the spirit of delinquency, he laughed aloud. "I only hope I'll still be around to see it happening."

Murugan joined in the laughter—joined in it, not as the sinisterly mirthful Tough Guy, but with one of those sudden changes of mood and expression that would make it, Will foresaw, so hard for him to play the Tough Guy part, as the triumphant urchin of a few minutes earlier. "The shock of their lives," he repeated happily.

"Have you made any specific plans?"

"I most certainly have," said Murugan. On his mobile face the triumphant urchin made way for the statesman, grave but condescendingly affable, at a press conference. "Top priority: get this place modernized. Look at what Rendang has been able to do because of its oil royalties."

"But doesn't Pala get any oil royalties?" Will questioned with that innocent air of total ignorance which he had found by long experience to be the best way of eliciting information from the simpleminded and the self-important.

"Not a penny," said Murugan. "And yet the southern end of the island is fairly oozing with the stuff. But except for a few measly little wells for home consumption, the old fogeys won't do anything about it. And what's more, they won't allow anyone else to do anything about it." The statesman was growing angry; there were hints now in his voice and expression of the Tough Guy. "All sorts of people have made offers—Southeast Asia Petroleum, Shell, Royal Dutch, Standard of California. But the bloody old fools won't listen."

"Can't you persuade them to listen?"

"I'll damn well *make* them listen," said the Tough Guy.

"That's the spirit!" Then, casually, "Which of the offers do you think of accepting?" he asked.

"Colonel Dipa's working with Standard of California, and he thinks it might be best if we did the same."

"I wouldn't do that without at least getting a few competing bids."

"That's what I think too. So does my mother."

"Very wise."

"My mother's all for Southeast Asia Petroleum. She knows the Chairman of the Board, Lord Aldehyde."

"She knows Lord Aldehyde? But how extraordinary!" The tone of delighted astonishment was thoroughly convincing. "Joe Aldehyde is a friend of mine. I write for his papers. I even serve as his private ambassador. Confidentially," he added, "that's why we took that trip to the copper mines. Copper is one of Joe's sidelines. But of course his real love is oil."

Murugan tried to look shrewd. "What would he be prepared to offer?"

Will picked up the cue and answered, in the best movie-tycoon style, "Whatever Standard offers plus a little more."

"Fair enough," said Murugan out of the same script, and nodded sagely. There was a long silence. When he spoke again, it was as the statesman granting an interview to representatives of the press.

"The oil royalties," he said, "will be used in the following manner: twenty-five per cent of all moneys received will go to World Reconstruction."

"May I ask," Will enquired deferentially, "precisely how you propose to reconstruct the world?"

"Through the Crusade of the Spirit. Do you know about the Crusade of the Spirit?"

"Of course. Who doesn't?"

"It's a great world movement," said the statesman gravely. "Like Early Christianity. Founded by my mother."

Will registered awe and astonishment.

"Yes, founded by my mother," Murugan repeated, and he added impressively, "I believe it's man's only hope."

"Quite," said Will Farnaby, "quite."

"Well, that's how the first twenty-five per cent of the royalties will be used," the statesman continued. "The remainder will go into an intensive program of industrialization." The tone changed again. "These old idiots here only want to industrialize in spots and leave all the rest as it was a thousand years ago."

"Whereas you'd like to go the whole hog. Industrialization for industrialization's sake."

"No, industrialization for the country's sake. Industrialization to make Pala strong. To make other people respect us. Look at Rendang. Within five years they'll be manufacturing all the rifles and mortars and ammunition they need. It'll be quite a long time before they can make tanks. But meanwhile they can buy them from Skoda with their oil money."

"How soon will they graduate to H-bombs?" Will asked ironically.

"They won't even try," Murugan answered. "But after all," he added, "H-bombs aren't the only absolute weapons." He pronounced the phrase with relish. It was evident that he found the taste of "absolute weapons" positively delicious. "Chemical and biological weapons—Colonel Dipa calls them the poor man's H-bombs. One of the first things I'll do is to build a big insecticide plant." Murugan laughed and winked an eye. "If you can make insecticides," he said, "you can make nerve gas."

Will remembered that still unfinished factory in the suburbs of Rendang-Lobo.

"What's that?" he had asked Colonel Dipa as they flashed past it in the white Mercedes.

"Insecticides," the Colonel had answered. And showing his gleaming white teeth in a genial smile, "We shall soon be exporting the stuff all over Southeast Asia."

At the time, of course, he had thought that the Colonel merely meant what he said. But now . . . Will shrugged his mental shoulders. Colonels will be colonels and boys, even boys like Murugan, will be gun-loving boys. There would always be plenty of jobs for special correspondents on the trail of death.

"So you'll strengthen Pala's army?" Will said aloud.

"Strengthen it? No—I'll create it. Pala doesn't have an army."

"None at all?"

"Absolutely nothing. They're all pacifists." The *p* was an explosion of disgust, the *s*'s hissed contemptuously. "I shall have to start from scratch."

"And you'll militarize as you industrialize, is that it?"

"Exactly."

Will laughed. "Back to the Assyrians! You'll go down in history as a true revolutionary."

"That's what I hope," said Murugan. "Because that's what my policy is going to be—Continuing Revolution."

"Very good!" Will applauded.

"I'll just be continuing the revolution that was started more than a hundred years ago by Dr. Robert's great-grandfather when he came to Pala and helped my great-great-grandfather to put through the first reforms. Some of the things they did were really wonderful. Not all of them, mind you," he qualified; and with the absurd solemnity of a schoolboy playing Polonius in an end-of-term performance of *Hamlet* he shook his curly head in grave, judicial disapproval. "But at least they *did* something. Whereas nowadays we're governed by a set of do-nothing conservatives. Conservatively primitive—they won't lift a finger to bring in modern improvements. And conservatively radical—they refuse to change any of the old bad revolutionary ideas that ought to be changed. They won't reform the reforms. And I tell you, some of those so-called reforms are absolutely disgusting."

"Meaning, I take it, that they have something to do with sex?"

Murugan nodded and turned away his face. To his astonishment, Will saw that he was blushing.

"Give me an example," he demanded.

But Murugan could not bring himself to be explicit.

"Ask Dr. Robert," he said, "ask Vijaya. *They* think that sort of thing is simply wonderful. In fact they all do. That's one of the reasons why nobody wants to change. They'd like everything to go on as it is, in the same old disgusting way, forever and ever."

"Forever and ever," a rich contralto voice teasingly repeated.

"Mother!" Murugan sprang to his feet.

Will turned and saw in the doorway a large florid woman

swathed (rather incongruously, he thought; for that kind of face and build usually went with mauve and magenta and electric blue) in clouds of white muslin. She stood there smiling with a conscious mysteriousness, one fleshy brown arm upraised, with its jeweled hand pressed against the doorjamb, in the post of the great actress, the acknowledged diva, pausing at her first entrance to accept the plaudits of her adorers on the other side of the footlights. In the background, waiting patiently for his cue, stood a tall man in a dove-gray Dacron suit whom Murugan, peering past the massive embodiment of maternity that almost filled the doorway, now greeted as Mr. Bahu.

Still in the wings, Mr. Bahu bowed without speaking.

Murugan turned again to his mother. "Did you *walk* here?" he asked. His tone expressed incredulity and an admiring solicitude. Walking here—how unthinkable! But if she *had* walked, what heroism! "All the way?"

"All the way, my baby," she echoed, tenderly playful. The uplifted arm came down, slid round the boy's slender body, pressed it, engulfed in floating draperies, against the enormous bosom, then released it again. "I had one of my Impulses." She had a way, Will noticed, of making you actually *hear* the capital letters at the beginning of the words she meant to emphasize. "My Little Voice said, 'Go and see this Stranger at Dr. Robert's house. Go!' 'Now?' I said. '*Malgré la chaleur?*' Which makes my Little Voice lose patience. 'Woman,' it says, 'hold your silly tongue and do as you're told.' So here I am, Mr. Farnaby." With hand outstretched and surrounded by a powerful aura of sandalwood oil, she advanced towards him.

Will bowed over the thick bejeweled fingers and mumbled something that ended in "Your Highness."

"Bahu!" she called, using the royal prerogative of the unadorned surname.

Responding to his long-awaited cue, the supporting actor made his entrance and was introduced as His Excellency, Abdul Bahu, the Ambassador of Rendang: "Abdul Pierre Bahu—*car sa mère est parisienne*. But he learned his English in New York."

He looked, Will thought as he shook the Ambassador's hand, like Savonarola—but a Savonarola with a monocle and a tailor in Savile Row.

"Bahu," said the Rani, "is Colonel Dipa's Brains Trust."

"Your Highness, if I may be permitted to say so, is much too kind to me and not nearly kind enough to the Colonel."

His words and manner were courtly to the point of being ironical, a parody of deference and self-abasement.

"The brains," he went on, "are where brains ought to be—in the head. As for me, I am merely a part of Rendang's sympathetic nervous system."

"*Et combien sympathique!*" said the Rani. "Among other things, Mr. Farnaby, Bahu is the Last of the Aristocrats. You should see his country place! Like *The Arabian Nights!* One claps one's hands—and instantly there are six servants ready to do one's bidding. One has a birthday—and there is a *fête nocturne* in the gardens. Music, refreshments, dancing girls; two hundred retainers carrying torches. The life of Harun al-Rashid, but with modern plumbing."

"It sounds quite delightful," said Will, remembering the villages through which he had passed in Colonel Dipa's white Mercedes—the wattled huts, the garbage, the children with ophthalmia, the skeleton dogs, the women bent double under enormous loads.

"And such taste," the Rani went on, "such as well-stored mind and, through it all" (she lowered her voice) "such a deep and unfailing Sense of the Divine."

Mr. Bahu bowed his head, and there was a silence.

Murugan, meanwhile, had pushed up a chair. Without so much as a backward glance—regally confident that someone must always, in the very nature of things, be at hand to guard against mishaps and loss of dignity—the Rani sat down with all the majestic emphasis of her hundred kilograms.

"I hope you don't feel that my visit is an intrusion," she said to Will. He assured her that he didn't; but she continued to apologize. "I would have given warning," she said, "I would have asked your permission. But my Little Voice says, 'No—you must go now.' Why? I cannot say. But no doubt we shall find out in due course." She fixed him with her large, bulging eyes and gave him a mysterious smile. "And now, first of all, how *are* you, dear Mr. Farnaby?"

"As you see, ma'am, in very good shape."

"Truly?" The bulging eyes scrutinized his face with an intentness that he found embarrassing. "I can see that you're the kind of heroically considerate man who will go on reassuring his friends even on his deathbed."

"You're very flattering," he said. "But as it happens, I *am* in good shape. Amazingly so, all things considered—miraculously so."

"Miraculous," said the Rani, "was the very word I used when I heard about your escape. It *was* a miracle."

"'As luck would have it,'" Will quoted again from *Erewhon*, "'Providence was on my side.'"

Mr. Bahu started to laugh; but noticing that the Rani had evidently failed to get the point, changed his mind and adroitly turned the sound of merriment into a loud cough.

"How true!" the Rani was saying, and her rich contralto thrillingly vibrated. "Providence is *always* on our side." And when Will raised a questioning eyebrow, "I mean," she elaborated, "in the eyes of those who Truly Understand" (capital T, capital U). "And this is true even when all things seem to conspire against us—*même dans le désastre.* You understand French, of course, Mr. Farnaby?" Will nodded. "It often comes to me more easily than my own native tongue, or English or Palanese. After so many years in Switzerland," she explained, "first at school. And again, later on, when my poor baby's health was so precarious" (she patted Murugan's bare arm) "and we had to go and live in the mountains. Which illustrates what I was saying about Providence always being on our side. When they told me that my little boy was on the brink of consumption, I forgot everything I'd ever learnt. I was mad with fear and anguish, I was indignant against God for having allowed such a thing to happen. What Utter Blindness! My baby got well, and those years among the Eternal Snows were the happiest of our lives—weren't they, darling?"

"The happiest of our lives," the boy agreed, with what almost sounded like complete sincerity.

The Rani smiled triumphantly, pouted her full red lips, and with a faint smack parted them again in a long-distance kiss. "So you see, my dear Farnaby," she went on, "you see. It's really self-evident. Nothing happens by Accident. There's a Great Plan, and within the Great Plan innumerable little plans. A little plan for each and every one of us."

"Quite," said Will politely. "Quite."

"There was a time," the Rani continued, "when I knew it only with my intellect. Now I know it with my heart. I really . . ." she paused for an instant to prepare for the utterance of the mystic majuscule, "Understand."

"Psychic as hell." Will remembered what Joe Aldehyde

had said of her. And surely that lifelong frequenter of séances should know.

"I take it, ma'am," he said, "that you're naturally psychic."

"From birth," she admitted. "But also and above all by training. Training, needless to say, in Something Else."

"Something else?"

"In the life of the Spirit. As one advances along the Path, all the *sidhis*, all the psychic gifts and miraculous powers, develop spontaneously."

"Is that so?"

"My mother," Murugan proudly assured him, "can do the most fantastic things."

"N'exagérons pas, chéri."

"But it's the truth," Murugan insisted.

"A truth," the Ambassador put in, "which I can confirm. And I confirm it," he added, smiling at his own expense, "with a certain reluctance. As a lifelong skeptic about these things, I don't like to see the impossible happening. But I have an unfortunate weakness for honesty. And when the impossible actually does happen, before my eyes, I'm compelled *malgré moi* to bear witness to the fact. Her Highness *does* do the *most* fantastic things."

"Well, if you like to put it that way," said the Rani, beaming with pleasure. "But never forget, Bahu, never forget. Miracles are of absolutely no importance. What's important is the Other Thing—the Thing one comes to at the end of the Path."

"After the Fourth Initiation," Murugan specified. "My mother . . ."

"Darling!" The Rani had raised a finger to her lips. "These are things one doesn't talk about."

"I'm sorry," said the boy. There was a long and pregnant silence.

The Rani closed her eyes, and Mr. Bahu, letting fall his monocle, reverentially followed suit and became the image of Savonarola in silent prayer. What was going on behind that austere, that almost fleshless mask of recollectedness? Will looked and wondered.

"May I ask," he said at last, "how you first came, ma'am, to find the Path?"

For a second or two the Rani said nothing, merely sat there with her eyes shut, smiling her Buddha smile of mysterious bliss. "Providence found it for me," she answered at last.

"Quite, quite. But there must have been an occasion, a place, a human instrument."

"I'll tell you." The lids fluttered apart and once again he found himself under the bright unswerving glare of those protuberant eyes of hers.

The place had been Lausanne; the time, the first year of her Swiss education; the chosen instrument, darling little Mme. Buloz. Darling little Mme. Buloz was the wife of darling old Professor Buloz, and old Professor Buloz was the man to whose charge, after careful enquiry and much anxious thought, she had been committed by her father, the late Sultan of Rendang. The Professor was sixty-seven, taught geology and was a Protestant of so austere a sect that, except for drinking a glass of claret with his dinner, saying his prayers only twice a day, and being strictly monogamous, he might almost have been a Muslim. Under such guardianship a princess of Rendang would be intellectually stimulated, while remaining morally and doctrinally intact. But the Sultan had reckoned without the Professor's wife. Mme. Buloz was only forty, plump, sentimental, bubblingly enthusiastic and, though officially of her husband's Protestant persuasion, a newly converted and intensely ardent Theosophist. In a room at the top of the tall house near the Place de la Riponne she had her Oratory, to which, whenever she could find time, she would secretly retire to do breathing exercises, practice concentration, and raise Kundalini. Strenuous disciplines! But the reward was transcendentally great. In the small hours of a hot summer night, while the darling old Professor lay rhythmically snoring two floors down, she had become aware of a Presence: the Master Koot Hoomi was with her.

The Rani made an impressive pause.

"Extraordinary," said Mr. Bahu.

"Extraordinary," Will dutifully echoed.

The Rani resumed her narrative. Irrepressibly happy, Mme. Buloz had been unable to keep her secret. She had dropped mysterious hints, had passed from hints to confidences, from confidences to an invitation to the Oratory and a course of instruction. In a very short time Koot Hoomi was bestowing greater favors upon the novice than upon her teacher.

"And from that day to this," she concluded, "the Master has helped me to Go Forward."

To go forward, Will asked himself, into what? Koot Hoomi only knew. But whatever it was that she had gone forward into, he didn't like it. There was an expression on that large florid face which he found peculiarly distasteful—an expression of domineering calm, of serene and unshakable self-esteem. She reminded him in a curious way of Joe Aldehyde. Joe was one of those happy tycoons who feel no qualms, but rejoice without inhibition in their money and in all that their money will buy in the way of influence and power. And here—albeit clothed in white muslin, mystic, wonderful—was another of Joe Aldehyde's breed: a female tycoon who had cornered the market, not in soya beans or copper, but in Pure Spirituality and the Ascended Masters, and was now happily rubbing her hands over the exploit.

"Here's one example of what He's done for me," the Rani went on. "Eight years ago—to be exact, on the twenty-third of November, 1952—the Master came to me in my morning Meditation. Came in Person, came in Glory. 'A great Crusade is to be launched,' He said, 'a World Movement to save Humanity from self-destruction. And you, my child, are the Appointed Instrument.' 'Me? A World movement? But that's absurd,' I said. 'I've never made a speech in my whole life. I've never written a word for publication. I've never been a leader or an organizer.' 'Nevertheless,' He said (and He gave one of these indescribably beautiful smiles of His), 'nevertheless it is you who will launch this Crusade—the World-Wide Crusade of the Spirit. You will be laughed at, you will be called a fool, a crank, a fanatic. The dogs bark; the Caravan passes. From tiny, laughable beginnings the Crusade of the Spirit is destined to become a Mighty Force. A force for Good, a force that will ultimately Save the World.' And with that He left me. Left me stunned, bewildered, scared out of my wits. But there was nothing for it; I had to obey. I *did* obey. And what happened? I made speeches, and He gave me eloquence. I accepted the burden of leadership and, because He was walking invisibly at my side, people followed me. I asked for help, and the money came pouring in. So here I am." She threw out her thick hands in a gesture of self-depreciation, she smiled a mystic smile. *A poor thing,* she seemed to be saying, *but not my own—my Master's, Koot Hoomi's.* "Here I am," she repeated.

"Here, praise God," said Mr. Bahu devoutly, "you are."

After a decent interval Will asked the Rani if she had always kept up the practices so providentially learned in Mme. Buloz's Oratory.

"Always," she answered. "I could no more do without Meditation than I could do without Food."

"Wasn't it rather difficult after you were married? I mean, before you went back to Switzerland. There must have been so many tiresome official duties."

"Not to mention all the *un*official ones," said the Rani in a tone that implied whole volumes of unfavorable comment upon her late husband's character, *Weltanschauung* and sexual habits. She opened her mouth to elaborate on the theme, then closed it again and looked at Murugan. "Darling," she called.

Murugan, who was absorbedly polishing the nails of his left hand upon the open palm of his right, looked up with a guilty start. "Yes, Mother?"

Ignoring the nails and his evident inattention to what she had been saying, the Rani gave him a seducing smile. "Be an angel," she said, "and go and fetch the car. My Little Voice doesn't say anything about *walking* back to the bungalow. It's only a few hundred yards," she explained to Will. "But in this heat, and at my age . . ."

Her words called for some kind of flattering rebuttal. But if it was too hot to walk, it was also too hot, Will felt, to put forth the very considerable amount of energy required for a convincing show of bogus sincerity. Fortunately a professional diplomat, a practiced courtier was on hand to make up for the uncouth journalist's deficiencies. Mr. Bahu uttered a peal of lighthearted laughter, then apologized for his merriment. "But it was really *too* funny! 'At my age,'" he repeated, and laughed again. "Murugan is not quite eighteen, and I happen to know how old—how *very* young—the Princess of Rendang was when she married the Raja of Pala."

Murugan, meanwhile, had obediently risen and was kissing his mother's hand.

"Now we can talk more freely," said the Rani when he had left the room. And freely—her face, her tone, her bulging eyes, her whole quivering frame registering the most intense disapproval—she now let fly. *De mortuis* . . . She wouldn't say anything about her husband except that he was a typical Palanese, a true representative of his country. For the sad truth was that Pala's smooth bright skin concealed the most horrible rottenness.

"When I think what they tried to do to my Baby, two years ago, when I was on my world tour for the Crusade of the Spirit." With a jingling of bracelets she lifted her hands in horror. "It was an agony for me to be parted from him for so long; but the Master had sent me on a Mission, and my Little Voice told me that it wouldn't be right for me to take my Baby with me. He'd lived abroad for so long. It was high time for him to get to know the country he was to rule. So I decided to leave him here. The Privy Council appointed a committee of guardianship. Two women with growing boys of their own and two men—one of whom, I regret to say" (more in sorrow than in anger), "was Dr. Robert MacPhail. Well, to cut a long story short, no sooner was I safely out of the country than those precious guardians, to whom I'd entrusted my Baby, my Only Son, set to work systematically—*systematically*, Mr. Farnaby—to undermine my influence. They tried to destroy the whole edifice of Moral and Spiritual Values which I had so laboriously built up over the years."

Somewhat maliciously (for of course he knew what the woman was talking about), Will expressed his astonishment. The *whole* edifice of moral and spiritual values? And yet nobody could have been kinder than Dr. Robert and the others, no Good Samaritans were ever more simply and effectively charitable.

"I'm not denying their kindness," said the Rani. "But after all kindness isn't the only virtue."

"Of course not," Will agreed, and he listed all the qualities that the Rani seemed most conspicuously to lack. "There's also sincerity. Not to mention truthfulness, humility, selflessness . . ."

"You're forgetting Purity," said the Rani severely. "Purity is fundamental, Purity is the *sine qua non*."

"But here in Pala, I gather, they don't think so."

"They most certainly do not," said the Rani. And she went on to tell him how her poor Baby had been deliberately exposed to impurity, even actively encouraged to indulge in it with one of those precocious, promiscuous girls of whom, in Pala, there were only too many. And when they found that he wasn't the sort of boy who would seduce a girl (for she had brought him up to think of Woman as essentially Holy), they had encouraged the girl to do her best to seduce *him*.

Had she, Will wondered, succeeded? Or had Antinoüs already been girlproofed by little friends of his own age or, still more effectively, by some older, more experienced and authoritative pederast, some Swiss precursor of Colonel Dipa?

"But that wasn't the worst." The Rani lowered her voice to a horrified stage whisper. "One of the mothers on the committee of guardianship—one of the *mothers*, mind you—advised him to take a course of lessons."

"What sort of lessons?"

"In what they euphemistically call Love." She wrinkled up her nose as though she had smelt raw sewage. "Lessons, if you please," and disgust turned into indignation, "from some Older Woman."

"Heavens!" cried the Ambassador.

"Heavens!" Will dutifully echoed. Those older women, he could see, were competitors much more dangerous, in the Rani's eyes, than even the most precociously promiscuous of girls. A mature instructress in love would be a rival mother, enjoying the monstrously unfair advantage of being free to go the limits of incest.

"They teach . . ." The Rani hesitated. "They teach Special Techniques."

"What sort of techniques?" Will enquired.

But she couldn't bring herself to go into the repulsive particulars. And anyhow it wasn't necessary, for Murugan (bless his heart!) had refused to listen to them. Lessons in immorality from someone old enough to be his mother—the very idea of it had made him sick. No wonder. He had been brought up to reverence the Ideal of Purity. "*Brahmacharya*, if you know what that means."

"Quite," said Will.

"And this is another reason why his illness was such a blessing in disguise, such a real godsend. I don't think I *could* have brought him up that way in Pala. There are too many bad influences here. Forces working against Purity, against the Family, even against Mother Love."

Will pricked up his ears. "Did they even reform mothers?"

She nodded. "You just can't imagine how far things have gone here. But Koot Hoomi knew what kind of dangers we would have to run in Pala. So what happens? My Baby falls ill, and the doctors order us to Switzerland. Out of harm's way."

"How was it," Will asked, "that Koot Hoomi let you go off on your Crusade? Didn't he foresee what would happen to Murugan as soon as your back was turned?"

"He foresaw everything," said the Rani. "The temptations,

the resistance, the massed assault by all the Powers of Evil and then, at the very last moment, the rescue. For a long time," she explained, "Murugan didn't tell me what was happening. But after three months the assaults of the Powers of Evil were too much for him. He dropped hints; but I was too completely absorbed in my Master's business to be able to take them. Finally he wrote me a letter in which it was all spelled out—in detail. I canceled my last four lectures in Brazil and flew home as fast as the jets would carry me. A week later we were back in Switzerland. Just my Baby and I—alone with the Master."

She closed her eyes, and an expression of gloating ecstasy appeared upon her face. Will looked away in distaste. This self-canonized world-savior, this clutching and devouring mother—had she ever, for a single moment, seen herself as others saw her? Did she have any idea of what she had done, what she was still doing, to her poor silly little son? To the first question the answer was certainly no. About the second one could only speculate. Perhaps she honestly didn't know what she had made of the boy. But perhaps, on the other hand, she *did* know. Knew and preferred what was happening with the Colonel to what might happen if the boy's education were taken in hand by a woman. The woman might supplant her; the Colonel, she knew, would not.

"Murugan told me that he intended to reform these so-called reforms."

"I can only pray," said the Rani in a tone that reminded Will of his grandfather, the Archdeacon, "that he'll be given the Strength and Wisdom to do it."

"And what do you think of his other projects?" Will asked. "Oil? Industries? An army?"

"Economics and politics aren't exactly my strong point," she answered with a little laugh which was meant to remind him that he was talking to someone who had taken the Fourth Initiation. "Ask Bahu what he thinks."

"I have no right to offer an opinion," said the Ambassador. "I'm an outsider, the representative of a foreign power."

"Not so very foreign," said the Rani.

"Not in your eyes, ma'am. And not, as you know very well, in mine. But in the eyes of the Palanese government—yes. Completely foreign."

"But that," said Will, "doesn't prevent you from having

opinions. It only prevents you from having the locally orthodox opinions. And incidentally," he added, "I'm not here in my professional capacity. You're not being interviewed, Mr. Ambassador. All this is strictly off the record."

"Strictly off the record, then, and strictly as myself and not as an official personage, I believe that our young friend is perfectly right."

"Which implies, of course, that you believe the policy of the Palanese government to be perfectly wrong."

"Perfectly wrong," said Mr. Bahu—and the bony, emphatic mask of Savonarola positively twinkled with his Voltairean smile—"perfectly wrong because all too perfectly right."

"Right?" the Rani protested. "Right?"

"Perfectly right," he explained, "because so perfectly designed to make every man, woman, and child on this enchanting island as perfectly free and happy as it's possible to be."

"But with a False Happiness," the Rani cried, "a freedom that's only for the Lower Self."

"I bow," said the Ambassador, duly bowing, "to Your Highness's superior insight. But still, high or low, true or false, happiness is happiness and freedom is most enjoyable. And there can be no doubt that the politics inaugurated by the original Reformers and developed over the years have been admirably well adapted to achieving these two goals."

"But you feel," said Will, "that these are undesirable goals?"

"On the contrary, everybody desires them. But unfortunately they're out of context, they've become completely irrelevant to the present situation of the world in general and Pala in particular."

"Are they more irrelevant now than they were when the Reformers first started to work for happiness and freedom?"

The Ambassador nodded. "In those days Pala was still completely off the map. The idea of turning it into an oasis of freedom and happiness made sense. So long as it remains out of touch with the rest of the world, an ideal society can be a viable society. Pala was completely viable, I'd say, until about 1905. Then, in less than a single generation, the world completely changed. Movies, cars, airplanes, radio. Mass production, mass slaughter, mass communication and, above all, plain mass—more and more people in bigger and bigger slums or suburbs. By 1930 any clear-sighted observer could have seen that, for three quarters of the human race, freedom and happiness were almost out of the question. Today, thirty years later, they're completely out of the question. And meanwhile the outside world has been closing in on this little island of freedom and happiness. Closing in steadily and inexorably, coming nearer and nearer. What was once a viable ideal is now no longer viable."

"So Pala will have to be changed—is that your conclusion?"

Mr. Bahu nodded. "Radically."

"Root and branch," said the Rani with a prophet's sadistic gusto.

"And for two cogent reasons," Mr. Bahu went on. "First, because it simply isn't possible for Pala to go on being different from the rest of the world. And, second, because it isn't right that it should be different."

"Not right for people to be free and happy?"

Once again the Rani said something inspirational about false happiness and the wrong kind of freedom.

Mr. Bahu deferentially acknowledged her interruption, then turned back to Will.

"Not right," he insisted. "Flaunting your blessedness in the face of so much misery—it's sheer hubris, it's a deliberate affront to the rest of humanity. It's even a kind of affront to God."

"God," the Rani murmured voluptuously, "God . . ."

Then, reopening her eyes, "These people in Pala," she added, "they don't believe in God. They only believe in Hypnotism and Pantheism and Free Love." She emphasized the words with indignant disgust.

"So now," said Will, "you're proposing to make them miserable in the hope that this will restore their faith in God. Well, that's one way of producing a conversion. Maybe it'll work. And maybe the end will justify the means." He shrugged his shoulders. "But I do see," he added, "that, good or bad, and regardless of what the Palanese may feel about it, this thing is going to happen. One doesn't have to be much of a prophet to foretell that Murugan is going to succeed. He's riding the wave of the future. And the wave of the future is undoubtedly a wave of crude petroleum. Talking of crudity and petroleum," he added, turning to the Rani, "I understand that you're acquainted with my old friend, Joe Aldehyde."

"You know Lord Aldehyde?"

"Well."

"So *that's* why my Little Voice was so insistent!" Closing her eyes again, she smiled to herself and slowly nodded her head. "Now I Understand." Then, in another tone, "How is that dear man?" she asked.

"Still characteristically himself," Will assured her.

"And what a rare self! *L'homme au cerf-volant*—that's what I call him."

"The man with the kite?" Will was puzzled.

"He does his work down here," she explained; "but he holds a string in his hand, and at the other end of the string is a kite, and the kite is forever trying to go higher, higher, Higher. Even while he's at work, he feels the constant Pull from Above, feels the Spirit tugging insistently at the flesh. Think of it! A man of affairs, a great Captain of Industry—and yet, for him, the only thing that Really Matters is the Immortality of the Soul."

Light dawned. The woman had been talking about Joe Aldehyde's addiction to spiritualism. He thought of those weekly séances with Mrs. Harbottle, the automatist; with Mrs. Pym, whose control was a Kiowa Indian called Bawbo; with Miss Tuke and her floating trumpet out of which a squeaky whisper uttered oracular words that were taken down in shorthand by Joe's private secretary: "*Buy Australian cement; don't be alarmed by the fall in Breakfast Foods; unload forty per cent of your rubber shares and invest the money in IBM and Westinghouse . . .*"

"Did he ever tell you," Will asked, "about that departed stockbroker who always knew what the market was going to do next week?"

"*Sidhis*," said the Rani indulgently. "Just *sidhis*. What else can you expect? After all, he's only a Beginner. And in this present life business is his karma. He was predestined to do what he's done, what he's doing, what he's going to do. And what he's going to do," she added impressively and paused in a listening pose, her finger lifted, her head cocked, "what he's going to do—that's what my Little Voice is saying—includes some great and wonderful things here in Pala."

What a spiritual way of saying, This is what I want to happen! Not as I will but as God wills—and by a happy coincidence God's will and mine are always identical. Will chuckled inwardly, but kept the straightest of faces.

"Does your Little Voice say anything about Southeast Asia Petroleum?" he asked.

The Rani listened again, then nodded. "Distinctly."

"But Colonel Dipa, I gather, doesn't say anything but 'Standard of California.' Incidentally," Will went on, "why does Pala have to worry about the Colonel's taste in oil companies?"

"My government," said Mr. Bahu sonorously, "is thinking in terms of a Five-Year Plan for Interisland Economic Co-ordination and Co-operation."

"Does Interisland Co-ordination and Co-operation mean that Standard has to be granted a monopoly?"

"Only if Standard's terms were more advantageous than those of its competitors."

"In other words," said the Rani, "only if there's nobody who will pay us more."

"Before you came," Will told her, "I was discussing this subject with Murugan. Southeast Asia Petroleum, I said, will give Pala whatever Standard gives Rendang plus a little more."

"Fifteen per cent more?"

"Let's say ten."

"Make it twelve and a half."

Will looked at her admiringly. For someone who had taken the Fourth Initiation she was doing pretty well.

"Joe Aldehyde will scream with agony," he said. "But in the end, I feel certain, you'll get your twelve and a half."

"It would certainly be a most attractive proposition," said Mr. Bahu.

"The only trouble is that the Palanese government won't accept it."

"The Palanese government," said the Rani, "will soon be changing its policy."

"You think so?"

"I KNOW it," the Rani answered in a tone that made it quite clear that the information had come straight from the Master's mouth.

"When the change of policy comes, would it help," Will asked, "if Colonel Dipa were to put in a good word for Southeast Asia Petroleum?"

"Undoubtedly."

Will turned to Mr. Bahu. "And would you be prepared, Mr. Ambassador, to put in a good word with Colonel Dipa?"

In polysyllables, as though he were addressing a plenary session of some international organization, Mr. Bahu hedged diplomatically. On the one hand, yes; but on the other hand, no. From one point of view, white; but from a different angle, distinctly black.

Will listened in polite silence. Behind the mask of Savonarola, behind the aristocratic monocle, behind the ambassadorial verbiage he could see and hear the Levantine broker in quest of his commission, the petty official cadging for a gratuity. And for her enthusiastic sponsorship of Southeast Asia Petroleum, how much had the royal initiate been promised? Something, he was prepared to bet, pretty substantial. Not for herself, of course, no *no!* For the Crusade of the Spirit, needless to say, for the greater glory of Koot Hoomi.

Mr. Bahu had reached the peroration of his speech to the international organization. "It must therefore be understood," he was saying, "that any positive action on my part must remain contingent upon circumstances as, when, and if these circumstances arise. Do I make myself clear?"

"Perfectly," Will assured him. "And now," he went on with deliberately indecent frankness, "let me explain my position in this matter. All *I'm* interested in is money. Two thousand pounds without having to do a hand's turn of work. A year of freedom just for helping Joe Aldehyde to get his hands on Pala."

"Lord Aldehyde," said the Rani, "is remarkably generous."

"Remarkably," Will agreed, "considering how little I can do in this matter. Needless to say, he'd be still more generous to anyone who could be of greater help."

There was a long silence. In the distance a mynah bird was calling monotonously for attention. Attention to avarice, attention to hypocrisy, attention to vulgar cynicism . . . There was a knock at the door.

"Come in," Will called out and, turning to Mr. Bahu, "Let's continue this conversation some other time," he said.

Mr. Bahu nodded.

"Come in," Will repeated.

Dressed in a blue skirt and a short buttonless jacket that left her midriff bare and only sometimes covered a pair of apple-round breasts, a girl in her late teens walked briskly into the room. On her smooth brown face a smile of friendliest greeting was punctuated at either end by dimples. "I'm

Nurse Appu," she began. "Radha Appu." Then, catching sight of Will's visitors, she broke off. "Oh, excuse me, I didn't know . . ."

She made a perfunctory *knicks* to the Rani.

Mr. Bahu, meanwhile, had courteously risen to his feet. "Nurse Appu," he cried enthusiastically. "My little ministering angel from the Shivapuram hospital. What a delightful surprise!"

For the girl, it was evident to Will, the surprise was far from delightful.

"How do you do, Mr. Bahu," she said without a smile and, quickly turning away, started to busy herself with the straps of the canvas bag she was carrying.

"Your Highness has probably forgotten," said Mr. Bahu; "but I had to have an operation last summer. For hernia," he specified. "Well, this young lady used to come and wash me every morning. Punctually at eight-forty-five. And now, after having vanished for all these months, here she is again!"

"Synchronicity," said the Rani oracularly. "It's all part of the Plan."

"I'm supposed to give Mr. Farnaby an injection," said the little nurse, looking up, still unsmiling, from her professional bag.

"Doctor's orders are doctor's orders," cried the Rani, overacting the role of royal personage deigning to be playfully gracious. "To hear is to obey. But where's my chauffeur?"

"Your chauffeur's here," called a familiar voice.

Beautiful as a vision of Ganymede, Murugan was standing in the doorway. A look of amusement appeared on the little nurse's face.

"Hullo, Murugan—I mean, Your Highness." She bobbed another curtsy, which he was free to take as a mark of respect or of ironic mockery.

"Oh, hullo, Radha," said the boy in a tone that was meant to be distantly casual. He walked past her to where his mother was sitting. "The car," he said, "is at the door. Or rather the so-called car." With a sarcastic laugh, "It's a Baby Austin, 1954 vintage," he explained to Will. "The best that this highly civilized country can provide for its royal family. Rendang gives its ambassador a Bentley," he added bitterly.

"Which will be calling for me at this address in about

ten minutes," said Mr. Bahu, looking at his watch. "So may I be permitted to take leave of you here, Your Highness?"

The Rani extended her hand. With all the piety of a good Catholic kissing a cardinal's ring, he bent over it; then, straightening himself up, he turned to Will.

"I'm assuming—perhaps unjustifiably—that Mr. Farnaby can put up with me for a little longer. May I stay?"

Will assured the Ambassador that he would be delighted.

"And I hope," said Mr. Bahu to the little nurse, "that there will be no objections on medical grounds?"

"Not on medical grounds," said the girl in a tone that implied the existence of the most cogent nonmedical objections.

Assisted by Murugan, the Rani hoisted herself out of her chair. "*Au revoir, mon cher* Farnaby," she said as she gave him her jeweled hand. Her smile was charged with a sweetness that Will found positively menacing.

"Good-bye, ma'am."

She turned, patted the little nurse's cheek, and sailed out of the room. Like a pinnace in the wake of a full-rigged ship of the line, Murugan trailed after her.

vi

"GOLLY!" THE LITTLE NURSE EXPLODED, WHEN THE DOOR was safely closed behind them.

"I entirely agree with you," said Will.

The Voltairean light twinkled for a moment on Mr. Bahu's evangelical face. "Golly," he repeated. "It was what I heard an English schoolboy saying when he first saw the Great Pyramid. The Rani makes the same kind of impression. Monumental. She's what the Germans call *eine grosse Seele.*" The twinkle had faded, the face was unequivocally Savonarola's, the words, it was obvious, were for publication.

The little nurse suddenly started to laugh.

"What's so funny?" Will asked.

"I suddenly saw the Great Pyramid all dressed up in white muslin," she gasped. "Dr. Robert calls it the mystic's uniform."

"Witty, very witty!" said Mr. Bahu. "And yet," he added diplomatically, "I don't know why mystics shouldn't wear uniforms, if they feel like it."

The little nurse drew a deep breath, wiped the tears of merriment from her eyes, and began to make her preparations for giving the patient his injection.

"I know exactly what you're thinking," she said to Will. "You're thinking I'm much too young to do a good job."

"I certainly think you're very young."

"You people go to a university at eighteen and stay there for four years. We start at sixteen and go on with our education till we're twenty-four—half-time study and half-time work. I've been doing biology and at the same time doing this job for two years. So I'm not quite such a fool as I look. Actually I'm a pretty good nurse."

"A statement," said Mr. Bahu, "which I can unequivocally confirm. Miss Radha is not merely a good nurse; she's an absolutely first-rate one."

But what he really meant, Will felt sure as he studied the expression on that face of a much-tempted monk, was that Miss Radha had a first-rate midriff, first-rate navel, and first-rate breasts. But the owner of the navel, midriff and breasts had clearly resented Savonarola's admiration, or at any rate the way it had been expressed. Hopefully, overhopefully, the rebuffed Ambassador was returning the attack.

The spirit lamp was lighted and, while the needle was being boiled, little Nurse Appu took her patient's temperature.

"Ninety-nine point two."

"Does that mean I have to be banished?" Mr. Bahu enquired.

"Not so far as he's concerned," the girl answered.

"So please stay," said Will.

The little nurse gave him his injection of antibiotic, then, from one of the bottles in her bag, stirred a tablespoonful of some greenish liquid into half a glass of water.

"Drink this."

It tasted like one of those herbal concoctions that health-food enthusiasts substitute for tea.

"What is it?" Will asked, and was told that it was an extract from a mountain plant related to valerian.

"It helps people to stop worrying," the little nurse explained, "without making them sleepy. We give it to convalescents. It's useful, too, in mental cases."

"Which am I? Mental or convalescent?"

"Both," she answered without hesitation.

Will laughed aloud. "That's what comes of fishing for compliments."

"I didn't mean to be rude," she assured him. "All I meant was that I've never met anybody from the outside who wasn't a mental case."

"Including the Ambassador?"

She turned the question back upon the questioner. "What do *you* think?"

Will passed it on to Mr. Bahu. "You're the expert in this field," he said.

"Settle it between yourselves," said the little nurse. "I've got to go and see about my patient's lunch."

Mr. Bahu watched her go; then, raising his left eyebrow, he let fall his monocle and started methodically to polish the lens with his handkerchief. "You're aberrated in one way," he said to Will. "I'm aberrated in another. A schizoid (isn't that what you are?) and, from the other side of the world, a paranoid. Both of us victims of the same twentieth-century plague. Not the Black Death, this time; the Gray Life. Were you ever interested in power?" he asked after a moment of silence.

"Never." Will shook his head emphatically. "One can't have power without committing oneself."

"And for you the horror of being committed outweighs the pleasure of pushing other people around?"

"By a factor of several thousand times."

"So it was never a temptation?"

"Never." Then after a pause, "Let's get down to business," Will added in another tone.

"To business," Mr. Bahu repeated. "Tell me something about Lord Aldehyde."

"Well, as the Rani said, he's remarkably generous."

"I'm not interested in his virtues, only his intelligence. How bright is he?"

"Bright enough to know that nobody does anything for nothing."

"Good," said Mr. Bahu. "Then tell him from me that for effective work by experts in strategic positions he must be prepared to lay out at least ten times what he's going to pay you."

"I'll write him a letter to that effect."

"And do it today," Mr. Bahu advised. "The plane leaves Shivapuram tomorrow evening, and there won't be another outgoing mail for a whole week."

"Thank you for telling me," said Will. "And now—Her Highness and the shockable stripling being gone—let's move on to the next temptation. What about sex?"

With the gesture of a man who tries to rid himself of a cloud of importunate insects, Mr. Bahu waved a brown and bony hand back and forth in front of his face. "Just a distraction, that's all. Just a nagging, humiliating vexation. But an intelligent man can always cope with it."

"How difficult it is," said Will, "to understand another man's vices!"

"You're right. Everybody should stick to the insanity that God has seen fit to curse him with. *Pecca fortiter*—that was Luther's advice. But make a point of sinning your own sins, not someone else's. And above all don't do what the people of this island do. Don't try to behave as though you were essentially sane and naturally good. We're all demented sinners in the same cosmic boat—and the boat is perpetually sinking."

"In spite of which, no rat is justified in leaving it. Is that what you're saying?"

"A few of them may sometimes try to leave. But they never get very far. History and the other rats will always see to it that they drown with the rest of us. That's why Pala doesn't have the ghost of a chance."

Carrying a tray, the little nurse re-entered the room.

"Buddhist food," she said, as she tied a napkin round Will's neck. "All except the fish. But we've decided that fishes are vegetables within the meaning of the act."

Will started to eat.

"Apart from the Rani and Murugan and us two here," he asked after swallowing the first mouthful, "how many people from the outside have you ever met?"

"Well, there was that group of American doctors," she answered. "They came to Shivapuram last year, while I was working at the Central Hospital."

"What were they doing here?"

"They wanted to find out why we have such a low rate of neurosis and cardiovascular trouble. Those doctors!" She shook her head. "I tell you, Mr. Farnaby, they really made my hair stand on end—made everybody's hair stand on end in the whole hospital."

"So you think our medicine's pretty primitive?"

"That's the wrong word. It isn't primitive. It's fifty per cent terrific and fifty per cent nonexistent. Marvelous antibiotics—but absolutely no methods for increasing resistance, so that antibiotics won't be necessary. Fantastic operations—but when it comes to teaching people the way of going through life without having to be chopped up, absolutely nothing. And it's the same all along the line. Alpha Plus for patching you up when you've started to fall apart; but Delta Minus for keeping you healthy. Apart from sewerage systems and synthetic vitamins, you don't seem to do anything at all about prevention. And yet you've got a proverb: prevention is better than cure."

"But cure," said Will, "is so much more dramatic than prevention. And for the doctors it's also a lot more profitable."

"Maybe for your doctors," said the little nurse. "Not for ours. Ours get paid for keeping people well."

"How is it to be done?"

"We've been asking that question for a hundred years, and we've found a lot of answers. Chemical answers, psychological answers, answers in terms of what you eat, how you make love, what you see and hear, how you feel about being who you are in this kind of world."

"And which are the best answers?"

"None of them is best without the others."

"So there's no panacea."

"How can there be?" And she quoted the little rhyme that every student nurse had to learn by heart on the first day of her training.

" 'I' am a crowd, obeying as many laws
As it has members. Chemically impure
Are all 'my' beings. There's no single cure
For what can never have a single cause."

"So whether it's prevention or whether it's cure, we attack on all the fronts at once. *All* the fronts," she insisted, "from diet to autosuggestion, from negative ions to meditation."

"Very sensible," was Will's comment.

"Perhaps a little *too* sensible," said Mr. Bahu. "Did you ever try to talk sense to a maniac?" Will shook his head. "I did once." He lifted the graying lock that slanted obliquely across his forehead. Just below the hairline a jagged scar stood out, strangely pale against the brown skin. "Luckily for me, the bottle he hit me with was pretty flimsy." Smoothing his ruffled hair, he turned to the little nurse. "Don't ever forget, Miss Radha; to the senseless nothing is more maddening than sense. Pala is a small island completely surrounded by twenty-nine hundred million mental cases. So beware of being too rational. In the country of the insane, the integrated man doesn't become king." Mr. Bahu's face was positively twinkling with Voltairean glee. "He gets lynched."

Will laughed perfunctorily, then turned again to the little nurse.

"Don't you have any candidates for the asylum?" he asked.

"Just as many as you have—I mean in proportion to the population. At least that's what the textbook says."

"So living in a sensible world doesn't seem to make any difference."

"Not to the people with the kind of body chemistry that'll turn them into psychotics. They're born vulnerable. Little troubles that other people hardly notice can bring them down. We're just beginning to find out what it is that makes them so vulnerable. We're beginning to be able to spot them in advance of a breakdown. And once they've been spotted, we can do something to raise their resistance. Prevention again—and, of course, on all the fronts at once."

"So being born into a sensible world will make a difference even for the predestined psychotic."

"And for the neurotics it has already made a difference. Your neurosis rate is about one in five or even four. Ours is about one in twenty. The one that breaks down gets treatment, on all fronts, and the nineteen who don't break down have had prevention on all the fronts. Which brings me back to those American doctors. Three of them were psychiatrists, and one of the psychiatrists smoked cigars without stopping and had a German accent. He was the one that was chosen to give us a lecture. What a lecture!" The little nurse held her head between her hands. "I never heard anything like it."

"What was it about?"

"About the way they treat people with neurotic symptoms. We just couldn't believe our ears. They *never* attack on all the fronts; they only attack on about half of one front. So far as they're concerned, the physical fronts don't exist. Except for a mouth and an anus, their patient doesn't have a body. He isn't an organism, he wasn't born with a constitution or a temperament. All he has is the two ends of a digestive tube, a family and a psyche. But what sort of psyche? Obviously not the whole mind, not the mind as it really is. How could it be that when they take no account of a person's anatomy, or biochemistry or physiology? Mind abstracted from body—that's the only front they attack on. And not even on the whole of that front. The man with the cigar kept talking about the unconscious. But the only unconscious they ever pay attention to is the negative unconscious, the garbage that people have tried to get rid of by burying it in the basement. Not a single word about the positive unconscious. No attempt to help the patient to open himself up to the life force or the Buddha Nature. And no attempt even to teach him to be a little more conscious in his everyday life. You know: 'Here and now, boys.' 'Attention.'" She gave an imitation of the mynah birds. "These people just leave the unfortunate neurotic to wallow in his old bad habits of never being all there in present time. The whole thing is just pure idiocy! No, the man with the cigar didn't even have *that* excuse; he was as clever as clever can be. So it's not idiocy. It must be something voluntary, something self-induced—like getting drunk or talking yourself into believing some piece of foolishness because it happens to be in the Scriptures. And then look at their idea of what's normal. Believe it or not, a normal human being is one who can have an orgasm and is adjusted to his society." Once again the little nurse held her head between her hands. "It's unimaginable! No question about what you do with your orgasms. No question about the quality of your feelings and thoughts and perceptions. And then what about the society you're supposed to be adjusted to? Is it a mad society or a sane one? And even if it's pretty sane, is it right that anybody should be *completely* adjusted to it?"

With another of his twinkling smiles, "Those whom God would destroy," said the Ambassador, "He first makes mad. Or alternatively, and perhaps even more effectively, He first makes them sane." Mr. Bahu rose and walked to the window. "My car has come for me. I must be getting back to Shivapuram and my desk." He turned to Will and treated him to a long and flowery farewell. Then, switching off the Ambassador, "Don't forget to write that letter," he said. "It's very important." He smiled conspiratorially and, passing his thumb back and forth across the first two fingers of his right hand, he counted out invisible money.

"Thank goodness," said the little nurse when he had gone.

"What was his offense?" Will enquired. "The usual thing?"

"Offering money to someone you want to go to bed with—but she doesn't like you. So you offer more. Is that usual where he comes from?"

"Profoundly usual," Will assured her.

"Well, I didn't like it."

"So I could see. And here's another question. What about Murugan?"

"What makes you ask?"

"Curiosity. I noticed that you'd met before. Was that when he was here two years ago without his mother?"

"How did you know about that?"

"A little bird told me—or rather an extremely massive bird."

"The Rani! She must have made it sound like Sodom and Gomorrah."

"But unfortunately I was spared the lurid details. Dark hints—that was all she gave me. Hints, for example, about veteran Messalinas giving lessons in love to innocent young boys."

"And did he need those lessons!"

"Hints, too, about a precocious and promiscuous girl of his own age."

Nurse Appu burst out laughing.

"Did you know her?"

"The precocious and promiscuous girl was me."

"You? Does the Rani know it?"

"Murugan only gave her the facts, not the names. For which I'm very grateful. You see, I'd behaved pretty badly. Losing my head about someone I didn't really love and hurting someone I did. Why is one so stupid?"

"The heart has its reasons," said Will, "and the endocrines have theirs."

There was a long silence. He finished the last of his cold boiled fish and vegetables. Nurse Appu handed him a plate of fruit salad.

"You've never seen Murugan in white satin pajamas," she said.

"Have I missed something?"

"You've no idea how beautiful he looks in white satin pajamas. Nobody has any right to be so beautiful. It's indecent. It's taking an unfair advantage."

It was the sight of him in those white satin pajamas from Sulka that had finally made her lose her head. Lose it so completely that for two months she had been someone else —an idiot who had gone chasing after a person who couldn't bear her and had turned her back on the person who had always loved her, the person she herself had always loved.

"Did you get anywhere with the pajama boy?" Will asked.

"As far as a bed," she answered. "But when I started to kiss him, he jumped out from between the sheets and locked himself in the bathroom. He wouldn't come out until I'd passed his pajamas through the transom and given him my word of honor that he wouldn't be molested. I can laugh about it now; but at the time, I tell you, at the time . . ." She shook her head. "Pure tragedy. They must have guessed, from the way I carried on, what had happened. Precocious and promiscuous girls, it was obvious, were no good. What he needed was regular lessons."

"And the rest of the story I know," said Will. "Boy writes to Mother, Mother flies home and whisks him off to Switzerland."

"And they didn't come back until about six months ago. And for at least half of that time they were in Rendang, staying with Murugan's aunt."

Will was on the point of mentioning Colonel Dipa, then remembered that he had promised Murugan to be discreet and said nothing.

From the garden came the sound of a whistle.

"Excuse me," said the little nurse and went to the window. Smiling happily at what she saw, she waved her hand. "It's Ranga."

"Who's Ranga?"

"That friend of mine I was talking about. He wants to ask you some questions. May he come in for a minute?"

"Of course."

She turned back to the window and made a beckoning gesture.

"This means, I take it, that the white satin pajamas are completely out of the picture."

She nodded. "It was only a one-act tragedy. I found my head almost as quickly as I'd lost it. And when I'd found it, there was Ranga, the same as ever, waiting for me." The door swung open and a lanky young man in gym shoes and khaki shorts came into the room.

"Ranga Karakuran," he announced as he shook Will's hand.

"If you'd come five minutes earlier," said Radha, "you'd have had the pleasure of meeting Mr. Bahu."

"Was *he* here?" Ranga made a grimace of disgust.

"Is he as bad as all that?" Will asked.

Ranga listed the indictments. "A: He hates us. B: He's Colonel Dipa's tame jackal. C: He's the unofficial ambassador of all the oil companies. D: The old pig made passes at Radha. And E: He goes about giving lectures about the need for a religious revival. He's even published a book about it. Complete with preface by someone at the Harvard

Divinity School. It's all part of the campaign against Palanese independence. God is Dipa's alibi. Why can't criminals be frank about what they're up to? All this disgusting idealistic hogwash—it makes one vomit."

Radha stretched out her hand and gave his ear three sharp tweaks.

"You little . . ." he began angrily; then broke off and laughed. "You're quite right," he said. "All the same, you didn't have to pull quite so hard."

"Is that what you always do when he gets worked up?" Will enquired of Radha.

"Whenever he gets worked up at the wrong moment, or over things he can't do anything about."

Will turned to the boy. "And do you ever have to tweak *her* ear?"

Ranga laughed. "I find it more satisfactory," he said, "to smack her bottom, Unfortunately, she rarely needs it."

"Does that mean she's better balanced than you are?"

"Better balanced? I tell you, she's abnormally sane."

"Whereas you're merely normal?"

"Maybe a little left of center." He shook his head. "I get horribly depressed sometimes—feel I'm no good for anything."

"Whereas in fact," said Radha, "he's so good that they've given him a scholarship to study biochemistry at the University of Manchester."

"What do you do with him when he plays these despairing, miserable-sinner tricks on you? Pull his ears?"

"That," she said, "and . . . well, other things." She looked at Ranga and Ranga looked at her. Then they both burst out laughing.

"Quite," said Will. "Quite. And these other things being what they are," he went on, "is Ranga looking forward to the prospect of leaving Pala for a couple of years?"

"Not much," Ranga admitted.

"But he has to go," said Radha firmly.

"And when he gets there," Will wondered, "is he going to be happy?"

"That's what I wanted to ask you," said Ranga.

"Well, you won't like the climate, you won't like the food, you won't like the noises or the smells or the architecture. But you'll almost certainly like the work and you'll probably find that you can like quite a lot of the people."

"What about the girls?" Radha enquired.

"How do you want me to answer *that* question?" he asked. "Consolingly or truthfully?"

"Truthfully."

"Well, my dear, the truth is that Ranga will be a wild success. Dozens of girls are going to find him irresistible. And some of those girls will be charming. How will you feel if *he* can't resist?"

"I'll be glad for his sake."

Will turned to Ranga. "And will you be glad if she consoles herself, while you're away, with another boy?"

"I'd like to be," he said. "But whether I actually shall be glad—that's another question."

"Will you make her promise to be faithful?"

"I won't make her promise anything."

"Even though she's your girl?"

"She's her own girl."

"And Ranga's his own boy," said the little nurse. "He's free to do what he likes."

Will thought of Babs's strawberry-pink alcove and laughed ferociously. "And free above all," he said, "to do what he doesn't like." He looked from one young face to the other and saw that he was being eyed with a certain astonishment. In another tone and with a different kind of smile, "But I'd forgotten," he added. "One of you is abnormally sane and the other is only a little left of center. So how can you be expected to understand what this mental case from the outside is talking about?" And without leaving them time to answer his question, "Tell me," he asked, "how long is it—" He broke off. "But perhaps I'm being indiscreet. If so, just tell me to mind my own business. But I *would* like to know, just as a matter of anthropological interest, how long you two have been friends."

"Do you mean 'friends'?" asked the little nurse. "Or do you mean 'lovers'?"

"Why not both, while we're about it?"

"Well, Ranga and I have been friends since we were babies. And we've been lovers—except for that miserable white pajama episode—since I was fifteen and a half and he was seventeen—just about two and a half years."

"And nobody objected?"

"Why should they?"

"Why, indeed," Will echoed. "But the fact remains

that, in my part of the world, practically everybody would have objected."

"What about other boys?" Ranga asked.

"In theory they are even more out of bounds than girls. In practice . . . Well, you can guess what happens when five or six hundred male adolescents are cooped up together in a boarding school. Does that sort of thing ever go on here?"

"Of course."

"I'm surprised."

"Surprised? Why?"

"Seeing that girls aren't out of bounds."

"But one kind of love doesn't exclude the other."

"And both are legitimate?"

"Naturally."

"So that nobody would have minded if Murugan had been interested in another pajama boy?"

"Not if it was a good sort of relationship."

"But unfortunately," said Radha, "the Rani had done such a thorough job that he couldn't be interested in anyone but her—and, of course, himself."

"No boys?"

"Maybe now. I don't know. All I know is that in my day there was nobody in his universe. No boys and, still more emphatically, no girls. Only Mother and masturbation and the Ascended Masters. Only jazz records and sports cars and Hitlerian ideas about being a Great Leader and turning Pala into what he calls a Modern State."

"Three weeks ago," said Ranga, "he and the Rani were at the palace, in Shivapuram. They invited a group of us from the university to come and listen to Murugan's ideas—on oil, on industrialization, on television, on armaments, on the Crusade of the Spirit."

"Did he make any converts?"

Ranga shook his head. "Why would anyone want to exchange something rich and good and endlessly interesting for something bad and thin and boring? We don't feel any need for your speedboats or your television, your wars and revolutions, your revivals, your political slogans, your metaphysical nonsense from Rome and Moscow. Did you ever hear of *maithuna*?" he asked.

"*Maithuna*? What's that?"

"Let's start with the historical background," Ranga answered; and with the engaging pedantry of an undergraduate delivering a lecture about matters which he himself has only lately heard of, he launched forth. "Buddhism came to Pala about twelve hundred years ago, and it came not from Ceylon, which is what one would have expected, but from Bengal, and through Bengal, later on, from Tibet. Result: we're Mahayanists, and our Buddhism is shot through and through with Tantra. Do you know what Tantra is?"

Will had to admit that he had only the haziest notion.

"And to tell you the truth," said Ranga, with a laugh that broke irrepressibly through the crust of his pedantry, "I don't really know much more than you do. Tantra's an enormous subject and most of it, I guess, is just silliness and superstition—not worth bothering about. But there's a hard core of sense. If you're a Tantrik, you don't renounce the world or deny its value; you don't try to escape into a Nirvana apart from life, as the monks of the Southern School do. No, you accept the world, and you make use of it; you make use of everything you do, of everything that happens to you, of all the things you see and hear and taste and touch, as so many means to your liberation from the prison of yourself."

"Good talk," said Will in a tone of polite skepticism.

"And something more besides," Ranga insisted. "That's the difference," he added—and youthful pedantry modulated into the eagerness of youthful prosclytism—"that's the difference between your philosophy and ours. Western philosophers, even the best of them—they're nothing more than good talkers. Eastern philosophers are often rather bad talkers, but that doesn't matter. Talk isn't the point. Their philosophy is pragmatic and operational. Like the philosophy of modern physics—except that the operations in question are psychological and the results transcendental. Your metaphysicians make statements about the nature of man and the universe; but they don't offer the reader any way of testing the truth of those statements. When *we* make statements, we follow them up with a list of operations that can be used for testing the validity of what we've been saying. For example, *tat tvam asi*, 'thou are That'—the heart of all our philosophy. *Tat tvam asi*," he repeated. "It looks like a proposition in metaphysics; but what it actually refers to is a psychological experience, and the operations by means of which the experience can be lived through are described by our philosophers, so that anyone who's willing to perform the necessary operations can test the validity of *tat tvam asi* for himself. The operations are called yoga, or dhyana, or Zen—or, in certain special circumstances, *maithuna*."

"Which brings us back to my original question. What *is maithuna*?"

"Maybe you'd better ask Radha."

Will turned to the little nurse. "What is it?"

"*Maithuna*," she answered gravely, "is the yoga of love."

"Sacred or profane?"

"There's no difference."

"That's the whole point," Ranga put in. "When you do *maithuna*, profane love *is* sacred love."

"*Buddhatvan yoshidyonisansritan*," the girl quoted.

"None of your Sanskrit! What does it mean?"

"How would you translate *Buddhatvan*, Ranga?"

"Buddhaness, Buddheity, the quality of being enlightened."

Radha nodded and turned back to Will. "It means that Buddhaness is in the *yoni*."

"In the *yoni*?" Will remembered those little stone emblems of the Eternal Feminine that he had bought, as presents for the girls at the office, from a hunchbacked vendor of *bondieuseries* at Benares. Eight annas for a black *yoni*; twelve for the still more sacred image of the *yoni-lingam*. "Literally in the *yoni*?" he asked. "Or metaphorically?"

"What a ridiculous question!" said the little nurse, and she laughed her clear unaffected laugh of pure amusement. "Do you think we make love metaphorically? *Buddhatvan yoshidyonisansritan*," she repeated. "It couldn't be more completely and absolutely literal."

"Did you ever hear of the Oneida Community?" Ranga now asked.

Will nodded. He had known an American historian who specialized in nineteenth-century communities. "But why do *you* know about it?" he asked.

"Because it's mentioned in all our textbooks of applied philosophy. Basically, *maithuna* is the same as what the Oneida people called Male Continence. And that was the same as what Roman Catholics mean by *coitus reservatus*."

"*Reservatus*," the little nurse repeated. "It always makes me want to laugh. 'Such a *reserved* young man'!" The dimples reappeared and there was a flash of white teeth.

"Don't be silly," said Ranga severely. "This is serious."

She expressed her contrition. "But *reservatus* was really too funny."

"In a word," Will concluded, "it's just birth control without contraceptives."

"But that's only the beginning of the story," said Ranga. "*Maithuna* is also something else. Something even more important." The undergraduate pedant had reasserted himself. "Remember," he went on earnestly, "remember the point that Freud was always harping on."

"Which point? There were so many."

"The point about the sexuality of children. What we're born with, what we experience all through infancy and childhood, is a sexuality that isn't concentrated on the genitals; it's a sexuality diffused throughout the whole organism. That's the paradise we inherit. But the paradise gets lost as the child grows up. *Maithuna* is the organized attempt to regain that paradise." He turned to Radha. "You've got a good memory," he said. "What's that phrase of Spinoza's that they quote in the applied philosophy book?"

" 'Make the body capable of doing many things,' " she recited. " 'This will help you to perfect the mind and so to come to the intellectual love of God.' "

"Hence all the yogas," said Ranga. "Including *maithuna*."

"And it's a real yoga," the girl insisted. "As good as raja yoga, or karma yoga, or bhakti yoga. In fact, a great deal better, so far as most people are concerned. *Maithuna* really gets them there."

"What's 'there'?" Will asked.

" 'There' is where you know."

"Know what?"

"Know who in fact you are—and believe it or not," she added, "*tat tvam asi*—thou art That, and so am I: That is me." The dimples came to life, the teeth flashed. "And That's also *him*." She pointed at Ranga. "Incredible, isn't it?" She stuck out her tongue at him. "And yet it's a fact."

Ranga smiled, reached out and with an extended forefinger touched the tip of her nose. "And not merely a fact," he said. "A revealed truth." He gave the nose a little tap. "A revealed truth," he repeated. "So mind your P's and Q's, young woman."

"What I'm wondering," said Will, "is why we aren't all enlightened—I mean, if it's just a question of making love with a rather special kind of technique. What's the answer to that?"

"I'll tell you," Ranga began.

But the girl cut him short. "Listen," she said, "listen!"

Will listened. Faint and far off, but still distinct, he heard the strange inhuman voice that had first welcomed him to Pala. "Attention," it was saying. "Attention. Attention . . ."

"That bloody bird again!"

"But that's the secret."

"Attention? But a moment ago you were saying it was something else. What about that young man who's so reserved?"

"That's just to make it easier to pay attention."

"And it *does* make it easier," Ranga confirmed. "And that's the whole point of *maithuna*. It's not the special technique that turns love-making into yoga; it's the kind of awareness that the technique makes possible. Awareness of one's sensations and awareness of the not-sensation in every sensation."

"What's a not-sensation?"

"It's the raw material for sensation that my not-self provides me with."

"And you can pay attention to your not-self?"

"Of course."

Will turned to the little nurse. "You too?"

"To myself," she answered, "and at the same time to my not-self. And to Ranga's not-self, and to Ranga's self, and to Ranga's body, and to my body and everything it's feeling. And to all the love and the friendship. And to the mystery of the other person—the perfect stranger, who's the other half of your own self, and the same as your not-self. And all the while one's paying attention to all the things that, if one were sentimental, or worse, if one were spiritual like the poor old Rani, one would find so unromantic and gross and sordid even. But they aren't sordid, because one's also paying attention to the fact that, when one's fully aware of them, those things are just as beautiful as all the rest, just as wonderful."

"*Maithuna* is dhyana," Ranga concluded. A new word, he evidently felt, would explain everything.

"But what is dhyana?" Will asked.

"Dhyana is contemplation."

"Contemplation."

Will thought of that strawberry-pink alcove above the

Charing Cross Road. Contemplation was hardly the word he would have chosen. And yet even there, on second thoughts, even there he had found a kind of deliverance. Those alienations in the changing light of Porter's Gin were alienations from his odious daytime self. They were also, unfortunately, alienations from all the rest of his being—alienations from love, from intelligence, from common decency, from all consciousness but that of an excruciating frenzy by corpse-light or in the rosy glow of the cheapest, vulgarest illusion. He looked again at Radha's shining face. What happiness! What a manifest conviction, not of the sin that Mr. Bahu was so determined to make the world safe for, but of its serene and blissful opposite! It was profoundly touching. But he refused to be touched. *Noli me tangere*—it was a categorical imperative. Shifting the focus of his mind, he managed to see the whole thing as reassuringly ludicrous. What shall we do to be saved? The answer is in four letters.

Smiling at his own little joke, "Were you taught *maithuna* at school?" he asked ironically.

"At school," Radha answered with a simple matter-of-factness that took all the Rabelaisian wind out of his sails.

"Everybody's taught it," Ranga added.

"And when does the teaching begin?"

"About the same time as trigonometry and advanced biology. That's between fifteen and fifteen and a half."

"And after they've learned *maithuna*, after they've gone out into the world and got married—that is, if you ever do get married?"

"Oh, we do, we do," Radha assured him.

"Do they still practice it?"

"Not all of them, of course. But a good many do."

"All the time?"

"Except when they want to have a baby."

"And those who don't want to have babies, but who might like to have a little change from *maithuna*—what do *they* do?"

"Contraceptives," said Ranga laconically.

"And are the contraceptives available?"

"Available! They're distributed by the government. Free, gratis, and for nothing—except of course that they have to be paid for out of taxes."

"The postman," Radha added, "delivers a thirty-night supply at the beginning of each month."

"And the babies don't arrive?"

"Only those we want. Nobody has more than three, and most people stop at two."

"With the result," said Ranga, reverting, with the statistics, to his pedantic manner, "that our population is increasing at less than a third of one per cent per annum. Whereas Rendang's increase is as big as Ceylon's—almost three per cent. And China's is two per cent, and India's about one point seven."

"I was in China only a month ago," said Will. "Terrifying! And last year I spent four weeks in India. And before India in Central America, which is outbreeding even Rendang and Ceylon. Has either of you been in Rendang-Lobo?"

Ranga nodded affirmatively.

"Three days in Rendang," he explained. "If you get into the Upper Sixth, it's part of the advanced sociology course. They let you see for yourself what the Outside is like."

"And what did you think of the Outside?" Will enquired.

Ranga answered with another question. "When you were in Rendang-Lobo, did they show you the slums?"

"On the contrary, they did their best to prevent me from seeing the slums. But I gave them the slip."

Gave them the slip, he was vividly remembering, on his way back to the hotel from that grisly cocktail party at the Rendang Foreign Office. Everybody who was anybody was there. All the local dignitaries and their wives—uniforms and medals, Dior and emeralds. All the important foreigners—diplomats galore, British and American oilmen, six members of the Japanese trade mission, a lady pharmacologist from Leningrad, two Polish engineers, a German tourist who just happened to be a cousin of Krupp von Bohlen, an enigmatic Armenian representing a very important financial consortium in Tangier, and, beaming with triumph, the fourteen Czech technicians who had come with last month's shipment of tanks and cannon and machine guns from Skoda. "And these are the people," he had said to himself as he walked down the marble steps of the Foreign Office into Liberty Square, "these are the people who rule the world. Twenty-nine hundred millions of us at the mercy of a few scores of politicians, a few thousands of tycoons and generals and moneylenders. Ye are the cyanide of the earth—and the cyanide will never, never lose its savor."

After the glare of the cocktail party, after the laughter and the luscious smells of canapés and Chanel-sprayed women, those alleys behind the brand-new Palace of Justice had seemed doubly dark and noisome. Those poor wretches camping out under the palm trees of Independence Avenue more totally abandoned by God and man than even the homeless, hopeless thousands he had seen sleeping like corpses in the streets of Calcutta. And now he thought of that little boy, that tiny potbellied skeleton, whom he had picked up, bruised and shaken by a fall from the back of the little girl, scarcely larger than himself, who was carrying him—had picked up and, led by the other child, had carried back, carried down, to the windowless cellar that, for nine of them (he had counted the dark ringwormy heads), was home.

"Keeping babies alive," he said, "healing the sick, preventing the sewage from getting into the water supply—one starts with doing things that are obviously and intrinsically good. And how does one end? One ends by increasing the sum of human misery and jeopardizing civilization. It's the kind of cosmic practical joke that God seems really to enjoy."

He gave the young people one of his flayed, ferocious grins.

"God has nothing to do with it," Ranga retorted, "and the joke isn't cosmic, it's strictly man-made. These things aren't like gravity or the second law of thermodynamics; they don't *have* to happen. They happen only if people are stupid enough to allow them to happen. Here in Pala we haven't allowed them to happen, so the joke hasn't been played on us. We've had good sanitation for the best part of a century—and still we're not overcrowded, we're not miserable, we're not under a dictatorship. And the reason is very simple: we chose to behave in a sensible and realistic way."

"How on earth were you able to choose?" Will asked.

"The right people were intelligent at the right moment," said Ranga. "But it must be admitted—they were also very lucky. In fact Pala as a whole has been extraordinarily lucky. It's had the luck, first of all, never to have been anyone's colony. Rendang has a magnificent harbor. That brought them an Arab invasion in the Middle Ages. We have no harbor, so the Arabs left us alone and we're still Buddhists or Shivaites—that is, when we're not Tantrik agnostics."

"Is that what *you* are?" Will enquired. "A Tantrik agnostic?"

"With Mahayana trimmings," Ranga qualified. "Well, to return to Rendang. After the Arabs it got the Portuguese. We didn't. No harbor, no Portuguese. Therefore no Catholic minority, no blasphemous nonsense about its being God's will that people should breed themselves into subhuman misery, no organized resistance to birth control. And that isn't our only blessing: After a hundred and twenty years of the Portuguese, Ceylon and Rendang got the Dutch. And after the Dutch came the English. We escaped both those infestations. No Dutch, no English, and therefore no planters, no coolie labor, no cash crops for export, no systematic exhaustion of our soil. Also no whisky, no Calvinism, no syphilis, no foreign administrators. We were left to go our own way and take responsibility for our own affairs."

"You certainly *were* lucky."

"And on top of that amazing good luck," Ranga went on, "there was the amazing good management of Murugan the Reformer and Andrew MacPhail. Has Dr. Robert talked to you about his great-grandfather?"

"Just a few words, that's all."

"Did he tell you about the founding of the Experimental Station?"

Will shook his head.

"The Experimental Station," said Ranga, "had a lot to do with our population policy. It all began with a famine. Before he came to Pala, Dr. Andrew spent a few years in Madras. The second year he was there, the monsoon failed. The crops were burnt up, the tanks and even the wells went dry. Except for the English and the rich, there was no food. People died like flies. There's a famous passage in Dr. Andrew's memoirs about the famine. A description and then a comment. He'd had to listen to a lot of sermons when he was a boy, and there was one he kept remembering now, as he worked among the starving Indians. 'Man cannot live by bread alone'—that was the text, and the preacher had been so eloquent that several people were converted. 'Man cannot live by bread alone.' But without bread, he now saw, there is no mind, no spirit, no inner light, no Father in Heaven. There is only hunger, there is only despair and then apathy and finally death."

"Another of the cosmic jokes," said Will. "And this one was formulated by Jesus himself. 'To those who have shall be given, and from those who have not shall be taken away even that which they have'—the bare possibility of being human. It's the cruelest of all God's jokes, and also the commonest. I've seen it being played on millions of men and women, millions of small children—all over the world."

"So you can understand why that famine made such an indelible impression on Dr. Andrew's mind. He was resolved, and so was his friend the Raja, that in Pala, at least, there should always be bread. Hence their decision to set up the Experimental Station. Rothamsted-in-the-Tropics was a great success. In a few years we had new strains of rice and maize and millet and breadfruit. We had better breeds of cattle and chickens. Better ways of cultivating and composting; and in the fifties we built the first superphosphate factory east of Berlin. Thanks to all these things people were eating better, living longer, losing fewer children. Ten years after the founding of Rothamsted-in-the-Tropics the Raja took a census. The population had been stable, more or less, for a century. Now it had started to rise. In fifty or sixty years, Dr. Andrew foresaw, Pala would be transformed into the kind of festering slum that Rendang is today. What was to be done? Dr. Andrew had read his Malthus. 'Food production increases arithmetically; population increased geometrically. Man has only two choices: he can either leave the matter to Nature, who will solve the population problem in the old familiar way, by famine, pestilence and war: or else (Malthus being a clergyman) he can keep down his numbers by moral restraint.' "

"Mor-ral r-restr-raint," the little nurse repeated, rolling her r's in the Indonesian parody of a Scottish divine. "Mor-ral r-restr-raint! Incidentally," she added, "Dr. Andrew had just married the Raja's sixteen-year-old niece."

"And that," said Ranga, "was yet another reason for revising Malthus. Famine on this side, restraint on that. Surely there must be some better, happier, humaner way between the Malthusian horns. And of course there was such a way even then, even before the age of rubber and spermicides. There were sponges, there was soap, there were condoms made of every known waterproof material from oiled silk to the blind gut of sheep. The whole armory of Paleo-Birth Control."

"And how did the Raja and his subjects react to Paleo-Birth Control? With horror?"

"Not at all. They were good Buddhists, and every good

Buddhist knows that begetting is merely postponed assassination. Do your best to get off the Wheel of Birth and Death, and for heaven's sake don't go about putting superfluous victims onto the Wheel. For a good Buddhist, birth control makes metaphysical sense. And for a village community of rice growers, it makes social and economic sense. There must be enough young people to work the fields and support the aged and the little ones. But not too many of them; for then neither the old nor the workers nor their children will have enough to eat. In the old days, couples had to have six children in order to raise two or three. Then came clean water and the Experimental Station. Out of six children five now survived. The old patterns of breeding had ceased to make sense. The only objection to Paleo-Birth Control was its crudity. But fortunately there was a more aesthetic alternative. The Raja was a Tantrik initiate and had learned the yoga of love. Dr. Andrew was told about *maithuna* and, being a true man of science, agreed to try it. He and his young wife were given the necessary instruction."

"With what results?"

"Enthusiastic approval."

"That's the way everybody feels about it," said Radha.

"Now, now, none of your sweeping generalizations! Some feel that way, others don't. Dr. Andrew was one of the enthusiasts. The whole matter was lengthily discussed. In the end they decided that contraceptives should be like education—free, tax-supported and, though not compulsory, as nearly as possible universal. For those who felt the need for something more refined, there would be instruction in the yoga of love."

"Do you mean to tell me that they got away with it?"

"It wasn't really so difficult. *Maithuna* was orthodox. People weren't being asked to do anything against their religion. On the contrary, they were being given a flattering opportunity to join the elect by learning something esoteric."

"And don't forget the most important point of all," the little nurse chimed in. "For women—*all* women, and I don't care what you say about sweeping generalizations—the yoga of love means perfection, means being transformed and taken out of themselves and completed." There was a brief silence. "And now," she resumed in another, brisker tone, "it's high time we left you to your siesta."

"Before you go," said Will, "I'd like to write a letter. Just a brief note to my boss to say that I'm alive and in no immediate danger of being eaten by the natives."

Radha went foraging in Dr. Robert's study and came back with paper, pencil and an envelope.

"*Veni, vidi,*" Will scrawled. "I was wrecked, I met the Rani and her collaborator from Rendang, who implies that he can deliver the goods in return for baksheesh to the tune (he was specific) of twenty thousand pounds. Shall I negotiate on this basis? If you cable *Proposed article OK,* I shall go ahead. If *No hurry for article* I shall let the matter drop. Tell my mother I am safe and shall soon be writing."

"There," he said as he handed the envelope, sealed and addressed, to Ranga. "May I ask you to buy me a stamp and get this off in time to catch tomorrow's plane?"

"Without fail," the boy promised.

Watching them go, Will felt a twinge of conscience. What charming young people! And here he was, plotting with Bahu and the forces of history to subvert their world. He comforted himself with the thought that, if he didn't do it, somebody else would. And even if Joe Aldehyde did get his concession, they could still go on making love in the style to which they were accustomed. Or couldn't they?

From the door the little nurse turned back for a final word. "No reading now," she wagged her finger at him. "Go to sleep."

"I never sleep during the day," Will assured her, with a certain perverse satisfaction.

vii

HE COULD NEVER GO TO SLEEP DURING THE DAY; BUT WHEN he looked next at his watch, the time was twenty-five past four, and he was feeling wonderfully refreshed. He picked up *Notes on What's What*, and resumed his interrupted reading:

> Give us this day our daily Faith, but deliver us, dear God, from Belief.

This was as far as he had got this morning; and now here was a new section, the fifth:

> Me as I think I am and me as I am in fact—sorrow, in other words, and the ending of sorrow. One third, more or less, of all the sorrow that the person I think I am must endure is unavoidable. It is the sorrow inherent in the human condition, the price we must pay for being sentient and self-conscious organisms, aspirants to liberation, but subject to the laws of nature and under orders to keep on marching, through irreversible time, through a world wholly indifferent to our well-being, toward decrepitude and the certainty of death. The remaining two thirds of all sorrow is homemade and, so far as the universe is concerned, unnecessary.

Will turned the page. A sheet of notepaper fluttered onto the bed. He picked it up and glanced at it. Twenty lines of small clear writing and at the bottom of the page the initials S. M. Not a letter evidently; a poem and therefore public property. He read:

> Somewhere between brute silence and last Sunday's
> Thirteen hundred thousand sermons;

Somewhere between
Calvin on Christ (God help us!) and the lizards;
Somewhere between seeing and speaking, somewhere
Between our soiled and greasy currency of words
And the first star, the great moths fluttering
About the ghosts of flowers,
Lies the clear place where I, no longer I,
Nevertheless remember
Love's nightlong wisdom of the other shore;
And, listening to the wind, remember too
That other night, that first of widowhood,
Sleepless, with death beside me in the dark.
Mine, mine, all mine, mine inescapably!
But I, no longer I,
In this clear place between my thought and silence
See all I had and lost, anguish and joys,
Glowing like gentians in the Alpine grass,
Blue, unpossessed and open.

"Like gentians," Will repeated to himself, and thought of that summer holiday in Switzerland when he was twelve; thought of the meadow, high above Grindelwald, with its unfamiliar flowers, its wonderful un-English butterflies; thought of the dark-blue sky and the sunshine and the huge shining mountains on the other side of the valley. And all his father had found to say was that it looked like an advertisement for Nestlé's milk chocolate. "Not even real chocolate," he had insisted with a grimace of disgust. "*Milk* chocolate." After which there had been an ironic comment on the water color his mother was painting—so badly (poor thing!) but with such loving and conscientious care. "The milk chocolate advertisement that Nestlé rejected." And now it was *his* turn. "Instead of just mooning about with your mouth open, like the village idiot, why not do something intelligent for a change? Put in some work on your German grammar, for example." And diving into the rucksack, he had pulled out, from among the hard-boiled eggs and the sandwiches, the abhorred little brown book. What a detestable man! And yet, if Susila was right, one ought to be able to see him now, after all these years, glowing like a gentian— Will glanced again at the last line of the poem—"blue, unpossessed and open."

"Well . . ." said a familiar voice.

He turned toward the door. "Talk of the devil," he said. "Or rather read what the devil has written." He held up the sheet of notepaper for her inspection.

Susila glanced at it. "Oh *that*," she said. "If only good intentions were enough to make good poetry!" She sighed and shook her head.

"I was trying to think of my father as a gentian," he went on. "But all I get is the persistent image of the most enormous turd."

"Even turds," she assured him, "can be seen as gentians."

"But only, I take it, in the place you were writing about—the clear place between thought and silence?"

Susila nodded.

"How do you get there?"

"You don't get there. There comes to you. Or rather there is really here."

"You're just like little Radha," he complained. "Parroting what the Old Raja says at the beginning of this book."

"If we repeat it," she said, "it's because it happens to be true. If we didn't repeat it, we'd be ignoring the facts."

"Whose facts?" he asked. "Certainly not mine."

"Not at the moment," she agreed. "But if you were to do the kind of things that the Old Raja recommends, they might be yours."

"Did *you* have parent trouble?" he asked after a little silence. "Or could you aways see turds as gentians?"

"Not at that age," she answered. "Children *have* to be Manichean dualists. It's the price we must all pay for learning the rudiments of being human. Seeing turds as gentians, or rather seeing both gentians and turds as Gentians with a capital G—that's a postgraduate accomplishment."

"So what did you do about your parents? Just grin and bear the unbearable? Or did your father and mother happen to be bearable?"

"Bearable separately," she answered. "Especially my father. But quite unbearable together—unbearable because they couldn't bear one another. A bustling, cheerful, outgoing woman married to a man so fastidiously introverted that she got on his nerves all the time—even, I suspect, in bed. She never stopped communicating, and he never started. With the result that he thought she was shallow and insincere, she thought he was heartless, contemptuous and without normal human feelings."

"I'd have expected that you people would know better than to walk into that kind of trap."

"We do know better," she assured him. "Boys and girls are specifically taught what to expect of people whose temperament and physique are very different from their own. Unfortunately, it sometimes happens that the lessons don't seem to have much effect. Not to mention the fact that in some cases the psychological distance between the people involved is really too great to be bridged. Anyhow, the fact remains that my father and mother never managed to make a go of it. They'd fallen in love with one another—goodness knows why. But when they came to close quarters, she found herself being constantly hurt by his inaccessibility, while *her* uninhibited good-fellowship made him fairly cringe with embarrassment and distaste. *My* sympathies were always with my father. Physically and temperamentally I'm very close to him, not in the least like my mother. I remember, even as a tiny child, how I used to shrink away from her exuberance. She was like a permanent invasion of one's privacy. She still is."

"Do you have to see a lot of her?"

"Very little. She has her own job and her own friends. In our part of the world 'Mother' is strictly the name of a function. When the function has been duly fulfilled, the title lapses; the ex-child and the woman who used to be called 'Mother' establish a new kind of relationship. If they get on well together, they continue to see a lot of one another. If they don't, they drift apart. Nobody expects them to cling, and clinging isn't equated with loving—isn't regarded as anything particularly creditable."

"So all's well *now*. But what about *then*? What happened when you were a child, growing up between two people who couldn't bridge the gulf that separated them? I know what *that* means—the fairy-story ending in reverse, 'And so they lived unhappily ever after.'"

"And I've no doubt," said Susila, "that if we hadn't been born in Pala, we would have lived unhappily ever after. As it was, we got on, all things considered, remarkably well."

"How did you manage to do that?"

"We didn't; it was all managed for us. Have you read what the Old Raja says about getting rid of the two thirds of sorrow that's homemade and gratuitous?"

Will nodded. "I was just reading it when you came in."

"Well, in the bad old days," she went on, "Palanese families could be just as victimizing, tyrant-producing and liar-creating as yours can be today. In fact they were so awful that Dr. Andrew and the Raja of the Reform decided that something had to be done about it. Buddhist ethics and primitive village communism were skillfully made to serve the purposes of reason, and in a single generation the whole family system was radically changed." She hesitated for a moment. "Let me explain," she went on, "in terms of my own particular case—the case of an only child of two people who couldn't understand one another and were always at cross-purposes or actually quarreling. In the old days, a little girl brought up in those surroundings would have emerged as either a wreck, a rebel, or a resigned hypocritical conformist. Under the new dispensation I didn't have to undergo unnecessary suffering, I wasn't wrecked or forced into rebellion or resignation. Why? Because from the moment I could toddle, I was free to escape."

"To escape?" he repeated. "To escape?" It seemed too good to be true.

"Escape," she explained, "is built into the new system. Whenever the parental Home Sweet Home becomes too unbearable, the child is allowed, is actively encouraged—and the whole weight of public opinion is behind the encouragement—to migrate to one of its other homes."

"How many homes does a Palanese child have?"

"About twenty on the average."

"Twenty? My God!"

"We all belong," Susila explained, "to an MAC—a Mutual Adoption Club. Every MAC consists of anything from fifteen to twenty-five assorted couples. Newly elected brides and bridegrooms, old-timers with growing children, grandparents and great-grandparents—everybody in the club adopts everyone else. Besides our own blood relations, we all have our quota of deputy mothers, deputy fathers, deputy aunts and uncles, deputy brothers and sisters, deputy babies and toddlers and teen-agers."

Will shook his head. "Making twenty families grow where only one grew before."

"But what grew before was *your* kind of family. The twenty are all our kind." As though reading instructions from a cookery book, "Take one sexually inept wage slave," she went on, "one dissatisfied female, two or (if preferred) three small television addicts; marinate in a mixture of Freudism and dilute Christianity; then bottle up tightly in a four-room flat and stew for fifteen years in their own juice. *Our* recipe is rather different: Take twenty sexually satisfied couples and their offspring; add science, intuition and humor in equal quantities; steep in Tantrik Buddhism and simmer indefinitely in an open pan in the open air over a brisk flame of affection."

"And what comes out of your open pan?" he asked.

"An entirely different kind of family. Not exclusive, like your families, and not predestined, not compulsory. An inclusive, unpredestined and voluntary family. Twenty pairs of fathers and mothers, eight or nine ex-fathers and ex-mothers, and forty or fifty assorted children of all ages."

"Do people stay in the same adoption club all their lives?"

"Of course not. Grown-up children don't adopt their own parents or their own brothers and sisters. They go out and adopt another set of elders, a different group of peers and juniors. And the members of the new club adopt them and, in due course, their children. Hybridization of microcultures—that's what our sociologists call the process. It's as beneficial, on its own level, as the hybridization of different strains of maize or chickens. Healthier relationships in more responsible groups, wider sympathies and deeper understandings. And the sympathies and understandings are for everyone in the MAC from babies to centenarians."

"Centenarians? What's your expectation of life?"

"A year or two more than yours," she answered. "Ten per cent of us are over sixty-five. The old get pensions, if they can't earn. But obviously pensions aren't enough. They need something useful and challenging to do; they need people they can care for and be loved by in return. The MAC's fulfill those needs."

"It all sounds," said Will, "suspiciously like the propaganda for one of the new Chinese communes."

"Nothing," she assured him, "could be less like a commune than an MAC. An MAC isn't run by the government, it's run by its members. And we're not militaristic. We're not interested in turning out good party members; we're only interested in turning out good human beings. We don't inculcate dogmas. And finally we don't take the children away from their parents; on the contrary, we give the children additional parents and the parents additional children. That means that even in the nursery we enjoy a certain degree of freedom; and our freedom increases as we grow older and can deal with a wider range of experience and take on greater responsibilities. Whereas in China there's no freedom at all. The children are handed over to official baby-tamers, whose business it is to turn them into obedient servants of the State. Things are a great deal better in your part of the world—better, but still quite bad enough. You escape the state-appointed baby-tamers; but your society condemns you to pass your childhood in an exclusive family, with only a single set of siblings and parents. They're foisted on you by hereditary predestination. You can't get rid of them, can't take a holiday from them, can't go to anyone else for a change of moral or psychological air. It's freedom, if you like—but freedom in a telephone booth."

"Locked in," Will elaborated, "(and I'm thinking now of myself) with a sneering bully, a Christian martyr, and a little girl who'd been frightened by the bully and blackmailed by the martyr's appeal to her better feelings into a state of quivering imbecility. That was the home from which, until I was fourteen and my aunt Mary came to live next door, I never escaped."

"And your unfortunate parents never escaped from *you.*"

"That's not quite true. My father used to escape into brandy and my mother into High Anglicanism. I had to serve out my sentence without the slightest mitigation. Fourteen years of family servitude. How I envy you! Free as a bird!"

"Not so lyrical! Free, let's say, as a developing human being, free as a future woman—but no freer. Mutual Adoption guarantees children against injustice and the worst consequences of parental ineptitude. It doesn't guarantee them against discipline, or against having to accept responsibilities. On the contrary, it increases the number of their responsibilities; it exposes them to a wide variety of disciplines. In your predestined and exclusive families, children, as you say, serve a long prison term under a single set of parental jailers. These parental jailers may, of course, be good, wise and intelligent. In that case the little prisoners will emerge more or less unscathed. But in point of fact most of your parental jailers are *not* conspicuously good, wise or intelligent. They're apt to be well-meaning but stupid, or not well-meaning and frivolous, or else neurotic, or occasionally downright malevolent, or frankly insane. So God help the young convicts committed by law and custom and religion to their tender mercies! But now consider what happens in a large, inclusive, voluntary family. No telephone booths, no predestined jailers. Here the children grow up in a world that's a working model of society at large, a small-scale but accurate version of the environment in which they're going to have to live when they're grown up. 'Holy,' 'healthy,' 'whole' —they all come from the same root and carry different overtones of the same meaning. Etymologically, and in fact, our kind of family, the inclusive and voluntary kind, is the genuine holy family. Yours is the *un*holy family."

"Amen," said Will, and thought again of his own childhood, thought too of poor little Murugan in the clutches of the Rani. "What happens," he asked after a pause, "when the children migrate to one of their other homes? How long do they stay there?"

"It all depends. When my children get fed up with me, they seldom stay away for more than a day or two. That's because, fundamentally, they're very happy at home. I wasn't, and so when *I* walked out, I'd sometimes stay away for a whole month."

"And did your deputy parents back you up against your real mother and father?"

"It's not a question of doing anything *against* anybody. All that's being backed up is intelligence and good feeling, and all that's being opposed is unhappiness and its avoidable causes. If a child feels unhappy in his first home, we do our best for him in fifteen or twenty second homes. Meanwhile the father and mother get some tactful therapy from the other members of their Mutual Adoption Club. In a few weeks the parents are fit to be with their children again, and the children are fit to be with their parents. But you mustn't think," she added, "that it's only when they're in trouble that children resort to their deputy parents and grandparents. They do it all the time, whenever they feel the need for a change or some kind of new experience. And it isn't just a social whirl. Wherever they go, as deputy children, they have their responsibilities as well as their rights—brushing the dog, for example, cleaning out the birdcages, minding the baby while the mother's doing something else. Duties as well as privileges—but not in one of your airless little telephone booths. Duties and privileges in a big, open, unpredestined, inclusive family, where all the seven ages of man and a dozen different skills and talents are represented, and in which children have experience of all the important and significant things that human beings do and suffer—working, playing, loving, getting old, being sick, dying . . ." She was silent, thinking of Dugald and Dugald's mother; then, deliberately changing her tone, "But what about *you?*" she went on. "I've been so busy talking about families that I haven't even asked you how you're feeling. You certainly *look* a lot better than when I saw you last."

"Thanks to Dr. MacPhail. And also thanks to someone who, I suspect, was definitely practicing medicine without a license. What on earth did you do to me yesterday afternoon?"

Susila smiled. "You did it to yourself," she assured him. "I merely pressed the buttons."

"Which buttons?"

"Memory buttons, imagination buttons."

"And that was enough to put me into a hypnotic trance?"

"If you like to call it that."

"What else can one call it?"

"Why call it anything? Names are such question-beggars. Why not be content with just knowing that it happened?"

"But what *did* happen?"

"Well, to begin with, we made some kind of contact, didn't we?"

"We certainly did," he agreed. "And yet I don't believe I even so much as looked at you."

He was looking at her now, though—looking and wondering, as he looked, who this strange little creature really was, what lay behind the smooth grave mask of the face, what the dark eyes were seeing as they returned his scrutiny, what she was thinking.

"How *could* you look at me?" she said. "You'd gone off on your vacation."

"Or was I pushed off?"

"Pushed? No." She shook her head. "Let's say seen off, helped off." There was a moment of silence. "Did you ever," she resumed, "try to do a job of work with a child hanging around?"

Will thought of the small neighbor who had offered to help him paint the dining-room furniture, and laughed at the memory of his exasperation.

"Poor little darling!" Susila went on. "He means so well, he's so anxious to help."

"But the paint's on the carpet, the fingerprints are all over the walls . . ."

"So that in the end you have to get rid of him. 'Run along, little boy! Go and play in the garden!' "

There was a silence.

"Well?" he questioned at last.

"Don't you see?"

Will shook his head.

"What happens when you're ill, when you've been hurt? Who does the repairing? Who heals the wounds and throws off the infection? Do *you?*"

"Who else?"

"You?" she insisted. "*You?* The person that feels the pain and does the worrying and thinks about sin and money and the future! Is *that* you capable of doing what has to be done?"

"Oh, I see what you're driving at."

"At last!" she mocked.

"Send *me* to play in the garden so that the grown-ups can do their work in peace. But who *are* the grown-ups?"

"Don't ask me," she answered. "That's a question for a neurotheologian."

"Meaning what?" he asked.

"Meaning precisely what it says. Somebody who thinks about people in terms, simultaneously, of the Clear Light of the Void and the vegetative nervous system. The grown-ups are a mixture of Mind and physiology."

"And the children?"

"The children are the little fellows who think they know better than the grown-ups."

"And so must be told to run along and play."

"Exactly."

"Is your sort of treatment standard procedure in Pala?" he asked.

"Standard procedure," she assured him. "In your part of the world doctors get rid of the children by poisoning them with barbiturates. We do it by talking to them about cathedrals and jackdaws." Her voice had modulated into a chant. "About white clouds floating in the sky, white swans floating on the dark, smooth, irresistible river of life . . ."

"Now, now," he protested. "None of that!"

A smile lit up the grave dark face, and she began to laugh. Will looked at her with astonishment. Here, suddenly, was a different person, another Susila MacPhail, gay, mischievous, ironical.

"I know your tricks," he added, joining in the laughter.

"Tricks?" Still laughing, she shook her head. "I was just explaining how I did it."

"I know exactly how you did it. And I also know that it works. What's more, I give you leave to do it again—whenever it's necessary."

"If you like," she said more seriously, "I'll show you how to press your own buttons. We teach it in all our elementary schools. The three R's plus rudimentary SD."

"What's that?"

"Self-Determination. Alias Destiny Control."

"Destiny Control?" He raised his eyebrows.

"No, no," she assured him, "we're not quite such fools as you seem to think. We know perfectly well that only a part of our destiny is controllable."

"And you control it by pressing your own buttons?"

"Pressing our own buttons and then visualizing what we'd like to happen."

"But does it happen?"

"In many cases it does."

"Simple!" There was a note of irony in his voice.

"Wonderfully simple," she agreed. "And yet, so far as I know, we're the only people who systematically teach DC to their children. *You* just tell them what they're supposed to do and leave it at that. Behave well, you say. But how? You never tell them. All you do is give them pep talks and punishments. Pure idiocy."

"Pure unadulterated idiocy," he agreed, remembering Mr. Crabbe, his housemaster, on the subject of masturbation, remembering the canings and the weekly sermons and the Commination Service on Ash Wednesday. "Cursed is he that lieth with his neighbor's wife. Amen."

"If your children take the idiocy seriously, they grow up to be miserable sinners. And if they don't take it seriously, they grow up to be miserable cynics. And if they react from miserable cynicism, they're apt to go Papist or Marxist. No wonder you have to have all those thousands of jails and churches and Communist cells."

"Whereas in Pala, I gather, you have very few."

Susila shook her head.

"No Alcatrazes here," she said. "No Billy Grahams or Mao Tse-tungs or Madonnas of Fatima. No hells on earth and no Christian pie in the sky, no Communist pie in the twenty-second century. Just men and women and their children trying to make the best of the here and now, instead of living somewhere else, as you people mostly do, in some other time, some other homemade imaginary universe. And it really isn't your fault. You're almost compelled to live that way because the present is so frustrating. And it's frustrating because you've never been taught how to bridge the gap between theory and practice, between your New Year's resolutions and your actual behavior."

"'For the good that I would,'" he quoted, "'I do not; and the evil that I would not, that I do.'"

"Who said that?"

"The man who invented Christianity—St. Paul."

"You see," she said, "the highest possible ideals, and no methods for realizing them."

"Except the supernatural method of having them realized by Somebody Else."

Throwing back his head, Will Farnaby burst into song.

> "There is a fountain fill'd with blood,
> Drawn from Emmanuel's veins,
> And sinners plunged beneath that flood
> Are cleansed of all their stains."

Susila had covered her ears. "It's really obscene," she said.

"My housemaster's favorite hymn," Will explained. "We used to sing it about once a week, all the time I was at school."

"Thank goodness," she said, "there was never any blood in Buddhism! Gautama lived till eighty and died from being too courteous to refuse bad food. Violent death always seems to call for more violent death. 'If you won't believe that you're redeemed by *my* redeemer's blood, I'll drown you in your own.' Last year I took a course at Shivapuram in the history of Christianity." Susila shuddered at the memory. "What a horror! And all because that poor ignorant man didn't know how to implement his good intentions."

"And most of us," said Will, "are still in the same old boat. The evil that we would not, that we do. And how!"

Reacting unforgivably to the unforgivable, Will Farnaby laughed derisively. Laughed because he had seen the goodness of Molly and then, with open eyes, had chosen the pink alcove and, with it, Molly's unhappiness, Molly's death, his own gnawing sense of guilt, and then the pain, out of all proportion to its low and essentially farcical cause, the agonizing pain that he had felt when Babs in due course did what any fool must have known she inevitably would do—turned him out of her infernal gin-illumined paradise, and took another lover.

"What's the matter?" Susila asked.

"Nothing. Why do you ask?"

"Because you're not very good at hiding your feelings. You were thinking of something that made you unhappy."

"You've got sharp eyes," he said, and looked away.

There was a long silence. Should he tell her? Tell her about Babs, about poor Molly, about himself, tell her all the dismal and senseless things he had never, even when he was drunk, told even his oldest friends? Old friends knew too much about one, too much about the other parties involved, too much about the grotesque and complicated game which (as an English gentleman who was also a bohemian, also a would-be poet, also—in mere despair, because he knew he could never be a good poet—a hard-boiled journalist, and the private agent, very well paid, of a rich man whom he despised) he was always so elaborately playing. No, old friends would never do. But from this dark little outsider, this stranger to whom he already owed so much and with whom, though he knew nothing about her, he was already so intimate, there would come no foregone conclusions, no *ex parte* judgments—would come perhaps, he found himself hoping (he who had trained himself never to hope!), some unexpected enlightenment, some positive and practical help. (And, God knew, he needed help—though God also knew only too well that he would never say so, never sink so low as to ask for it.)

Like a muezzin in his minaret, one of the talking birds began to shout from the tall palm beyond the mango trees, "Here and now, boys. Here and now, boys."

Will decided to take the plunge—but to take it indirectly,

by talking first, not about his problems, but about hers. Without looking at Susila (for that, he felt, would be indecent), he began to speak.

"Dr. MacPhail told me something about . . . about what happened to your husband."

The words turned a sword in her heart; but that was to be expected, that was right and inevitable. "It'll be four months next Wednesday," she said. And then, meditatively, "Two people," she went on after a little silence, "two separate individuals—but they add up to something like a new creation. And then suddenly half of this new creature is amputated; but the other half doesn't die—can't die, *mustn't* die."

"Mustn't die?"

"For so many reasons—the children, oneself, the whole nature of things. But needless to say," she added, with a little smile that only accentuated the sadness in her eyes, "needless to say the reasons don't lessen the shock of the amputation or make the aftermath any more bearable. The only thing that helps is what we were talking about just now—Destiny Control. And even that . . ." She shook her head. "DC can give you a completely painless childbirth. But a completely painless bereavement—no. And of course that's as it should be. It wouldn't be right if you could take away all the pain of a bereavement; you'd be less than human."

"Less than human," he repeated. "Less than human . . ." Three short words; but how completely they summed him up! "The really terrible thing," he said aloud, "is when you know it's your fault that the other person died."

"Were *you* married?" she asked.

"For twelve years. Until last spring . . ."

"And now she's dead?"

"She died in an accident."

"In an accident? Then how was it your fault?"

"The accident happened because . . . well, because the evil that I didn't want to do, I did. And that day it came to a head. The hurt of it confused and distracted her, and I let her drive away in the car—let her drive away into a head-on collision."

"Did you love her?"

He hesitated for a moment, then slowly shook his head.

"Was there somebody else—somebody you cared for more?"

"Somebody I couldn't have cared for less." He made a grimace of sardonic self-mockery.

"And that was the evil you didn't want to do, but did?"

"Did and went on doing until I'd killed the woman I ought to have loved, but didn't. Went on doing it even after I'd killed her, even though I hated myself for doing it—yes, and really hated the person who made me do it."

"Made you do it, I suppose, by having the right kind of body?"

Will nodded, and there was a silence.

"Do you know what it's like," he asked at length, "to feel that nothing is quite real—including yourself?"

Susila nodded. "It sometimes happens when one's just on the point of discovering that everything, including oneself, is much more real than one ever imagined. It's like shifting gears: you have to go into neutral before you change into high."

"Or low," said Will. "In my case, the shift wasn't up, it was down. No, not even down; it was into reverse. The first time it happened I was waiting for a bus to take me home from Fleet Street. Thousands upon thousands of people, all on the move, and each of them unique, each of them the center of the universe. Then the sun came out from behind a cloud. Everything was extraordinarily bright and clear; and suddenly, with an almost audible click, they were all maggots."

"Maggots?"

"You know, those little pale worms with black heads that one sees on rotten meat. Nothing had changed, of course; people's faces were the same, their clothes were the same. And yet they were all maggots. Not even real maggots—just the ghosts of maggots, just the illusion of maggots. And I was the illusion of a spectator of maggots. I lived in that maggot world for months. Lived in it, worked in it, went out to lunch and dinner in it—all without the least interest in what I was doing. Without the least enjoyment or relish, completely desireless and, as I discovered when I tried to make love to a young woman I'd had occasional fun with in the past, completely impotent."

"What did you expect?"

"Precisely that."

"Then why on earth . . . ?"

Will gave her one of his flayed smiles and shrugged his shoulders. "As a matter of scientific interest. I was an entomologist investigating the sex life of the phantom maggot."

"After which, I suppose, everything seemed even more unreal."

"Even more," he agreed, "if that was possible."

"But what brought on the maggots in the first place?"

"Well, to begin with," he answered, "I was my parents' son. By Bully Boozer out of Christian Martyr. And on top of being my parents' son," he went on after a little pause, "I was my aunt Mary's nephew."

"What did your aunt Mary have to do with it?"

"She was the only person I ever loved, and when I was sixteen she got cancer. Off with the right breast; then, a year later, off with the left. And after that nine months of X rays and radiation sickness. Then it got into the liver, and that was the end. I was there from start to finish. For a boy in his teens it was a liberal education—but *liberal*."

"In what?" Susila asked.

"In Pure and Applied Pointlessness. And a few weeks after the close of my private course in the subject came the grand opening of the public course. World War II. Followed by the nonstop refresher course of Cold War I. And all this time I'd been wanting to be a poet and finding out that I simply don't have what it takes. And then, after the war, I had to go into journalism to make money. What I wanted was to go hungry, if necessary, but try to write something decent—good prose at least, seeing that it couldn't be good poetry. But I'd reckoned without those darling parents of mine. By the time he died, in January of 'forty-six, my father had got rid of all the little money our family had inherited and by the time she was blessedly a widow, my mother was crippled with arthritis and had to be supported. So there I was in Fleet Street, supporting her with an ease and a success that were completely humiliating."

"Why humiliating?"

"Wouldn't you be humiliated if you found yourself making money by turning out the cheapest, flashiest kind of literary forgery? I was a success because I was so irremediably second-rate."

"And the net result of it all was maggots?"

He nodded. "Not even real maggots: phantom maggots. And here's where Molly came into the picture. I met her at a high-class maggot party in Bloomsbury. We were introduced, we made some politely inane conversation about nonobjective painting. Not wanting to see any more maggots, I didn't look at her; but she must have been looking at me. Molly had very pale gray-blue eyes," he added parenthetically, "eyes that saw everything—she was incredibly observant, but observed without malice or censoriousness, seeing the evil, if it was there, but never condemning it, just feeling enormously sorry for the person who was under compulsion to think those thoughts and do that odious kind of thing. Well, as I say, she must have been looking at me while we talked; for suddenly she asked me why I was so sad. I'd had a couple of drinks and there was nothing impertinent or offensive about the way she asked the question; so I told her about the maggots. 'And you're one of them,' I finished up, and for the first time I looked at her. 'A blue-eyed maggot with a face like one of the holy women in attendance at a Flemish crucifixion.'"

"Was she flattered?"

"I think so. She'd stopped being a Catholic; but she still had a certain weakness for crucifixions and holy women. Anyhow, next morning she called me at breakfast time. Would I like to drive down into the country with her? It was Sunday and, by a miracle, fine. I accepted. We spent an hour in a hazel copse, picking primroses and looking at the little white windflowers. One doesn't pick the windflowers," he explained, "because in an hour they're withered. I did a lot of looking in that hazel copse—looking at flowers with the naked eye and then looking into them through the magnifying glass that Molly had brought with her. I don't know why, but it was extraordinarily therapeutic—just looking into the hearts of primroses and anemones. For the rest of the day I saw no maggots. But Fleet Street was still there, waiting for me, and by lunchtime on Monday the whole place was crawling with them as thickly as ever. Millions of maggots. But now I knew what to do about them. That evening I went to Molly's studio."

"Was she a painter?"

"Not a real painter, and she knew it. Knew it and didn't resent it, just made the best of having no talent. She didn't paint for art's sake; she painted because she liked looking at things, liked the process of trying meticulously to reproduce what she saw. That evening she gave me a canvas and a palette, and told me to do likewise."

"And did it work?"

"It worked so well that when a couple of months later I cut

open a rotten apple, the worm at its center wasn't a maggot—not subjectively, I mean. Objectively, yes; it was all that a maggot should be, and that's how I portrayed it, how we both portrayed it—for we always painted the same things at the same time."

"What about the other maggots, the phantom maggots outside the apple?"

"Well, I still had relapses, especially in Fleet Street and at cocktail parties; but the maggots were definitely fewer, definitely less haunting. And meanwhile something new was happening in the studio. I was falling in love—falling in love because love is catching and Molly was so obviously in love with me—why, God only knows."

"I can see several possible reasons why. She might have loved you because . . ." Susila eyed him appraisingly and smiled. "Well, because you're quite an attractive kind of queer fish."

He laughed. "Thank you for a handsome compliment."

"On the other hand," Susila went on, "(and this isn't quite so complimentary), she might have loved you because you made her feel so damned sorry for you."

"That's the truth, I'm afraid. Molly was a born Sister of Mercy."

"And a Sister of Mercy, unfortunately, isn't the same as a Wife of Love."

"Which I duly discovered," he said.

"After your marriage, I suppose."

Will hesitated for a moment. "Actually," he said, "it was before. Not because, on her side, there had been any urgency of desire, but only because she was so eager to do anything to please me. Only because, on principle, she didn't believe in conventions and was all for freely loving, and more surprisingly" (he remembered the outrageous things she would so casually and placidly give utterance to even in his mother's presence) "all for freely talking about that freedom."

"You knew it beforehand," Susila summed up, "and yet you still married her."

Will nodded his head without speaking.

"Because you were a gentleman, I take it, and a gentleman keeps his word."

"Partly for that rather old-fashioned reason, but also because I was in love with her."

"*Were* you in love with her?"

"Yes. No, I don't know. But at the time I *did* know. At least I thought I knew. I was really convinced that I was really in love with her. And I knew, I still know, why I was convinced. I was grateful to her for having exorcised those maggots. And besides the gratitude there was respect. There was admiration. She was so much better and honester than I was. But unfortunately, you're right: a Sister of Mercy isn't the same as a Wife of Love. But I was ready to take Molly on her own terms, not on mine. I was ready to believe that her terms were better than mine."

"How soon," Susila asked, after a long silence, "did you start having affairs on the side?"

Will smiled his flayed smile. "Three months to the day after our wedding. The first time was with one of the secretaries at the office. Goodness, what a bore! After that there was a young painter, a curlyheaded little Jewish girl whom Molly had helped with money while she was studying at the Slade. I used to go to her studio twice a week, from five to seven. It was almost three years before Molly found out about it."

"And, I gather, she was upset?"

"Much more than I'd ever thought she'd be."

"So what did you do about it?"

Will shook his head. "This is where it begins to get complicated," he said. "I had no intention of giving up my cocktail hours with Rachel; but I hated myself for making Molly so unhappy. At the same time I hated her for being unhappy. I resented her suffering and the love that had made her suffer; I felt that they were unfair, a kind of blackmail to force me to give up my innocent fun with Rachel. By loving me so much and being so miserable about what I was doing—what she really forced me to do—she was putting pressure on me, she was trying to restrict my freedom. But meanwhile she was genuinely unhappy; and though I hated her for blackmailing me with her unhappiness, I was filled with pity for her. Pity," he repeated, "not compassion. Compassion is suffering-with, and what I wanted at all costs was to spare myself the pain her suffering caused me, and avoid the painful sacrifices by which I could put an end to her suffering. Pity was my answer, being sorry for her from the outside, if you see what I mean—sorry for her as a spectator, an aesthete, a connoisseur in excruciations. And this aesthetic pity of mine was so intense, every time her unhappiness came to a head, that I could almost mistake it for love. Almost, but never quite. For when I expressed my pity in physical tenderness (which I did because that was the only way of putting a temporary stop to her unhappiness and to the pain her unhappiness was inflicting on me), that tenderness was always frustrated before it could come to its natural consummation. Frustrated because, by temperament, she was only a Sister of Mercy, not a wife. And yet, on every level but the sensual, she loved me with a total commitment —a commitment that called for an answering commitment on my part. But I wouldn't commit myself, maybe I genuinely couldn't. So instead of being grateful for her self-giving, I resented it. It made claims on me, claims that I refused to acknowledge. So there we were, at the end of every crisis, back at the beginning of the old drama—the drama of a love incapable of sensuality self-committed to a sensuality incapable of love and evoking strangely mixed responses of guilt and exasperation, of pity and resentment, sometimes of real hatred (but always with an undertone of remorse), the whole accompanied by, contrapuntal to, a succession of furtive evenings with my little curlyheaded painter."

"I hope at least they were enjoyable," said Susila.

He shrugged his shoulders. "Only moderately. Rachel could never forget that she was an intellectual. She had a way of asking what one thought of Piero di Cosimo at the most inopportune moments. The real enjoyment and of course the real agony—I never experienced them until Babs appeared on the scene."

"When was that?"

"Just over a year ago. In Africa."

"Africa?"

"I'd been sent there by Joe Aldehyde."

"That man who owns newspapers?"

"*And* all the rest. He was married to Molly's aunt Eileen. An exemplary family man, I may add. That's why he's so serenely convinced of his own righteousness, even when he's engaged in the most nefarious financial operations."

"And you're working for him?"

Will nodded. "That was his wedding present to Molly—a job for me on the Aldehyde papers at almost twice the salary I'd been getting from my previous employers. Princely! But then he was very fond of Molly."

"How did he react to Babs?"

"He never knew about her—never knew that there was any reason for Molly's accident."

"So he goes on employing you for your dead wife's sake?"

Will shrugged his shoulders. "The excuse," he said, "is that I have my mother to support."

"And of course you wouldn't enjoy being poor."

"I certainly wouldn't."

There was a silence.

"Well," said Susila at last, "let's get back to Africa."

"I'd been sent there to do a series on Negro Nationalism. Not to mention a little private hanky-panky in the business line for Uncle Joe. It was on the plane, flying home from Nairobi. I found myself sitting next to her."

"Next to the young woman you couldn't have liked less?"

"Couldn't have liked less," he repeated, "or disapproved of more. But if you're an addict you've got to have your dope—the dope that you know in advance is going to destroy you."

"It's a funny thing," she said reflectively, "but in Pala we have hardly any addicts."

"Not even sex addicts?"

"The sex addicts are also person addicts. In other words, they're lovers."

"But even lovers sometimes hate the people they love."

"Naturally. Because I always have the same name and the same nose and eyes, it doesn't follow that I'm always the same woman. Recognizing that fact and reacting to it sensibly—that's part of the Art of Loving."

As succinctly as he could, Will told her the rest of the story. It was the same story, now that Babs had come on the scene, as it had been before—the same but much more so. Babs had been Rachel raised, so to speak, to a higher power—Rachel squared, Rachel to the *n*th. And the unhappiness that, because of Babs, he had inflicted upon Molly was proportionately greater than anything she had had to suffer on account of Rachel. Proportionately greater, too, had been his own exasperation, his own resentful sense of being blackmailed by her love and suffering, his own remorse and pity, his own determination, in spite of the remorse and the pity, to go on getting what he wanted, what he hated himself for wanting, what he resolutely refused to do without. And meanwhile Babs had become more demanding, was claiming ever more and more of his time—time not only in the strawberry-pink alcove, but also outside, in restaurants, and nightclubs, at her horrible friends' cocktail parties, on weekends in the country. "Just you and me, darling," she would say, "all alone together." All alone together in an isolation that gave him the opportunity to plumb the almost unfathomable depths of her mindlessness and vulgarity. But through all his boredom and distaste, all his moral and intellectual repugnance, the craving persisted. After one of those dreadful weekends, he was as hopelessly a Babs addict as he had been before. And on her side, on her own Sister-of-Mercy level, Molly had remained, in spite of everything, no less hopelessly a Will Farnaby addict. Hopelessly so far as *he* was concerned—for his one wish was that she should love him less and allow him to go to hell in peace. But, so far as Molly herself was concerned, the addiction was always and irrepressibly hopeful. She never ceased to expect the transfiguring miracle that would change him into the kind, unselfish, loving Will Farnaby whom (in the teeth of all the evidence, all the repeated disappointments) she stubbornly insisted on regarding as his true self. It was only in the course of that last fatal interview, only when (stifling his pity and giving free rein to his resentment of her blackmailing unhappiness) he had announced his intention of leaving her and going to live with Babs—it was only then that hope had finally given place to hopelessness. "Do you mean it, Will—do you really mean it?" "I really mean it." It was in hopelessness, in utter hopelessness, that she had walked out to the car, had driven away into the rain—into her death. At the funeral, when the coffin was lowered into the grave, he had promised himself that he would never see Babs again. Never, never, never again. That evening, while he was sitting at his desk trying to write an article on "What's Wrong With Youth," trying not to remember the hospital, the open grave, and his own responsibility for everything that had happened, he was startled by the shrill buzzing of the doorbell. A belated message of condolence, no doubt . . . He had opened, and there, instead of the telegram, was Babs—dramatically without makeup and all in black.

"My poor, poor Will!" They had sat down on the sofa in the living room, and she had stroked his hair and both of them had cried.

"When pain and anguish wring the brow, a ministering

angel thou." An hour later, needless to say, they were naked and in bed. After which he had moved, earth to earth, into the pink alcove. Within three months, as any fool could have foreseen, Babs had begun to tire of him; within four, an absolutely divine man from Kenya had turned up at a cocktail party. One thing had led to another and when, three days later, Babs came home, it was to prepare the alcove for a new tenant and give notice to the old.

"Do you really mean it, Babs?"

She really meant it.

There was a rustling in the bushes outside the window and an instant later, startlingly loud and slightly out of time, "Here and now, boys," shouted a talking bird.

"Shut up!" Will shouted back.

"Here and now, boys," the mynah repeated. "Here and now, boys. Here and—"

"Shut up!"

There was silence.

"I had to shut him up," Will explained, "because of course he's absolutely right. Here, boys; now, boys. Then and there are absolutely irrelevant. Or aren't they? What about your husband's death, for example? Is *that* irrelevant?"

Susila looked at him for a moment in silence, then slowly nodded her head. "In the context of what I have to do now --yes, completely irrelevant. That's something I had to learn."

"Does one learn how to forget?"

"It isn't a matter of forgetting. What one has to learn is how to remember and yet be free of the past. How to be there with the dead and yet still be here, on the spot, with the living." She gave him a sad little smile and added, "It isn't easy."

"It isn't easy," Will repeated. And suddenly all his defenses were down, all his pride had left him. "Will you help me?" he asked.

"It's a bargain," she said, and held out her hand.

A sound of footsteps made them turn their heads. Dr. MacPhail had entered the room.

viii

"GOOD EVENING, MY DEAR. GOOD EVENING, MR. FARNABY."

The tone was cheerful—not, Susila was quick to notice, with any kind of synthetic cheerfulness, but naturally, genuinely. And yet, before coming here, he must have stopped at the hospital, must have seen Lakshmi as Susila herself had seen her only an hour or two since, more dreadfully emaciated than ever, more skull-like and discolored. Half a long lifetime of love and loyalty and mutual forgiveness—and in another day or two it would be all over; he would be alone. But sufficient unto the day is the evil thereof—sufficient unto the place and the person. "One has no right," her father-in-law had said to her one day as they were leaving the hospital together, "one has no right to inflict one's sadness on other people. And no right, of course, to pretend that one isn't sad. One just has to accept one's grief and one's absurd attempts to be a stoic. Accept, accept . . ." His voice broke. Looking up at him, she saw that his face was wet with tears. Five minutes later they were sitting on a bench, at the edge of the lotus pool, in the shadow of the huge stone Buddha. With a little plop, sharp and yet liquidly voluptuous, an unseen frog dived from its round leafy platform into the water. Thrusting up from the mud, the thick green stems with their turgid buds broke through into the air, and here and there the blue or rosy symbols of enlightenment had opened their petals to the sun and the probing visitations of flies and tiny beetles and the wild bees from the jungle. Darting, pausing in mid-flight, darting again, a score of glittering blue and green dragonflies were hawking for midges.

"*Tathata,*" Dr. Robert had whispered. "Suchness."

For a long time they sat there in silence. Then, suddenly, he had touched her shoulder.

"Look!"

She lifted her eyes to where he was pointing. Two small

parrots had perched on the Buddha's right hand and were going through the ritual of courtship.

"Did you stop again at the lotus pool?" Susila asked aloud.

Dr. Robert gave her a little smile and nodded his head.

"How was Shivapuram?" Will enquired.

"Pleasant enough in itself," the doctor answered. "Its only defect is that it's so close to the outside world. Up here one can simply ignore the organized insanities and get on with one's work. Down there, with all those antennae and listening posts and channels of communication that a government has to have, the outside world is perpetually breathing down one's neck. One hears it, feels it, smells it—yes, *smells* it."

"Has anything more than usually disastrous happened since I've been here?"

"Nothing out of the ordinary at your end of the world. I wish I could say the same about *our* end."

"What's the trouble?"

"The trouble is our next-door neighbor, Colonel Dipa. To begin with, he's made another deal with the Czechs."

"More armaments?"

"Sixty million dollars' worth. It was on the radio this morning."

"But what on earth for?"

"The usual reasons. Glory and power. The pleasures of vanity and the pleasures of bullying. Terrorism and military parades at home; conquests and Te Deums abroad. And that brings me to the second item of unpleasant news. Last night the Colonel delivered another of his celebrated Greater Rendang speeches."

"Greater Rendang? What's that?"

"You may well ask," said Dr. Robert. "Greater Rendang is the territory controlled by the Sultans of Rendang-Lobo between 1447 and 1483. It included Rendang, the Nicobar Islands, about thirty per cent of Sumatra and the whole of Pala. Today, it's Colonel Dipa's *Irredenta*."

"Seriously?"

"With a perfectly straight face. No, I'm wrong. With a purple, distorted face and at the top of a voice that he has trained, after long practice, to sound exactly like Hitler's. Greater Rendang or death!"

"But the great powers would never allow it."

"Maybe they wouldn't like to see him in Sumatra. But Pala—that's another matter." He shook his head. "Pala, unfortunately, is in nobody's good books. We don't want the Communists; but neither do we want the capitalists. Least of all do we want the wholesale industrialization that both parties are so anxious to impose on us—for different reasons, of course. The West wants it because our labor costs are low and investors' dividends will be correspondingly high. And the East wants it because industrialization will create a proletariat, open fresh fields for Communist agitation and may lead in the long run to the setting up of yet another People's Democracy. We say no to both of you, so we're unpopular everywhere. Regardless of their ideologies, all the Great Powers may prefer a Rendang-controlled Pala with oil fields to an independent Pala without. If Dipa attacks us, they'll say it's most deplorable; but they won't lift a finger. And when he takes us over and calls the oilmen in, they'll be delighted."

"What can you do about Colonel Dipa?" Will asked.

"Except for passive resistance, nothing. We have no army and no powerful friends. The Colonel has both. The most we can do, if he starts making trouble, is to appeal to the United Nations. Meanwhile we shall remonstrate with the Colonel about this latest Greater Rendang effusion. Remonstrate through our minister in Rendang-Lobo, and remonstrate with the great man in person when he pays his state visit to Pala ten days from now."

"A state visit?"

"For the young Raja's coming-of-age celebrations. He was asked a long time ago, but he never let us know for certain whether he was coming or not. Today it was finally settled. We'll have a summit meeting as well as a birthday party. But let's talk about something more rewarding. How did you get on today, Mr. Farnaby?"

"Not merely well—gloriously. I had the honor of a visit from your reigning monarch."

"Murugan?"

"Why didn't you tell me he was your reigning monarch?"

Dr. Robert laughed. "You might have asked for an interview."

"Well, I didn't. Nor from the Queen Mother."

"Did the Rani come too?"

"At the command of her Little Voice. And, sure enough, the Little Voice sent her to the right address. My boss, Joe Aldehyde, is one of her dearest friends."

"Did she tell you that she's trying to bring your boss here, to exploit our oil?"

"She did indeed."

"We turned down his latest offer less than a month ago. Did you know that?"

Will was relieved to be able to answer quite truthfully that he didn't. Neither Joe Aldehyde nor the Rani had told him of this most recent rebuff. "My job," he went on, a little less truthfully, "is in the wood-pulp department, not in petroleum." There was a silence. "What's my status here?" he asked at last. "Undesirable alien?"

"Well, fortunately you're not an armament salesman."

"Nor a missionary," said Susila.

"Nor an oilman—though on that count you might be guilty by association."

"Nor even, so far as we know, a uranium prospector."

"Those," Dr. Robert concluded, "are the Alpha Plus undesirables. As a journalist you rank as a Beta. Not the kind of person we should ever dream of inviting to Pala. But also not the kind who, having managed to get here, requires to be summarily deported."

"I'd like to stay here for as long as it's legally possible," said Will.

"May I ask why?"

Will hesitated. As Joe Aldehyde's secret agent and a reporter with a hopeless passion for literature, he had to stay long enough to negotiate with Bahu and earn his year of freedom. But there were other, more avowable reasons. "If you don't object to personal remarks," he said, "I'll tell you."

"Fire away," said Dr. Robert.

"The fact is that, the more I see of you people the better I like you. I want to find out more about you. And in the process," he added, glancing at Susila, "I might find out some interesting things about myself. How long shall I be allowed to stay?"

"Normally we'd turn you out as soon as you're fit to travel. But if you're seriously interested in Pala, above all if you're seriously interested in yourself—well, we might stretch a point. Or shouldn't we stretch that point? What do you say, Susila? After all, he *does* work for Lord Aldehyde."

Will was on the point of protesting again that his job was in the wood-pulp department; but the words stuck in his throat and he said nothing. The seconds passed. Dr. Robert repeated his question.

"Yes," Susila said at last, "we'd be taking a certain risk. But personally . . . personally I'd be ready to take it. Am I right?" she turned to Will.

"Well, I think you can trust me. At least I hope you can." He laughed, trying to make a joke of it; but to his annoyance and embarrassment, he felt himself blushing. Blushing for what? he demanded resentfully of his conscience. If anybody was being double-crossed, it was Standard of California. And once Dipa had moved in, what difference would it make who got the concession? Which would you rather be eaten by—a wolf or a tiger? So far as the lamb is concerned, it hardly seems to matter. Joe would be no worse than his competitors. All the same, he wished he hadn't been in such a hurry to send off that letter. And why, why couldn't that dreadful woman have left him in peace?

Through the sheet he felt a hand on his undamaged knee. Dr. Robert was smiling down at him.

"You can have a month here," he said. "I'll take full responsibility for you. And we'll do our best to show you everything."

"I'm very grateful to you."

"When in doubt," said Dr. Robert, "always act on the assumption that people are more honorable than you have any solid reason for supposing they are. That was the advice the Old Raja gave me when I was a young man." Turning to Susila, "Let's see," he said, "how old were you when the Old Raja died?"

"Just eight."

"So you remember him pretty well."

Susila laughed. "Could anyone ever forget the way he used to talk about himself. 'Quote "I" (unquote) like sugar in my tea.' What a darling man."

"And what a great one!"

Dr. MacPhail got up and, crossing to the bookcase that stood between the door and the wardrobe, pulled out of its lowest shelf a thick red album, much the worse for tropical weather and fish insects. "There's a picture of him somewhere," he said as he turned over the pages. "Here we are."

Will found himself looking at the faded snapshot of a little old Hindu in spectacles and a loincloth, engaged in emptying the contents of an extremely ornate silver sauceboat over a small squat pillar.

"What *is* he doing?" he asked.

"Anointing a phallic symbol with melted butter," the doctor answered. "It was a habit my poor father could never break him of."

"Did your father disapprove of phalluses?"

"No, *no*," said Dr. MacPhail. "My father was all for them. It was the *symbol* that he disapproved of."

"Why the symbol?"

"Because he thought that people ought to take their religion warm from the cow, if you see what I mean. Not skimmed or pasteurized or homogenized. Above all not canned in any kind of theological or liturgical container."

"And the Raja had a weakness for containers?"

"Not for containers in general. Just this one particular tin can. He'd always felt a special attachment to the family lingam. It was made of black basalt, and was at least eight hundred years old."

"I see," said Will Farnaby.

"Buttering the family lingam—it was an act of piety, it expressed a beautiful sentiment about a sublime idea. But even the sublimest of ideas is totally different from the cosmic mystery it's supposed to stand for. And the beautiful sentiments connected with the sublime idea—what do they have in common with the direct experience of the mystery? Nothing whatsoever. Needless to say, the Old Raja knew all this perfectly well. Better than my father. He'd drunk the milk as it came from the cow, he'd actually *been* the milk. But the buttering of lingams was a devotional practice he just couldn't bear to give up. And, I don't have to tell you, he should never have been asked to give it up. But where symbols were concerned, my father was a puritan. He'd amended Goethe—*Alles vergängliche ist* NICHT *ein Gleichnis*. His ideal was pure experimental science at one end of the spectrum and pure experimental mysticism at the other. Direct experience on every level and then clear, rational statements about those experiences. Lingams and crosses, butter and holy water, sutras, gospels, images, chanting—he'd have liked to abolish them all."

"Where would the arts have come in?" Will questioned.

"They wouldn't have come in at all," Dr. MacPhail answered. "And that was my father's blindest spot—poetry. He said he liked it; but in fact he didn't. Poetry for its own sake, poetry as an autonomous universe, out there, in the space between direct experience and the symbols of science—that was something he simply couldn't understand. Let's find his picture."

Dr. MacPhail turned back the pages of the album and pointed to a craggy profile with enormous eyebrows.

"What a Scotsman!" Will commented.

"And yet his mother and his grandmother were Palanese."

"One doesn't see a trace of them."

"Whereas his grandfather, who hailed from Perth, might almost have passed for a Rajput."

Will peered into the ancient photograph of a young man with an oval face and black side-whiskers, leaning his elbow on a marble pedestal on which, bottom upwards, stood his inordinately tall top hat.

"Your great-grandfather?"

"The first MacPhail of Pala. Dr. Andrew. Born 1822, in the Royal Burgh, where *his* father, James MacPhail, owned a rope mill. Which was properly symbolical; for James was a devout Calvinist, and being convinced that he himself was one of the elect, derived a deep and glowing satisfaction from the thought of all those millions of his fellow men going through life with the noose of predestination about their necks, and Old Nobodaddy Aloft counting the minutes to spring the trap."

Will laughed.

"Yes," Dr. Robert agreed, "it does seem pretty comic. But it didn't then. Then it was serious—much more serious than the H-bomb is today. It was known for certain that ninety-nine point nine per cent of the human race were condemned to everlasting brimstone. Why? Either because they'd never heard of Jesus; or, if they had, because they couldn't believe sufficiently strongly that Jesus had delivered them from the brimstone. And the proof that they didn't believe sufficiently strongly was the empirical, observable fact that their souls were not at peace. Perfect faith is defined as something that produces perfect peace of mind. But perfect peace of mind is something that practically nobody possesses. Therefore practically nobody possesses perfect faith. Therefore practically everybody is predestined to eternal punishment. *Quod erat demonstrandum.*"

"One wonders," said Susila, "why they didn't all go mad."

"Fortunately most of them believed only with the tops of their heads. Up here." Dr. MacPhail tapped his bald spot. "With the tops of their heads they were convinced it was the Truth with the largest possible T. But their glands and their guts knew better—knew that it was all sheer bosh. For most of them, Truth was true only on Sundays, and then only in a strictly Pickwickian sense. James MacPhail knew all this and was determined that *his* children should not be mere Sabbath-day believers. They were to believe every word of the sacred nonsense even on Mondays, even on half-holiday afternoons; and they were to believe with their whole being, not merely up there, in the attic. Perfect faith and the perfect peace that goes with it were to be forced into them. How? By giving them hell now and threatening them with hell hereafter. And if, in their devilish perversity, they refused to have perfect faith, and be at peace, give them more hell and threaten hotter fires. And meanwhile tell them that good works are as filthy rags in the sight of God; but punish them ferociously for every misdemeanor. Tell them that by nature they're totally depraved, then beat them for being what they inescapably are."

Will Farnaby turned back to the album.

"Do you have a picture of this delightful ancestor of yours?"

"We had an oil painting," said Dr. MacPhail. "But the dampness was too much for the canvas, and then the fish insects got into it. He was a splendid specimen. Like a High Renaissance picture of Jeremiah. You know—majestic, with an inspired eye and the kind of prophetic beard that covers such a multitude of physiognomic sins. The only relic of him that remains is a pencil drawing of his house."

He turned back another page and there it was.

"Solid granite," he went on, "with bars on all the windows. And, inside that cozy little family Bastille, what systematic inhumanity! Systematic inhumanity in the name, needless to say, of Christ and for righteousness' sake. Dr. Andrew left an unfinished autobiography, so we know all about it."

"Didn't the children get any help from their mother?"

Dr. MacPhail shook his head.

"Janet MacPhail was a Cameron and as good a Calvinist as James himself. Maybe an even better Calvinist than he was. Being a woman, she had further to go, she had more instinctive decencies to overcome. But she did overcome them—heroically. Far from restraining her husband, she urged him on, she backed him up. There were homilies before breakfast and at the midday dinner; there was the catechism on Sundays and learning the Epistles by heart; and every evening, when the day's delinquencies had been added up and assessed, methodical whipping, with a whalebone riding switch on the bare buttocks, for all six children, girls as well as boys, in order of seniority."

"It always makes me feel slightly sick," said Susila. "Pure sadism."

"No, not *pure*," said Dr. MacPhail. "Applied sadism. Sadism with an ulterior motive, sadism in the service of an ideal, as the expression of a religious conviction. And that's a subject," he added, turning to Will, "that somebody ought to make a historical study of—the relation between theology and corporal punishment in childhood. I have a theory that, wherever little boys and girls are systematically flagellated, the victims grow up to think of God as 'Wholly Other'—isn't that the fashionable argot in your part of the world? Wherever, on the contrary, children are brought up without being subjected to physical violence, God is immanent. A people's theology reflects the state of its children's bottoms. Look at the Hebrews—enthusiastic child-beaters. And so were all good Christians in the Ages of Faith. Hence Jehovah, hence Original Sin and the infinitely offended Father of Roman and Protestant orthodoxy. Whereas among Buddhists and Hindus education has always been nonviolent. No laceration of little buttocks—therefore *tat tvam asi*, thou art That, mind from Mind is not divided. And look at the Quakers. They were heretical enough to believe in the Inner Light, and what happened? They gave up beating their children and were the first Christian denomination to protest against the institution of slavery."

"But child-beating," Will objected, "has quite gone out of fashion nowadays. And yet it's precisely at this moment that it has become modish to hold forth about the Wholly Other."

Dr. MacPhail waved the objection away. "It's just a case of reaction following action. By the second half of the nineteenth century freethinking humanitarianism had become so strong that even good Christians were influenced by it and stopped beating their children. There were no weals on the younger generation's posterior; consequently, it ceased to think of God as the Wholly Other and proceeded to invent New Thought, Unity, Christian Science—all the semi-Oriental heresies in which God is the Wholly Identical. The movement was well under way in William James's day, and it's been gathering momentum ever since. But thesis always invites antithesis and in due course the heresies begat Neo-Orthodoxy. Down with the Wholly Identical and back to the Wholly Other! Back to Augustine, back to Martin Luther—back, in a word, to the two most relentlessly flagellated bottoms in the whole history of Christian thought. Read the *Confessions*, read the *Table Talk*. Augustine was beaten by his schoolmaster and laughed at by his parents when he complained. Luther was systematically flogged not only by his teachers and his father, but even by his loving mother. The world has been paying for the scars on his buttocks ever since. Prussianism and the Third Reich—without Luther and his flagellation theology these monstrosities could never have come into existence. Or take the flagellation theology of Augustine, as carried to its logical conclusions by Calvin and swallowed whole by pious folk like James MacPhail and Janet Cameron. Major premise: God is Wholly Other. Minor premise: man is totally depraved. Conclusion: Do to your children's bottoms what was done to yours, what your Heavenly Father has been doing to the collective bottom of humanity ever since the Fall: whip, whip, whip!"

There was a silence. Will Farnaby looked again at the drawing of the granite person in the rope walk, and thought of all the grotesque and ugly phantasies promoted to the rank of supernatural facts, all the obscene cruelties inspired by those phantasies, all the pain inflicted and the miseries endured because of them. And when it wasn't Augustine with his "benignant asperity," it was Robespierre, it was Stalin; when it wasn't Luther exhorting the princes to kill the peasants, it was a genial Mao reducing them to slavery.

"Don't you sometimes despair?" he asked.

Dr. MacPhail shook his head. "We don't despair," he said, "because we know that things don't necessarily *have* to be as bad as in fact they've always been."

"We know that they can be a great deal better," Susila added. "Know it because they already *are* a great deal better, here and now, on this absurd little island."

"But whether we shall be able to persuade you people to follow our example, or whether we shall even be able to preserve our tiny oasis of humanity in the midst of your worldwide wilderness of monkeys—that, alas," said Dr. MacPhail, "is another question. One's justified in feeling extremely pessimistic about the current situation. But despair, radical despair—no, I can't see any justification for that."

"Not even when you read history?"

"Not even when I read history."

"I envy you. How do you manage to do it?"

"By remembering what history is—the record of what human beings have been impelled to do by their ignorance and the enormous bumptiousness that makes them canonize their ignorance as a political or religious dogma."

He turned again to the album. "Let's get back to the house in the Royal Burgh, back to James and Janet, and the six children whom Calvin's God, in His inscrutable malevolence, had condemned to their tender mercies. 'The rod and reproof bring wisdom; but a child left to himself bringeth his mother to shame.' Indoctrination reinforced by psychological stress and physical torture—the perfect Pavlovian setup. But, unfortunately for organized religion and political dictatorship, human beings are much less reliable as laboratory animals than dogs. On Tom, Mary and Jean the conditioning worked as it was meant to work. Tom became a minister, and Mary married a minister and duly died in childbirth. Jean stayed at home, nursed her mother through a long grim cancer and for the next twenty years was slowly sacrificed to the aging and finally senile and driveling patriarch. So far, so good. But with Annie, the fourth child, the pattern changed. Annie was pretty. At eighteen she was proposed to by a captain of dragoons. But the captain was an Anglican and his views on total depravity and God's good pleasure were criminally incorrect. The marriage was forbidden. It looked as though Annie were predestined to share the fate of Jean. She stuck it out for ten years; then, at twenty-eight, she got herself seduced by the second mate of an East Indiaman. There were seven weeks of almost frantic happiness—the first she had ever known. Her face was transfigured by a kind of supernatural beauty, her body glowed with life. Then the Indiaman sailed for a two-year voyage for Madras and Macao. Four months later, pregnant, friendless and despairing, Annie threw herself into the Tay. Meanwhile Alexander, the next in line, had run away from school and joined a company of actors. In the house by the rope walk nobody, thenceforward, was ever allowed to refer to his existence. And finally there was Andrew, the youngest, the Benjamin. What a model child! He was obedient, he loved his lessons, he learned the Epistles by heart faster and more accurately than any of the other children had done. Then, just in time to restore her faith in human wickedness, his mother caught him one evening playing with his genitals. He was whipped till the blood came; was caught again a few weeks later and again whipped, sentenced to solitary confinement on bread and water, told that he had almost certainly committed the sin against the Holy Ghost and that it was undoubtedly on account of that sin that his mother had been afflicted with cancer. For the rest of his childhood Andrew was haunted by recurrent nightmares of hell. Haunted, too, by recurrent temptations and, when he succumbed to them—which of course he did, but always in the privacy of the latrine at the bottom of the garden—by yet more terrifying visions of the punishments in store for him."

"And to think," Will Farnaby commented, "to think that people complain about modern life having no meaning! Look at what life was like when it *did* have a meaning. A tale told by an idiot or a tale told by a Calvinist? Give me the idiot every time."

"Agreed," said Dr. MacPhail. "But mightn't there be a third possibility? Mightn't there be a tale told by somebody who is neither an imbecile nor a paranoiac?"

"Somebody, for a change, completely sane," said Susila.

"Yes, for a change," Dr. MacPhail repeated. "For a blessed change. And luckily, even under the old dispensation, there were always plenty of people whom even the most diabolic upbringing couldn't ruin. By all the rules of the Freudian and Pavlovian games, my great-grandfather ought to have grown up to be a mental cripple. In fact, he grew up to be a mental athlete. Which only shows," Dr. Robert added parenthetically, "how hopelessly inadequate your two highly touted systems of psychology really are. Freudism and behaviorism—poles apart but in complete agreement when it comes to the facts of the built-in, congenital differences between individuals. How do your pet psychologists deal with these facts? Very simply. They ignore them. They blandly pretend that the facts aren't there. Hence their complete inability to cope with the human situation as it really exists, or even to explain it theoretically. Look at what happened, for example, in this particular case. Andrew's brothers and sisters were either tamed by their conditioning or destroyed. Andrew was neither destroyed nor tamed. Why? Because the roulette wheel of heredity had stopped turning at a lucky number. He had a more resilient constitution than the others, a different anatomy, different biochemistry and different temperament. His parents did their worst, as they had done with all the rest of their unfortunate brood. Andrew came through with flying colors, almost without a scar."

"In spite of the sin against the Holy Ghost?"

"That, happily, was something he got rid of during his first year of medical studies at Edinburgh. He was only a boy—just over seventeen. (They started young in those days.) In the dissecting room the boy found himself listening to the extravagant obscenities and blasphemies with which his fellow students kept up their spirits among the slowly rotting cadavers. Listening at first with horror, with a sickening fear that God would surely take vengeance. But nothing happened. The blasphemers flourished, the loud-mouthed fornicators escaped with nothing worse than a dose, every now and then, of the clap. Fear gave place in Andrew's mind to a wonderful sense of relief and deliverance. Greatly daring, he began to risk a few ribald jokes of his own. His first utterance of a four-letter word—what a liberation, what a genuinely religious experience! And meanwhile, in his spare time, he read *Tom Jones*, he read Hume's 'Essay on Miracles,' he read the infidel Gibbon. Putting the French he had learned at school to good account, he read La Mettrie, he read Dr. Cabanis. Man is a machine, the brain secretes thought as the liver secretes bile. How simple it all was, how luminously obvious! With all the fervor of a convert at a revival meeting, he decided for atheism. In the circumstances it was only to be expected. You can't stomach St. Augustine any more, you can't go on repeating the Athanasian rigmarole. So you pull the plug and send them down the drain. What bliss! But not for very long. Something, you discover, is missing. The experimental baby was flushed out with the theological dirt and soapsuds. But nature abhors a vacuum. Bliss gives place to a chronic discomfort, and now you're afflicted, generation after generation, by a succession of Wesleys, Puseys, Moodys and Billys—Sunday and Graham—all working like beavers to pump the theology back out of the cesspool. They hope, of course, to recover the baby. But they never succeed. All that a revivalist can do is to siphon up a little of the dirty water. Which, in due course, has to be thrown out again. And so on, indefinitely. It's really too boring and, as Dr. Andrew came at last to realize, wholly unnecessary. Meanwhile here he was, in the first flush of his new-found freedom. Excited, exultant—but quietly excited, exultant behind that appearance of grave and courteous detachment which he habitually presented to the world."

"What about his father?" Will asked. "Did they have a battle?"

"No battle. Andrew didn't like battles. He was the sort of man who always goes his own way, but doesn't advertise the fact, doesn't argue with people who prefer another road. The old man was never given the opportunity of putting on his Jeremiah act. Andrew kept his mouth shut about Hume and La Mettrie and went through the traditional motions. But when his training was finished, he just didn't come home. Instead, he went to London and signed up, as surgeon and naturalist, on HMS *Melampus*, bound for the South Seas with orders to chart, survey, collect specimens and protect Protestant missionaries and British interests. The cruise of the *Melampus* lasted for a full three years. They called at Tahiti, they spent two months on Samoa and a month in the Marquesas group. After Perth, the islands seemed like Eden—but an Eden innocent unfortunately not only of Calvinism and capitalism and industrial slums, but also of Shakespeare and Mozart, also of scientific knowledge and logical thinking. It was paradise, but it wouldn't do, it wouldn't do. They sailed on. They visited Fiji and the Carolines and the Solomons. They charted the northern coast of New Guinea and, in Borneo, a party went ashore, trapped a pregnant orangutan and climbed to the top of Mount Kinabalu. Then followed a week at Panay, a fortnight in the Mergui Archipelago. After which they headed west to the Andamans and from the Andamans to the mainland of India. While ashore, my great-grandfather was thrown from his horse and broke his right leg. The captain of the *Melampus* found another surgeon and sailed for home. Two months later, as good as new, Andrew was practicing medicine at Madras. Doctors were scarce in those days and sickness fearfully common. The young man began to prosper. But life among the merchants and officials of the presidency was oppressively boring. It was an exile, but an exile without any of the compensations of exile, an exile without adventure or strangeness, a banishment merely to the provinces, to the tropical equivalent of Swansea or Huddersfield. But still he resisted the temptation to book a passage on the next homebound ship. If he stuck it out for five years, he would have enough money to buy a good practice in Edinburgh—no, in London, in the West End. The future beckoned, rosy and golden. There would be a wife, preferably with auburn hair and a modest competence. There would be four or five children—happy, unwhipped and atheistic. And his practice would grow, his patients would be drawn from circles ever more exalted. Wealth, reputation, dignity, even a knighthood. Sir Andrew MacPhail stepping out of his brougham in Belgrave Square. The great Sir Andrew, physician to the Queen. Summoned to St. Petersburg to operate on the Grand Duke, to the Tuileries, to the Vatican, to the Sublime Porte. Delightful phantasies! But the facts, as it turned out, were to be far more interesting. One fine morning a brown-skinned stranger called at the surgery. In halting English he gave an account of himself. He was from Pala and had been commanded by His Highness, the Raja, to seek out and bring back with him a skillful surgeon from the West. The rewards would be princely. *Princely,* he insisted. There and then Dr. Andrew accepted the invitation. Partly, of course, for the money; but mostly because he was bored, because he needed a change, needed a taste of adventure. A trip to the Forbidden Island—the lure was irresistible."

"And remember," Susila interjected, "in those days Pala was much more forbidden than it is now."

"So you can imagine how eagerly young Dr. Andrew jumped at the opportunity now offered by the Raja's ambassador. Ten days later his ship dropped anchor off the north coast of the forbidden island. With his medicine chest, his bag of instruments, and a small tin trunk containing his clothes and a few indispensable books, he was rowed in an outrigger canoe through the pounding surf, carried in a palanquin through the streets of Shivapuram and set down in the inner courtyard of the royal palace. His royal patient was eagerly awaiting him. Without being given time to shave or change his clothes, Dr. Andrew was ushered into the presence—the pitiable presence of a small brown man in his early forties, terribly emaciated under his rich brocades, his face so swollen and distorted as to be barely human, his voice reduced to a hoarse whisper. Dr. Andrew examined him. From the maxillary antrum, where it had its roots, a tumor had spread in all directions. It had filled the nose, it had pushed up into the socket of the right eye, it had half blocked the throat. Breathing had become difficult, swallowing acutely painful, and sleep an impossibility—for whenever he dropped off, the patient would choke and wake up frantically struggling for air. Without radical surgery, it was obvious, the Raja would be dead within a couple of months. *With* radical surgery, much sooner. Those were the good old days, remember—the good old days of septic operations without benefit of chloroform. Even in the most favorable circumstances surgery was fatal to one patient out of four. Where conditions were less propitious, the odds declined—fifty-fifty, thirty to seventy, zero to a hundred. In the present case the prognosis could hardly have been worse. The patient was already weak and the operation would be long, difficult and excruciatingly painful. There was a good chance that he would die on the operating table and a virtual certainty that, if he survived, it would only be to die a few days later of blood poisoning. But if he should die, Dr. Andrew now reflected, what would be the fate of the alien surgeon who had killed a king? And, during the operation, who would hold the royal patient down while he writhed under the knife? Which of his servants or courtiers would have the strength of mind to disobey, when the master screamed in agony or positively commanded them to let him go?

"Perhaps the wisest thing would be to say, here and now, that the case was hopeless, that he could do nothing, and ask to be sent back to Madras forthwith. Then he looked again at the sick man. Through the grotesque mask of his poor deformed face the Raja was looking at him intently—looking with the eyes of a condemned criminal begging the judge for mercy. Touched by the appeal, Dr. Andrew gave him a smile of encouragement and all at once, as he patted the thin hand, he had an idea. It was absurd, crackbrained, thoroughly discreditable; but all the same, all the same . . .

"Five years before, he suddenly remembered, while he was still at Edinburgh, there had been an article in *The Lancet,* an article denouncing the notorious Professor Elliotson for his advocacy of animal magnetism. Elliotson had had the effrontery to talk of painless operations performed on patients in the mesmeric trance.

"The man was either a gullible fool or an unscrupulous knave. The so-called evidence for such nonsense was manifestly worthless. It was all sheer humbug, quackery, downright fraud—and so on for six columns of righteous indignation. At the time—for he was still full of La Mettrie and Hume and Cabanis—Dr. Andrew had read the article with a glow of orthodox approval. After which he had forgotten about the very existence of animal magnetism. Now, at the Raja's bedside, it all came back to him—the mad professor, the magnetic passes, the amputations without pain, the low death rate and the rapid recoveries. Perhaps, after all, there might be something in it. He was deep in these thoughts when, breaking a long silence, the sick man spoke to him. From a young sailor who had deserted his ship at Rendang-Lobo and somehow made his way across the Strait, the Raja had learned to speak English with remarkable fluency, but also, in faithful imitation of his teacher, with a strong Cockney accent. That Cockney accent," Dr. MacPhail repeated with a little laugh. "It turns up again and again in my great-grandfather's memoirs. There was something, to him, inexpressibly improper about a king who spoke like Sam Weller. And in this case the impropriety was more than merely social. Besides being a king, the Raja was a man of intellect and the most exquisite refinement; a man, not only of deep religious convictions (any crude oaf can have deep religious convictions), but also of deep religious experience and spiritual insight. That such a man should express himself in Cockney was something that an Early Victorian Scotsman who had read *The Pickwick Papers* could never get over. Nor, in spite of all my great-grandfather's tactful coaching, could the Raja ever get over his impure diphthongs and dropped aitches. But all that was in the future. At their first tragic meeting, that shocking, lower-class accent seemed strangely touching. Laying the palms of his hands together in a gesture of supplication, the sick man whispered, ' 'Elp me, Dr. MacPhile, 'elp me.'

"The appeal was decisive. Without any further hesitation, Dr. Andrew took the Raja's thin hands between his own and began to speak in the most confident tone about a wonderful new treatment recently discovered in Europe and employed as yet by only a handful of the most eminent physicians. Then, turning to the attendants who had been hovering all this time in the background, he ordered them out of the room. They did not understand the words; but his tone and accompanying gestures were unmistakably clear. They bowed and withdrew. Dr. Andrew took off his coat, rolled up his shirt sleeves and started to make those famous magnetic passes, about which he had read with so much skeptical amusement in *The Lancet*. From the crown of the head, over the face and down the trunk to the epigastrium, again and again until the patient falls into a trance—'or until' (he remembered the derisive comments of the anonymous writer of the article) 'until the presiding charlatan shall choose to say that his dupe is now under the magnetic influence.' Quackery, humbug and fraud. But all the same, all the same . . . He worked away in silence. Twenty passes, fifty passes. The sick man sighed and closed his eyes. Sixty, eighty, a hundred, a hundred and twenty. The heat was stifling, Dr. Andrew's shirt was drenched with sweat, and his arms ached. Grimly he repeated the same absurd gesture. A hundred and fifty, a hundred and seventy-five, two hundred. It was all fraud and humbug; but all the same he was determined to make this poor devil go to sleep, even if it took him the whole day to do it. 'You are going to sleep,' he said aloud as he made the two hundred and eleventh pass. 'You are going to sleep.' The sick man seemed to sink more deeply into his pillows, and suddenly Dr. Andrew caught the sound of a rattling wheeze. 'This time,' he added quickly, 'you are not going to choke. There's plenty of room for the air to pass, and you're not going to choke.' The Raja's breathing grew quiet. Dr. Andrew made a few more passes, then decided that it would be safe to take a rest. He mopped his face, then rose, stretched his arms and took a couple of turns up and down the room. Sitting down again by the bed, he took one of the Raja's sticklike wrists and felt for the pulse. An hour before it had been running at almost a hundred; now the rate had fallen to seventy. He raised the arm: the hand hung limp like a dead man's. He let go, and the arm dropped by its own weight and lay, inert and unmoving, where it had fallen. 'Your Highness,' he said, and again, more loudly, 'Your Highness.' There was no answer. It was all quackery, humbug and fraud, but all the same it worked, it obviously worked."

A large, brightly colored mantis fluttered down onto the rail at the foot of the bed, folded its pink and white wings, raised its small flat head, and stretched out its incredibly muscular front legs in the attitude of prayer. Dr. MacPhail pulled out a magnifying glass and bent forward to examine it.

"*Gongylus gongyloides,*" he pronounced. "It dresses itself up to look like a flower. When unwary flies and moths come sailing in to sip the nectar, it sips *them.* And if it's a female, she eats her lovers." He put the glass away and leaned back in his chair. "What one likes most about the universe," he said to Will Farnaby, "is its wild improbability. *Gongylus gongyloides, Homo sapiens,* my great-grandfather's introduction to Pala and hypnosis—what could be more unlikely?"

"Nothing," said Will. "Except perhaps *my* introduction to Pala and hypnosis, Pala via a shipwreck and a precipice; hypnosis by way of a soliloquy about an English cathedral."

Susila laughed. "Fortunately I didn't have to make all those passes over you. In this climate! I really admire Dr. Andrew. It sometimes takes three hours to anesthetize a person with the passes."

"But in the end he succeeded?"

"Triumphantly."

"And did he actually perform the operation?"

"Yes, he actually performed the operation," said Dr. MacPhail. "But not immediately. There had to be a long preparation. Dr. Andrew began by telling his patient that henceforward he would be able to swallow without pain. Then, for the next three weeks, he fed him up. And between meals he put him into trance and kept him asleep until it was time for another feeding. It's wonderful what your body will do for you if you only give it a chance. The Raja gained twelve pounds and felt like a new man. A new man full of new hope and confidence. He *knew* he was going to come through his ordeal. And so, incidentally, did Dr. Andrew. In the process of fortifying the Raja's faith he had fortified his own. It was not a blind faith. The operation, he felt quite certain, was going to be successful. But this unshakable confidence did not prevent him from doing everything that might contribute to its success. Very early in the proceedings he started to work on the trance. The trance, he kept telling his patient, was becoming deeper every day, and on the day of the operation it would be much deeper than it had ever been before. It would also last longer. 'You'll sleep,' he assured the Raja, 'for four full hours after the operation's over; and when you awake, you won't feel the slightest pain.' Dr. Andrew made these affirmations with a mixture of total skepticism and complete confidence. Reason and past experience assured him that all this was impossible. But in the present context past experience had proved to be irrelevant. The impossible had already happened, several times. There was no reason why it shouldn't happen again. The important thing was to *say* that it would happen—so he said it, again and again. All this was good; but better still was Dr. Andrew's invention of the rehearsal."

"Rehearsal of what?"

"Of the surgery. They ran through the procedure half a dozen times. The last rehearsal was on the morning of the operation. At six, Dr. Andrew came to the Raja's room and, after a little cheerful talk, began to make the passes. In a few minutes the patient was in deep trance. Stage by stage, Dr. Andrew described what he was going to do. Touching the cheekbone near the Raja's right eye, he said, 'I begin by stretching the skin. And now with this scalpel' (and he drew the tip of a pencil across the cheek) 'I make an incision. You feel no pain, of course—not even the slightest discomfort. And now the underlying tissues are being cut and you still feel nothing at all. You just lie there, comfortably asleep, while I dissect the cheek back to the nose. Every now and then I stop to tie a blood vessel; then I go on again. And when that part of the work is done, I'm ready to start on the tumor. It has its roots there in the antrum and it has grown upwards, under the cheekbone, into the eye socket, and downwards into the gullet. And as I cut it loose, you lie there as before, feeling nothing, perfectly comfortable, completely relaxed. And now I lift your head.' Suiting his action to the words, he lifted the Raja's head and bent it forward on the limp neck. 'I lift it and bend it so that you can get rid of the blood that's run down into your mouth and throat. Some of the blood has got into your windpipe, and you cough a little to get rid of it; but it doesn't wake you.' The Raja coughed once or twice, then, when Dr. Andrew released his hold, dropped back onto the pillows, still fast asleep. 'And you don't choke even when I work on the lower end of the tumor in your gullet.' Dr. Andrew opened the Raja's mouth and thrust two fingers down his throat. 'It's just a question of pulling it loose, that's all. Nothing in that to make you choke. And if you have to cough up the blood, you can do it in your sleep. Yes, in your sleep, in this deep, deep sleep.'

"That was the end of the rehearsal. Ten minutes later, after making some more passes and telling his patient to sleep still more deeply, Dr. Andrew began the operation. He stretched the skin, he made the incision, he dissected the cheek, he cut the tumor away from its roots in the antrum. The Raja lay there perfectly relaxed, his pulse firm and steady at seventy-five, feeling no more pain than he had felt during the make-believe of the rehearsal. Dr. Andrew worked on the throat; there was no choking. The blood flowed into the windpipe; the Raja coughed but did not awake. Four hours after the operation was over, he was still sleeping; then, punctual to the minute, he opened his eyes, smiled at Dr. Andrew between his bandages and asked, in his singsong Cockney, when the operation was to start. After a feeding and a sponging, he was given some more passes and told to sleep for four more hours and to get well quickly. Dr. Andrew kept it up for a full week. Sixteen hours of trance each day, eight of waking. The Raja suffered almost no pain and, in spite of the thoroughly septic conditions under which the operation had been performed and the dressings renewed, the wounds healed without suppuration. Remembering the horrors he had witnessed in the Edinburgh infirmary, the yet more frightful horrors of the surgical wards at Madras, Dr. Andrew could hardly believe his eyes. And now he was given another opportunity to prove to himself what animal magnetism could do. The Raja's eldest daughter was in the ninth month of her first pregnancy. Impressed by what he had done for her husband, the Rani sent for Dr. Andrew. He found her sitting with a frail frightened girl of sixteen, who knew just enough broken Cockney to be able to tell him she was going to die—she and her baby too. Three black birds had confirmed it by flying on three successive days across her path. Dr. Andrew did not try to argue with her. Instead, he asked her to lie down, then started to make the passes. Twenty minutes later the girl was in a deep trance. In *his* country, Dr. Andrew now assured her, black birds were lucky—a presage of birth and joy. She would bear her child easily and without pain. Yes, with no more pain than her father had felt during his operation. No pain at all, he promised, no pain whatsoever.

"Three days later, and after three or four more hours of intensive suggestion, it all came true. When the Raja woke up for his evening meal, he found his wife sitting by his bed. 'We have a grandson,' she said, 'and our daughter is well. Dr. Andrew has said that tomorrow you may be carried to her room, to give them both your blessing.' At the end of a month the Raja dissolved the Council of Regency and resumed his royal powers. Resumed them, in gratitude to the man who had saved his life and (the Rani was convinced of it) his daughter's life as well, with Dr. Andrew as his chief adviser."

"So he didn't go back to Madras?"

"Not to Madras. Not even to London. He stayed here in Pala."

"Trying to change the Raja's accent?"

"And trying, rather more successfully, to change the Raja's kingdom."

"Into what?"

"That was a question he couldn't have answered. In those early days he had no plan—only a set of likes and dislikes. There were things about Pala that he liked, and plenty of others that he didn't like at all. Things about Europe that he detested, and things he passionately approved of. Things he had seen on his travels that seemed to make good sense, and things that filled him with disgust. People, he was beginning to understand, are at once the beneficiaries and the victims of their culture. It brings them to flower; but it also nips them in the bud or plants a canker at the heart of the blossom. Might it not be possible, on this forbidden island, to avoid the cankers, minimize the nippings, and make the individual blooms more beautiful? That was the question to which, implicitly at first, then with a growing awareness of what they were really up to, Dr. Andrew and the Raja were trying to find an answer."

"And *did* they find an answer?"

"Looking back," said Dr. MacPhail, "one's amazed by what those two men accomplished. The Scottish doctor and the Palanese king, the Calvinist-turned-atheist and the pious Mahayana Buddhist—what a strangely assorted pair! But a pair, very soon, of firm friends; a pair, moreover, of complementary temperaments and talents, with complementary philosophies and complementary stocks of knowledge, each man supplying the other's deficiencies, each stimulating and fortifying the other's native capacities. The Raja's was an acute and subtle mind; but he knew nothing of the world beyond the confines of his island, nothing of physical science, nothing of European technology, European art, European ways of thinking. No less intelligent, Dr. Andrew knew nothing, of course, about Indian painting and poetry and philosophy. He also knew nothing, as he gradually discovered, about the science of the human mind and the art of living. In the months that followed the operation each became the other's pupil and the other's teacher. And of course that was only a beginning. They were not merely private citizens concerned with their private improvement. The Raja had a million subjects and Dr. Andrew was virtually his prime minister. Private improvement was to be the preliminary to public improvement. If the king and the doctor were now teaching one another to make the best of both worlds—the Oriental and the European, the ancient and the modern—it was in order to help the whole nation to do the same. To make the best of both worlds—what am I saying? To make the best of *all* the worlds—the worlds already realized within the various cultures and, beyond them, the worlds of still unrealized potentialities. It was an enormous ambition, an ambition totally impossible of fulfillment; but at least it had the merit of spurring them on, of making them rush in where angels feared to tread—with results that sometimes proved, to everybody's astonishment, that they had not been quite such fools as they looked. They never succeeded, of course, in making the best of all the worlds; but by dint of boldly trying they made the best of many more worlds than any merely prudent or sensible person would have dreamed of being able to reconcile and combine."

" 'If the fool would persist in his folly,' " Will quoted from *The Proverbs of Hell*, " 'he would become wise.' "

"Precisely," Dr. Robert agreed. "And the most extravagant folly of all is the folly described by Blake, the folly that the Raja and Dr. Andrew were now contemplating—the enormous folly of trying to make a marriage between hell and heaven. But if you persist in that enormous folly, what an enormous reward! Provided, of course, that you persist intelligently. Stupid fools get nowhere; it's only the knowledgeable and clever ones whose folly can make them wise or produce good results. Fortunately these two fools *were* clever.

Clever enough, for example, to embark on their folly in a modest and appealing way. They began with pain relievers. The Palanese were Buddhists. They knew how misery is related to mind. You cling, you crave, you assert yourself—and you live in a homemade hell. You become detached—and you live in peace. 'I show you sorrow,' the Buddha had said, 'and I show you the ending of sorrow.' Well, here was Dr. Andrew with a special kind of mental detachment which would put an end at least to one kind of sorrow, namely, physical pain. With the Raja himself or, for the women, the Rani and her daughter acting as interpreters, Dr. Andrew gave lessons in his new-found art to groups of midwives and physicians, of teachers, mothers, invalids. Painless childbirth—and forthwith all the women of Pala were enthusiastically on the side of the innovators. Painless operations for stone and cataract and hemorrhoids—and they had won the approval of all the old and the ailing. At one stroke more than half the adult population became their allies, prejudiced in their favor, friendly in advance, or at least open-minded, toward the next reform."

"Where did they go from pain?" Will asked.

"To agriculture and language. To bread and communication. They got a man out from England to establish Rothamstead-in-the-Tropics, and they set to work to give the Palanese a second language. Pala was to remain a forbidden island; for Dr. Andrew wholeheartedly agreed with the Raja that missionaries, planters and traders were far too dangerous to be tolerated. But, while the foreign subversives must not be allowed to come in, the natives must somehow be helped to get out—if not physically, at least with their minds. But their language and their archaic version of the Brahmi alphabet were a prison without windows. There could be no escape for them, no glimpse of the outside world until they had learned English and could read the Latin script. Among the courtiers, the Raja's linguistic accomplishments had already set a fashion. Ladies and gentlemen larded their conversation with scraps of Cockney, and some of them had even sent to Ceylon for English-speaking tutors. What had been a mode was now transformed into a policy. English schools were set up and a staff of Bengali printers, with their presses and their fonts of Caslon and Bodoni were imported from Calcutta. The first English book to be published at

Shivapuram was a selection from *The Arabian Nights*, the second, a translation of *The Diamond Sutra*, hitherto available only in Sanskrit and in manuscript. For those who wished to read about Sindbad and Marouf, and for those who were interested in the Wisdom of the Other Shore, there were now two cogent reasons for learning English. That was the beginning of the long educational process that turned us at last into a bilingual people. We speak Palanese when we're cooking, when we're telling funny stories, when we're talking about love or making it. (Incidentally, we have the richest erotic and sentimental vocabulary in Southeast Asia.) But when it comes to business, or science, or speculative philosophy, we generally speak English. And most of us prefer to write in English. Every writer needs a literature as his frame of reference; a set of models to conform to or depart from. Pala had good painting and sculpture, splendid architecture, wonderful dancing, subtle and expressive music—but no real literature, no national poets or dramatists or storytellers. Just bards reciting Buddhist and Hindu myths; just a lot of monks preaching sermons and splitting metaphysical hairs. Adopting English as our stepmother tongue, we gave ourselves a literature with one of the longest pasts and certainly the widest of presents. We gave ourselves a background, a spiritual yardstick, a repertory of styles and techniques, an inexhaustible source of inspiration. In a word, we gave ourselves the possibility of being creative in a field where we had never been creative before. Thanks to the Raja and my great-grandfather, there's an Anglo-Palanese literature—of which, I may add, Susila here is a contemporary light."

"On the dim side," she protested.

Dr. MacPhail shut his eyes, and, smiling to himself, began to recite:

"Thus-Gone to Thus-Gone, I with a Buddha's hand
Offer the unplucked flower, the frog's soliloquy
Among the lotus leaves, the milk-smeared mouth
At my full breast and love and, like the cloudless
Sky that makes possible mountains and setting moon,
This emptiness that is the womb of love
This poetry of silence."

He opened his eyes again. "And not only this poetry of

silence," he said. "This science, this philosophy, this theology of silence. And now it's high time you went to sleep." He rose and moved towards the door. "I'll go and get you a glass of fruit juice."

ix

"'PATRIOTISM IS NOT ENOUGH.' BUT NEITHER IS ANYTHING else. Science is not enough, religion is not enough, art is not enough, politics and economics are not enough, nor is love, nor is duty, nor is action however disinterested, nor, however sublime, is contemplation. Nothing short of everything will really do."

"Attention!" shouted a faraway bird.

Will looked at his watch. Five to twelve. He closed his *Notes on What's What* and picking up the bamboo alpenstock which had once belonged to Dugald MacPhail, he set out to keep his appointment with Vijaya and Dr. Robert. By the short cut the main building of the Experimental Station was less than a quarter of a mile from Dr. Robert's bungalow. But the day was oppressively hot, and there were two flights of steps to be negotiated. For a convalescent with his right leg in a splint, it was a considerable journey.

Slowly, painfully, Will made his way along the winding path and up the steps. At the top of the second flight he halted to take breath and mop his forehead; then keeping close to the wall, where there was still a narrow strip of shade, he moved on towards a signboard marked LABORATORY.

The door beneath the board was ajar; he pushed it open and found himself on the threshold of a long, high-ceilinged room. There were the usual sinks and worktables, the usual glass-fronted cabinets full of bottles and equipment, the usual smells of chemicals and caged mice. For the first moment Will was under the impression that the room was untenanted, but no—almost hidden from view by a bookcase that projected at right angles from the wall, young Murugan was seated at a table, intently reading. As quietly as he could—for it was always amusing to take people by surprise—Will advanced into the room. The whirring of an electric fan covered the sound of his approach, and it was not until he was within a few feet of the bookcase that Murugan became aware of his presence. The boy started guiltily, shoved his book with panic haste into a leather briefcase and, reaching for another, smaller volume that lay open on the table beside the briefcase, drew it within reading range. Only then did he turn to face the intruder.

Will gave him a reassuring smile. "It's only me."

The look of angry defiance gave place, on the boy's face, to one of relief.

"I thought it was . . ." He broke off, leaving the sentence unfinished.

"You thought it was someone who would bawl you out for not doing what you're supposed to do—is that it?"

Murugan grinned and nodded his curly head.

"Where's everyone else?" Will asked.

"They're out in the fields—pruning or pollinating or something." His tone was contemptuous.

"And so, the cats being away, the mouse duly played. What were you studying so passionately?"

With innocent disingenuousness, Murugan held up the book he was now pretending to read. "It's called *Elementary Ecology,*" he said.

"So I see," said Will. "But what I asked you was what *were* you reading?"

"Oh, that," Murugan shrugged his shoulders. "You wouldn't be interested."

"I'm interested in everything that anyone tries to hide," Will assured him. "Was it pornography?"

Murugan dropped his playacting and looked genuinely offended. "Who do you take me for?"

Will was on the point of saying that he took him for an average boy, but checked himself. To Colonel Dipa's pretty young friend, "Average boy" might sound like an insult or an innuendo. Instead he bowed with mock politeness. "I beg Your Majesty's pardon," he said. "But I'm still curious," he added in another tone. "May I?" He laid a hand on the bulging briefcase.

Murugan hesitated for a moment, then forced a laugh. "Go ahead."

"What a tome!" Will pulled the ponderous volume out of the bag and laid it on the table. "Sears, Roebuck and Co.," he read aloud, "Spring and Summer Catalog."

"It's last year's," said Murugan apologetically. "But I don't suppose there's been much change since then."

"There," Will assured him, "you're mistaken. If the styles weren't completely changed every year, there'd be no reason for buying new things before the old ones are worn out. You don't understand the first principles of modern consumerism." He opened at random. " 'Soft Platform Wedgies in Wide Widths.' " Opened at another place and found the description and image of a Whisper-Pink Bra in Dacron and Pima cotton. Turned the page and here, *memento mori*, was what the bra-buyer would be wearing twenty years later—A Strap-Controlled Front, Cupped to Support Pendulous Abdomen.

"It doesn't get really interesting," said Murugan, "until near the end of the book. It has thirteen hundred and fifty-eight pages," he added parenthetically. "Imagine! Thirteen hundred and fifty-eight!"

Will skipped the next seven hundred and fifty pages.

"Ah, this is more like it," he said. " 'Our Famous .22 Revolvers and Automatics.' " And here, a little further on, were the Fibre Glass Boats, here were the High Thrust Inboard Engines, here was a 12-hp Outboard for only $234.95—and the Fuel Tank was included. "That's extraordinarily generous!"

But Murugan, it was evident, was no sailor. Taking the book, he leafed impatiently through a score of additional pages.

"Look at this Italian Style Motor Scooter!" And while Will looked, Murugan read aloud. " 'This sleek Speedster gives up to 110 Miles per Gallon of Fuel.' Just imagine!" His normally sulky face was glowing with enthusiasm. "And you can get up to sixty miles per gallon even on this 14.5-hp Motorcycle. And it's guaranteed to do seventy-five miles an hour—*guaranteed!*"

"Remarkable!" said Will. Then, curiously, "Did somebody in America send you this glorious book?" he asked.

Murugan shook his head. "Colonel Dipa gave it to me."

"Colonel Dipa?" What an odd kind of present from Hadrian to Antinoüs! He looked again at the picture of the motorbike, then back at Murugan's glowing face. Light dawned; the Colonel's purpose revealed itself. *The serpent tempted me, and I did eat.* The tree in the midst of the garden was called the Tree of Consumer Goods, and to the inhabitants of every underdeveloped Eden the tiniest taste of its fruit, and even the sight of its thirteen hundred and fifty-eight leaves, had power to bring the shameful knowledge that, industrially speaking, they were stark-naked. The future Raja of Pala was being made to realize that he was no more than the untrousered ruler of a tribe of savages.

"You ought," Will said aloud, "to import a million of these catalogues and distribute them—gratis, of course, like contraceptives—to all your subjects."

"What for?"

"To whet their appetite for possessions. Then they'll start clamoring for Progress—oil wells, armaments, Joe Aldehyde, Soviet technicians."

Murugan frowned and shook his head. "It wouldn't work."

"You mean, they wouldn't be tempted? Not even by Sleek Speedsters and Whisper-Pink Bras? But that's incredible!"

"It may be incredible," said Murugan bitterly, "but it's a fact. They're just not interested."

"Not even the young ones?"

"I'd say especially the young ones."

Will Farnaby pricked up his ears. This lack of interest was profoundly interesting. "Can you guess why?" he asked.

"I don't guess," the boy answered. "I know." And as though he had suddenly decided to stage a parody of his mother, he began to speak in a tone of righteous indignation that was absurdly out of keeping with his age and appearance. "To begin with, they're much too busy with . . ." He hesitated, then the abhorred word was hissed out with a disgustful emphasis. "With *sex.*"

"But everybody's busy with sex. Which doesn't keep them from whoring after sleek speedsters."

"Sex is different here," Murugan insisted.

"Because of the yoga of love?" Will asked, remembering the little nurse's rapturous face.

The boy nodded. "They've got something that makes them think they're perfectly happy, and they don't want anything else."

"What a blessed state!"

"There's nothing blessed about it," Murugan snapped. "It's just stupid and disgusting. No progress, only sex, sex, sex. And of course that beastly dope they're all given."

"Dope?" Will repeated in some astonishment. Dope in a place where Susila had said there were no addicts? "What kind of dope?"

"It's made out of toadstools. *Toadstools!*" He spoke in a comical caricature of the Rani's vibrant tone of outraged spirituality.

"Those lovely red toadstools that gnomes used to sit on?"

"No, these are yellow. People used to go out and collect them in the mountains. Nowadays the things are grown in special fungus beds at the high Altitude Experimental Station. Scientifically cultivated dope. Pretty, isn't it?"

A door slammed and there was a sound of voices, of footsteps approaching along a corridor. Abruptly, the indignant spirit of the Rani took flight, and Murugan was once again the conscience-stricken schoolboy furtively trying to cover up his delinquencies. In a trice *Elementary Ecology* had taken the place of Sears, Roebuck, and the suspiciously bulging briefcase was under the table. A moment later, stripped to the waist and shining like oiled bronze with the sweat of labor in the noonday sun, Vijaya came striding into the room. Behind him came Dr. Robert. With the air of a model student, interrupted in the midst of his reading by trespassers from the frivolous outside world, Murugan looked up from his book. Amused, Will threw himself at once wholeheartedly into the part that had been assigned to him.

"It was I who got here too early," he said in response to Vijaya's apologies for their being so late. "With the result that our young friend here hasn't been able to get on with his lessons. We've been talking our heads off."

"What about?" Dr. Robert asked.

"Everything. Cabbages, kings, motor scooters, pendulous abdomens. And when you came in, we'd just embarked on toadstools. Murugan was telling me about the fungi that are used here as a source of dope."

"What's in a name?" said Dr. Robert, with a laugh. "Answer, practically everything. Having had the misfortune to be brought up in Europe, Murugan calls it dope and feels about it all the dispproval that, by conditioned reflex, the dirty word evokes. We, on the contrary, give the stuff good names—the *moksha*-medicine, the reality revealer, the truth-and-beauty pill. And we know, by direct experience, that the good names are deserved. Whereas our young friend here has no firsthand knowledge of the stuff and can't be persuaded even to give it a try. For him, it's dope and dope is something that, by definition, no decent person ever indulges in."

"What does His Highness say to that?" Will asked.

Murugan shook his head. "All it gives you is a lot of illusions," he muttered. "Why should I go out of my way to be made a fool of?"

"Why indeed?" said Vijaya with good-humored irony. "Seeing that, in your normal condition, you alone of the human race are never made a fool of and never have illusions about anything!"

"I never said that," Murugan protested. "All I mean is that I don't want any of your false *samadhi.*"

"How do you know it's false?" Dr. Robert enquired.

"Because the real thing only comes to people after years and years of meditation and *tapas* and . . . well, you know —not going with women."

"Murugan," Vijaya explained to Will, "is one of the Puritans. He's outraged by the fact that, with four hundred milligrams of *moksha*-medicine in their bloodstreams, even beginners—yes, and even boys and girls who make love together—can catch a glimpse of the world as it looks to someone who has been liberated from his bondage to the ego."

"But it isn't real," Murugan insisted.

"Not real!" Dr. Robert repeated. "You might as well say that the experience of feeling well isn't real."

"You're begging the question," Will objected. "An experience can be real in relation to something going on inside your skull but completely irrelevant to anything outside."

"Of course," Dr. Robert agreed.

"*Do* you know what goes on inside your skull, when you've taken a dose of the mushroom?"

"We know a little."

"And we're trying all the time to find out more," Vijaya added.

"For example," said Dr. Robert, "we've found that the people whose EEG doesn't show any alpha-wave activity when they're relaxed aren't likely to respond significantly to the *moksha*-medicine. That means that, for about fifteen per cent of the population, we have to find other approaches to liberation."

"Another thing we're just beginning to understand," said

Vijaya, "is the neurological correlate of these experiences. What's happening in the brain when you're having a vision? And what's happening when you pass from a premystical to a genuinely mystical state of mind?"

"Do you know?" Will asked.

"'Know' is a big word. Let's say we're in a position to make some plausible guesses. Angels and New Jerusalems and Madonnas and Future Buddhas—they're all related to some kind of unusual stimulation of the brain areas of primary projection—the visual cortex, for example. Just how the *moksha*-medicine produces those unusual stimuli we haven't yet found out. The important fact is that, somehow or other, it does produce them. And somehow or other, it also does something unusual to the silent areas of the brain, the areas not specifically concerned with perceiving, or moving, or feeling."

"And how do the silent areas respond?" Will enquired.

"Let's start with what they *don't* respond with. They don't respond with visions or auditions, they don't respond with telepathy or clairvoyance or any other kind of parapsychological performance. None of that amusing premystical stuff. Their response is the full-blown mystical experience. You know—One in all and All in one. The basic experience with its corollaries—boundless compassion, fathomless mystery and meaning."

"Not to mention joy," said Dr. Robert, "inexpressible joy."

"And the whole caboodle is inside your skull," said Will. "Strictly private. No reference to any external fact except a toadstool."

"Not real," Murugan chimed in. "That's exactly what I was trying to say."

"You're assuming," said Dr. Robert, "that the brain *produces* consciousness. I'm assuming that it transmits consciousness. And my explanation is no more farfetched than yours. How on earth can a set of events belonging to one order be experienced as a set of events belonging to an entirely different and incommensurable order? Nobody has the faintest idea. All one can do is to accept the facts and concoct hypotheses. And one hypothesis is just about as good, philosophically speaking, as another. You say that the *moksha*-medicine does something to the silent areas of the brain which causes them to produce a set of subjective events to which people have given the name 'mystical experience.' *I* say that the *moksha*-medicine does something to the silent areas of the brain which opens some kind of neurological sluice and so allows a larger volume of Mind with a large 'M' to flow into your mind with a small 'm.' You can't demonstrate the truth of your hypothesis, and I can't demonstrate the truth of mine. And even if you could prove that I'm wrong, would it make any practical difference?"

"I'd have thought it would make all the difference," said Will.

"Do you like music?" Dr. Robert asked.

"More than most things."

"And what, may I ask, does Mozart's G-Minor Quintet refer to? Does it refer to Allah? Or Tao? Or the second person of the Trinity? Or the Atman-Brahman?"

Will laughed. "Let's hope not."

"But that doesn't make the experience of the G-Minor Quintet any less rewarding. Well, it's the same with the kind of experience that you get with the *moksha*-medicine, or through prayer and fasting and spiritual exercises. Even if it doesn't refer to anything outside itself, it's still the most important thing that ever happened to you. Like music, only incomparably more so. And if you give the experience a chance, if you're prepared to go along with it, the results are incomparably more therapeutic and transforming. So maybe the whole thing does happen inside one's skull. Maybe it *is* private and there's no unitive knowledge of anything but one's own physiology. Who cares? The fact remains that the experience can open one's eyes and make one blessed and transform one's whole life." There was a long silence. "Let me tell you something," he resumed, turning to Murugan. "Something I hadn't intended to talk about to anybody. But now I feel that perhaps I have a duty, a duty to the throne, a duty to Pala and all its people—an obligation to tell you about this very private experience. Perhaps the telling may help you to be a little more understanding about your country and its ways." He was silent for a moment; then in a quietly matter-of-fact tone, "I suppose you know about my wife," he went on.

His face still averted, Murugan nodded. "I was sorry," he mumbled, "to hear she was so ill."

"It's a matter of a few days now," said Dr. Robert. "Four or five at the most. But she's still perfectly lucid, perfectly conscious of what's happening to her. Yesterday she asked me if we could take the *moksha*-medicine together. We'd taken it together," he added parenthetically, "once or twice each year for the last thirty-seven years—ever since we decided to get married. And now once more—for the last time, the last, last time. There was a risk involved, because of the damage to the liver. But we decided it was a risk worth taking. And as it turned out, we were right. The *moksha*-medicine—the dope, as you prefer to call it—hardly upset her at all. All that happened to her was the mental transformation."

He was silent, and Will suddenly became aware of the squeak and scrabble of caged rats and, through the open window, the babel of tropical life and the call of a distant mynah bird. "Here and now, boys. Here and now . . ."

"You're like that mynah," said Dr. Robert at last. "Trained to repeat words you don't understand or know the reason for, '*It isn't real. It isn't real.*' But if you'd experienced what Lakshmi and I went through yesterday you'd know better. You'd know it was much more real than what you call reality. More real than what you're thinking and feeling at this moment. More real than the world before your eyes. But *not real* is what you've been taught to say. *Not real, not real.*" Dr. Robert laid a hand affectionately on the boy's shoulder. "You've been told that we're just a set of self-indulgent dope takers, wallowing in illusions and false *samadhis*. Listen, Murugan—forget all the bad language that's been pumped into you. Forget it at least to the point of making a single experiment. Take four hundred milligrams of *moksha*-medicine and find out for yourself what it does, what it can tell you about your own nature, about this strange world you've got to live in, learn in, suffer in, and finally die in. Yes, even you will have to die one day—maybe fifty years from now, maybe tomorrow. Who knows? But it's going to happen, and one's a fool if one doesn't prepare for it." He turned to Will. "Would you like to come along while we take our shower and get into some clothes?"

Without waiting for an answer, he walked out through the door that led into that central corridor of the long building. Will picked up his bamboo staff and, accompanied by Vijaya, followed him out of the room.

"Do you suppose that made any impression on Murugan?" he asked Vijaya when the door had closed behind them.

Vijaya shrugged his shoulders. "I doubt it."

"What with his mother," said Will, "and his passion for internal-combustion engines, he's probably impervious to anything you people can say. You should have heard him on the subject of motor scooters!"

"We have heard him," said Dr. Robert, who had halted in front of a blue door and was waiting for them to come up with him. "Frequently. When he comes of age, scooters are going to become a major political issue."

Vijaya laughed. "To scoot or not to scoot, that is the question."

"And it isn't only in Pala that it's the question," Dr. Robert added. "It's the question that every underdeveloped country has to answer one way or the other."

"And the answer," said Will, "is always the same. Wherever I've been—and I've been almost everywhere—they've opted wholeheartedly for scooting. All of them."

"Without exception," Vijaya agreed. "Scooting for scooting's sake, and to hell with all considerations of fulfillment, self-knowledge, liberation. Not to mention common or garden health or happiness."

"Whereas *we*," said Dr. Robert, "have always chosen to adapt our economy and technology to human beings—not our human beings to somebody else's economy and technology. We import what we can't make; but we make an import only what we can afford. And what we can afford is limited not merely by our supply of pounds and marks and dollars, but also primarily—*primarily*," he insisted—"by our wish to be happy, our ambition to become fully human. Scooters, we've decided after carefully looking into the matter, are among the things—the very numerous things—we simply can't afford. Which is something poor little Murugan will have to learn the hard way—seeing that he hasn't learned, and doesn't want to learn, the easy way."

"Which is the easy way?" Will asked.

"Education and reality-revealers. Murugan has had neither. Or rather he's had the opposite of both. He's had miseducation in Europe—Swiss governesses, English tutors, American movies, everybody's advertisements—and he's had reality eclipsed for him by his mother's brand of spirituality. So it's no wonder he pines for scooters."

"But his subjects, I gather, do not."

"Why should they? They've been taught from infancy to be fully aware of the world, and to enjoy their awareness.

And, on top of that, they have been shown the world and themselves and other people as these are illumined and transfigured by reality-revealers. Which helps them, of course, to have an intenser awareness and a more understanding enjoyment, so that the most ordinary things, the most trivial events, are seen as jewels and miracles. Jewels and miracles," he repeated emphatically. "So why should we resort to scooters or whisky or television or Billy Graham or any other of your distractions and compensations?"

"'Nothing short of everything will really do,'" Will quoted. "I see now what the Old Raja was talking about. You can't be a good economist unless you're also a good psychologist. Or a good engineer without being the right kind of metaphysician."

"And don't forget all the other sciences," said Dr. Robert. "Pharmacology, sociology, physiology, not to mention pure and applied autology, neurotheology, metachemistry, mycomysticism, and the ultimate science," he added, looking away so as to be more alone with his thoughts of Lakshmi in the hospital, "the science that sooner or later we shall all have to be examined in—thanatology." He was silent for a moment; then, in another tone, "Well, let's go and get washed up," he said and, opening the blue door, led the way into a long changing room with a row of showers and wash basins at one end and, on the opposite wall, tiers of lockers and a large hanging cupboard.

Will took a seat and while his companions lathered themselves at the basins, went on with their conversations.

"Would it be permissible," he asked, "for a miseducated alien to try a truth-and-beauty pill?"

The answer was another question. "Is your liver in good order?" Dr. Robert enquired.

"Excellent."

"And you don't seem to be more than mildly schizophrenic. So I can't see any counterindication."

"Then I can make the experiment?"

"Whenever you like."

He stepped into the nearest shower stall and turned on the water. Vijaya followed suit.

"Aren't you supposed to be intellectuals?" Will asked when the two men had emerged again and were drying themselves.

"We do intellectual work," Vijaya answered.

"Then why all this horrible honest toil?"

"For a very simple reason: this morning I had some spare time."

"So did I," said Dr. Robert.

"So you went out into the fields and did a Tolstoy act."

Vijaya laughed. "You seem to imagine we do it for ethical reasons."

"Don't you?"

"Certainly not. I do muscular work, because I have muscles; and if I don't use my muscles I shall become a bad-tempered sitting-addict."

"With nothing between the cortex and the buttocks," said Dr. Robert. "Or rather with everything—but in a condition of complete unconsciousness and toxic stagnation. Western intellectuals are all sitting-addicts. That's why most of you are so repulsively unwholesome. In the past even a duke had to do a lot of walking, even a moneylender, even a metaphysician. And when they weren't using their legs, they were jogging about on horses. Whereas now, from the tycoon to his typist, from the logical positivist to the positive thinker, you spend nine tenths of your time on foam rubber. Spongy seats for spongy bottoms—at home, in the office, in cars and bars, in planes and trains and buses. No moving of legs, no struggles with distance and gravity—just lifts and planes and cars, just foam rubber and an eternity of sitting. The life force that used to find an outlet through striped muscle gets turned back on the viscera and the nervous system, and slowly destroys them."

"So you take to digging and delving as a form of therapy?"

"As prevention—to make therapy unnecessary. In Pala even a professor, even a government official, generally puts in two hours of digging and delving each day."

"As part of his duties?"

"And as part of his pleasure."

Will made a grimace. "It wouldn't be part of *my* pleasure."

"That's because you weren't taught to use your mind-body in the right way," Vijaya explained. "If you'd been shown how to do things with the minimum of strain and the maximum of awareness, you'd enjoy even honest toil."

"I take it that your children all get this kind of training."

"From the first moment they start doing for themselves. For example, what's the proper way of handling yourself while you're buttoning your clothes?" And suiting action to words, Vijaya started to button the shirt he had just slipped into. "We answer the question by actually putting their heads and bodies into the physiologically best position. And we encourage them at the same time to notice how it feels to be in the physiologically best position, to be aware of what the process of doing up buttons consists of in terms of touches and pressures and muscular sensations. By the time they're fourteen they've learned how to get the most and the best—objectively and subjectively—out of any activity they may undertake. And that's when we start them working. Ninety minutes a day at some kind of manual job."

"Back to good old child labor!"

"Or rather," said Dr. Robert, "forward from bad new child idleness. You don't allow your teen-agers to work; so they have to blow off steam in delinquency or else throttle down steam till they're ready to become domesticated sitting-addicts. And now," he added, "it's time to be going. I'll lead the way."

In the laboratory, when they entered, Murugan was in the act of locking his briefcase against all prying eyes. "I'm ready," he said and, tucking the thirteen hundred and fifty-eight pages of the Newest Testament under his arm, he followed them out into the sunshine. A few minutes later, crammed into an ancient jeep, the four of them were rolling along the road that led, past the paddock of the white bull, past the lotus pool and the huge stone Buddha, out through the gate of the Station Compound to the highway. "I'm sorry we can't provide more comfortable transportation," said Vijaya as they bumped and rattled along.

Will patted Murugan's knee. "This is the man you should be apologizing to," he said. "The one whose soul yearns for Jaguars and Thunderbirds."

"It's a yearning, I'm afraid," said Dr. Robert from the back seat, "that will have to remain unsatisfied."

Murugan made no comment, but smiled the secret contemptuous smile of one who knows better.

"We can't import toys," Dr. Robert went on. "Only essentials."

"Such as?"

"You'll see in a moment." They rounded a curve, and there beneath them were the thatched roofs and tree-shaded gardens of a considerable village. Vijaya pulled up at the side of the road and turned off the motor. "You're looking at New Rothamsted," he said. "Alias Madalia. Rice, vegetables, poultry, fruit. Not to mention two potteries and a furniture factory. Hence those wires." He waved his hand in the direction of the long row of pylons that climbed up the terraced slope behind the village, dipped out of sight over the ridge, and reappeared, far away, marching up from the floor of the next valley towards the green belt of mountain jungle and the cloudy peaks beyond and above. "That's one of the indispensable imports—electrical equipment. And when the waterfalls have been harnessed and you've strung up the transmission lines, here's something else with a high priority." He directed a pointing finger at a windowless block of cement that rose incongruously from among the wooden houses near the upper entrance to the village.

"What is it?" Will asked. "Some kind of electric oven?"

"No, the kilns are over on the other side of the village. This is the communal freezer."

"In the old days," Dr. Robert explained, "we used to lose about half of all the perishables we produced. Now we lose practically nothing. Whatever we grow is for us, not for the circumambient bacteria."

"So now you have enough to eat."

"More than enough. We eat better than any other country in Asia, and there's a surplus for export. Lenin used to say that electricity plus socialism equals communism. Our equations are rather different. Electricity minus heavy industry plus birth control equals democracy and plenty. Electricity plus heavy industry minus birth control equals misery, totalitarianism and war."

"Incidentally," Will asked, "who owns all this? Are you capitalists or state socialists?"

"Neither. Most of the time we're co-operators. Palanese agriculture has always been an affair of terracing and irrigation. But terracing and irrigation call for pooled efforts and friendly agreements. Cutthroat competition isn't compatible with rice-growing in a mountainous country. Our people found it quite easy to pass from mutual aid in a village community to streamlined co-operative techniques for buying and selling and profit sharing and financing."

"Even co-operative financing?"

Dr. Robert nodded. "None of those bloodsucking usurers that you find all over the Indian countryside. And no commercial banks in your Western style. Our borrowing and lending system was modeled on those credit unions that Wilhelm Raiffeisen set up more than a century ago in Germany. Dr. Andrew persuaded the Raja to invite one of Raiffeisen's young men to come here and organize a co-operative banking system. It's still going strong."

"And what do you use for money?" Will asked.

Dr. Robert dipped into his trouser pocket and pulled out a handful of silver, gold and copper.

"In a modest way," he explained, "Pala's a gold-producing country. We mine enough to give our paper a solid metallic backing. And the gold supplements our exports. We can pay spot cash for expensive equipment like those transmission lines and the generators at the other end."

"You seem to have solved your economic problems pretty successfully."

"Solving them wasn't difficult. To begin with, we never allowed ourselves to produce more children than we could feed, clothe, house, and educate into something like full humanity. Not being overpopulated, we have plenty. But, although we have plenty, we've managed to resist the temptation that the West has now succumbed to—the temptation to overconsume. We don't give ourselves coronaries by guzzling six times as much saturated fat as we need. We don't hypnotize ourselves into believing that two television sets will make us twice as happy as one television set. And finally we don't spend a quarter of the gross national product preparing for World War III or even World War's baby brother, Local War MMMCCCXXXIII. Armaments, universal debt, and planned obsolescence—those are the three pillars of Western prosperity. If war, waste, and moneylenders were abolished, you'd collapse. And while you people are overconsuming the rest of the world sinks more and more deeply into chronic disaster. Ignorance, militarism and breeding, these three—and the greatest of these is breeding. No hope, not the slightest possibility, of solving the economic problem until *that's* under control. As population rushes up, prosperity goes down." He traced the descending curve with an outstretched finger. "And as prosperity goes down, discontent and rebellion" (the forefinger moved up again), "political ruthlessness and one-party rule, nationalism and bellicosity begin to rise. Another ten or fifteen years of uninhibited breeding, and the whole world, from China to Peru via Africa and the Middle East, will be fairly crawling with Great

Leaders, all dedicated to the suppression of freedom, all armed to the teeth by Russia or America or, better still, by both at once, all waving flags, all screaming for *Lebensraum.*"

"What about Pala?" Will asked. "Will *you* be blessed with a Great Leader ten years from now?"

"Not if we can help it," Dr. Robert answered. "We've always done everything possible to make it very difficult for a Great Leader to arise."

Out of the corner of his eye Will saw that Murugan was making a face of indignant and contemptuous disgust. In his fancy Antinoüs evidently saw himself as a Carlylean Hero. Will turned back to Dr. Robert.

"Tell me how you do it," he said.

"Well, to begin with we don't fight wars or prepare for them. Consequently, we have no need for conscription, or military hierarchies, or a unified command. Then there's our economic system: it doesn't permit anybody to become more than four or five times as rich as the average. That means that we don't have any captains of industry or omnipotent financiers. Better stiill, we have no omnipotent politicians or bureaucrats. Pala's a federation of self-governing units, geographical units, professional units, economic units—so there's plenty of scope for small-scale initiative and democratic leaders, but no place for any kind of dictator at the head of a centralized government. Another point: we have no established church, and our religion stresses immediate experience and deplores belief in unverifiable dogmas and the emotions which that belief inspires. So we're preserved from the plagues of popery, on the one hand, and fundamentalist revivalism, on the other. And along with transcendental experience we systematically cultivate skepticism. Discouraging children from taking words too seriously, teaching them to analyze whatever they hear or read—this is an integral part of the school curriculum. Result: the eloquent rabble-rouser, like Hitler or our neighbor across the Strait, Colonel Dipa, just doesn't have a chance here in Pala."

This was too much for Murugan. Unable to contain himself, "But look at the energy Colonel Dipa generates in his people," he burst out. "Look at all the devotion and self-sacrifice. We don't have anything like that here."

"Thank God," said Dr. Robert devoutly.

"Thank God," Vijaya echoed.

"But these things are good," the boy protested. "I admire them."

"I admire them too," said Dr. Robert. "Admire them in the same way as I admire a typhoon. Unfortunately that kind of energy and devotion and self-sacrifice happens to be incompatible with liberty, not to mention reason and human decency. But decency, reason and liberty are what Pala has been working for, ever since the time of your namesake, Murugan the Reformer."

From under his seat Vijaya pulled out a tin box and, lifting the lid, distributed a first round of cheese and avocado sandwiches. "We'll have to eat as we go." He started the motor and with one hand, the other being busy with his sandwich, swung the little car onto the road. "Tomorrow," he said to Will, "I'll show you the sights of the village, and the still more remarkable sight of my family eating their lunch. Today we have an appointment in the mountains."

Near the entrance to the village he turned the jeep into a side road that went winding steeply up between terraced fields of rice and vegetables, interspersed with orchards and, here and there, plantations of young trees destined, Dr. Robert explained, to supply the pulp mills of Shivapuram with their raw material.

"How many papers does Pala support?" Will enquired and was surprised to learn that there was only one. "Who enjoys the monopoly? The government? The party in power? The local Joe Aldehyde?"

"Nobody enjoys a monopoly," Dr. Robert assured him. "There's a panel of editors representing half a dozen different parties and interests. Each of them gets his allotted space for comment and criticism. The reader's in a position to compare their arguments and make up his own mind. I remember how shocked I was the first time I read one of your big-circulation newspapers. The bias of the headlines, the systematic one-sidedness of the reporting and the commentaries, the catchwords and slogans instead of argument. No serious appeal to reason. Instead, a systematic effort to install conditioned reflexes in the minds of the voters—and, for the rest, crime, divorce, anecdotes, twaddle, anything to keep them distracted, anything to prevent them from thinking."

The car climbed on and now they were on a ridge between two headlong descents, with a tree-fringed lake down at the bottom of a gorge to their left and to the right a broader valley where, between two tree-shaded villages, like an incongruous piece of pure geometry, sprawled a huge factory.

"Cement?" Will questioned.

Dr. Robert nodded. "One of the indispensable industries. We produce all we need and a surplus for export."

"And those villages supply the manpower?"

"In the intervals of agriculture and work in the forest and the sawmills."

"Does that kind of part-time system work well?"

"It depends what you mean by 'well.' It doesn't result in maximum efficiency. But then in Pala maximum efficiency isn't the categorical imperative that it is with you. You think first of getting the biggest possible output in the shortest possible time. We think first of human beings and their satisfactions. Changing jobs doesn't make for the biggest output in the fewest days. But most people like it better than doing one kind of job all their lives. If it's a choice between mechanical efficiency and human satisfaction, we choose satisfaction."

"When I was twenty," Vijaya now volunteered, "I put in four months at that cement plant—and after that ten weeks making superphosphates and then six months in the jungle, as a lumberjack."

"All this ghastly honest toil!"

"Twenty years earlier," said Dr. Robert, "I did a stint at the copper smelters. After which I had a taste of the sea on a fishing boat. Sampling all kinds of work—it's part of everybody's education. One learns an enormous amount that way—about things and skills and organizations, about all kinds of people and their ways of thinking."

Will shook his head. "I'd still rather get it out of a book."

"But what you can get out of a book is never *it*. At bottom," Dr. Robert added, "all of you are still Platonists. You worship the word and abhor matter!"

"Tell that to the clergymen," said Will. "They're always reproaching us with being crass materialists."

"Crass," Dr. Robert agreed, "but crass precisely because you're such inadequate materialists. Abstract materialism—that's what you profess. Whereas we make a point of being materialists concretely—materialistic on the wordless levels of seeing and touching and smelling, of tensed muscles and dirty hands. Abstract materialism is as bad as abstract idealism; it makes immediate spiritual experience almost impossible. Sampling different kinds of work in concrete materialism is the first, indispensable step in our education for concrete spirituality."

"But even the most concrete materialism," Vijaya qualified, "won't get you very far unless you're fully conscious of what you're doing and experiencing. You've got to be completely aware of the bits of matter you're handling, the skills you're practicing, the people you work with."

"Quite right," said Dr. Robert. "I ought to have made it clear that concrete materialism is only the raw stuff of a fully human life. It's through awareness, complete and constant awareness, that we transform it into concrete spirituality. Be fully aware of what you're doing, and work becomes the yoga of work, play becomes the yoga of play, everyday living becomes the yoga of everyday living."

Will thought of Ranga and the little nurse. "And what about love?"

Dr. Robert nodded. "That too. Awareness transfigures it, turns love-making into the yoga of love-making."

Murugan gave an imitation of his mother looking shocked.

"Psychophysical means to a transcendental end," said Vijaya, raising his voice against the grinding screech of the low gear into which he had just shifted, "that, primarily, is what all these yogas are. But they're also something else, they're also devices for dealing with the problems of power." He shifted back to a quieter gear and lowered his voice to its normal tone. "The problems of power," he repeated. "And they confront you on every level of organization—every level, from national governments down to nurseries and honeymooning couples. For it isn't merely a question of making things hard for the Great Leaders. There are all the millions of small-scale tyrants and persecutors, all the mute inglorious Hitlers, the village Napoleons, the Calvins and Torquemadas of the family. Not to mention all the brigands and bullies stupid enough to get themselves labeled as criminals. How does one harness the enormous power these people generate and set it to work in some useful way—or at least prevent it from doing harm?"

"That's what I want you to tell me," said Will. "Where do you start?"

"We start everywhere at once," Vijaya answered. "But

since one can't say more than one thing at a time, let's begin by talking about the anatomy and physiology of power. Tell him about your biochemical approach to the subject, Dr. Robert."

"It started," said Dr. Robert, "nearly forty years ago, while I was studying in London. Started with prison visiting on weekends and reading history whenever I had a free evening. History and prisons," he repeated. "I discovered that they were closely related. The record of the crimes, follies and misfortunes of mankind (that's Gibbon, isn't it?) and the place where unsuccessful crimes and follies are visited with a special kind of misfortune. Reading my books and talking to my jailbirds, I found myself asking questions. What kind of people became dangerous delinquents—the grand delinquents of the history books, the little ones of Pentonville and Wormwood Scrubbs? What kinds of people are moved by the lust for power, the passion to bully and domineer? And the ruthless ones, the men and women who know what they want and have no qualms about hurting and killing in order to get it, the monsters who hurt and kill, not for profit, but gratuitously, because hurting and killing are such fun—who *are* they? I used to discuss these questions with the experts—doctors, phychologists, social scientists, teachers. Mantegazza and Galton had gone out of fashion, and most of my experts assured me that the only valid answers to these questions were answers in terms of culture, economics, and the family. It was all a matter of mothers and toilet training, of early conditioning and traumatic environments. I was only half convinced. Mothers and toilet training and the circumambient nonsense—these were obviously important. But were they *all*-important? In the course of my prison visiting I'd begun to see evidence of some kind of a built-in pattern —or rather of two kinds of built-in patterns; for dangerous delinquents and power-loving troublemakers don't belong to a single species. Most of them, as I was beginning to realize even then, belong to one or other of two distinct and dissimilar species—the Muscle People and the Peter Pans. I've specialized in the treatment of Peter Pans."

"The boys who never grow up?" Will queried.

"'Never' is the wrong word. In real life Peter Pan always ends by growing up. He merely grows up too late—grows up physiologically more slowly than he grows up in terms of birthdays."

"What about girl Peter Pans?"

"They're very rare. But the boys are as common as blackberries. You can expect one Peter Pan among every five or six male children. And among problem children, among the boys who can't read, won't learn, don't get on with anyone, and finally turn to the more violent forms of delinquency, seven out of ten turn out, if you take an X ray of the bones of the wrist, to be Peter Pans. The rest are mostly Muscle People of one sort or another."

"I'm trying to think," said Will, "of a good historical example of a delinquent Peter Pan."

"You don't have to go far afield. The most recent, as well as the best and biggest, was Adolf Hitler."

"Hitler?" Murugan's tone was one of shocked astonishment. Hitler was evidently one of his heroes.

"Read the Führer's biography," said Dr. Robert. "A Peter Pan if ever there was one. Hopeless at school. Incapable either of competing or co-operating. Envying all the normally successful boys—and, because he envied, hating them and, to make himself feel better, despising them as inferior beings. Then came the time for puberty. But Adolf was sexually backward. Other boys made advances to girls, and the girls responded. Adolf was too shy, too uncertain of his manhood. And all the time incapable of steady work, at home only in the compensatory Other World of his fancy. There, at the very least, he was Michelangelo. Here, unfortunately, he couldn't draw. His only gifts were hatred, low cunning, a set of indefatigable vocal cords and a talent for nonstop talking at the top of his voice from the depths of his Peter-Panic paranoia. Thirty or forty million deaths and heaven knows how many billions of dollars—that was the price the world had to pay for little Adolf's retarded maturation. Fortunately most of the boys who grow up too slowly never get a chance of being more than minor delinquents. But even minor delinquents, if there are enough of them, can exact a pretty stiff price. That's why we try to nip them in the bud—or rather, since we're dealing with Peter Pans, that's why we try to make their nipped buds open out and grow."

"And do you succeed?"

Dr. Robert nodded. "It isn't hard. Particularly if you start early enough. Between four and a half and five all our children get a thorough examination. Blood tests, psychological tests, somatotyping; then we X ray their wrists and give them an EEG. All the cute little Peter Pans are spotted without fail, and appropriate treatment is started immediately. Within a year practically all of them are perfectly normal. A crop of potential failures and criminals, potential tyrants and sadists, potential misanthropes and revolutionaries for revolution's sake, has been transformed into a crop of useful citizens who can be governed *adandena asatthena*—without punishment and without a sword. In your part of the world delinquency is still left to clergymen, social workers and the police. Nonstop sermons and supportive therapy; prison sentences galore. With what results? The delinquency rate goes steadily up and up. No wonder. Words about sibling rivalry and hell and the personality of Jesus are no substitutes for biochemistry. A year in jail won't cure a Peter Pan of his endocrine disbalance or help the ex-Peter Pan to get rid of his psychological consequences. For Peter-Panic delinquency, what you need is early diagnosis and three pink capsules a day before meals. Given a tolerable environment, the result will be sweet reasonableness and a modicum of the cardinal virtues within eighteen months. Not to mention a fair chance, where before there hadn't been the faintest possibility, of eventual *prajnaparamita* and *karuna*, eventual wisdom and compassion. And now get Vijaya to tell you about the Muscle People. As you may perhaps have observed, he's one of them." Leaning forward, Dr. Robert thumped the giant's broad back. "Solid beef!" And he added, "How lucky for us poor shrimps that the animal isn't savage."

Vijaya took one hand off the wheel, beat his chest and uttered a loud ferocious roar. "Don't tease the gorilla," he said, and laughed good-humoredly. Then, "Think of the other great dictator," he said to Will, "think of Joseph Vissarionovich Stalin. Hitler's the supreme example of the delinquent Peter Pan. Stalin's the supreme example of the delinquent Muscle Man. Predestined, by his shape, to be an extravert. Not one of your soft, round, spill-the-beans extraverts who pine for indiscriminate togetherness. No—the trampling, driving extravert, the one who always feels impelled to Do Something and is never inhibited by doubts or qualms, by sympathy or sensibility. In his will, Lenin advised his successors to get rid of Stalin: the man was too fond of power and too apt to abuse it. But the advice came too late. Stalin was already so firmly entrenched that he couldn't be ousted. Ten years later his power was absolute. Trotsky had been scotched; all his old friends had been bumped off. Now, like God among the choiring angels, he was alone in a cozy little heaven peopled only by flatterers and yes-men. And all the time he was ruthlessly busy, liquidating kulaks, organizing collectives, building an armament industry, shifting reluctant millions from farm to factory. Working with a tenacity, a lucid efficiency of which the German Peter Pan, with his apocalyptic phantasies and his fluctuating moods, was utterly incapable. And in the last phase of the war, compare Stalin's strategy with Hitler's. Cool calculation pitted against compensatory daydreams, clear-eyed realism against the rhetorical nonsense that Hitler had finally talked himself into believing. Two monsters, equal in delinquency, but profoundly dissimilar in temperament, in unconscious motivation, and finally in efficiency. Peter Pans are wonderfully good at starting wars and revolutions; but it takes Muscle Men to carry them through to a successful conclusion. Here's the jungle," Vijaya added in another tone, waving a hand in the direction of a great cliff of trees that seemed to block their further ascent.

A moment later they had left the glare of the open hillside and had plunged into a narrow tunnel of green twilight that zigzagged up between walls of tropical foliage. Creepers dangled from the overarching branches and between the trunks of huge trees grew ferns and dark-leaved rhododendrons with a dense profusion of shrubs and bushes that for Will, as he looked about him, were namelessly unfamiliar. The air was stiflingly damp and there was a hot, acrid smell of luxuriant green growth and of that other kind of life which is decay. Muffled by the thick foliage, Will heard the ringing of distant axes, the rhythmic screech of a saw. The road turned yet once more and suddenly the green darkness of the tunnel gave place to sunshine. They had entered a clearing in the forest. Tall and broad-shouldered, half a dozen almost naked woodcutters were engaged in lopping the branches from a newly felled tree. In the sunshine hundreds of blue and amethyst butterflies chased one another, fluttering and soaring in an endless random dance. Over a fire at the further side of the clearing an old man was slowly stirring the contents of an iron caldron. Nearby a small tame deer, fine-limbed and elegantly dappled, was quietly grazing.

"Old friends," said Vijaya, and shouted something in

Palanese. The woodcutters shouted back and waved their hands. Then the road swung sharply to the left and they were climbing again up the green tunnel between the trees.

"Talk of Muscle Men," said Will as they left the clearing. "Those were really splendid specimens."

"That kind of physique," said Vijaya, "is a standing temptation. And yet among all these men—and I've worked with scores of them—I've never met a single bully, a single potentially dangerous power lover."

"Which is just another way," Murugan broke in contemptuously, "of saying that nobody here has any ambition."

"What's the explanation?" Will asked.

"Very simple, so far as the Peter Pans are concerned. They're never given a chance to work up an appetite for power. We cure them of their delinquency before it's had time to develop. But the Muscle Men are different. They're just as muscular here, just as tramplingly extraverted, as they are with you. So why don't they turn into Stalins or Dipas, or at the least into domestic tyrants? First of all, our social arrangements offer them very few opportunities for bullying their families, and our political arrangements make it practically impossible for them to domineer on any larger scale. Second, we train the Muscle Men to be aware and sensitive, we teach them to enjoy the commonplaces of everyday existence. This means that they always have an alternative —innumerable alternatives—to the pleasure of being the boss. And finally we work directly on the love of power and domination that goes with this kind of physique in almost all its variations. We canalize this love of power and we deflect it—turn it away from people and on to things. We give them all kinds of difficult tasks to perform—strenuous and violent tasks that exercise their muscles and satisfy their craving for domination—but satisfy it at nobody's expense and in ways that are either harmless or positively useful."

"So these splendid creatures fell trees instead of felling people—is that it?"

"Precisely. And when they've had enough of the woods, they can go to sea, or try their hands at mining, or take it easy, relatively speaking, on the rice paddies."

Will Farnaby suddenly laughed.

"What's the joke?"

"I was thinking of my father. A little woodchopping might have been the making of him—not to mention the salvation of his wretched family. Unfortunately he was an English gentleman. Woodchopping was out of the question."

"Didn't he have *any* physical outlet for his energies?"

Will shook his head. "Besides being a gentleman," he explained, "my father thought he was an intellectual. But an intellectual doesn't hunt or shoot or play golf; he just thinks and drinks. Apart from brandy, my father's only amusements were bullying, auction bridge, and the theory of politics. He fancied himself as a twentieth-century version of Lord Acton—the last, lonely philosopher of Liberalism. You should have heard him on the iniquities of the modern omnipotent state! 'Power corrupts. Absolute power corrupts absolutely. *Absolutely.*' After which he'd down another brandy and go back with renewed gusto to his favorite pastime—trampling on his wife and children."

"And if Acton himself didn't behave in that way," said Dr. Robert, "it was merely because he happened to be virtuous and intelligent. There was nothing in his theories to restrain a delinquent Muscle Man or an untreated Peter Pan from trampling on anyone he could get his feet on. That was Acton's fatal weakness. As a political theorist he was altogether admirable. As a practical psychologist he was almost nonexistent. He seems to have thought that the power problem could be solved by good social arrangements, supplemented, of course, by sound morality and a spot of revealed religion. But the power problem has its roots in anatomy and biochemistry and temperament. Power has to be curbed on the legal and political levels; that's obvious. But it's also obvious that there must be prevention on the individual level. On the level of instinct and emotion, on the level of the glands and the viscera, the muscles and the blood. If I can ever find the time, I'd like to write a little book on human physiology in relation to ethics, religion, politics and law."

"Law," Will echoed. "I was just gong to ask you about law. Are you absolutely swordless and punishmentless? Or do you still need judges and policemen?"

"We still need them," said Dr. Robert. "But we don't need nearly so many of them as you do. In the first place, thanks to preventive medicine and preventive education, we don't commit many crimes. And in the second place, most of the few crimes that are committed are dealt with by the criminal's MAC. Group therapy within a community that has assumed group responsibility for the delinquent. And in difficult cases the group therapy is supplemented by medical treatment and a course of *moksha*-medicine experiences, directed by somebody with an exceptional degree of insight."

"So where do the judges come in?"

"The judge listens to the evidence, decides whether the accused person is innocent or guilty, and if he's guilty, remands him to his MAC and, where it seems advisable, to the local panel of medical and mycomystical experts. At stated intervals the experts and the MAC report back to the judge. When the reports are satisfactory, the case is closed."

"And if they're never satisfactory?"

"In the long run," said Dr. Robert, "they always are."

There was a silence.

"Did you ever do any rock climbing?" Vijaya suddenly asked.

Will laughed. "How do you think I came by my game leg?"

"That was forced climbing. Did you ever climb for fun?"

"Enough," said Will, "to convince me that I wasn't much good at it."

Vijaya glanced at Murugan. "What about you, while you were in Switzerland?"

The boy blushed deeply and shook his head. "You can't do any of those things," he muttered, "if you have a tendency to TB."

"What a pity!" said Vijaya. "It would have been so good for you."

Will asked, "Do people do a lot of climbing in these mountains?"

"Climbing's an integral part of the school curriculum."

"For everybody?"

"A little for everybody. With more advanced rock work for the full-blown Muscle People—that's about one in twelve of the boys and one in twenty-seven of the girls. We shall soon be seeing some youngsters tackling their first post-elementary climb."

The green tunnel widened, brightened, and suddenly they were out of the dripping forest on a wide shelf of almost level ground, walled in on three sides by red rocks that towered up two thousand feet and more into a succession of jagged crests and isolated pinnacles. There was a freshness in the air and, as they passed from sunshine into the shadow of a floating island of cumulus, it was almost cool. Dr. Robert leaned forward and pointed, through the windshield, at a group of white buildings on a little knoll near the center of the plateau.

"That's the High Altitude Station," he said. "Seven thousand feet up, with more than five thousand acres of good flat land, where we can grow practically anything that grows in southern Europe. Wheat and barely; green peas and cabbages, lettuce and tomatoes (the fruit won't set where night temperatures are over sixty-eight); gooseberries, strawberries, walnuts, greengages, peaches, apricots. Plus all the valuable plants that are native to high mountains at this latitude—including the mushrooms that our young friend here so violently disapproves of."

"Is this the place we're bound for?" Will asked.

"No, we're going higher." Dr. Robert pointed to the last outpost of the range, a ridge of dark-red rock from which the land sloped down on one side to the jungle and on the other mounted precipitously towards an unseen summit lost in the clouds. "Up to the old Shiva temple where the pilgrims used to come every spring and autumn equinox. It's one of my favorite places in the whole island. When the children were small, we used to go up there for picnics, Lakshmi and I, almost every week. How many years ago!" A note of sadness had come into his voice. He sighed and, leaning back in his seat, closed his eyes.

They turned off the road that led to the High Altitude Station and began to climb again.

"Entering the last, worst lap," said Vijaya. "Seven hairpin turns and half a mile of unventilated tunnel."

He shifted into first gear and conversation became impossible. Ten minutes later they had arrived.

x

CAUTIOUSLY MANEUVERING HIS IMMOBILIZED LEG, WILL climbed out of the car and looked about him. Between the red soaring crags to the south and the headlong descents in every other direction the crest of the ridge had been leveled, and at the midpoint of this long narrow terrace stood the temple—a great red tower of the same substance as the mountains, massive, four-sided, vertically ribbed. A thing of symmetry in contrast with the rocks, but regular not as Euclidean abstractions are regular; regular with the pragmatic geometry of a living thing. Yes, of a living thing; for all the temple's richly textured surfaces, all its bounding contours against the sky curved organically inwards, narrowing as they mounted towards a ring of marble, above which the red stone swelled out again, like the seed capsule of a flowering plant, into a flattened, many-ribbed dome that crowned the whole.

"Built about fifty years before the Norman Conquest," said Dr. Robert.

"And looks," Will commented, "as though it hadn't been built by anybody—as though it had grown out of the rock. Grown like the bud of an agave, on the point of rocketing up into a twelve-foot stalk and an explosion of flowers."

Vijaya touched his arm. "Look," he said. "A party of Elementaries coming down."

Will turned towards the mountain and saw a young man in nailed boots and climbing clothes working his way down a chimney in the face of the precipice. At a place where the chimney offered a convenient resting place he halted and, throwing back his head, gave utterance to a loud Alpine yodel. Fifty feet above him a boy came out from behind a buttress of rock, lowered himself from the ledge on which he was standing and started down the chimney.

"Does it tempt you?" Vijaya asked, turning to Murugan.

Heavily overacting the part of the bored, sophisticated adult who has something better to do than watch the children at play, Murugan shrugged his shoulders. "Not in the slightest." He moved away and, sitting down on the weatherworn carving of a lion, pulled a gaudily bound American magazine out of his pocket and started to read.

"What's the literature?" Vijaya asked.

"*Science Fiction.*" There was a ring of defiance in Murugan's voice.

Dr. Robert laughed. "Anything to escape from Fact."

Pretending not to have heard him, Murugan turned a page and went on reading.

"He's pretty good," said Vijaya, who had been watching the young climber's progress. "They have an experienced man at each end of the rope," he added. "You can't see the number-one man. He's behind that buttress in a parallel chimney thirty or forty feet higher up. There's a permanent iron spike up there, where you can belay the rope. The whole party could fall, and they'd be perfectly safe."

Spread-eagled between footholds in either wall of the narrow chimney, the leader kept shouting up instructions and encouragement. Then, as the boy approached, he yielded his place, climbed down another twenty feet and, halting, yodeled again. Booted and trousered, a tall girl with her hair in pigtails appeared from behind the buttress and lowered herself into the chimney.

"Excellent!" said Vijaya approvingly as he watched her.

Meanwhile, from a low building at the foot of the cliff—the tropical version, evidently, of an Alpine hut—a group of young people had come out to see what was happening. They belonged, Will was told, to three other parties of climbers who had taken their Postelementary Test earlier in the day.

"Does the best team win a prize?" Will asked.

"Nobody wins anything," Vijaya answered. "This isn't a competition. It's more like an ordeal."

"An ordeal," Dr. Robert explained, "which is the first stage of their initiation out of childhood into adolescence. An ordeal that helps them to understand the world they'll have to live in, helps them to realize the omnipresence of death, the essential precariousness of all existence. But after the ordeal comes the revelation. In a few minutes these boys and girls will be given their first experience of the *moksha-*

medicine. They'll all take it together, and there'll be a religious ceremony in the temple."

"Something like the Confirmation Service?"

"Except that this is more than just a piece of theological rigmarole. Thanks to the *moksha*-medicine, it includes an actual experience of the real thing."

"The real thing?" Will shook his head. "Is there such a thing? I wish I could believe it."

"You're not being asked to believe it," said Dr. Robert. "The real thing isn't a proposition; it's a state of being. We don't teach our children creeds or get them worked up over emotionally charged symbols. When it's time for them to learn the deepest truths of religion, we set them to climb a precipice and then give them four hundred milligrams of revelation. Two firsthand experiences of reality, from which any reasonably intelligent boy or girl can derive a very good idea of what's what."

"And don't forget the dear old power problem," said Vijaya. "Rock climbing's a branch of applied ethics; it's another preventive substitute for bullying."

"So my father ought to have been an Alpinist as well as a woodchopper."

"One may laugh," said Vijaya, duly laughing. "But the fact remains that it works. It works. First and last I've climbed my way out of literally scores of the ugliest temptations to throw my weight around—and my weight being considerable," he added, "incitements were correspondingly strong."

"There seems to be only one catch," said Will. "In the process of climbing your way out of temptation, you might fall and . . ." Suddenly remembering what had happened to Dugald MacPhail, he broke off.

It was Dr. Robert who finished the sentence. "Might fall," he said slowly, "and kill yourself. Dugald was climbing alone," he went on after a little pause. "Nobody knows what happened. The body wasn't found till the next day." There was a long silence.

"Do you still think this is a good idea?" Will asked, pointing with his bamboo staff at the tiny figures crawling so laboriously on the face of that headlong wilderness of naked rock.

"I still think it's a good idea," said Dr. Robert.

"But poor Susila. . . ."

"Yes, poor Susila," Dr. Robert repeated. "And poor children, poor Lakshmi, poor me. But if Dugald hadn't made a habit of risking his life, it might have been poor everybody for other reasons. Better court the danger of killing yourself than court the danger of killing other people, or at the very least making them miserable. Hurting them because you're naturally aggressive and too prudent, or too ignorant, to work off your aggression on a precipice. And now," he continued in another tone, "I want to show you the view."

"And *I'll* go and talk to those boys and girls." Vijaya walked away towards the group at the foot of the red crags.

Leaving Murugan to his *Science Fiction,* Will followed Dr. Robert through a pillared gateway and across the wide stone platform that surrounded the temple. At one corner of this platform stood a small domed pavilion. They entered and, crossing to the wide unglazed window, looked out. Rising to the line of the horizon, like a solid wall of jade and lapis, was the sea. Below them, after a sheer fall of a thousand feet, lay the green of the jungle. Beyond the jungle, folded vertically into combe and buttress, terraced horizontally into a huge man-made staircase of innumerable fields, the lower slopes went steeply down into a wide plain, at whose furthest verge, between the market gardens and the palm-fringed beach, stretched a considerable city. Seen from this high vantage point in its shining completeness, it looked like the tiny, meticulous painting of a city in a medieval book of hours.

"There's Shivapuram," said Dr. Robert. "And that complex of buildings on the hill beyond the river—that's the great Buddhist temple. A little earlier than Borobudur, and the sculpture is as fine as anything in Further India." There was a silence. "This little summerhouse," he resumed, "is where we used to eat our picnics when it was raining. I shall never forget the time when Dugald (he must have been about ten) amused himself by climbing up here on the window ledge and standing on one leg in the attitude of the dancing Shiva. Poor Lakshmi, she was scared out of her wits. But Dugald was a born steeplejack. Which only makes the accident even more incomprehensible." He shook his head; then, after another silence, "The last time we all came up here," he said, "was eight or nine months ago. Dugald was still alive and Lakshmi wasn't yet too weak for a day's outing with her grandchildren. He did that Shiva stunt again for the benefit of Tom Krishna and Mary Sarojini. On one leg; and he kept his arms moving so fast that one could have sworn there were four of them." Dr. Robert broke off. Picking up a flake of mortar from the floor, he tossed it out of the window. "Down, down, down . . . Empty space. *Pascal avait son gouffre*. How strange that this should be at once the most powerful symbol of death and the most powerful symbol of the fullest, intensest life." Suddenly his face lighted up. "Do you see that hawk?"

"A hawk?"

Dr. Robert pointed to where, halfway between their eyrie and the dark roof of the forest, a small brown incarnation of speed and rapine lazily wheeled on unmoving wings. "It reminds me of a poem that the Old Raja once wrote about this place." Dr. Robert was silent for a moment, then started to recite:

"Up here, you ask me,
Up here aloft where Shiva
Dances above the world,
What the devil do I think I'm doing?

No answer, friend—except
That hawk below us turning,
Those black and arrowy swifts
Trailing long silver wires across the air—
The shrillness of their crying.

How far, you say, from the hot plains,
How far, reproachfully, from all my people!
And yet how close! For here between the cloudy
Sky and the sea below, suddenly visible,
I read their luminous secret and my own."

"And the secret, I take it, is this empty space."

"Or rather what this empty space is the symbol of—the Buddha Nature in all our perpetual perishing. Which reminds me . . ." He looked at his watch.

"What's next on the program?" Will asked as they stepped out into the glare.

"The service in the temple," Dr. Robert answered. "The young climbers will offer their accomplishment to Shiva—in other words, to their own Suchness visualized as God. After which they'll go on to the second part of their initiation—the experience of being liberated from themselves."

"By means of the *moksha*-medicine?"

Dr. Robert nodded. "Their leaders give it them before they leave the Climbing Association's hut. Then they come over to the temple. The stuff starts working during the service. Incidentally," he added, "the service is in Sanskrit, so you won't understand a word of it. Vijaya's address will be in English—he speaks in his capacity as president of the Climbing Association. So will mine. And of course the young people will mostly talk in English."

Inside the temple there was a cool, cavernous darkness, tempered only by the faint daylight filtering in through a pair of small latticed windows and by the seven lamps that hung, like a halo of yellow, quivering stars, above the head of the image on the altar. It was a copper statue, no taller than a child, of Shiva. Surrounded by a flame-fringed glory, his four arms gesturing, his braided hair wildly flying, his right foot treading down a dwarfish figure of the most hideous malignity, his left foot gracefully lifted, the god stood there, frozen in mid-ecstasy. No longer in their climbing dress, but sandaled, bare-breasted and in shorts or brightly colored skirts, a score of boys and girls, together with the six young men who had acted as their leaders and instructors, were sitting cross-legged on the floor. Above them, on the highest of the altar steps, an old priest, shaven and yellow-robed, was intoning something sonorous and incomprehensible. Leaving Will installed on a convenient ledge, Dr. Robert tiptoed over to where Vijaya and Murugan were sitting and squatted down beside them.

The splendid rumble of Sanskrit gave place to a high nasal chant, and the chanting in due course was succeeded by a litany, priestly utterance alternating with congregational response.

And now incense was burned in a bass thurible. The old priest held up his two hands for silence, and through a long pregnant time of the most perfect stillness the thread of gray incense smoke rose straight and unwavering before the god, then as it met the draft from the windows broke and was lost to view in an invisible cloud that filled the whole dim space with the mysterious fragrance of another world. Will opened his eyes and saw that, alone of all the congregation, Murugan was restlessly fidgeting. And not merely fidgeting—making faces of impatient disapproval. He himself had never climbed; therefore climbing was merely silly. He himself had always refused to try the *moksha*-medicine; therefore those who used it were beyond the pale. His mother believed in the Ascended Masters and chatted regularly with Koot Hoomi; therefore the image of Shiva was a vulgar idol. What an eloquent pantomime, Will thought as he watched the boy. But alas for poor little Murugan, nobody was paying the slightest attention to his antics.

"Shivayanama," said the old priest, breaking the long silence, and again, "Shivayanama." He made a beckoning gesture.

Rising from her place, the tall girl whom Will had seen working her way down the precipice mounted the altar steps. Standing on tiptoe, her oiled body gleaming like a second copper statue in the light of the lamps, she hung a garland of pale-yellow flowers on the uppermost of Shiva's two left arms. Then, laying palm to palm, she looked up into the god's serenely smiling face and, in a voice that faltered at first, but gradually grew steadier, began to speak:

"O you the creator, you the destroyer, you who sustain
and make an end,
Who in sunlight dance among the birds and the
children at their play,
Who at midnight dance among corpses in the
burning grounds,
You Shiva, you dark and terrible Bhairava,
You Suchness and Illusion, the Void and All Things,
You are the lord of life, and therefore I have
brought you flowers;
You are the lord of death, and therefore I have
brought you my heart—
This heart that is now your burning ground.
Ignorance there and self shall be consumed with fire.
That you may dance, Bhairava, among the ashes.
That you may dance, Lord Shiva, in a place of flowers,
And I dance with you."

Raising her arms, the girl made a gesture that hinted at the ecstatic devotion of a hundred generations of dancing worshipers, then turned away and walked back into the twilight.

"Shivayanama," somebody cried out. Murugan snorted contemptuously as the refrain was taken up by other young voices. "Shivayanama, Shivayanama . . ." The old priest started to intone another passage from the Scriptures. Halfway through his recitation a small gray bird with a crimson head flew in through one of the latticed windows, fluttered wildly around the altar lamps, then, chattering in loud indignant terror, darted out again. The chanting continued, swelled to a climax, and ended in the whispered prayer for peace: *Shanti shanti shanti.* The old priest now turned towards the altar, picked up a long taper and, borrowing flame from one of the lamps above Shiva's head, proceeded to light seven other lamps that hung within a deep niche beneath the slab on which the dancer stood. Glinting on polished convexities of metal, their light revealed another statue—this time of Shiva and Parvati, of the Arch-Yogin seated and, while two of his four hands held aloft the symbolic drum and fire, caressing with the second pair the amorous Goddess, with her twining legs and arms, by whom, in this eternal embrace of bronze, he was bestridden. The old priest waved his hand. This time it was a boy, dark-skinned and powerfully muscled, who stepped into the light. Bending down, he hung the garland he was carrying about Parvati's neck; then, twisting the long flower chain, dropped a second loop of white orchids over Shiva's head.

"Each is both," he said.

"Each is both," the chorus of young voices repeated.

Murugan violently shook his head.

"O you who are gone," said the dark-skinned boy, "who are gone, who are gone to the other shore, who have landed on the other shore, O you enlightenment and you other enlightenment, you liberation made one with liberation, you compassion in the arms of infinite compassion."

"Shivayanama."

He went back to his place. There was a long silence. Then Vijaya rose to his feet and began to speak.

"Danger," he said, and again, "danger. Danger deliberately and yet lightly accepted. Danger shared with a friend, a group of friends. Shared consciously, shared to the limits of awareness so that the sharing and the danger become a yoga. Two friends roped together on a rock face. Sometimes three friends or four. Each totally aware of his own straining muscles, his own skill, his own fear, and his own spirit transcending the fear. And each, of course, aware at the same time of all the others, concerned for them, doing the right things to make sure that they'll be safe. Life at its highest pitch of bodily and mental tension, life more abundant, more inestimably precious, because of the ever-present threat of death. But after the yoga of danger there's the yoga of the summit, the yoga of rest and letting go, the yoga of complete and total receptiveness, the yoga that consists in consciously accepting what is given as it is given, without censorship by your busy moralistic mind, without any additions from your stock of secondhand ideals, your even larger stock of wishful phantasies. You just sit there with muscles relaxed and a mind open to the sunlight and the clouds, open to distance and the horizon, open in the end to that formless, wordless Not-Thought which the stillness of the summit permits you to divine, profound and enduring, within the twittering flux of your everyday thinking.

"And now it's time for the descent, time for a second bout of the yoga of danger, time for a renewal of tension and the awareness of life in its glowing plenitude as you hang precariously on the brink of destruction. Then at the foot of the precipice you unrope, you go striding down the rocky path toward the first trees. And suddenly you're in the forest, and another kind of yoga is called for—the yoga of the jungle, the yoga that consists of being totally aware of life at the near-point, jungle life in all its exuberance and its rotting, crawling squalor, all its melodramatic ambivalence of orchids and centipedes, of leeches and sunbirds, of the drinkers of nectar and the drinkers of blood. Life bringing order out of chaos and ugliness, life performing its miracles of birth and growth, but performing them, it seems, for no other purpose than to destroy itself. Beauty and horror, beauty," he repeated, "and horror. And then suddenly, as you come down from one of your expeditions in the mountains, suddenly you know that there's a reconciliation. And not merely a reconciliation. A fusion, an identity. Beauty made one with horror in the yoga of the jungle. Life reconciled with the perpetual imminence of death in the yoga of danger. Emptiness identified with selfhood in the Sabbath yoga of the summit."

There was silence. Murugan yawned ostentatiously. The old priest lighted another stick of incense and, muttering, waved it before the dancer, waved it again around the cosmic love-making of Shiva and the Goddess.

"Breathe deeply," said Vijaya, "and as you breathe pay attention to this smell of incense. Pay your whole attention to it; know it for what it is—an ineffable fact beyond words, beyond reason and explanation. Know it in the raw. Know it as a mystery. Perfume, women and prayer—those were the three things that Mohammed loved above all others. The inexplicable data of breathed incense, touched skin, felt love and beyond them, the mystery of mysteries, the One in plurality, the Emptiness that is all, the Suchness totally present in every appearance, at every point and instant. So breathe," he repeated, "breathe," and in a final whisper, as he sat down, "breathe."

"Shivayanama," murmured the old priest ecstatically.

Dr. Robert rose and started towards the altar, then halted, turned back, and beckoned to Will Farnaby.

"Come and sit with me," he whispered, when Will had caught up with him. "I'd like you to see their faces."

"Shan't I be in the way?"

Dr. Robert shook his head, and together they moved forward, climbed and, three quarters of the way up the altar stair, sat down side by side in the penumbra between darkness and the light of the lamps. Very quietly Dr. Robert began to talk about Shiva-Nataraja, the Lord of the Dance.

"Look at his image," he said. "Look at it with these new eyes that the *moksha*-medicine has given you. See how it breathes and pulses, how it grows out of brightness into brightness ever more intense. Dancing through time and out of time, dancing everlastingly and in the eternal now. Dancing and dancing in all the worlds at once. Look at him."

Scanning those upturned faces, Will noted, now in one, now in another, the dawning illuminations of delight, recognition, understanding, the signs of worshiping wonder that quivered on the brinks of ecstasy or terror.

"Look closely," Dr. Robert insisted. "Look still more closely." Then, after a long minute of silence, "Dancing in all the worlds at once," he repeated. "In *all* the worlds. And first of all in the world of matter. Look at the great round halo, fringed with the symbols of fire, within which the god is dancing. It stands for Nature, for the world of mass and energy. Within it Shiva-Nataraja dances the dance of endless becoming and passing away. It's his *lila*, his cosmic play. Playing for the sake of playing, like a child. But this child is the Order of Things. His toys are galaxies, his playground is infinite space and between finger and finger every interval is a thousand million light-years. Look at him there on the altar. The image is man-made, a little contraption of copper only four feet high. But Shiva-Nataraja fills the universe, *is* the universe. Shut your eyes and see him towering into the night, follow the boundless stretch of those arms and the wild hair infinitely flying.

"Nataraja at play among the stars and in the atoms. But also," he added, "also at play within every living thing, every sentient creature, every child and man and woman. Play for play's sake. But now the playground is conscious, the dance floor is capable of suffering. To us, this play without purpose seems a kind of insult. What we would really like is a God who never destroys what he has created. Or if there must be pain and death, let them be meted out by a God of righteousness, who will punish the wicked and reward the good with everlasting happiness. But in fact the good get hurt, the innocent suffer. Then let there be a God who sympathizes and brings comfort. But Nataraja only dances. His play is a play impartially of death and of life, of all evils as well as of all goods. In the uppermost of his right hands he holds the drum that summons being out of not-being. Rub-a-dub-dub—the creation tattoo, the cosmic reveille. But now look at the uppermost of his left hands. It brandishes the fire by which all that has been created is forthwith destroyed. He dances this way—what happiness! Dances that way—and oh, the pain, the hideous fear, the desolation! Then hop, skip and jump. Hop into perfect health. Skip into cancer and senility. Jump out of the fullness of life into nothingness, out of nothingness again into life. For Nataraja it's all play, and the play is an end in itself, everlastingly purposeless. He dances because he dances, and the dancing is his *maha-sukha*, his infinite and eternal bliss. Eternal bliss," Dr. Robert repeated and again, but questioningly, "Eternal bliss?" He shook his head. "For us there's no bliss, only the oscillation between happiness and terror and a sense of outrage at the thought that our pains are as integral a part of Nataraja's dance as our pleasures, our dying as our living. Let's quietly think about that for a little while."

The seconds passed, the silence deepened. Suddenly, startlingly, one of the girls began to sob. Vijaya left his place and, kneeling down beside her, laid a hand on her shoulder. The sobbing died down.

"Suffering and sickness," Dr. Robert resumed at last, "old age, decrepitude, death. *I show you sorrow.* But that wasn't the only thing the Buddha showed us. He also showed us the ending of sorrow."

"Shivayanama," the old priest cried triumphantly.

"Open your eyes again and look at Nataraja up there on the altar. Look closely. In his upper right hand, as you've already seen, he holds the drum that calls the world into existence and in his upper left hand he carries the destroying fire. Life and death, order and disintegration, impartially. But now look at Shiva's other pair of hands. The lower right hand is raised and the palm is turned outwards. What does that gesture signify? It signifies, 'Don't be afraid; it's All Right.' But how can anyone in his senses fail to be afraid? How can anyone pretend that evil and suffering are all right, when it's so obvious that they're all wrong? Nataraja has the answer. Look now at his lower left hand. He's using it to point down at his feet. And what are his feet doing? Look closely and you'll see that the right foot is planted squarely on a horrible little subhuman creature—the demon, Muyalaka. A dwarf, but immensely powerful in his malignity, Muyalaka is the embodiment of ignorance, the manifestation of greedy, possessive selfhood. Stamp on him, break his back! And that's precisely what Nataraja is doing. Trampling the little monster down under his right foot. But notice that it isn't at this trampling right foot that he points his finger; it's at the left foot, the foot that, as he dances, he's in the act of raising from the ground. And why does he point at it? Why? That lifted foot, that dancing defiance of the force of gravity—it's the symbol of release, of *moksha*, of liberation. Nataraja dances in all the worlds at once—in the world of physics and chemistry, in the world of ordinary, all-too-human experience, in the world finally of Suchness, of Mind, of the Clear Light. . . . And now," Dr. Robert went on after a moment of silence, "I want you to look at the other statue, the image of Shiva and the Goddess. Look at them there in their little cave of light. And now shut your eyes and see them again—shining, alive, glorified. How beautiful! And in their tenderness what depths of meaning! What wisdom beyond all spoken wisdoms in that sensual experience of spiritual fusion and atonement! Eternity in love with time. The One joined in marriage to the many, the relative made absolute by its union with the One. Nirvana identified with samsara, the manifestation in time and flesh and feeling of the Buddha Nature."

"*Shivayanama.*" The old priest lighted another stick of incense and softly, in a succession of long-drawn melismata, began to chant something in Sanskrit. On the young faces before him Will could read the marks of a listening serenity, the hardly perceptible, ecstatic smile that welcomes a sudden insight, a revelation of truth or of beauty. In the background, meanwhile, Murugan sat wearily slumped against a pillar, picking his exquisitely Grecian nose.

"Liberation," Dr. Robert began again, "the ending of sorrow, ceasing to be what you ignorantly think you are and becoming what you are in fact. For a little while, thanks to the *moksha*-medicine, you will know what it's like to be what in fact you are, what in fact you always have been. What a timeless bliss! But, like everything else, this timelessness is transient. Like everything else, it will pass. And when it has passed, what will you do with this experience? What will you do with all the other similar experiences that the *moksha*-medicine will bring you in the years to come? Will you merely enjoy them as you would enjoy an evening at the puppet show, and then go back to business as usual, back to behaving like the silly delinquents you imagine yourselves to be? Or, having glimpsed, will you devote your lives to the business, not at all as usual, of being what you are in fact? All that we older people can do with our teachings, all that Pala can do for you with its social arrangements, is to provide you with techniques and opportunities. And all that the *moksha*-medicine can do is to give you a succession of beatific glimpses, an hour or two, every now and then, of enlightening and liberating grace. It remains for you to decide whether you'll co-operate with the grace and take those opportunities. But that's for the future. Here and now, all you have to do is to follow the mynah bird's advice: Attention! Pay attention and you'll find yourselves, gradually or suddenly, becoming aware of the great primordial facts behind these symbols on the altar."

"Shivayanama!" The old priest waved his stick of incense. At the foot of the altar steps the boys and girls sat motionless as statues. A door creaked, there was a sound of footsteps. Will turned his head and saw a short, thickset man picking his way between the young contemplatives. He mounted the steps and, bending down, murmured something in Dr. Robert's ear, then turned and walked back towards the door.

Dr. Robert laid a hand on Will's knee. "It's a royal command," he whispered, with a smile and a shrug of the shoulders. "That was the man in charge of the Alpine hut. The Rani has just telephoned to say that she has to see Murugan as soon as possible. It's urgent." Laughing noiselessly, he rose and helped Will to his feet.

xi

WILL FARNABY HAD MADE HIS OWN BREAKFAST AND, WHEN Dr. Robert returned from his early-morning visit to the hospital, was drinking his second cup of Palanese tea and eating toasted breadfruit with pumelo marmalade.

"Not too much pain in the night," was Dr. Robert's response to his enquiries. "Lakshmi had four or five hour of good sleep, and this morning she was able to take some broth."

They could look forward, he continued, to another day of respite. And so, since it tired the patient to have him there all the time, and since life, after all, had to go on and be made the best of, he had decided to drive up to the High Altitude Station and put in a few hours' work on the research team in the pharmaceutical laboratory.

"Work on the *moksha*-medicine?"

Dr. Robert shook his head. "That's just a matter of repeating a standard operation—something for technicians, not for the researchers. *They're* busy with something new."

And he began to talk about the indoles recently isolated from the ololiuqui seeds that had been brought in from Mexico last year and were now being grown in the station's botanic garden. At least three different indoles, of which one seemed to be extremely potent. Animal experiments indicated that it affected the reticular system. . . .

Left to himself, Will sat down under the overhead fan and went on with his reading of the *Notes on What's What*:

> We cannot reason ourselves out of our basic irrationality. All we can do is to learn the art of being irrational in a reasonable way.
>
> In Pala, after three generations of Reform, there are no sheeplike flocks and no ecclesiastical Good Shepherds to shear and castrate; there are no bovine or swinish herds

and no licensed drovers, royal or military, capitalistic or revolutionary, to brand, confine and butcher. There are only voluntary associations of men and women on the road to full humanity.

Tunes or pebbles, processes or substantial things? "Tunes," answer Buddhism and modern science. "Pebbles," say the classical philosophers of the West. Buddhism and modern science think of the world in terms of music. The image that comes to mind when one reads the philosophers of the West is a figure in a Byzantine mosaic, rigid, symmetrical, made up of millions of little squares of some stony material and firmly cemented to the walls of a windowless basilica.

The dancer's grace and, forty years on, her arthritis—both are functions of the skeleton. It is thanks to an inflexible framework of bones that the girl is able to do her pirouettes, thanks to the same bones, grown a little rusty, that the grandmother is condemned to a wheelchair. Analogously, the firm support of a culture is the prime-condition of all individual originality and creativeness; it is also their principal enemy. The thing in whose absence we cannot possibly grow into a complete human being is, all too often, the thing that prevents us from growing.

A century of research on the *moksha*-medicine has clearly shown that quite ordinary people are perfectly capable of having visionary or even fully liberating experiences. In this respect the men and women who make and enjoy high culture are no better off than the lowbrows. High experience is perfectly compatible with low symbolic expression.

The expressive symbols created by Palanese artists are no better than the expressive symbols created by artists elsewhere. Being the products of happiness and a sense of fulfillment, they are probably less moving, perhaps less satisfying aesthetically, than the tragic or compensatory symbols created by victims of frustration and ignorance, of tyranny, war and guilt-fostering, crime-inciting superstitions. Palanese superiority does not lie in symbolic expression but in an art which, though higher and far more valuable than all the rest, can yet be practiced by everyone—the art of adequately experiencing, the art of becoming more intimately acquainted with all the worlds that, as human beings, we find ourselves inhabiting. Palanese culture is not to be judged as (for lack of any better criterion) we judge other cultures. It is not to be judged by the accomplishments of a few gifted manipulators of artistic or philosophical symbols. No, it is to be judged by what all the members of the community, the ordinary as well as the extraordinary, can and do experience in every contingency and at each successive intersection of time and eternity.

The telephone bell had started to ring. Should he let it ring or would it be better to answer and let the caller know that Dr. Robert was out for the day? Deciding on the second course, Will lifted the receiver.

"Dr. MacPhail's bungalow," he said, in a parody of secretarial efficiency. "But the doctor is out for the day."

"*Tant mieux,*" said the rich royal voice at the other end of the wire. "How are you, *mon cher* Farnaby?"

Taken aback, Will stammered out his thanks for Her Highness' gracious enquiry.

"So they took you," said the Rani, "to see one of their so-called initiations yesterday afternoon."

Will had recovered sufficiently from his surprise to respond with a neutral word and in the most noncommittal of tones. "It was most remarkable," he said.

"Remarkable," said the Rani, dwelling emphatically on the spoken equivalents of pejorative and laudatory capital letters, "but only as the Blasphemous Caricature of TRUE Initiation. They've never learned to make the elementary distinction between the Natural Order and the Supernatural."

"Quite," Will murmured. "Quite . . ."

"What did you say?" the voice at the other end of the line demanded.

"Quite," Will repeated more loudly.

"I'm glad you agree. But I didn't call you," the Rani went on, "to discuss the difference between the Natural and the Supernatural—Supremely Important as that difference is. No, I called you about a more urgent matter."

"Oil?"

"Oil," she confirmed. "I've just received a very disquieting communication from my Personal Representative in Rendang. Very Highly Placed," she added parenthetically, "and invariably Well Informed."

Will found himself wondering which of all those sleek and

much bemedaled guests at the Foreign Office cocktail party had double-crossed his fellow double-crossers—himself, of course, included.

"Within the last few days," the Rani went on, "representatives of no less than three Major Oil Companies, European and American, have flown into Rendang-Lobo. My informant tells me that they're already working on the four or five Key Figures in the Administration who might, at some future date, be influential in deciding who is to get the concession for Pala."

Will clicked his tongue disapprovingly.

Considerable sums, she hinted, had been, if not directly offered, at least named and temptingly dangled.

"Nefarious," he commented.

Nefarious, the Rani agreed, was the word. And that was why Something must be Done About It, and Done Immediately. From Bahu she had learned that Will had already written to Lord Aldehyde, and within a few days a reply would doubtless be forthcoming. But a few days were too long. Time was of the essence—not only because of what those rival companies were up to, but also (and the Rani lowered her voice mysteriously) for Other Reasons. "Now, now!" her Little Voice kept exhorting. "Now, without delay!" Lord Aldehyde must be informed by cable of what was happening (the faithful Bahu, she added parenthetically, had offered to transmit the message in code by way of the Rendang Legation in London) and along with the information must go an urgent request that he empower his Special Correspondent to take such steps—at this stage the appropriate steps would be predominantly of a financial nature—as might be necessary to secure the triumph of their Common Cause.

"So with your permission," the voice concluded, "I'll tell Bahu to send the cable immediately. In our joint names, Mr. Farnaby, yours and Mine. I hope, *mon cher*, that this will be agreeable to you."

It wasn't at all agreeable, but there seemed to be no excuse, seeing that he had already written that letter to Joe Aldehyde, for demurring. And so, "Yes, of course," he cried with a show of enthusiasm belied by his long dubious pause, before the words were uttered, in search of an alternative answer. "We ought to get the reply sometime tomorrow," he added.

"We shall get it tonight," the Rani assured him.

"Is that possible?"

"With God" (*con espressione*) "all things are possible."

"Quite," he said, "quite. But still . . ."

"I go by what my Little Voice tells me. 'Tonight,' it's saying. And 'he will give Mr. Farnaby carte blanche'—carte blanche," she repeated with gusto. " 'And Farnaby will be completely successful.' "

"I wonder?" he said doubtfully.

"You *must* be successful."

"Must be?"

"Must be," she insisted.

"Why?"

"Because it was *God* who inspired me to launch the Crusade of the Spirit."

"I don't quite get the connection."

"Perhaps I oughtn't to tell you," she said. Then, after a moment of silence, "But after all, why not? If Our Cause triumphs, Lord Aldehyde has promised to back the Crusade with all his resources. And since God wants the Crusade to succeed, Our Cause cannot fail to triumph."

"Q.E.D.," he wanted to shout, but restrained himself. It wouldn't be polite. And anyhow this was no joking matter.

"Well, I must call Bahu," said the Rani. "*A bientôt*, my dear Farnaby." And she rang off.

Shrugging his shoulders, Will turned back to the *Notes on What's What*. What else was there do do?

> Dualism . . . Without it there can hardly be good literature. With it, there most certainly can be no good life.
>
> "I" affirms a separate and abiding me-substance; "am" denies the fact that all existence is relationship and change. "I am." Two tiny words, but what an enormity of untruth! The religiously-minded dualist calls homemade spirits from the vasty deep; the nondualist calls the vasty deep into his spirit or, to be more accurate, he finds that the vasty deep is already there.

There was the noise of an approaching car, then silence as the motor was turned off, then the slamming of a door and the sound of footsteps on gravel, on the steps of the veranda.

"Are you ready?" called Vijaya's deep voice.

Will put down the *Notes on What's What*, picked up his bamboo staff, and hoisting himself to his feet, walked to the front door.

"Ready and champing at the bit," he said as he stepped out onto the veranda.

"Then let's go." Vijaya took his arm. "Careful of these steps," he recommended.

Dressed all in pink and with corals round her neck and in her ears, a plump, round-faced woman in her middle forties was standing beside the jeep.

"This is Leela Rao," said Vijaya. "Our librarian, secretary, treasurer, and general keeper-in-order. Without her we'd be lost."

She looked, Will thought as he shook hands with her, like a browner version of one of those gentle but inexhaustibly energetic English ladies who, when their children are grown, go in for good works or organized culture. Not too intelligent, poor dears; but how selfless, how devoted, how genuinely good—and, alas, how boring!

"I was hearing of you," Mrs. Rao volunteered as they rattled along past the lotus pond and out onto the highway, "from my young friends, Radha and Ranga."

"I hope," said Will, "that they approved of me as heartily as I approved of them."

Mrs. Rao's face brightened with pleasure. "I'm so glad you like them!"

"Ranga's exceptionally bright," Vijaya put in.

And so delicately balanced, Mrs. Rao elaborated, between introversion and the outside world. Always tempted—and how strongly!—to escape into the Arhat's Nirvana or the scientists' beautifully tidy little paradise of pure abstraction. Always tempted, but often resisting temptation; for Ranga, the Arhat-scientist, was also another kind of Ranga, a Ranga capable of compassion, ready, if one knew how to make the right kind of appeal, to lay himself open to the concrete realities of life, to be aware, concerned and actively helpful. How fortunate for him and for everyone else that he had found a girl like little Radha, a girl so intelligently simple, so humorous and tender, so richly endowed for love and happiness! Radha and Ranga, Mrs. Rao confided, had been among her favorite pupils.

Pupils, Will patronizingly assumed, in some kind of Buddhist Sunday school. But in fact, as he was now flabbergasted to learn, it was in the yoga of love that this devoted settlement worker had been, for the past six years and in the intervals of librarianship, instructing the young. By the kinds of methods, Will supposed, that Murugan had shrunk from and the Rani, in her all but incestuous possessiveness, had found so outrageous. He opened his mouth to question her. But his reflexes had been conditioned in higher latitude and by settlement workers of another species. The questions simply refused to pass his lips. And now it was too late to ask them. Mrs. Rao had begun to talk about her other avocation.

"If you knew," she was saying, "what trouble we have with books in this climate! The paper rots, the glue liquefies, the bindings disintegrate, the insects devour. Literature and the tropics are really incompatible."

"And if one's to believe your Old Raja," said Will, "literature is incompatible with a lot of other local features besides your climate—incompatible with human integrity, incompatible with philosophical truth, incompatible with individual sanity and a decent social system, incompatible with everything except dualism, criminal lunacy, impossible aspiration, and unnecessary guilt. But never mind." He grinned ferociously. "Colonel Dipa will put everything right. After Pala has been invaded and made safe for war and oil and heavy industry, you'll undoubtedly have a Golden Age of literature and theology."

"I'd like to laugh," said Vijaya. "The only trouble is that you're probably right. I have an uncomfortable feeling that my children will grow up to see your prophecy come true."

They left their jeep, parked between an oxcart and a brand-new Japanese lorry, at the entrance to the village, and proceeded on foot. Between thatched houses, set in gardens shaded by palms and papayas and breadfruit trees, the narrow street led to a central market place. Will halted and, leaning on his bamboo staff, looked around him. On one side of the square stood a charming piece of Oriental rococo with a pink stucco façade and gazebos at the four corners—evidently the town hall. Facing it, on the opposite side of the square, rose a small temple of reddish stone, with a central tower on which, tier after tier, a host of sculptured figures recounted the legends of the Buddha's progress from spoiled child to Tathagata. Between these two monuments, more than half of the open space was covered by a huge banyan tree. Along its winding and shadowy aisles were ranged the stalls of a score of merchants and market women. Slanting down through chinks in the green vaulting overhead, the long probes of sunlight picked out here a row of black-and-yellow water jars, there a silver bracelet, a painted wooden toy, a bolt of cotton print; here a pile of fruits, and a girl's gaily flowered bodice, there the flash of laughing teeth and eyes, the ruddy gold of a naked torso.

"Everybody looks so healthy," Will commented, as they made their way between the stalls under the great tree.

"They look healthy because they *are* healthy," said Mrs. Rao.

"And happy—for a change." He was thinking of the faces he had seen in Calcutta, in Manila, in Rendang-Lobo—the faces, for that matter, one saw every day in Fleet Street and the Strand. "Even the women," he noted, glancing from face to face, "even the women look happy."

"They don't have ten children," Mrs. Rao explained.

"They don't have ten children where I come from," said Will. "In spite of which . . . 'Marks of weakness marks of woe.'" He halted for a moment to watch a middle-aged market woman weighing out slices of sun-dried breadfruit for a very young mother with a baby in a carrying bag on her back. "There's a kind of radiance," he concluded.

"Thanks to *maithuna*," said Mrs. Rao triumphantly. "Thanks to the yoga of love." Her face shone with a mixture of religious fervor and professional pride.

They walked out from under the shade of the banyan, across a stretch of fierce sunlight, up a flight of worn steps, and into the gloom of the temple. A golden Bodhisattva loomed, gigantic, out of the darkness. There was a smell of incense and fading flowers, and from somewhere behind the statue the voice of an unseen worshiper was muttering an endless litany. Noiselessly, on bare feet, a little girl came hurrying in from a side door. Paying no attention to the grown-ups she climbed with the agility of a cat onto the altar and laid a spray of white orchids on the statue's upturned palm. Then, looking up into the huge golden face, she murmured a few words, shut her eyes for a moment, murmured again, then turned, scrambled down and, softly singing to herself, went out by the door through which she had entered.

"Charming," said Will, as he watched her go. "Couldn't be

prettier. But precisely what does a child like that think she's doing? What kind of religion is she supposed to be practicing?"

"She's practicing," Vijaya explained, "the local brand of Mahayana Buddhism, with a bit of Shivaism, probably, on the side."

"And do you highbrows encourage this kind of thing?"

"We neither encourage nor discourage. We accept it. Accept it as we accept that spider web up there on the cornice. Given the nature of spiders, webs are inevitable. And given the nature of human beings, so are religions. Spiders can't help making flytraps, and men can't help making symbols. That's what the human brain is there for—to turn the chaos of given experience into a set of manageable symbols. Sometimes the symbols correspond fairly closely to some of the aspects of the external reality behind our experience; then you have science and common sense. Sometimes, on the contrary, the symbols have almost no connection with external reality; then you have paranoia and delirium. More often there's a mixture, part realistic and part fantastic; that's religion. Good religion or bad religion—it depends on the blending of the cocktail. For example, in the kind of Calvinism that Dr. Andrew was brought up in, you're given only the tiniest jigger of realism to a whole jugful of malignant fancy. In other cases the mixture is more wholesome. Fifty-fifty, or even sixty-forty, even seventy-thirty in favor of truth and decency. Our local Old-Fashioned contains a remarkably small admixture of poison."

Will nodded. "Offerings of white orchids to an image of compassion and enlightenment—it certainly seems harmless enough. And after what I saw yesterday, I'd be prepared to put in a good word for cosmic dancing and divine copulation."

"And remember," said Vijaya, "this sort of thing isn't compulsory. Everybody's given a chance to go further. You asked what that child thinks she's doing. I'll tell you. With one part of her mind, she thinks she's talking to a person —an enormous, divine person who can be cajoled with orchids into giving her what she wants. But she's already old enough to have been told about the profounder symbols behind Amitabha's statue and about the experiences that give birth to those profounder symbols. Consequently with another part of her mind she knows perfectly well that Amitabha isn't a person. She even knows, because it's been explained to her, that if prayers are sometimes answered it's because, in this very odd psychophysical world of ours, ideas have a tendency, if you concentrate your mind on them, to get themselves realized. She knows too that this temple isn't what she still likes to think it is—the house of Buddha. She knows it's just a diagram of her own unconscious mind—a dark little cubby-hole with lizards crawling upside down on the ceiling and cockroaches in all the crevices. But at the heart of the verminous darkness sits Enlightenment. And that's another thing the child is doing—she's unconsciously learning a lesson about herself, she's being told that if she'd only stop giving herself suggestions to the contrary, she might discover that her own busy little mind is also Mind with a large M."

"And how soon will the lesson be learned? When will she stop giving herself those suggestions?"

"She may never learn. A lot of people don't. On the other hand, a lot of people do."

He took Will's arm and led him into the deeper darkness behind the image of Enlightenment. The chanting grew more distinct, and there, hardly visible in the shadows, sat the chanter—a very old man, naked to the waist and, except for his moving lips, as rigidly still as Amitabha's golden statue.

"What's he intoning?" Will asked.

"Something in Sanskrit."

Seven incomprehensible syllables, again and again.

"Good old vain repetition!"

"Not necessarily vain," Mrs. Rao objected. "Sometimes it really gets you somewhere."

"It gets you somewhere," Vijaya elaborated, "not because of what the words mean or suggest, but simply because they're being repeated. You could repeat *Hey Diddle Diddle* and it would work just as well as *Om* or *Kyrie Eleison* or *La ila illa 'llah*. It works because when you're busy with the repetition of *Hey Diddle Diddle* or the name of God, you can't be entirely preoccupied with yourself. The only trouble is that you can hey-diddle-diddle yourself downwards as well as upwards—down into the not-thought of idiocy as well as up into the not-thought of pure awareness."

"So, I take it, you wouldn't recommend this kind of thing," said Will, "to our little friend with the orchids?"

"Not unless she were unusually jittery or anxious. Which

she isn't. I know her very well; she plays with my children."

"Then what would you do in her case?"

"Among other things," said Vijaya, "I'd take her, in another year or so, to the place we're going to now."

"What place?"

"The meditation room."

Will followed him through an archway and along a short corridor. Heavy curtains were parted and they stepped into a large whitewashed room with a long window, to their left, that opened onto a little garden planted with banana and breadfruit trees. There was no furniture, only a scattering on the floor of small square cushions. On the wall opposite the window hung a large oil painting. Will gave it a glance, then approached to look into it more closely.

"My word!" he said at last. "Who is it by?"

"Gobind Singh."

"And who's Gobind Singh?"

"The best landscape painter Pala ever produced. He died in 'forty-eight."

"Why haven't we ever seen anything by him?"

"Because we like his work too well to export any of it."

"Good for you," said Will. "But bad for us." He looked again at the picture. "Did this man ever go to China?"

"No; but he studied with a Cantonese painter who was living in Pala. And of course he'd seen plenty of reproductions of Sung landscapes."

"A Sung master," said Will, "who chose to paint in oils and was interested in chiaroscuro."

"Only after he went to Paris. That was in 1910. He struck up a friendship with Vuillard."

Will nodded. "One might have guessed as much from this extraordinary richness of texture." He went on looking at the picture in silence. "Why do you hang it in the meditation room?" he asked at last.

"Why do you suppose?" Vijaya countered.

"Is it because this thing is what you call a diagram of the mind?"

"The temple was a diagram. This is something much better. It's an actual manifestation. A manifestation of Mind with a large M in an individual mind in relation to a landscape, to canvas and to the experience of painting. It's a picture, incidentally, of the next valley to the west. Painted from the place where the power lines disappear over the ridge."

"What clouds!" said Will. "And the light!"

"The light," Vijaya elaborated, "of the last hour before dusk. It's just stopped raining and the sun has come out again, brighter than ever. Bright with the preternatural brightness of slanting light under a ceiling of cloud, the last, doomed, afternoon brightness that stipples every surface it touches and deepens every shadow."

"Deepens every shadow," Will repeated to himself, as he looked into the picture. The shadow of that huge, high continent of cloud, darkening whole mountain ranges almost to blackness; and in the middle distance the shadows of island clouds. And between dark and dark was the blaze of young rice, or the red heat of plowed earth, the incandescence of naked limestone, the sumptuous darks and diamond glitter of evergreen foliage. And here at the center of the valley stood a group of thatched houses, remote and tiny, but how clearly seen, how perfect and articulate, how profoundly significant! Yes, significant. But when you asked yourself, "Of what?" you found no answer. Will put the question into words.

"What do they mean?" Vijaya repeated. "They mean precisely what they are. And so do the mountains, so do the clouds, so do the lights and darks. And that's why this is a genuinely religious image. Pseudoreligious pictures always refer to something else, something beyond the things they represent—some piece of metaphysical nonsense, some absurd dogma from the local theology. A genuinely religious image is always intrinsically meaningful. So that's why we hang this kind of painting in our meditation room."

"Always landscapes?"

"Almost always. Landscapes can really remind people of who they are."

"Better than scenes from the life of a saint or savior?"

Vijaya nodded. "It's the difference, to begin with, between objective and subjective. A picture of Christ or Buddha is merely the record of something observed by a behaviorist and interpreted by a theologian. But when you're confronted with a landscape like this, it's psychologically impossible for you to look at it with the eyes of a J. B. Watson or the mind of a Thomas Aquinas. You're almost forced to submit to your immediate experience; you're practically compelled to perform an act of self-knowing."

"Self-knowing?"

"Self-knowing," Vijaya insisted. "This view of the next valley is a view, at one remove, of your own mind, of everybody's mind as it exists above and below the level of personal history. Mysteries of darkness; but the darkness teems with life. Apocalypses of light; and the light shines out as brightly from the flimsy little houses as from the trees, the grass, the blue spaces between the clouds. We do our best to disprove the fact, but a fact it remains; man is as divine as nature, as infinite as the Void. But that's getting perilously close to theology, and nobody was ever saved by a notion. Stick to the data, stick to the concrete facts." He pointed a finger at the picture. "The fact of half a village in sunshine and half in shadow and in secret. The fact of those indigo mountains and of the more fantastic mountains of vapor above them. The fact of blue lakes in the sky, lakes of pale green and raw sienna on the sunlit earth. The fact of this grass in the foreground, this clump of bamboos only a few yards down the slope, and the fact, at the same time, of those faraway peaks and the absurd little houses two thousand feet below in the valley. Distance," he added parenthetically, "their ability to express the fact of distance—that's yet another reason why landscapes are the most genuinely religious pictures."

"Because distance lends enchantment to the view?"

"No; because it lends reality. Distance reminds us that there's a lot more to the universe than just people—that there's even a lot more to people than just people. It reminds us that there are mental spaces inside our skulls as enormous as the spaces out there. The experience of distance, of inner distance and outer distance, of distance in time and distance in space—it's the first and fundamental religious experience. 'O Death in life, the days that are no more'—and O the places, the infinite number of places that are not *this* place! Past pleasures, past unhappinesses and insights—all so intensely alive in our memories and yet all dead, dead without hope of resurrection. And the village down there in the valley so clearly seen even in the shadow, so real and indubitable, and yet so hopelessly out of reach, incommunicado. A picture like this is the proof of man's capacity to accept all the deaths in life, all the yawning absences surrounding every presence. To my mind," Vijaya added, "the worst feature of your nonrepresentational art is its systematic two-dimensionality, its refusal to take account of the universal experience of distance. As a colored object, a piece of abstract expressionism can be very handsome. It can also serve as a kind of glorified Rorschach inkblot. Everybody can find in it a symbolic expression of his own fears, lusts, hatreds, and daydreams. But can one ever find in it those more than human (or should one say those other than all too human) facts that one discovers in oneself when the mind is confronted by the outer distances of nature, or by the simultaneously inner and outer distances of a painted landscape like this one we're looking at? All I know is that in your abstractions I don't find the realities that reveal themselves here, and I doubt if anyone else can. Which is why this fashionable abstract nonobjective expressionism of yours is so fundamentally irreligious—and also, I may add, why even the best of it is so profoundly boring, so bottomlessly trivial."

"Do you come here often?" Will asked after a silence.

"Whenever I feel like meditating in a group rather than alone."

"How often is that?"

"Once every week or so. But of course some people like to do it oftener—and some much more rarely, or even never. It depends on one's temperament. Take our friend Susila, for example—she needs big doses of solitude; so she hardly ever comes to the meditation room. Whereas Shanta (that's my wife) likes to look in here almost every day."

"So do I," said Mrs. Rao. "But that's only to be expected," she added with a laugh. "Fat people enjoy company—even when they're meditating."

"And do you meditate on this picture?" Will asked.

"Not *on* it. *From* it, if you see what I mean. Or rather parallel with it. I look at it, and the other people look at it, and it reminds us all of who we are and what we aren't, and how what we aren't might turn into who we are."

"Is there any connection," Will asked, "between what you've been talking about and what I saw up there in the Shiva temple?"

"Of course there is," she answered. "The *moksha*-medicine takes you to the same place as you get to in meditation."

"So why bother to meditate?"

"You might as well ask, Why bother to eat your dinner?"

"But, according to you, the *moksha*-medicine *is* dinner."

"It's a banquet," she said emphatically. "And that's precisely why there has to be meditation. You can't have banquets every day. They're too rich and they last too long. Besides, banquets are provided by a caterer; *you* don't have any part in the preparation of them. For your everyday diet you have to do your own cooking. The *moksha*-medicine comes as an occasional treat."

"In theological terms," said Vijaya, "the *moksha*-medicine prepares one for the reception of gratuitous graces—premystical visions or the full-blown mystical experiences. Meditation is one of the ways in which one co-operates with those gratuitous graces."

"How?"

"By cultivating the state of mind that makes it possible for the dazzling ecstatic insights to become permanent and habitual illuminations. By getting to know oneself to the point where one won't be compelled by one's unconscious to do all the ugly, absurd, self-stultifying things that one so often finds oneself doing."

"You mean, it helps one to be more intelligent?"

"Not more intelligent in relation to science or logical argument—more intelligent on the deeper level of concrete experiences and personal relationships."

"More intelligent on *that* level," said Mrs. Rao, "even though one may be very stupid upstairs." She patted the top of her head. "I'm too dumb to be any good at the things that Dr. Robert and Vijaya are good at—genetics and biochemistry and philosophy and all the rest. And I'm no good at painting or poetry or acting. No talents and no cleverness. So I ought to feel horribly inferior and depressed. But in fact I don't—thanks entirely to the *moksha*-medicine and meditation. No talents or cleverness. But when it comes to living, when it comes to understanding people and helping them, I feel myself growing more and more sensitive and skillful. And when it comes to what Vijaya calls gratuitous graces . . ." She broke off. "You could be the greatest genius in the world, but you wouldn't have anything more than what I've been given. Isn't that true, Vijaya?"

"Perfectly true."

She turned back to Will. "So you see, Mr. Farnaby, Pala's the place for stupid people. The greatest happiness of the greatest number—and we stupid ones *are* the greatest number. People like Dr. Robert and Vijaya and my darling Ranga—we recognize their superiority, we know very well that their kind of intelligence is enormously important. But we also know that our kind of intelligence is just as important. And we don't envy them, because we're given just as much as they are. Sometimes even more."

"Sometimes," Vijaya agreed, "even more. For the simple reason that a talent for manipulating symbols tempts its possessors into habitual symbol manipulation, and habitual symbol manipulation is an obstacle in the way of concrete experiencing and the reception of gratuitous graces."

"So you see," said Mrs. Rao, "you don't have to feel too sorry for us." She looked at her watch. "Goodness, I shall be late for Dillip's dinner if I don't hurry."

She started briskly towards the door.

"Time, time, time," Will mocked. "Time even in this place of timeless meditation. Time for dinner breaking incorrigibly into eternity." He laughed. Never take yes for an answer. The nature of things is always no.

Mrs. Rao halted for a moment and looked back at him.

"But sometimes," she said with a smile, "it's eternity that miraculously breaks into time—even into dinnertime. Goodbye." She waved her hand and was gone.

"Which is better," Will wondered aloud as he followed Vijaya through the dark temple, out into the noonday glare, "which is better—to be born stupid into an intelligent society or intelligent into an insane one?"

xii

"HERE WE ARE," SAID VIJAYA, WHEN THEY HAD REACHED the end of the short street that led downhill from the market-place. He opened a wicket gate and ushered his guest into a tiny garden, at the further end of which, on its low stilts, stood a small thatched house.

From behind the bungalow a yellow mongrel dog rushed out and greeted them with a frenzy of ecstatic yelps and jumps and tail-waggings. A moment later a large green parrot, with white cheeks and a bill of polished jet, came swooping down from nowhere and landed with a squawk and a noisy fluttering of wings on Vijaya's shoulder.

"Parrots for you," said Will, "mynahs for little Mary Sarojini. You people seem to be on remarkably good terms with the local fauna."

Vijaya nodded. "Pala is probably the only country in which an animal theologian would have no reason for believing in devils. For animals everywhere else, Satan, quite obviously, is *Homo sapiens*."

They climbed the steps to the veranda and walked through the open front door into the bungalow's main living room. Seated on a low chair near the window, a young woman in blue was nursing her baby son. She lifted a heart-shaped face that narrowed down from a broad forehead to a delicately pointed chin, and gave them a welcoming smile.

"I've brought Will Farnaby," said Vijaya as he bent down to kiss her.

Shanta held out her free hand to the stranger.

"I hope Mr. Farnaby doesn't object to nature in the raw," she said. As though to give point to her words, the baby withdrew his mouth from the brown nipple, and belched. A white bubble of milk appeared between his lips, swelled up and burst. He belched again, then resumed his sucking. "Even at eight months," she added, "Rama's table manners are still rather primitive."

"A fine specimen," said Will politely. He was not much interested in babies and had always been thankful for those repeated miscarriages which had frustrated all Molly's hopes and longings for a child. "Who's he going to look like—you or Vijaya?"

Shanta laughed and Vijaya joined in, enormously, an octave lower.

"He certainly won't look like Vijaya," she answered.

"Why not?"

"For the sufficient reason," said Vijaya, "that I'm not genetically responsible."

"In other words, the baby isn't Vijaya's son."

Will looked from one laughing face to the other, then shrugged his shoulders. "I give up."

"Four years ago," Shanta explained, "we produced a pair of twins who are the living image of Vijaya. This time we thought it would be fun to have a complete change. We decided to enrich the family with an entirely new physique and temperament. Did you ever hear of Gobind Singh?"

"Vijaya has just been showing me his painting in your meditation room."

"Well, that's the man we chose for Rama's father."

"But I understood he was dead."

Shanta nodded. "But his soul goes marching along."

"What do you mean?"

"DF and AI."

"DF and AI?"

"Deep Freeze and Artificial Insemination."

"Oh, I see."

"Actually," said Vijaya, "we developed the techniques of AI about twenty years before you did. But of course we couldn't do much with it until we had electric power and reliable refrigerators. We got those in the late twenties. Since then we've been using AI in a big way."

"So you see," Shanta chimed in, "my baby might grow up to be a painter—that is, if that kind of talent is inherited. And even if it isn't he'll be a lot more endomorphic and viscerotonic than his brothers or either of his parents. Which is going to be very interesting and educative for everybody concerned."

"Do many people go in for this kind of thing?" Will asked.

"More and more. In fact I'd say that practically all the couples who decide to have a third child now go in for AI. So do quite a lot of those who mean to stop at number two. Take my family, for example. There's been some diabetes among my father's people; so they thought it best—he and my mother—to have both their children by AI. My brother's descended from three generation of dancers and, genetically, I'm the daughter of Dr. Robert's first cousin, Malcolm Chakravarti-MacPhail, who was the Old Raja's private secretary."

"And the author," Vijaya added, "of the best history of Pala. Chakravarti-MacPhail was one of the ablest men of his generation."

Will looked at Shanta, then back again at Vijaya.

"And has the ability been inherited?" he asked.

"So much so," Vijaya answered, "that I have the greatest difficulty in maintaining my position of masculine superiority. Shanta has more brains than I have; but fortunately she can't compete with my brawn."

"Brawn," Shanta repeated sarcastically, "*brawn* . . . I seem to remember a story about a young lady called Delilah."

"Incidentally," Vijaya went on, "Shanta has thirty-two half brothers and twenty-nine half sisters. And more than a third of them are exceptionally bright."

"So you're improving the race."

"Very definitely. Give us another century, and our average IQ will be up to a hundred and fifteen."

"Whereas *ours,* at the present rate of progress, will be down to about eighty-five. Better medicine—more congenital deficiencies preserved and passed on. It'll make things a lot easier for future dictators." At the thought of this cosmic joke he laughed aloud. Then, after a silence, "What about the ethical and religious aspects of AI?" he asked.

"In the early days," said Vijaya, "there were a good many conscientious objectors. But now the advantages of AI have been so clearly demonstrated, most married couples feel that it's more moral to take a shot at having a child of superior quality than to run the risk of slavishly reproducing whatever quirks and defects may happen to run in the husband's family. Meanwhile the theologians have got busy. AI has been justified in terms of reincarnation and the theory of karma. Pious fathers now feel happy at the thought that they're giving their wife's children a chance of creating a better destiny for themselves and their posterity."

"A better destiny?"

"Because they carry the germ plasm of a better stock. And the stock is better because it's the manifestation of a better karma. We have a central bank of superior stocks. Superior stocks of every variety of physique and temperament. In *your* kind of environment, most people's heredity never gets a fair chance. In ours, it does. And incidentally we have excellent genealogical and anthropometric records going back as far as the eighteen-seventies. So you see we're not working entirely in the dark. For example, we know that Gobind Singh's maternal grandmother was a gifted medium and lived to ninety-six."

"So you see," said Shanta, "we may even have a centenarian clairvoyant in the family." The baby belched again. She laughed. "The oracle has spoken—as usual, very enigmatically." Turning to Vijaya, "If you want lunch to be ready on time," she added, "you'd better go and do something about it. Rama's going to keep me busy for at least another ten minutes."

Vijaya rose, laid one hand on his wife's shoulder and with the other gently rubbed the baby's brown back.

Shanta bent down and passed her cheek across the top of the child's downy head. "It's father," she whispered. "Good father, good, good. . . ."

Vijaya administered a final pat, then straightened himself up. "You were wondering," he said to Will, "how it is that we get on so well with the local fauna. I'll show you." He raised his hand. "Polly. Polly." Cautiously, the big bird stepped from his shoulder to the extended forefinger. "Polly's a good bird," he chanted. "Polly's a very good bird." He lowered his hand to the point where a contact was made between the bird's body and the child's, then moved it slowly, feathers against brown skin, back and forth, back and forth. "Polly's a good bird," he repeated, "a good bird."

The parrot uttered a succession of low chuckles, then leaned forward from its perch on Vijaya's finger and very gently nibbled at the child's tiny ear.

"Such a good bird," Shanta whispered, taking up the refrain. "Such a *good* bird."

"Dr. Andrew picked up the idea," said Vijaya, "while he was serving as a naturalist on the *Melampus*. From a tribe in northern New Guinea. Neolithic people; but like you Christians and us Buddhists, they believed in love. And unlike us and you, they'd invented some very practical ways of making their belief come true. This technique was one of their happiest discoveries. Stroke the baby while you're feeding him; it doubles his pleasure. Then, while he's sucking and being caressed, introduce him to the animal or person you want him to love. Rub his body against theirs; let there be a warm physical contact between child and love object. At the same time repeat some word like 'good.' At first he'll understand only your tone of voice. Later on, when he learns to speak, he'll get the full meaning. Food plus caress plus contact plus 'good' equals love. And love equals pleasure, love equals satisfaction."

"Pure Pavlov."

"But Pavlov purely for a good purpose. Pavlov for friendliness and trust and compassion. Whereas you prefer to use Pavlov for brainwashing, Pavlov for selling cigarettes and vodka and patriotism. Pavlov for the benefit of dictators, generals, and tycoons."

Refusing any longer to be left out in the cold, the yellow mongrel had joined the group and was impartially licking every piece of sentient matter within its reach—Shanta's arm, Vijaya's hand, the parrot's feet, the baby's backside. Shanta drew the dog closer and rubbed the child against its furry flank.

"And this is a good good dog," she said. "Dog Toby, good good dog Toby."

Will laughed. "Oughtn't I to get into the act?"

"I was going to suggest it," Shanta answered, "only I was afraid you'd think it was beneath your dignity."

"You can take my place," said Vijaya. "I must go and see about our lunch."

Still carrying the parrot, he walked out through the door that led into the kitchen. Will pulled up his chair and, leaning forward, began to stroke the child's tiny body.

"This is another man," Shanta whispered. "A good man, baby. A *good* man."

"How I wish it were true!" he said with a rueful little laugh.

"Here and now it *is* true." And bending down again over the child, "He's a good man," she repeated. "A good good man."

He looked at her blissful, secretly smiling face, he felt the smoothness and warmth of the child's tiny body against his fingertips. Good, good, good . . . He too might have known this goodness—but only if his life had been completely different from what in fact, in senseless and disgusting fact, it was. So never take yes for an answer, even when, as now, yes is self-evident. He looked again with eyes deliberately attuned to another wavelength of value, and saw the caricature of a Memling altarpiece. "Madonna with Child, Dog, Pavlov and Casual Acquaintance." And suddenly he could almost understand, from the inside, why Mr. Bahu so hated these people. Why he was so bent—in the name, as usual and needless to say, of God—on their destruction.

"Good," Shanta was still murmuring to her baby, "good, good, good."

Too good—that was their crime. It simply wasn't permissible. And yet how precious it was! And how passionately he wished that he might have had a part in it! "Pure sentimentality!" he said to himself; and then aloud, "Good, good, good," he echoed ironically. "But what happens when the child grows a little bigger and discovers that a lot of things and people are thoroughly bad, bad, bad?"

"Friendliness evokes friendliness," she answered.

"From the friendly—yes. But not from the greedy, not from the power lovers, not from the frustrated and embittered. For them, friendliness is just weakness, just an invitation to exploit, to bully, to take vengeance with impunity."

"But one has to run the risk, one has to make a beginning. And luckily no one's immortal. The people who've been conditioned to swindling and bullying and bitterness will all be dead in a few years. Dead, and replaced by men and women brought up in the new way. It happened with us; it can happen with you."

"It *can* happen," he agreed. "But in the context of H-bombs and nationalism and fifty million more people every single year, it almost certainly won't."

"You can't tell till you try."

"And we shan't try as long as the world is in its present state. And, of course, it will remain in its present state until we do try. Try and, what's more, succeed at least as well as you've succeeded. Which brings me back to my original question. What happens when good, good, good discovers that, even in Pala, there's a lot of bad, bad, bad? Don't the children get some pretty unpleasant shocks?"

"We try to inoculate them against those shocks."

"How? By making things unpleasant for them while they're still young?"

"Not unpleasant. Let's say *real.* We teach them love and confidence, but we expose them to reality, reality in *all* its aspects. And then give them responsibilities. They're made to understand that Pala isn't Eden or the Land of Cockaigne. It's a nice place all right. But it will remain nice only if everybody works and behaves decently. And meanwhile the facts of life are the facts of life. Even here."

"What about the facts of life in those bloodcurdling snakes I met halfway up the precipice? You can say 'good, good, good' as much as you like; but snakes will still bite."

"You mean, they still *can* bite. But will they in fact make use of their ability?"

"Why shouldn't they?"

"Look over there," said Shanta. He turned his head and saw that what she was pointing at was a niche in the wall behind him. Within the niche was a stone Buddha, about half life-size, seated upon a curiously grooved cylindrical pedestal and surmounted by a kind of lead-shaped canopy that tapered down behind him into a broad pillar. "It's a small replica," she went on, "of the Buddha in the Station Compound—you know, the huge figure by the lotus pool."

"Which is a magnificent piece of sculpture," he said. "And the smile really gives one an inkling of what the Beatific Vision must be like. But what has it got to do with snakes?"

"Look again."

He looked. "I don't see anything specially significant."

"Look harder."

The seconds passed. Then, with a shock of surprise, he noticed something strange and even disquieting. What he had taken for an oddly ornamented cylindrical pedestal had suddenly revealed itself as a huge coiled snake. And that downward tapering canopy under which the Buddha was sitting was the expanded hood, with the flattened head at the center of its leading edge, of a giant cobra.

"My God!" he said. "I hadn't noticed. How unobservant can one be?"

"Is this the first time you've seen the Buddha in this context?"

"The first time. Is there some legend?"

She nodded. "One of my favorites. You know about the Bodhi Tree, of course?"

"Yes, I know about the Bodhi Tree."

"Well, that wasn't the only tree that Gautama sat under at the time of his Enlightenment. After the Bodhi Tree, he sat for seven days under a banyan, called the Tree of the Goatherd. And after that he moved on to the Tree of Muchalinda."

"Who was Muchalinda?"

"Muchalinda was the King of the Snakes and, being a god, he knew what was happening. So when the Buddha sat down under his tree, the Snake King crawled out of his hole, yards and yards of him, to pay Nature's homage to Wisdom. Then a great storm blew up from the west. The divine cobra wrapped its coils round the more than divine man's body, spread its hood over his head and, for the seven days his contemplation lasted, sheltered the Tathagata from the wind and rain. So there he sits to this day, with cobra beneath him, cobra above him, conscious simultaneously of cobra and the Clear Light and their ultimate identity."

"How very different," said Will, "from *our* view of snakes!"

"And your view of snakes is supposed to be God's view—remember Genesis."

"'I will put enmity between thee and the woman,'" he quoted, "'and between her seed and thy seed.'"

"But Wisdom never puts enmity anywhere. All those senseless pointless cockfights between Man and Nature, between Nature and God, between the Flesh and the Spirit! Wisdom doesn't make those insane separations."

"Nor does Science."

"Wisdom takes Science in its stride and goes a stage further."

"And what about totemism?" Will went on. "What about the fertility cults? *They* didn't make any separations. Were *they* Wisdom?"

"Of course they were—primitive Wisdom, Wisdom on the neolithic level. But after a time people begin to get self-conscious and the old Dark Gods come to seem disreputable. So the scene changes. Enter the Gods of Light, enter the Prophets, enter Pythagoras and Zoroaster, enter the Jains and the early Buddhists. Between them they usher in the Age of the Cosmic Cockfight–Ormuzd versus Ahriman, Jehovah versus Satan and the Baalim, Nirvana as opposed to Samsara, appearance over against Plato's Ideal Reality. And except in the minds of a few Tankriks and Mahayanists and Taoists and heretical Christians, the cockfight went on for the best part of two thousand years."

"After which?" he questioned.

"After which you get the beginnings of modern biology."

Will laughed. " 'God said, Let Darwin be,' and there was Nietzsche, Imperialism and Adolf Hitler."

"All that," she agreed. "But also the possibility of a new kind of Wisdom for everybody. Darwin took the old totemism and raised it to the level of biology. The fertility cults reappeared as genetics and Havelock Ellis. And now it's up to us to take another half turn up the spiral. Darwinism was the old neolithic Wisdom turned into scientific concepts. The new conscious Wisdom–the kind of Wisdom that was prophetically glimpsed in Zen and Taoism and Tantra–is biological theory realized in living practice, is Darwinism raised to the level of compassion and spiritual insight. So you see," she concluded, "there isn't any earthly reason–much less any heavenly reason–why the Buddha, or anyone else for that matter, shouldn't contemplate the Clear Light as manifested in a snake."

"Even though the snake might kill him?"

"Even though it might kill him."

"And even though it's the oldest and most universal of phallic symbols?"

Shanta laughed. " 'Meditate under the Tree of Muchalinda' –that's the advice we give to every pair of lovers. And in the intervals between those loving meditations remember what you were taught as children; snakes are your brothers; snakes have a right to your compassion and your respect; snakes, in a word, are good, good, good."

"Snakes are also poisonous, poisonous, poisonous."

"But if you remember that they're just as good as they're poisonous, and act accordingly, they won't use their poison."

"Who says so?"

"It's an observable fact. People who aren't frightened of snakes, people who don't approach them with the fixed belief that the only good snake is a dead snake, hardly ever get bitten. Next week I'm borrowing our neighbor's pet python.

For a few days I'll be giving Rama his lunch and dinner in the coils of the Old Serpent."

From outside the house came the sound of high-pitched laughter, then a confusion of children's voices interrupting one another in English and Palanese. A moment later, looking very tall and maternal by comparison with her charges, Mary Sarojini walked into the room flanked by a pair of identical four-year-olds and followed by the sturdy cherub who had been with her when Will first opened his eyes on Pala.

"We picked up Tara and Arjuna at the kindergarten," Mary Sarojini explained as the twins hurled themselves upon their mother.

With the baby in one arm and the other round the two little boys, Shanta smiled her thanks. "That was very kind of you."

It was Tom Krishna who said, "You're welcome." He stepped forward and, after a moment of hesitation, "I was wondering . . ." he began, then broke off and looked appealingly at his sister. Mary Sarojini shook her head.

"What were you wondering?" Shanta enquired.

"Well, as a matter of fact, we were both wondering . . . I mean, could we come and have dinner with you?"

"Oh, I see." Shanta looked from Tom Krishna's face to Mary Sarojini's and back again. "Well, you'd better go and ask Vijaya if there's enough to eat. He's doing the cooking today."

"Okay," said Tom Krishna without enthusiasm. With slow reluctant steps he crossed the room and went out through the door into the kitchen. Shanta turned to Mary Sarojini. "What happened?"

"Well, Mother's told him at least fifty times that she doesn't like his bringing lizards into the house. But this morning he did it again. So she got very cross with him."

"And you decided you'd better come and have dinner here?"

"If it isn't convenient, Shanta, we could try the Raos or the Rajajinnadasas."

"I'm quite sure it will be convenient," Shanta assured her. "I only thought it would be good for Tom Krishna to have a little talk with Vijaya."

"You're perfectly right," said Mary Sarojini gravely. Then, very businesslike, "Tara, Arjuna," she called. "Come with me to the bathroom and we'll get washed up. They're pretty grubby," she said to Shanta as she led them away.

Will waited until they were out of earshot, then turned to Shanta. "I take it that I've just been seeing a Mutual Adoption Club in action."

"Fortunately," said Shanta, "in very mild action. Tom Krishna and Mary Sarojini get on remarkably well with their mother. There's no personal problem there—only the problem of destiny, the enormous and terrible problem of Dugald's being dead."

"Will Susila marry again?" he asked.

"I hope so. For everybody's sake. Meanwhile, it's good for the children to spend a certain amount of time with one or other of their deputy fathers. Specially good for Tom Krishna. Tom Krishna's just reaching the age when little boys discover their maleness. He still cries like a baby; but the next moment he's bragging and showing off and bringing lizards into the house—just to prove he's two hundred per cent a he-man. That's why I sent him to Vijaya. Vijaya's everything Tom Krishna likes to imagine he is. Three yards high, two yards wide, terrifically strong, immensely competent. When he tells Tom Krishna how he ought to behave, Tom Krishna listens—listens as he would never listen to me or his mother saying the same things. And Vijaya *does* say the same things as we would say. Because, on top of being two hundred per cent male, he's almost fifty per cent sensitive-feminine. So, you see, Tom Krishna is really getting the works. And now," she concluded, looking down at the sleeping child in her arms, "I must put this young man to bed and get ready for lunch."

xiii

WASHED AND BRUSHED, THE TWINS WERE ALREADY IN THEIR high chairs. Mary Sarojini hung over them like a proud but anxious mother. At the stove Vijaya was ladling rice and vegetables out of an earthenware pot. Cautiously and with an expression on his face of focused concentration, Tom Krishna carried each bowl, as it was filled, to the table.

"There!" said Vijaya when the last brimming bowl had been sent on its way. He wiped his hands, walked over to the table and took his seat. "Better tell our guest about grace," he said to Shanta.

Turning to Will, "In Pala," she explained, "we don't say grace *before* meals. We say it *with* meals. Or rather we don't *say* grace; we chew it."

"Chew it?"

"Grace is the first mouthful of each course—chewed and chewed until there's nothing left of it. And all the time you're chewing you pay attention to the flavor of the food, to its consistency and temperature, to the pressures on your teeth and the feel of the muscles in your jaws."

"And meanwhile, I suppose, you give thanks to the Enlightened One, or Shiva, or whoever it may be?"

Shanta shook her head emphatically. "That would distract your attention, and attention is the whole point. Attention to the experience of something given, something you haven't invented. not the memory of a form of words addressed to somebody in your imagination." She looked round the table. "Shall we begin?"

"Hurrah!" the twins shouted in unison, and picked up their spoons.

For a long minute there was a silence, broken only by the twins who had not yet learned to eat without smacking their lips.

"May we swallow now?" asked one of the little boys at last.

Shanta nodded. Everyone swallowed. There was a clinking of spoons and a burst of talk from full mouths.

"Well," Shanta enquired, "what did your grace taste like?"

"It tasted," said Will, "like a long succession of different things. Or rather a succession of variations on the fundamental theme of rice and turmeric and red peppers and zucchini and something leafy that I don't recognize. It's interesting how it doesn't remain the same. I'd never really noticed that before."

"And while you were paying attention to these things, you were momentarily delivered from daydreams, from memories, from anticipations, from silly notions—from all the symptoms of *you*."

"Isn't tasting *me*?"

Shanta looked down the length of the table to her husband. "What would you say, Vijaya?"

"I'd say it was halfway between me and not-me. Tasting is not-me doing something for the whole organism. And at the same time tasting is me being conscious of what's happening. And that's the point of our chewing-grace—to make the me more conscious of what the not-me is up to."

"Very nice," was Will's comment. "But what's the point of the point?"

It was Shanta who answered. "The point of the point," she said, "is that when you've learned to pay closer attention to more of the not-you in the environment (that's the food) and more of the not-you in your own organism (that's your taste sensations), you may suddenly find yourself paying attention to the not-you on the further side of consciousness, or perhaps it would be better," Shanta went on, "to put it the other way round. The not-you on the further side of consciousness will find it easier to make itself known to a you that has learned to be more aware of its not-you on the side of physiology." She was interrupted by a crash, followed by a howl from one of the twins. "After which," she continued as she wiped up the mess on the floor, "one has to consider the problem of me and not-me in relation to people less than forty-two inches high. A prize of sixty-four thousand crores of rupees will be given to anyone who comes up with a foolproof solution." She wiped the child's eyes, had him blow his nose, then gave him a kiss and went to the stove for another bowl of rice.

"What are your chores for this afternoon?" Vijaya asked when lunch was over.

"We're on scarecrow duty," Tom Krishna answered importantly.

"In the field just below the schoolhouse," Mary Sarojini added.

"Then I'll take you there in the car," said Vijaya. Turning to Will Farnaby, "Would you like to come along?" he asked.

Will nodded. "And if it's permissible," he said, "I'd like to see the school, while I'm about it—sit in, maybe, at some of the classes."

Shanta waved good-bye to them from the veranda and a few minutes later they came in sight of the parked jeep.

"The school's on the other side of the village," explained Vijaya as he started the motor. "We have to take the bypass. It goes down and then up again."

Down through terraced fields of rice and maize and sweet potatoes, then on the level, along a contour line, with a muddy little fishpond on the left and an orchard of breadfruit trees on the right, and finally up again through more fields, some green, some golden—and there was the schoolhouse, white and spacious under its towering shade trees.

"And down there," said Mary Sarojini, "are our scarecrows."

Will looked in the direction she was pointing. In the nearest of the terraced fields below them the yellow rice was almost ready to harvest. Two small boys in pink loincloths and a little girl in a blue skirt were taking turns at pulling the strings that set in motion two life-sized marionettes attached to poles at either end of the narrow field. The puppets were of wood, beautifully carved and clothed, not in rags, but in the most splendid draperies. Will looked at them in astonishment.

"Solomon in all his glory," he exclaimed, "was not arrayed like one of these."

But then Solomon, he went on to reflect, was only a king; these gorgeous scarecrows were beings of a higher order. One was a Future Buddha, the other a delightfully gay, East Indian version of God the Father as one sees him in the Sistine Chapel, swooping down over the newly created Adam. With each tug of the string the Future Buddha wagged his head, uncrossed his legs from the lotus posture, danced a brief fandango in the air, then crossed them again and sat motionless for a moment until another jerk of the string once more disturbed his meditations. God the Father, meanwhile, waved his outstretched arm, wagged his forefinger in portentous warning, opened and shut his horsehair-fringed mouth and rolled a pair of eyes which, being made of glass, flashed comminatory fire at any bird that dared to approach the rice. And all the time a brisk wind was fluttering his draperies, which were bright yellow, with a bold design—in brown, white and black—of tigers and monkeys, while the Future Buddha's magnificent robes of red and orange rayon bellied and flapped around him with an Aeolian jingling of dozens of little silver bells.

"Are all your scarecrows like this?" Will asked.

"It was the Old Raja's idea," Vijaya answered. "He wanted to make the children understand that all gods are homemade, and that it's we who pull their strings and so give them the power to pull ours."

"Make them dance," said Tom Krishna, "make them wiggle." He laughed delightedly.

Vijaya stretched out an enormous hand and patted the child's dark curly head. "That's the spirit!" And turning back to Will, "*Quote* 'gods' *unquote,*" he said in what was evidently an imitation of the Old Raja's manner "—their one great merit apart from scaring birds and *quote* 'sinners' *unquote*, and occasionally, perhaps, consoling the miserable, consists in this: being raised aloft on poles, they have to be looked up at; and when anyone looks up, even at a god, he can hardly fail to see the sky beyond. And what's the sky? Air and scattered light; but also a symbol of that boundless and (excuse the metaphor) *pregnant* emptiness out of which everything, the living and the inanimate, the puppet makers and their divine marionettes, emerge into the universe we know—or rather that we think we know."

Mary Sarojini, who had been listening intently, nodded her head. "Father used to say," she volunteered, "that looking up at birds in the sky was even better. Birds aren't words, he used to say. Birds are real. Just as real as the sky." Vijaya brought the car to a standstill. "Have a good time," he said as the children jumped out. "Make them dance and wiggle."

Shouting, Tom Kirshna and Mary Sarojini ran down to join the little group in the field below the road.

"And now for the more solemn aspects of education." Vijaya turned the jeep into the driveway that led up to the schoolhouse. "I'll leave the car here and walk back to the station. When you've had enough, get someone to drive you home." He turned off the ignition and handed Will the key.

In the school office Mrs. Narayan, the Principal, was talking across her desk to a white-haired man with a long, rather doleful face like the face of a lined and wrinkled bloodhound.

"Mr. Chandra Menon," Vijaya explained when the introductions had been made, "is our Under-Secretary of Education."

"Who is paying us," said the Principal, "one of his periodical visits of inspection."

"And who thoroughly approves of what he sees," the Under-Secretary added with a courteous bow in Mrs. Narayan's direction.

Vijaya excused himself. "I have to get back to my work," he said and moved towards the door.

"Are you specially interested in education?" Mr. Menon enquired.

"Specially ignorant would be more like it," Will answered. "I was merely brought up, never educated. That's why I'd like to have a look at the genuine article."

"Well, you've come to the right place," the Under-Secretary assured him. "New Rothamsted is one of our best schools."

"What's your criterion of a good school?" Will asked.

"Success."

"In what? Winning scholarships? Getting ready for jobs? Obeying the local categorical imperatives?"

"All that, of course," said Mr. Menon. "But the fundamental question remains. What are boys and girls for?"

Will shrugged his shoulders. "The answer depends on where you happen to be domiciled. For example, what are boys and girls for in America? Answer: for mass consumption. And the corollaries of mass consumption are mass communications, mass advertising, mass opiates in the form of television, meprobamate, positive thinking, and cigarettes. And now that Europe has made the breakthrough into mass production, what will its boys and girls be for? For mass consumption and all the rest—just like the boys and girls in America. Whereas in Russia there's a different answer. Boys and girls are for strengthening the national state. Hence all those engineers and science teachers, not to mention fifty divisions ready for instant combat and equipped with everything from tanks to H-bombs and long-range rockets. And in China it's the same, but a good deal more so. What are boys and girls for there? For cannon fodder, industry fodder, agriculture fodder, road-building fodder. So East is East and West is West—for the moment. But the twain may meet in one or other of two ways. West may get so frightened of East they it will give up thinking that boys and girls are for mass consumption and decide instead that they're for cannon fodder and strengthening the state. Alternatively East may find itself under such pressure from the appliance-hungry masses who long to go Western, that it will have to change its mind and say that boys and girls are really for mass consumption. But that's for the future. As of now, the current answers to your question are mutually exclusive."

"And both of the answers," said Mr. Menon, "are different from ours. What are Palanese boys and girls for? Neither for mass consumption, nor for strengthening the state. The state has to exist, of course. And there has to be enough for everybody. That goes without saying. It's only on those conditions that boys and girls can discover what in fact they are for—only on those conditions that we can do anything about it."

"And what in fact *are* they for?"

"For actualization, for being turned into full-blown human beings."

Will nodded. "*Notes on What's What,*" he commented. "Become what you really are."

"The Old Raja," said Mr. Menon, "was mainly concerned with what people really are on the level that's beyond individuality. And of course we're just as much interested in that as he was. But our first business is elementary education, and elementary education has to deal with individuals in all their diversity of shape, size, temperament, gifts and deficiencies. Individuals in their transcendent unity are the affair of higher education. That begins in adolescence and is given concurrently with advanced elementary education."

"Begins, I take it," said Will, "with the first experience of the *moksha*-medicine."

"So you've heard about the *moksha*-medicine?"

"I've even seen it in action."

"Dr. Robert," the Principal explained, "took him yesterday to see an initiation."

"By which," added Will, "I was profoundly impressed. When I think of *my* religious training . . ." He left the sentence eloquently unfinished.

"Well, as I was saying," Mr. Menon continued, "adolescents get both kinds of education concurrently. They're helped to experience their transcendental unity with all other sentient beings and at the same time they're learning, in their psychology and physiology classes, that each one of us has his own constitutional uniqueness, everybody's different from everybody else."

"When I was at school," said Will, "the pedagogues did their best to iron out those differences, or at least to plaster them over with the same Late Victorian ideal—the ideal of the scholarly but Anglican football-playing gentleman. But now tell me what *you* do about the fact that everybody's different from everybody else."

"We begin," said Mr. Menon, "by assessing the differences. Precisely who or what, anatomically, biochemically and psychologically, is this child? In the organic hierarchy, which takes precedence—his gut, his muscles, or his nervous system? How near does he stand to the three polar extremes? How harmonious or how disharmonious is the mixture of his component elements, physical and mental? How great is his inborn wish to dominate, or to be sociable, or to retreat into his inner world? And how does he do his thinking and perceiving and remembering? Is he a visualizer or a non-visualizer? Does his mind work with images or with words, with both at once, or with neither? How close to the surface is his storytelling faculty? Does he see the world as Wordsworth and Traherne saw it when they were children? And, if so, what can be done to prevent the glory and the freshness from fading into the light of common day? Or, in more general terms, how can we educate children on the conceptual level without killing their capacity for intense non-verbal experience? How can we reconcile analysis with vision? And there are dozens of other questions that must be asked and answered. For example, does this child absorb all the vitamins in his food or is he subject to some chronic deficiency that, if it isn't recognized and treated, will lower his vitality, darken his mood, make him see ugliness, feel boredom and think foolishness or malice? And what about his blood sugar? What about his breathing? What about his posture and the way he uses his organism when he's working, playing, studying? And there are all the questions that have to do with special gifts. Does he show signs of having a talent for music, for mathematics, for handling words, for observing accurately and for thinking logically and imaginatively about what he has observed? And finally how suggestible is he going to be when he grows up? All children are good hypnotic subjects—so good that four out of five of them can be talked into somnambulism. In adults the proportion is reversed. Four out of five of them can never be talked into somnambulism. Out of any hundred children, which are the twenty who will grow up to be suggestible to the pitch of somnambulism?"

"Can you spot them in advance?" Will asked. "And if so, what's the point of spotting them?"

"We *can* spot them," Mr. Menon answered. "And it's very important that they should be spotted. Particularly important in *your* part of the world. Politically speaking, the twenty per cent that can be hypnotized easily and to the limit is the most dangerous element in your societies."

"Dangerous?"

"Because these people are the propagandist's predestined victims. In an old-fashioned, prescientific democracy, any spellbinder with a good organization behind him can turn that twenty per cent of potential somnambulists into an army of regimented fanatics dedicated to the greater glory and power of their hypnotist. And under a dictatorship these same potential somnambulists can be talked into implicit faith and mobilized as the hard core of the omnipotent party. So you see it's very important for any society that values liberty to be able to spot the future somnambulists when they're young. Once they've been spotted, they can be hypnotized and systematically trained *not* to be hypnotizable by the enemies of liberty. And at the same time, of course, you'd be well advised to reorganize your social arrangements so as to make it difficult or impossible for the enemies of liberty to arise or have any influence."

"Which is the state of things, I gather, in Pala?"

"Precisely," said Mr. Menon. "And that's why *our* potential somnambulists don't constitute a danger."

"Then why do you go to the trouble of spotting them in advance?"

"Because, if it's properly used, their gift is so valuable."

"For Destiny Control?" Will questioned, remembering

those therapeutic swans and all the things that Susila had said about pressing one's own buttons.

The Under-Secretary shook his head. "Destiny Control doesn't call for anything more than a light trance. Practically everybody's capable of that. The potential somnambulists are the twenty per cent who can go into very deep trance. And it's in very deep trance—and only in very deep trance—that a person can be taught how to distort time."

"Can *you* distort time?" Will enquired.

Mr. Menon shook his head. "Unfortunately I could never go deep enough. Everything I know had to be learned the long, slow way. Mrs. Narayan was more fortunate. Being one of the privileged twenty per cent, she could take all kinds of educational short cuts that were completely closed to the rest of us."

"What sort of short cuts?" Will asked, turning to the Principal.

"Short cuts to memorizing," she answered, "short cuts to calculating and thinking and problem solving. One starts by learning how to experience twenty seconds as ten minutes, a minute as half an hour. In deep trance it's really very easy. You listen to the teacher's suggestions and you sit there quietly for a long, long time. Two full hours—you'd be ready to take your oath on it. When you've been brought back, you look at your watch. Your experience of two hours was telescoped into exactly four minutes of clock time."

"How?"

"Nobody knows how," said Mr. Menon. "But all those anecdotes about drowning men seeing the whole of their life unfolding before them in a few seconds are substantially true. The mind and the nervous system—or rather some minds and some nervous systems—happen to be capable of this curious feat; that's all that anybody knows. We discovered the fact about sixty years ago, and since then we've been exploiting it. Exploiting it, among other things, for educational purposes."

"For example," Mrs. Narayan resumed, "here's a mathematical problem. In your normal state it might take you the best part of half an hour to solve. But now you distort time to the point where one minute is subjectively the equivalent of thirty minutes. Then you set to work on your problem. Thirty subjective minutes later it's solved. But thirty subjective minutes are one clock minute. Without the least sense of rush or strain you've been working as fast as one of those extraordinary calculating boys, who turn up from time to time. Future geniuses like Ampère and Gauss, or future idiots like Dase—but all of them, by some built-in trick of time distortion, capable of getting through an hour's hard work in a couple of minutes—sometimes in a matter of seconds. I'm only an average student; but I could go into deep trance, which meant that I could be taught how to telescope my time into a thirtieth of its normal span. Result: I was able to cover far more intellectual ground than I could possibly have covered if I'd had to do all my learning in the ordinary way. You can imagine what happens when somebody with a genius IQ is also capable of time distortion. The results are fantastic!"

"Unfortunately," said Mr. Menon, "they're not very common. In the last two generations we've had precisely two time distorters of real genius, and only five or six runners-up. But what Pala owes to those few is incalculable. So it's no wonder that we keep a sharp lookout for potential somnambulists!"

"Well, you certainly ask plenty of searching questions about your little pupils," Will concluded after a brief silence. "What do you do when you've found the answers?"

"We start educating accordingly," said Mr. Menon. "For example, we ask questions about every child's physique and temperament. When we have the answers, we sort out all the shyest, tensest, most overresponsive and introverted children, and assemble them in a single group. Then, little by little, the group is enlarged. First a few children with tendencies towards indiscriminate sociability are introduced. Then one or two little muscle men and muscle women—children with tendencies towards aggressiveness and love of power. It's the best method, we've found, for getting little boys and girls at the three polar extremes to understand and tolerate one another. After a few months of carefully controlled mixing, they're ready to admit that people with a different kind of hereditary makeup have just as good a right to exist as they have."

"And the principle," said Mrs. Narayan, "is explicitly taught as well as progressively applied. In the lower forms we do the teaching in terms of analogies with familiar animals. Cats like to be by themselves. Sheep like being together. Martens are fierce and can't be tamed. Guinea pigs are gentle and friendly. Are you a cat person or a sheep person, a guinea-pig person or a marten person? Talk about it in animal parables, and even very small children can understand the fact of human diversity and the need for mutual forbearance, mutual forgiveness."

"And later on," said Mr. Menon, "when they come to read the *Gita,* we tell them about the link between constitution and religion. Sheep people and guinea-pig people love ritual and public ceremonies and revivalistic emotion; their temperamental preferences can be directed into the Way of Devotion. Cat people like to be alone, and their private broodings can become the Way of Self-Knowledge. Marten people want to *do* things, and the problem is how to transform their driving aggressiveness into the Way of Disinterested Action."

"And the way to the Way of Disinterested Action is what I was looking at yesterday," said Will. "The way that leads through woodchopping and rock climbing—is that it?"

"Woodchopping and rock climbing," said Mr. Menon, "are special cases. Let's generalize and say that the way to *all* the Ways leads through the redirection of power."

"What's that?"

"The principle is very simple. You take the power generated by fear or envy or too much noradrenalin, or else by some built-in urge that happens, at the moment, to be out of place—you take it and, instead of using it to do something unpleasant to someone else, instead of repressing it and so doing something unpleasant to yourself, you consciously direct it along a channel where it can do something useful, or, if not useful, at least harmless."

"Here's a simple case," said the Principal. "An angry or frustrated child has worked up enough power for a burst of crying, or bad language, or a fight. If the power generated is sufficient for any of those things, it's sufficient for running, or dancing, more than sufficient for five deep breaths. I'll show you some dancing later on. For the moment, let's confine ourselves to breathing. Any irritated person who takes five deep breaths releases a lot of tension and so makes it easier for himself to behave rationally. So we teach our children all kinds of breathing games, to be played whenever they're angry or upset. Some of the games are competitive. Which of two antagonists can inhale most deeply and say 'OM' on the outgoing breath for the longest time? It's a duel that ends, almost without fail, in reconciliation. But of course there are many occasions when competitive breathing is out of place. So here's a little game that an exasperated child can play on his own, a game that's based on the local folklore. Every Palanese child has been brought up on Buddhist legends, and in most of these pious fairy stories somebody has a vision of a celestial being. A Bodhisattva, say, in an explosion of lights, jewels and rainbows. And along with the glorious vision there's always an equally glorious olfaction; the fireworks are accompanied by an unutterably delicious perfume. Well, we take these traditional phantasies—which are all based, needless to say, on actual visionary experiences of the kind induced by fasting, sensory deprivation or mushrooms—and we set them to work. Violent feelings, we tell the children, are like earthquakes. They shake us so hard that cracks appear in the wall that separates our private selves from the shared, universal Buddha Nature. You get cross, something inside of you cracks and, through the crack, out comes a whiff of the heavenly smell of enlightenment. Like champak, like ylang-ylang, like gardenias—only infinitely more wonderful. So don't miss this heavenliness that you've accidentally released. It's there every time you get cross. Inhale it, breathe it in, fill your lungs with it. Again and again."

"And they actually do it?"

"After a few weeks of teaching, most of them do it as a matter of course. And, what's more, a lot of them really smell that perfume. The old repressive 'Thou shalt not' has been translated into a new expressive and rewarding 'Thou shalt.' Potentially harmful power has been redirected into channels where it's not merely harmless, but may actually do some good. And meanwhile, of course, we've been giving the children systematic and carefully graduated training in perception and the proper use of language. They're taught to pay attention to what they see and hear, and at the same time they're asked to notice how their feelings and desires affect what they experience of the outer world, and how their language habits affect not only their feelings and desires but even their sensations. What my ears and my eyes record is one thing; what the words I use and the mood I'm in and the purposes I'm pursuing allow me to perceive, make sense of and act upon is something quite different. So you see it's all brought together into a single educational process. What we give the children is simultaneously a training in perceiving and imagining, a training in applied physiology and psychology, a training in practical ethics and practical religion, a training in the proper use of language, and a training in self-knowledge. In a word, a training of the whole mind-body in all its aspects."

"What's the relevance," Will asked, "of all this elaborate training of the mind-body to formal education? Does it help a child to do sums, or write grammatically, or understand elementary physics?"

"It helps a lot," said Mr. Menon. "A trained mind-body learns more quickly and more thoroughly than an untrained one. It's also more capable of relating facts to ideas, and both of them to its own ongoing life." Suddenly and surprisingly—for that long melancholy face gave one the impression of being incompatible with any expression of mirth more emphatic than a rather weary smile—he broke into a loud long peal of laughter.

"What's the joke?"

"I was thinking of two people I met last time I was in England. At Cambridge. One of them was an atomic physicist, the other was a philosopher. Both extremely eminent. But one had a mental age, outside the laboratory, of about eleven and the other was a compulsive eater with a weight problem that he refused to face. Two extreme examples of what happens when you take a clever boy, give him fifteen years of the most intensive formal education and totally neglect to do anything for the mind-body which has to do the learning and the living."

"And your system, I take it, doesn't produce that kind of academic monster?"

The Under-Secretary shook his head. "Until I went to Europe, I'd never seen anything of the kind. They're grotesquely funny," he added. "But, goodness, how pathetic! And, poor things, how curiously repulsive!"

"Being pathetically and curiously repulsive—that's the price we pay for specialization."

"For specialization," Mr. Menon agreed, "but not in the sense you people ordinarily use the word. Specialization in that sense is necessary and inevitable. No specialization, no civilization. And if one educates the whole mind-body along with the symbol-using intellect, that kind of necessary specialization won't do much harm. But you people don't educate the mind-body. Your cure for too much scientific specialization is a few more courses in the humanities. Excellent! Every education ought to include courses in the humanities. But don't let's be fooled by the name. By themselves, the humanities don't humanize. They're simply another form of specialization on the symbolic level. Reading Plato or listening to a lecture on T. S. Eliot doesn't educate the whole human being; like courses in physics or chemistry, it merely educates the symbol manipulator and leaves the rest of the living mind-body in its pristine state of ignorance and ineptitude. Hence all those pathetic and repulsive creatures that so astonished me on my first trip abroad."

"What about formal education?" Will now asked. "What about indispensable information and the necessary intellectual skills? Do you teach the way we do?"

"We teach the way you're probably going to teach in another ten or fifteen years. Take mathematics, for example. Historically mathematics began with the elaboration of useful tricks, soared up into metaphysics and finally explained itself in terms of structure and logical transformations. In our schools we reverse the historical process. We begin with structure and logic; then, skipping the metaphysics, we go on from general principles to particular applications."

"And the children understand?"

"Far better than they understand when one starts with utilitarian tricks. From about five onwards practically any intelligent child can learn practically anything, provided always that you present it to him in the right way. Logic and structure in the form of games and puzzles. The children play and, incredibly quickly, they catch the point. After which you can go on to practical applications. Taught in this way, most children can learn at least three times as much, four times as thoroughly, in half the time. Or consider another field where one can use games to implant an understanding of basic principles. All scientific thinking is in terms of probability. The old eternal verities are merely a high degree of likeliness; the immutable laws of nature are just statistical averages. How does one get these profoundly unobvious notions into children's heads? By playing roulette with them, by spinning coins and drawing lots. By teaching them all kinds of games with cards and boards and dice."

"Evolutionary Snakes and Ladders—that's the most popular game with the little ones," said Mrs. Narayan. "Another great favorite is Mendelian Happy Families."

"And a little later," Mr. Menon added, "we introduce them to a rather complicated game played by four people with a pack of sixty specially designed cards divided into three suits. Psychological bridge, we call it. Chance deals you your hand, but the way you play it is a matter of skill, bluff and co-operation with your partner."

"Psychology, Mendelism, Evolution—your education seems to be heavily biological," said Will.

"It *is*," Mr. Menon agreed. "Our primary emphasis isn't on physics and chemistry; it's on the sciences of life."

"Is that a matter of principle?"

"Not entirely. It's also a matter of convenience and economic necessity. We don't have the money for large-scale research in physics and chemistry, and we don't really have any practical need for that kind of research—no heavy industries to be made more competitive, no armaments to be made more diabolical, not the faintest desire to land on the backside of the moon. Only the modest ambition to live as fully human beings in harmony with the rest of life on this island at this latitude on this planet. We can take the results of your researches in physics and chemistry and apply them, if we want to or can afford it, to our own purposes. Meanwhile we'll concentrate on the research which promises to do us the greatest good—in the sciences of life and mind. If the politicians in the newly independent countries had any sense," he added, "they'd do the same. But they want to throw their weight around; they want to have armies, they want to catch up with the motorized television addicts of America and Europe. You people have no choice," he went on. "You're irretrievably committed to applied physics and chemistry, with all their dismal consequences, military, political and social. But the underdeveloped countries aren't committed. They don't *have* to follow your example. They're still free to take the road *we've* taken—the road of applied biology, the road of fertility control and the limited production and selective industrialization which fertility control makes possible, the road that leads towards happiness from the inside out, through health, through awareness, through a change in one's attitude towards the world; not towards the mirage of happiness from the outside in, through toys and pills and nonstop distractions. They could still choose our way; but they don't want to, they want to be exactly like you, God help them. And as they can't possibly do what you've done—at any rate within the time they've set themselves—they're foredoomed to frustration and disappointment, predestined to the misery of social breakdown and anarchy, and then to the misery of enslavement by tyrants. It's a completely foreseeable tragedy, and they're walking into it with their eyes open."

"And we can't do anything about it," the Principal added.

"Can't do anything," said Mr. Menon, "except go on doing what we're doing now and hoping against hope that the example of a nation that has found a way of being happily human may be imitated. There's very little chance of it; but it just might happen."

"Unless Greater Rendang happens first."

"Unless Greater Rendang happens first," Mr. Menon gravely agreed. "Meanwhile we have to get on with our job, which is education. Is there anything more that you'd like to hear about, Mr. Farnaby?"

"Lots more," said Will. "For example, how early do you start your science teaching?"

"We start it at the same time we start multiplication and division. First lessons in ecology."

"Ecology? Isn't that a bit complicated?"

"That's precisely the reason why we begin with it. Never give children a chance of imagining that anything exists in isolation. Make it plain from the very first that all living is relationship. Show them relationships in the woods, in the fields, in the ponds and streams, in the village and the country around it. Rub it in."

"And let me add," said the Principal, "that we always teach the science of relationship in conjunction with the ethics of relationship. Balance, give and take, no excesses—it's the rule in nature and, translated out of fact into morality, it *ought* to be the rule among people. As I said before, children find it very easy to understand an idea when it's presented to them in a parable about animals. We give them an up-to-date version of Aesop's Fables. Not the old anthropomorphic fictions, but true ecological fables with built-in, cosmic morals. And another wonderful parable for children is the story of erosion. We don't have any good examples of erosion here; so we show them photographs of what has happened in

Rendang, in India and China, in Greece and the Levant, in Africa and America—all the places where greedy, stupid people have tried to take without giving, to exploit without love or understanding. Treat Nature well, and Nature will treat you well. Hurt or destroy Nature, and Nature will soon destroy you. In a Dust Bowl, 'Do as you would be done by' is self-evident—much easier for a child to recognize and understand than in an eroded family or village. Psychological wounds don't show—and anyhow children know so little about their elders. And, having no standards of comparison, they tend to take even the worst situation for granted, as though it were part of the nature of things. Whereas the difference between ten acres of meadow and ten acres of gullies and blowing sand is obvious. Sand and gullies are parables. Confronted by them, it's easy for the child to see the need for conservation and then to go on from conservation to morality —easy for him to go on from the Golden Rule in relation to plants and animals and the earth that supports them to the Golden Rule in relation to human beings. And here's another important point. The morality to which a child goes on from the facts of ecology and the parables of erosion is a universal ethic. There are no Chosen People in nature, no Holy Lands, no Unique Historical Revelations. Conservation morality gives nobody an excuse for feeling superior, or claiming special privileges. 'Do as you would be done by' applies to our dealings with all kinds of life in every part of the world. We shall be permitted to live on this planet only for as long as we treat all nature with compassion and intelligence. Elementary ecology leads straight to elementary Buddhism."

"A few weeks ago," said Will after a moment of silence, "I was looking at Thorwald's book about what happened in eastern Germany between January and May of 1945. Have either of you read it?"

They shook their heads.

"Then don't," Will advised. "I was in Dresden five months after the February bombing. Fifty or sixty thousand civilians —mostly refugees running away from the Russians—burned alive in a single night. And all because little Adolf had never learned ecology," he smiled his flayed ferocious smile, "never been taught the first principles of conservation." One made a joke of it because it was too horrible to be talked about seriously.

Mr. Menon rose and picked up his briefcase.

"I must be going." He shook hands with Will. It had been a pleasure, and he hoped that Mr. Farnaby would enjoy his stay in Pala. Meanwhile, if he wanted to know more about Palanese education, he had only to ask Mrs. Narayan. Nobody was better qualified to act as a guide and instructor.

"Would you like to visit some of the classrooms?" Mrs. Narayan asked, when the Under-Secretary had left.

Will rose and followed her out of the room and along a corridor.

"Mathematics," said the Principal as she opened a door. "And this is the Upper Fifth. Under Mrs. Anand."

Will bowed as he was introduced. The white-haired teacher gave a welcoming smile and whispered, "We're deep, as you see, in a problem."

He looked about him. At their desks a score of boys and girls were frowning, in a concentrated, pencil-biting silence, over their notebooks. The bent heads were sleek and dark. Above the white or khaki shorts, above the long gaily colored skirts, the golden bodies glistened in the heat. Boys' bodies that showed the cage of the ribs beneath the skin, girls' bodies, fuller, smoother, with the swell of small breasts, firm, high-set, elegant as the inventions of a rococo sculptor of nymphs. And everyone took them completely for granted. What a comfort, Will reflected, to be in a place where the Fall was an exploded doctrine!

Meanwhile Mrs. Anand was explaining—*sotto voce* so as not to distract the problem solvers from their task—that she always divided her classes into two groups. The group of the visualizers, who thought in geometrical terms, like the ancient Greeks, and the group of the nonvisualizers who preferred algebra and imageless abstractions. Somewhat reluctantly Will withdrew his attention from the beautiful unfallen world of young bodies and resigned himself to taking an intelligent interest in human diversity and the teaching of mathematics.

They took their leave at last. Next door, in a pale-blue classroom decorated with paintings of tropical animals, Bodhisattvas and their bosomy Shaktis, the Lower Fifth were having their biweekly lesson in Elementary Applied Philosophy. Breasts here were smaller, arms thinner and less muscular. These philosophers were only a year away from childhood.

"Symbols are public," the young man at the blackboard was saying as Will and Mrs. Narayan entered the room. He drew a row of little circles, numbered them 1, 2, 3, 4, and *n*. "These are people," he explained. Then from each of the little circles he drew a line that connected it with a square at the left of the board. S he wrote in the center of the square. "S is the system of symbols that the people use when they want to talk to one another. They all speak the same language—English, Palanese, Eskimo, it depends where they happen to live. Words are public; they belong to all the speakers of a given language; they're listed in dictionaries. And now let's look at the things that happen out there." He pointed through the open window. Gaudy against a white cloud, half a dozen parrots came sailing into view, passed behind a tree and were gone. The teacher drew a second square at the opposite side of the board, labeled it E for "events" and connected it by lines to the circles. "What happens out there is public—or at least fairly public," he qualified. "And what happens when somebody speaks or writes words—that's also public. But the things that go on inside these little circles are private. Private." He laid a hand on his chest. "Private." He rubbed his forehead. "Private." He touched his eyelids and the tip of his nose with a brown forefinger. "Now let's make a simple experiment. Say the word 'pinch.'"

"Pinch," said the class in ragged unison. "Pinch . . ."

"P-I-N-C-H—pinch. That's public, that's something you can look up in the dictionary. But now pinch yourselves. Hard! Harder!"

To an accompaniment of giggles, of *aies* and *ows*, the children did as they were told.

"Can anybody feel what the person sitting next to him is feeling?"

There was a chorus of noes.

"So it looks," said the young man, "as though there were—let's see, how many are we?" He ran his eyes over the desks before him. "It looks as though there were twenty-three distinct and separate pains. Twenty-three in this one room. Nearly three thousand million of them in the whole world. Plus the pains of all the animals. And each of these pains is strictly private. There's no way of passing the experience from one center of pain to another center of pain. No communication except indirectly through S." He pointed to the square at the left of the board, then to the circles at the center. "Private pains here in 1, 2, 3, 4, and *n*. News about private pains out here at S, where you can say 'pinch,' which is a public word listed in a dictionary. And notice this: there's only one public word, 'pain,' for three thousand million private experiences, each of which is probably about as different from all the others as my nose is different from your noses and your noses are different from one another. A word only stands for the ways in which things or happenings of the same general kind are like one another. That's why the word is public. And, being public, it can't possibly stand for the ways in which happenings of the same general kind are unlike one another."

There was a silence. Then the teacher looked up and asked a question.

"Does anyone here know about Mahakasyapa?"

Several hands were raised. He pointed his finger at a little girl in a blue skirt and a necklace of shells sitting in the front row.

"You tell us, Amiya."

Breathlessly and with a lisp, Amiya began.

"Mahakathyapa," she said, "wath the only one of the dithipleth that underthtood what the Buddha wath talking about."

"And what was he talking about?"

"He wathn't talking. That'th why they didn't underthtand."

"But Mahakasyapa understood what he was talking about even though he wasn't talking—is that it?"

The little girl nodded. That was it exactly. "They thought he wath going to preatth a thermon," she said, "but he didn't. He jutht picked a flower and held it up for everybody to look at."

"And that was the sermon," shouted a small boy in a yellow loincloth, who had been wriggling in his seat, hardly able to contain his desire to impart what he knew. "But nobody could underthand that kind of a thermon. Nobody but Mahakathyapa."

"So what did Mahakasyapa say when the Buddha held up that flower?"

"Nothing!" the yellow loincloth shouted triumphantly.

"He jutht thmiled," Amiya elaborated. "And that thowed

the Buddha that he underthtood what it wath all about. So he thmiled back, and they jutht that there, thmiling and thmiling."

"Very good," said the teacher. "And now," he turned to the yellow loincloth, "let's hear what you think it was that Mahakasyapa understood."

There was a silence. Then, crestfallen, the child shook his head. "I don't know," he mumbled.

"Does anyone else know?"

There were several conjectures. Perhaps he'd understood that people get bored with sermons—even the Buddha's sermons. Perhaps he liked flowers as much as the Compassionate One did. Perhaps it was a white flower, and that made him think of the Clear Light. Or perhaps it was blue, and that was Shiva's color.

"Good answers," said the teacher. "Especially the first one. Sermons *are* pretty boring—especially for the preacher. But here's a question. If any of your answers had been what Mahakasyapa understood when Buddha held up the flower, why didn't he come out with it in so many words?"

"Perhapth he wathn't a good thpeaker."

"He was an excellent speaker."

"Maybe he had a sore throat."

"If he'd had a sore throat, he wouldn't have smiled so happily."

"*You* tell us," called a shrill voice from the back of the room.

"Yes, *you* tell us," a dozen other voices chimed in.

The teacher shook his head. "If Mahakasyapa and the Compassionate One couldn't put it into words, how can I? Meanwhile let's take another look at these diagrams on the blackboard. Public words, more or less public events, and then people, completely private centers of pain and pleasure. "*Completely* private?" he questioned. "But perhaps that isn't quite true. Perhaps, after all, there is some kind of communication between the circles—not in the way I'm communicating with you now, through words, but directly. And maybe that was what the Buddha was talking about when his wordless flower-sermon was over. 'I have the treasure of the unmistakable teachings,' he said to his disciples, 'the wonderful Mind of Nirvana, the true form without form, beyond all words, the teaching to be given and received outside of all doctrines. This I have now handed to Mahakasyapa.'" Picking up the chalk again, he traced a rough ellipse that enclosed within its boundaries all the other diagrams on the board—the little circles representing human beings, the square that stood for events, and the other square that stood for words and symbols. "All separate," he said, "and yet all one. People, events, words—they're all manifestations of Mind, of Suchness, of the Void. What Buddha was implying and what Mahakasyapa understood was that one can't speak these teachings, one can only *be* them. Which is something you'll all discover when the moment comes for your initiation."

"Time to move on," the Principal whispered. And when the door had closed behind them, and they were standing again in the corridor, "We use this same kind of approach," she said to Will, "in our science teaching, beginning with botany."

"Why with botany?"

"Because it can be related so easily to what was being talked about just now—the Mahakasyapa story."

"Is that your starting point?"

"No, we start prosaically with the textbook. The children are given all the obvious, elementary facts, tidily arranged in the standard pigeonholes. Undiluted botany—that's the first stage. Six or seven weeks of it. After which they get a whole morning of what we call bridge building. Two and a half hours during which we try to make them relate everything they've learned in the previous lessons to art, language, religion, self-knowledge."

"Botany and self-knowledge—how do you build *that* bridge?"

"It's really quite simple," Mrs. Narayan assured him. "Each of the children is given a common flower—a hibiscus, for example, or better still (because the hibiscus has no scent) a gardenia. Scientifically speaking, what is a gardenia? What does it consist of? Petals, stamens, pistil, ovary, and all the rest of it. The children are asked to write a full analytical description of the flower, illustrated by an accurate drawing. When that's done there's a short rest period, at the close of which the Mahakasyapa story is read to them and they're asked to think about it. Was Buddha giving a lesson in botany? Or was he teaching his disciples something else? And, if so, what?"

"What indeed?"

"And of course, as the story makes clear, there's no answer that can be put into words. So we tell the boys and girls to stop thinking and just look. 'But don't look analytically,' we tell them, 'don't look as scientists, even as gardeners. Liberate yourselves from everything you know and look with complete innocence at this infinitely improbably thing before you. Look at it as though you'd never seen anything of the kind before, as though it had no name and belonged to no recognizable class. Look at it alertly but passively, receptively, without labeling or judging or comparing. And as you look at it, inhale its mystery, breathe in the spirit of sense, the smell of the wisdom of the Other Shore.' "

"All this," Will commented, "sounds very like what Dr. Robert was saying at the initiation ceremony."

"Of course it does," said Mrs. Narayan. "Learning to take the Mahakasyapa's-eye view of things is the best preparation for the *moksha*-medicine experience. Every child who comes to initiation comes to it after a long education in the art of being receptive. First the gardenia as a botanical specimen. Then the same gardenia in its uniqueness, the gardenia as the artist sees it, the even more miraculous gardenia seen by the Buddha and Mahakasyapa. And it goes without saying," she added, "that we don't confine ourselves to flowers. Every course the children take is punctuated by periodical bridge-building sessions. Everything from dissected frogs to the spiral nebulae, it all gets looked at receptively as well as conceptually, as a fact of aesthetic or spiritual experience as well as in terms of science or history or economics. Training in receptivity is the complement and antidote to training in analysis and symbol manipulation. Both kinds of training are absolutely indispensable. If you neglect either of them you'll never grow into a fully human being."

There was a silence. "How should one look at other people?" Will asked at last. "Should one take the Freud's-eye view or the Cézanne's-eye view? The Proust's-eye view or the Buddha's-eye view?"

Mrs. Narayan laughed. "Which view are you taking of me?" she asked.

"Primarily, I suppose, the sociologist's-eye view," he answered. "I'm looking at you as the representative of an unfamiliar culture. But I'm also being aware of you receptively. Thinking, if you don't mind my saying so, that you seem to have aged remarkably well. Well aesthetically, well intellectually and psychologically, and well spiritually, whatever that word means—and if I make myself receptive it means something important. Whereas, if I choose to project instead of taking in, I can conceptualize it into pure nonsense." He uttered a mildly hyenalike laugh.

"If one chooses to," said Mrs. Narayan, "one can always substitute a bad ready-made notion for the best insights of receptivity. The question is, why should one want to make that kind of choice? Why shouldn't one choose to listen to both parties and harmonize their views? The analyzing tradition-bound concept maker and the alertly passive insight receiver—neither is infallible; but both together can do a reasonably good job."

"Just how effective is your training in the art of being receptive?" Will now enquired.

"There are degrees of receptivity," she answered. "Very little of it in a science lesson, for example. Science starts with observation; but the observation is always selective. You have to look at the world through a lattice of projected concepts. Then you take the *moksha*-medicine, and suddenly there are hardly any concepts. You don't select and immediately classify what you experience; you just take it in. It's like that poem of Wordsworth's, 'Bring with you a heart that watches and receives.' In these bridge-building sessions I've been describing there's still quite a lot of busy selecting and projecting, but not nearly so much as in the preceding science lessons. The children don't suddenly turn into little Tathagatas; they don't achieve the pure receptivity that comes with the *moksha*-medicine. Far from it. All one can say is that they learn to go easy on names and notions. For a little while they're taking in a lot more than they give out."

"What do you make them do with what they've taken in?"

"We merely ask them," Mrs. Narayan answered, with a smile, "to attempt the impossible. The children are told to translate their experience into words. As a piece of pure, unconceptualized giveness, what *is* this flower, this dissected frog, this planet at the other end of the telescope? What does it mean? What does it make you think, feel, imagine, remember? Try to put it down on paper. You won't succeed, of course; but try all the same. It'll help you to understand the difference between words and events, between knowing about things and being acquainted with them. 'And when you've finished writing,' we tell them, 'look at the flower again and, after you've looked, shut your eyes for a minute or two. Then draw what came to you when your eyes were closed. Draw whatever it may have been—something vague or vivid, something like the flower itself or something entirely different. Draw what you saw or even what you didn't see, draw it and color it with your paints or crayons. Then take another rest and, after that, compare your first drawing with the second; compare the scientific description of the flower with what you wrote about it when you weren't analyzing what you saw, when you behaved as though you didn't know anything about the flower and just permitted the mystery of its existence to come to you, like that, out of the blue. Then compare your drawings and writings with the drawings and writings of the other boys and girls in the class. You'll notice that the analytical descriptions and illustrations are very similar, whereas the drawings and writings of the other kind are very different one from another. How is all this connected with what you have learned in school, at home, in the jungle, in the temple?' Dozens of questions, and all of them insistent. The bridges have to be built in all directions. One starts with botany—or any other subject in the school curriculum—and one finds oneself, at the end of a bridge-building session, thinking about the nature of language, about different kinds of experience, about metaphysics and the conduct of life, about analytical knowledge and the wisdom of the Other Shore."

"How on earth," Will asked, "did you ever manage to teach the teachers who now teach the children to build these bridges?"

"We began teaching teachers a hundred and seven years ago," said Mrs. Narayan. "Classes of young men and women who had been educated in the traditional Palanese way. You know—good manners, good agriculture, good arts and crafts, tempered by folk medicine, old-wives' physics and biology and a belief in the power of magic and the truth of fairy tales. No science, no history, no knowledge of anything going on in the outside world. But these future teachers were pious Buddhists; most of them practiced meditation and all of them had read or listened to quite a lot of Mahayana philosophy. That meant that in the fields of applied metaphysics and psychology they'd been educated far more thoroughly and far more realistically than any group of future teachers in your part of the world. Dr. Andrew was a scientifically trained, antidogmatic humanist, who had discovered the value of pure and applied Mahayana. His friend, the Raja, was a Tantrik Buddhist, who had discovered the value of pure and applied science. Both, consequently, saw very clearly that, to be capable of teaching children to become fully human in a society fit for fully human beings to live in, a teacher would first have to be taught how to make the best of both worlds."

"And how did those early teachers feel about it? Didn't they resist the process?"

Mrs. Narayan shook her head. "They didn't resist, for the good reason that nothing precious had been attacked. Their Buddhism was respected. All they were asked to give up was the old-wives' science and the fairy tales. And in exchange for those they got all kinds of much more interesting facts and much more useful theories. And these exciting things from your Western world of knowledge and power and progress were now to be combined with, and in a sense subordinated to, the theories of Buddhism and the psychological facts of applied metaphysics. There was really nothing in that best-of-both-worlds program to offend the susceptibilities of even the touchiest and most ardent of religious patriots."

"I'm wondering about *our* future teachers," said Will after a silence. "At this late stage, would they be teachable? Could they possibly learn to make the best of both worlds?"

"Why not? They wouldn't have to give up any of the things that are really important to them. The non-Christian could go on thinking about man and the Christian could go on worshiping God. No change, except that God would have to be thought of as immanent and man would have to be thought of as potentially self-transcendent."

"And you think they'd make those changes without any fuss?" Will laughed. "You're an optimist."

"An optimist," said Mrs. Narayan, "for the simple reason that, if one tackles a problem intelligently and realistically, the results are apt to be fairly good. This island justifies a certain optimism. And now let's go and have a look at the dancing class."

They crossed a tree-shaded courtyard and, pushing through a swing door, passed out of silence into the rhythmic beat of a drum and the screech of fifes repeating over and over again a short pentatonic tune that to Will's ears sounded vaguely Scotch.

"Live music or canned?" he asked.

"Japanese tape," Mrs. Narayan answered laconically. She opened a second door that gave access to a large gymnasium where two bearded young men and an amazingly agile little old lady in black satin slacks were teaching some twenty or thirty little boys and girls the steps of a lively dance.

"What's this?" Will asked. "Fun or education?"

"Both," said the Principal. "And it's also applied ethics. Like those breathing exercises we were talking about just now—only more effective because so much more violent."

"So stamp it out," the children were chanting in unison. And they stamped their small sandaled feet with all their might. "So stamp it out!" A final furious stamp and they were off again, jigging and turning, into another movement of the dance.

"This is called the Rakshasi Hornpipe," said Mrs. Narayan.

"Rakshasi?" Will questioned. "What's that?"

"A Rakshasi is a species of demon. Very large, and exceedingly unpleasant. All the ugliest passions personified. The Rakshasi Hornpipe is a device for letting off those dangerous heads of steam raised by anger and frustration."

"So stamp it out!" The music had come round again to the choral refrain. "So stamp it out!"

"Stamp again," cried the little old lady setting a furious example. "Harder! Harder!"

"Which did more," Will speculated, "for morality and rational behavior—the Bacchic orgies or the *Republic*? the *Nicomachean Ethics* or corybantic dancing?"

"The Greeks," said Mrs. Narayan, "were much too sensible to think in terms of either-or. For them, it was always not-only-but-also. Not only Plato and Aristotle, but also the maenads. Without those tension-reducing hornpipes, the moral philosophy would have been impotent, and without the moral philosophy the hornpipers wouldn't have known where to go next. All we've done is to take a leaf out of the old Greek book."

"Very good!" said Will approvingly. Then remembering (as sooner or later, however keen his pleasure and however genuine his enthusiasm, he always did remember) that he was the man who wouldn't take yes for an answer, he suddenly broke into laughter. "Not that it makes any difference in the long run," he said. "Corybantism couldn't stop the Greeks from cutting one another's throats. And when Colonel

Dipa decides to move, what will your Rakshasi Hornpipes do for you? Help you to reconcile yourselves to your fate, perhaps—that's all."

"Yes, that's all," said Mrs. Narayan. "But being reconciled to one's fate—that's already a great achievement."

"You seem to take it all very calmly."

"What would be the point of taking it hysterically? It wouldn't make our political situation any better; it would merely make our personal situation a good deal worse."

"So stamp it out," the children shouted again in unison, and the boards trembled under their pounding feet. "So stamp it out."

"Don't imagine," Mrs. Narayan resumed, "that this is the only kind of dancing we teach. Redirecting the power generated by bad feelings is important. But equally important is directing good feelings and right knowledge into expression. Expressive movements, in this case, expressive gesture. If you had come yesterday, when our visiting master was here, I could have shown you how we teach that kind of dancing. Not today unfortunately. He won't be here again before Tuesday."

"What sort of dancing does he teach?"

Mrs. Narayan tried to describe it. No leaps, no high kicks, no running. The feet always firmly on the ground. Just bendings and sideways motions of the knees and hips. All expression confined to the arms, wrists and hands, to the neck and head, the face and, above all, the eyes. Movement from the shoulders upwards and outwards—movement intrinsically beautiful and at the same time charged with symbolic meaning. Thought taking shape in ritual and stylized gesture. The whole body transformed into a hieroglyph, a succession of hieroglyphs, or attitudes modulating from significance to significance like a poem or a piece of music. Movements of the muscles representing movements of Consciousness, the passage of Suchness into the many, of the many into the immanent and ever-present One.

"It's meditation in action," she concluded. "It's the metaphysics of the Mahayana expressed, not in words, but through symbolic movements and gestures."

They left the gymnasium by a different door from that through which they had entered and turned left along a short corridor.

"What's the next item?" Will asked.

"The Lower Fourth," Mrs. Narayan answered, "and they're working on Elementary Practical Psychology."

She opened a green door.

"Well, now you know," Will heard a familiar voice saying. "Nobody *has* to feel pain. You told yourselves that the pin wouldn't hurt—and it didn't hurt."

They stepped into the room and there, very tall in the midst of a score of plump or skinny little brown bodies, was Susila MacPhail. She smiled at them, pointed to a couple of chairs in a corner of the room, and turned back to the children. "Nobody *has* to feel pain," she repeated. "But never forget: pain always means that something is wrong. You've learned to shut pain off, but don't do it thoughtlessly, don't do it without asking yourselves the question: What's the reason for this pain? And if it's bad, or if there's no obvious reason for it, tell your mother about it, or your teacher, or any grown-up in your Mutual Adoption Club. *Then* shut off the pain. Shut it off knowing that, if anything needs to be done, it will be done. Do you understand? . . . And now," she went on, after all the questions had been asked and answered. "Now let's play some pretending games. Shut your eyes and pretend you're looking at that poor old mynah bird with one leg that comes to school every day to be fed. Can you see him?"

Of course they could see him. The one-legged mynah was evidently an old friend.

"See him just as clearly as you saw him today at lunchtime. And don't stare at him, don't make any effort. Just see what comes to you, and let your eyes shift—from his beak to his tail, from his bright little round eye to his one orange leg."

"I can hear him too," a little girl volunteered. "He's saying '*Karuna, karuna!*' "

"That's not true," another child said indignantly. "He's saying 'Attention!' "

"He's saying both those things," Susila assured them. "And probably a lot of other words besides. But now we're going to do some real pretending. Pretend that there are two one-legged mynah birds. Three one-legged mynah birds. Four one-legged mynah birds. Can you see all four of them?"

They could.

"Four one-legged mynah birds at the four corners of a square, and a fifth one in the middle. And now let's make them change their color. They're white now. Five white mynah birds with yellow heads and one orange leg. And now the heads are blue. Bright blue—and the rest of the bird is pink. Five pink birds with blue heads. And they keep changing. They're purple now. Five purple birds with white heads and each of them has one pale-green leg. Goodness, what's happening! There aren't five of them; there are ten. No, twenty, fifty, a hundred. Hundreds and hundreds. Can you see them?" Some of them could—without the slightest difficulty; and for those who couldn't go the whole hog, Susila proposed more modest goals.

"Just make twelve of them," she said. "Or if twelve is too many, make ten, make eight. That's still an awful lot of mynahs. And now," she went on, when all the children had conjured up all the purple birds that each was capable of creating, "now they're gone." She clapped her hands. "Gone! Every single one of them. There's nothing there. And now you're not going to see mynahs, you're going to see *me*. One me in yellow. Two mes in green. Three mes in blue with pink spots. Four mes in the brightest red you ever saw." She clapped her hands again. "All gone. And this time it's Mrs. Narayan and that funny-looking man with a stiff leg who came in with her. Four of each of them. Standing in a big circle in the gymnasium. And now they're dancing the Rakshasi Hornpipe. 'So stamp it out, so stamp it out.'"

There was a general giggle. The dancing Wills and Principals must have looked richly comical.

Susila snapped her fingers.

"Away with them! Vanish! And now each of you sees three of your mothers and three of your fathers running round the playground. Faster, faster, faster! And suddenly they're not there any more. And then they *are* there. But next moment they aren't. They are there, they aren't. They are, they aren't . . ."

The giggles swelled into squeals of laughter and at the height of the laughter a bell rang. The lesson in Elementary Practical Psychology was over.

"What's the point of it all?" Will asked when the children had run off to play and Mrs. Narayan had returned to her office.

"The point," Susila answered, "is to get people to understand that we're not *completely* at the mercy of our memory and our phantasies. If we're disturbed by what's going on inside our heads, we can do something about it. It's all a question of being shown what to do and then practicing—the way one learns to write or play the flute. What those children you saw here were being taught is a very simple technique—a technique that we'll develop later on into a method of liberation. Not complete liberation, of course. But half a loaf is a great deal better than no bread. This technique won't lead you to the discovery of your Buddha Nature: but it may help you to prepare for that discovery—help you by liberating you from the hauntings of your own painful memories, your remorses, your causeless anxieties about the future."

"'Hauntings,'" Will agreed, "is the word."

"But one doesn't *have* to be haunted. Some of the ghosts can be laid quite easily. Whenever one of them appears, just give it the imagination treatment. Deal with it as we dealt with those mynahs, as we dealt with you and Mrs. Narayan. Change its clothes, give it another nose, multiply it, tell it to go away, call it back again and make it do something ridiculous. Then abolish it. Just think what you could have done about your father, if someone had taught you a few of these simple little tricks when you were a child! You thought of him as a terrifying ogre. But that wasn't necessary. In your fancy you could have turned the ogre into a grotesque. Into a whole chorus of grotesques. Twenty of them doing a tap dance and singing, 'I dreamt I dwelt in marble halls.' A short course in Elementary Practical Psychology, and your whole life might have been different."

How would he have dealt with Molly's death, Will wondered as they walked out towards the parked jeep. What rites of imaginative exorcism could he have practiced on that white, musk-scented succubus who was the incarnation of his frantic and abhorred desires?

But here was the jeep. Will handed Susila the keys and laboriously hoisted himself into his seat. Very noisily, as though it were under some neurotic compulsion to overcompensate for its diminutive stature, a small and aged car approached from the direction of the village, turned into the driveway and, still clattering and shuddering, came to a halt beside the jeep.

They turned. There, leaning out of the window of the royal Baby Austin, was Murugan, and beyond him, vast in white muslin and billowy like a cumulus cloud, sat the Rani. Will bowed in her direction and evoked the most gracious of smiles, which was switched off as soon as she turned to Susila, whose greeting was acknowledged only with the most distant of nods.

"Going for a drive?" Will asked politely.

"Only as far as Shivapuram," said the Rani.

"If this wretched little crate will hold together that long," Murugan added bitterly. He turned the ignition key. The motor gave a last obscene hiccup and died.

"There are some people we have to see," the Rani went on. "Or rather One Person," she added in a tone charged with conspiratorial significance. She smiled at Will and very nearly winked.

Pretending not to understand that she was talking about Bahu, Will uttered a noncommittal "Quite," and commiserated with her on all the work and worry that the preparations for next week's coming-of-age party must entail.

Murugan interrupted him. "What are you doing out here?" he asked.

"I've spent the afternoon taking an intelligent interest in Palanese education."

"Palanese education," the Rani echoed. And again, sorrowfully, "Palanese" (pause) "Education." She shook her head.

"Personally," said Will, "I liked everything I saw and heard of it—from Mr. Menon and the Principal to Elementary Practical Psychology, as taught," he added, trying to bring Susila into the conversation, "by Mrs. MacPhail here."

Still studiedly ignoring Susila, the Rani pointed a thick accusing finger at the scarecrows in the field below.

"Have you seen *those*, Mr. Farnaby?"

He had indeed. "And where but in Pala," he asked, "can one find scarecrows which are simultaneously beautiful, efficient, and metaphysically significant?"

"And which," said the Rani in a voice that was vibrant with a kind of sepulchral indignation, "not only scare the birds away from the rice; they also scare little children away from the very idea of God and His Avatars." She raised her hand. "Listen!"

Tom Krishna and Mary Sarojini had been joined by five or six small companions and were making a game of tugging at the strings that worked the supernatural marionettes. From the group came a sound of shrill voices piping in unison. At their second repetition, Will made out the words of the chantey.

> Pully, hauly, tug with a will;
> The gods wiggle-waggle, but the sky stands still.

"Bravo!" he said, and laughed.

"I'm afraid I can't be amused," said the Rani severely. "It isn't funny. It's Tragic, *Tragic.*"

Will stuck to his guns. "I understand," he said, "that these charming scarecrows were an invention of Murugan's grandfather."

"Murugan's grandfather," said the Rani, "was a very remarkable man. Remarkably intelligent, but no less remarkably perverse. Great gifts—but, alas, how maleficently used! And what made it all so much worse, he was full of False Spirituality."

"False Spirituality?" Will eyed the enormous specimen of True Spirituality and, through the reek of hot petroleum products, inhaled the incenselike, otherworldly smell of sandalwood. "False Spirituality?" And suddenly he found himself wondering—wondering and then, with a shudder, imagining—what the Rani would look like if suddenly divested of her mystic's uniform and exposed, exuberantly and steatopygously naked, to the light. And now multiply her into a trinity of undressed obesities, into two trinities, ten trinities. Applied Practicial Psychology—with a vengeance!

"Yes, False Spirituality," the Rani was repeating. "Talking about Liberation; but always, because of his obstinate refusal to follow the True Path, always working for greater Bondage. Acting the part of humility. But in his heart, he was so full of pride, Mr. Farnaby, that he refused to recognize any Spiritual Authority Higher than his own. The Masters, the Avatare, the Great Tradition—they meant nothing to him. Nothing at all. Hence those dreadful scarecrows. Hence that blasphemous rhyme that the children have been taught to sing. When I think of those Poor Innocent Little Ones being deliberately perverted, I find it hard to contain myself, Mr. Farnaby, I find it . . ."

"Listen, Mother," said Murugan, who had been glancing impatiently and ever more openly at his wrist watch, "if we want to be back by dinnertime we'd better get going." His tone was rudely authoritative. Being at the wheel of a car—even of this senile Baby Austin—made him feel, it was evident, considerably larger than life. Without waiting for the Rani's answer he started the motor, shifted into low and, with a wave of the hand, drove off.

"Good riddance," said Susila.

"Don't you love your dear Queen?"

"She makes my blood boil."

"So stamp it out," Will chanted teasingly.

"You're quite right," she agreed, with a laugh. "But unfortunately this was an occasion when it just wasn't feasible to do a Rakshasi Hornpipe." Her face brightened with a sudden flash of mischief, and without warning she punched him, surprisingly hard, in the ribs. "There!" she said. "Now I feel much better."

xiv

SHE STARTED THE MOTOR AND THEY DROVE OFF—DOWN TO the bypass, up again to the high road beyond the other end of the village, and on into the compound of the Experimental Station. Susila pulled up at a small thatched bungalow like all the others. They climbed the six steps that led up to the veranda and entered a whitewashed living room.

To the left was a wide window with a hammock slung between the two wooden pillars at either side of the projecting bay. "For you," she said, pointing to the hammock. "You can put your leg up." And when Will had lowered himself into the net, "What shall we talk about?" she asked as she pulled up a wicker chair and sat down beside him.

"What about the good, the true and the beautiful? Or maybe," he grinned, "the ugly, the bad and the even truer."

"I'd thought," she said, ignoring his attempt at a witticism, "that we might go on where we left off last time—go on talking about *you*."

"That was precisely what I was suggesting—the ugly, the bad and the truer than all official truth."

"Is this just an exhibition of your conversational style?" she asked. "Or do you really want to talk about yourself?"

"Really," he assured her, "desperately. Just as desperately as I *don't* want to talk about myself. Hence, as you may have noticed, my unflagging interest in art, science, philosophy, politics, literature—any damned thing rather than the only thing that ultimately has any importance."

There was a long silence. Then in a tone of casual reminiscence, Susila began to talk about Wells Cathedral, about the calling of the jackdaws, about the white swans floating between the reflections of the floating clouds. In a few minutes he too was floating.

"I was very happy all the time I was at Wells," she said. "Wonderfully happy. And so were you, weren't you?"

Will made no answer. He was remembering those days in the green valley, years ago, before he and Molly were married, before they were lovers. What peace! What a solid, living maggotless world of springing grass and flowers! And between them had flowed the kind of natural, undistorted feeling that he hadn't experienced since those far-off days when Aunt Mary was alive. The only person he had ever really loved—and here, in Molly, was her successor. What blessedness! Love transposed into another key—but the melody, the rich and subtle harmonies were the same. And then, on the fourth night of their stay, Molly had knocked on the wall that separated their rooms, and he had found her door ajar, had groped his way in darkness to the bed where, conscientiously naked, the Sister of Mercy was doing her best to play the part of the Wife of Love. Doing her best and (how disastrously!) failing.

Suddenly, as happened almost every afternoon, there was a loud rushing of wind and, muffled by distance, a hollow roaring of rain on thick foliage—a roaring that grew louder and louder as the shower approached. A few seconds passed, and then the raindrops were hammering insistently on the windowpanes. Hammering as they had hammered on the windows of his study that day of their last interview. "Do you really mean it, Will?"

The pain and shame of it made him want to cry aloud. He bit his lip.

"What are you thinking of?" Susila asked.

It wasn't a matter of thinking. He was actually seeing her, actually hearing her voice. "Do you really mean it, Will?" And through the sound of the rain he heard himself answering, "I really mean it."

On the windowpane—was it here? or was it there, was it then?—the roar had diminished, as the gust spent itself, to a pattering whisper.

"What are you thinking of?" Susila insisted.

"I'm thinking of what I did to Molly."

"What was it that you did to Molly?"

He didn't want to answer; but Susila was inexorable.

"Tell me what it was that you did."

Another violent gust made the windows rattle. It was raining harder now—raining, it seemed to Will Farnaby, on purpose, raining in such a way that he would *have* to go on remembering what he didn't want to remember, would be compelled to say out loud the shameful things he must at all costs keep to himself.

"Tell me."

Reluctantly and in spite of himself, he told her.

"'Do you really mean it, Will?'" And because of Babs—*Babs*, God help him! *Babs*, believe it or not!—he really did mean it, and she had walked out into the rain.

"The next time I saw her was in the hospital."

"Was it still raining?" Susila asked.

"Still raining."

"As hard as it's raining now?"

"Very nearly." And what Will heard was no longer this afternoon shower in the tropics but the steady drumming on the window of the little room where Molly lay dying.

"It's me," he was saying through the sound of the rain, "it's Will." Nothing happened; and then suddenly he felt the almost imperceptible movement of Molly's hand within his own. The voluntary pressure and then, after a few seconds, the involuntary release, the total limpness.

"Tell me again, Will."

He shook his head. It was too painful, too humiliating.

"Tell me again," she insisted. "It's the only way."

Making an enormous effort, he started to tell the odious story yet once more. Did he really mean it? Yes, he really meant it—meant to hurt, meant perhaps (did one ever know what one really intended?) to kill. *All for Babs, or the World Well Lost.* Not *his* world, of course—Molly's world and, at the center of that world, the life that had created it. Snuffed out for the sake of that delicious smell in the darkness, of those muscular reflexes, that enormity of enjoyment, those consummate and intoxicatingly shameless skills.

"Good-bye, Will." And the door had closed behind her with a faint, dry click.

He wanted to call her back. But Babs's lover remembered the skills, the reflexes, and within its aura of musk, a body agonizing in the extremity of pleasure. Remembered these things and, standing at the window, watched the car move away through the rain, watched and was filled, as it turned the corner, with a shameful exultation. Free at last! Even freer, as he discovered three hours later in the hospital, than he had supposed. For now he was feeling the last faint pressure of her fingers; feeling the final message of her love. And then the message was interrupted. The hand went limp and now, suddenly, appallingly, there was no sound of breathing. "Dead," he whispered, and felt himself choking. "Dead."

"Suppose it hadn't been your fault," said Susila, breaking a long silence. "Suppose that she'd suddenly died without your having had anything to do with it. Wouldn't that have been almost as bad?"

"What do you mean?" he asked.

"I mean, it's more than just feeling guilty about Molly's death. It's death itself, death as such, that you find so terrible." She was thinking of Dugald now. "So senselessly evil."

"Senselessly evil," he repeated. "Yes, perhaps that's why I had to be a professional execution watcher. Just because it was all so senseless, so utterly bestial. Following the smell of death from one end of the earth to the other. Like a vulture. Nice comfortable people just don't have any idea what the world is like. Not exceptionally, as it was during the war, but all the time. All the time." And as he spoke he was seeing, in a vision as brief and comprehensive and intensely circumstantial as a drowning man's, all the hateful scenes he had witnessed in the course of those well-paid pilgrimages to every hellhole and abattoir revolting enough to qualify as News. Negroes in South Africa, the man in the San Quentin gas chamber, mangled bodies in an Algerian farmhouse, and everywhere mobs, everywhere policemen and paratroopers, everywhere those dark-skinned children, stick-legged, potbellied, with flies on their raw eyelids, everywhere the nauseating smells of hunger and disease, the awful stench of death. And then suddenly, through the stench of death, mingled and impregnated with the stench of death, he was breathing the musky essence of Babs. Breathing the essence of Babs and remembering his little joke about the chemistry of purgatory and paradise. Purgatory is tetraethylene diamine and sulfureted hydrogen; paradise, very definitely, is symtrinitropsibutyl toluene, with an assortment of organic impurities—ha—ha—ha! (Oh, the delights of social life!) And then, quite suddenly, the odors of love and death gave place to a rank animal smell—a smell of dog.

The wind swelled up again into violence and the driving raindrops hammered and splashed against the panes.

"Are you still thinking of Molly?" Susila asked.

"I was thinking of something I'd completely forgotten," he

answered. "I can't have been more than four years old when it happened, and now it's all come back to me. Poor Tiger."

"Who was poor Tiger?" she questioned.

Tiger, his beautiful red setter. Tiger, the only source of light in that dismal house where he had spent his childhood. Tiger, dear dear Tiger. In the midst of all that fear and misery, between the two poles of his father's sneering hate of everything and everybody and his mother's self-conscious self-sacrifice, what effortless good will, what spontaneous friendliness, what a bounding, barking irrepressible joy! His mother used to take him on her knee and tell him about God and Jesus. But there was more God in Tiger than in all her Bible stories. Tiger, so far as he was concerned, was the Incarnation. And then one day the Incarnation came down with distemper.

"What happened then?" Susila asked.

"His basket's in the kitchen, and I'm there, kneeling beside it. And I'm stroking him—but his fur feels quite different from what it felt like before he was sick. Kind of sticky. And there's a bad smell. If I didn't love him so much, I'd run away, I couldn't bear to be near him. But I do love him, I love him more than anything or anybody. And while I stroke him, I keep telling him that he'll soon be well again. Very soon—tomorrow morning. And then all of a sudden he starts to shudder, and I try to stop the shuddering by holding his head between my hands. But it doesn't do any good. The trembling turns into a horrible convulsion. It makes me feel sick to look at it, and I'm frightened. I'm dreadfully frightened. Then the shuddering and the twitching die down and in a little while he's absolutely still. And when I lift his head and then let go, the head falls back—thump, like a piece of meat with a bone inside."

Will's voice broke, the tears were streaming down his cheeks, he was shaken by the sobs of a four-year-old grieving for his dog and confronted by the awful, inexplicable fact of death. With the mental equivalent of a click and a little jerk, his consciousness seemed to change gear. He was an adult again, and he had ceased to float.

"I'm sorry." He wiped his eyes and blew his nose. "Well, that was my first introduction to the Essential Horror. Tiger was my friend, Tiger was my only consolation. That was something, obviously, that the Essential Horror couldn't tolerate. And it was the same with my Aunt Mary. The only person I ever really loved and admired and completely trusted; and, Christ, what the Essential Horror did to her!"

"Tell me," said Susila.

Will hesitated, then, shrugging his shoulders, "Why not?" he said. "Mary Frances Farnaby, my father's younger sister. Married at eighteen, just a year before the outbreak of the First World War, to a professional soldier. Frank and Mary, Mary and Frank—what harmony, what happiness!" He laughed. "Even outside of Pala there one can find occasional islands of decency. Tiny little atolls, or even, every now and then, a full-blown Tahiti—but always totally surrounded by the Essential Horror. Two young people on their private Pala. Then, one fine morning, it was August 4, 1914, Frank went overseas with the Expeditionary Force, and on Christmas Eve Mary gave birth to a deformed child that survived long enough for her to see for herself what the E.H. can do when it really tries. Only God can make a microcephalous idiot. Three months later, needless to say, Frank was hit by a piece of shrapnel and died in due course of gangrene. . . . All that," Will went on after a little silence, "was before my time. When I first knew her, in the twenties, Aunt Mary was devoting herself to the aged. Old people in institutions, old people cooped up in their own homes, old people living on and on as a burden to their children and grandchildren. Struldbrugs, Tithonuses. And the more hopeless the decrepitude, the more crotchety and querulous the character, the better. As a child, how I hated Aunt Mary's old people! They smelt bad, they were frighteningly ugly, they were always boring and generally cross. But Aunt Mary really loved them—loved them through thick and thin, loved them in spite of everything. My mother used to talk a lot about Christian charity; but somehow one never believed what she said, just as one never felt any love in all the self-sacrificing things she was always forcing herself to do—no love, only duty. Whereas with Aunt Mary one was never in the slightest doubt. Her love was like a kind of physical radiation, something one could almost sense as heat or light. When she took me to stay with her in the country and later, when she came to town and I used to go and see her almost every day, it was like escaping from a refrigerator into the sunshine. I could feel myself coming alive in that light of hers, that radiating warmth. Then the Essential Horror got busy again. At the beginning she made a joke of it. 'Now I'm an Amazon,' she said after the first operation."

"Why an Amazon?" Susila asked.

"The Amazons had their right breast amputated. They were warriors and the breast got in the way when they were shooting with the long bow. 'Now I'm an Amazon,'" he repeated, and with his mind's eye could see the smile on that strong aquiline face, could hear, with his mind's ear, the tone of amusement in that clear, ringing voice. "But a few months later the other breast had to be cut off. After that there were the X rays, the radiation sickness and then, little by little, the degradation." Will's face took on its look of flayed ferocity. "If it weren't so unspeakably hideous, it would be really funny. What a masterpiece of irony! Here was a soul that radiated goodness and love and heroic charity. Then, for no known reason, something went wrong. Instead of flouting it, a little piece of her body started to obey the second law of thermodynamics. And as the body broke down, the soul began to lose its virtue, its very identity. The heroism went out of her, the love and the goodness evaporated. For the last months of her life she was no more the Aunt Mary I had loved and admired; she was somebody else, somebody (and this was the ironist's final and most exquisite touch) almost indistinguishable from the worst and weakest of the old people she had once befriended and been a tower of strength to. She had to be humiliated and degraded; and when the degradation was complete, she was slowly, and with a great deal of pain, put to death in solitude. In solitude," he insisted. "For of course nobody can help, nobody can ever be present. People may stand by while you're suffering and dying; but they're standing by in another world. In *your* world you're absolutely alone. Alone in your suffering and your dying, just as you're alone in love, alone even in the most completely shared pleasure."

The essences of Babs and of Tiger, and when the cancer had gnawed a hole in the liver and her wasted body was impregnated with that strange, aromatic smell of contaminated blood, the essence of Aunt Mary dying. And in the midst of those essences, sickeningly or intoxicatedly aware of them, was an isolated consciousness, a child's, a boy's, a man's, forever isolated, irremediably alone. "And on top of everything else," he went on, "this woman was only forty-two. She didn't want to die. She refused to accept what was being done to her. The Essential Horror had to drag her down by main force. I was there; I saw it happening."

"And that's why you're the man who won't take yes for an answer?"

"How can anyone take yes for an answer?" he countered. "Yes is just pretending, just positive thinking. The facts, the basic and ultimate facts, are always no. Spirit? No! Love? No! Sense, meaning, achievement? No!"

Tiger exuberantly alive and joyful and full of God. And then Tiger transformed by the Essential Horror into a packet of garbage, which the vet had to come and be paid for removing. And after Tiger, Aunt Mary. Maimed and tortured, dragged in the mud, degraded and finally, like Tiger, transformed into a packet of garbage—only this time it was the undertaker who had removed it, and a clergyman was hired to make believe that it was all, in some sublime and Pickwickian sense, perfectly O.K. Twenty years later another clergyman had been hired to repeat the same strange rigmarole over Molly's coffin. "*If after the manner of men I have fought with beasts at Ephesus, what advantageth it me, if the dead rise not? let us eat and drink; for tomorrow we die.*"

Will uttered another of his hyena laughs. "What impeccable logic, what sensibility, what ethical refinement!"

"But you're the man who won't take yes for an answer. So why raise any objections?"

"I oughtn't to," he agreed. "But one remains an aesthete, one likes to have the no said with style. 'Let us eat and drink, for tomorrow we die.' " He screwed up his face in an expression of disgust.

"And yet," said Susila, "in a certain sense the advice is excellent. Eating, drinking, dying—three primary manifestations of the universal and impersonal life. Animals live that impersonal and universal life without knowing its nature. Ordinary people know its nature but don't live it and, if ever they think seriously about it, refuse to accept it. An enlightened person knows it, lives it, and accepts it completely. He eats, he drinks, and in due course he dies—but he eats with a difference, drinks with a difference, dies with a difference."

"And rises again from the dead?" he asked sarcastically.

"That's one of the questions the Buddha always refused to discuss. Believing in eternal life never helped anybody to live in eternity. Nor, of course, did *dis*believing. So stop all your pro-ing and con-ing (that's the Buddha's advice) and get on with the job."

"Which job?"

"Everybody's job—enlightenment. Which means, here and now, the preliminary job of practicing all the yogas of increased awareness."

"But I don't want to be more aware," said Will. "I want to be less aware. Less aware of horrors like Aunt Mary's death and the slums of Rendang-Lobo. Less aware of hideous sights and loathsome smells—even of some delicious smells," he added as he caught, through the remembered essences of dog and cancer of the liver, a civetlike whiff of the pink alcove. "Less aware of my fat income and other people's subhuman poverty. Less aware of my own excellent health in an ocean of malaria and hookworm, of my own safely sterilized sex fun in the ocean of starving babies. '*Forgive them, for they know not what they do.*' What a blessed state of affairs! But unfortunately I do know what I'm doing. Only too well. And here you go, asking me to be even more aware than I am already."

"I'm not asking anything," she said. "I'm merely passing on the advice of a succession of shrewd old birds, beginning with Gautama and ending with the Old Raja. Start by being fully aware of what you think you are. It'll help you to become aware of what you are in fact."

He shrugged his shoulders. "One thinks one's something unique and wonderful at the center of the universe. But in fact one's merely a slight delay in the ongoing march of entropy."

"And that precisely is the first half of the Buddha's message. Transience, no permanent soul, inevitable sorrow. But he didn't stop there, the message had a second half. This temporary slowdown of entropy is also pure undiluted Suchness. This absence of a permanent soul is also the Buddha Nature."

"Absence of a soul—that's easy to cope with. But what about the presence of cancer, the presence of slow degradation? What about hunger and overbreeding and Colonel Dipa? Are *they* pure Suchness?"

"Of course. But, needless to say, it's desperately difficult for the people who are deeply involved in any of those evils to discover their Buddha Nature. Public health and social reform are the indispensable preconditions of any kind of general enlightenment."

"But in spite of public health and social reform, people still die. Even in Pala," he added ironically.

"Which is why the corollary of welfare has to be dhyana —all the yogas of living and dying, so that you can be aware, even in the final agony, of who in fact, and in spite of everything, you really are."

There was a sound of footsteps on the planking of the veranda, and a childish voice called, "Mother!"

"Here I am, darling," Susila called back.

The front door was flung open and Mary Sarojini came hurrying into the room.

"Mother," she said breathlessly, "they want you to come at once. It's Granny Lakshmi. She's . . ." Catching sight for the first time of the figure in the hammock, she started and broke off. "Oh! I didn't know *you* were here."

Will waved his hand to her without speaking. She gave him a perfunctory smile, then turned back to her mother. "Granny Lakshmi suddenly got much worse," she said, "and Grandpa Robert is still up at the High Altitude Station, and they can't get through to him on the telephone."

"Did you run all the way?"

"Except where it's really *too* steep."

Susila put her arm round the child and kissed her, then very brisk and businesslike, rose to her feet.

"It's Dugald's mother," she said.

"Is she . . . ?" He glanced at Mary Sarojini, then back at Susila. Was death taboo? Could one mention it before children?

"You mean, is she dying?"

He nodded.

"We've been expecting it, of course," Susila went on. "But not today. Today she seemed a little better." She shook her head. "Well, I have to go and stand by—even if it *is* another world. And actually," she added, "it isn't quite so completely other as you think. I'm sorry we had to leave our business unfinished; but there'll be other opportunities. Meanwhile what do you want to do? You can stay here. Or I'll drop you at Dr. Robert's. Or you can come with me and Mary Sarojini."

"As a professional execution watcher?"

"*Not* as a professional execution watcher," she answered emphatically. "As a human being, as someone who needs to know how to live and then how to die. Needs it as urgently as we all do."

"Needs it," he said, "a lot more urgently than most. But shan't I be in the way?"

"If you can get out of your own way, you won't be in anyone else's."

She took his hand and helped him out of the hammock. Two minutes later they were driving past the lotus pool and the huge Buddha meditating under the cobra's hood, past the white bull, out through the main gate of the compound. The rain was over, in a green sky enormous clouds glowed like archangels. Low in the west the sun was shining with a brightness that seemed almost supernatural.

> *Soles occidere et redire possunt;*
> *nobis cum semel occidit brevis lux,*
> *nox est perpetua una dormienda.*
> *Da mi basia mille.*

Sunsets and death; death and therefore kisses; kisses and consequently birth and then death for yet another generation of sunset watchers.

"What do you say to people who are dying?" he asked. "Do you tell *them* not to bother their heads about immortality and get on with the job?"

"If you like to put it that way—yes, that's precisely what we do. Going on being aware—it's the whole art of dying."

"And you teach the art?"

"I'd put it another way. We help them to go on practicing the art of living even while they're dying. Knowing who in fact one is, being conscious of the universal and impersonal life that lives itself through each of us—that's the art of living, and that's what one can help the dying to go on practicing. To the very end. Maybe beyond the end."

"Beyond?" he questioned. "But you said that was something that the dying aren't supposed to think about."

"They're not being asked to think *about* it. They're being helped, if there is such a thing, to experience it. If there is such a thing," she repeated, "if the universal life goes on, when the separate me-life is over."

"Do you personally think it does go on?"

Susila smiled. "What I personally think is beside the

point. All that matters is what I may impersonally experience —while I'm living, when I'm dying, maybe when I'm dead."

She swung the car into a parking space and turned off the engine. On foot they entered the village. Work was over for the day and the main street was so densely thronged that it was hard for them to pass.

"I'm going ahead by myself," Susila announced. Then to Mary Sarojini, "Be at the hospital in about an hour," she said. "Not before." She turned and, threading her way between the slowly promenading groups, was soon lost to view.

"You're in charge now," said Will, smiling down at the child by his side.

Mary Sarojini nodded gravely and took his hand. "Let's go and see what's happening in the square," she said.

"How old is your Granny Lakshmi?" Will asked as they started to make their way along the crowded street.

"I don't really know," Mary Sarojini answered. "She *looks* terribly old. But maybe that's because she's got cancer."

"Do you know what cancer is?" he asked.

Mary Sarojini knew perfectly well. "It's what happens when part of you forgets all about the rest of you and carries on the way people do when they're crazy—just goes on blowing itself up and blowing itself up as if there was nobody else in the whole world. Sometimes you can do something about it. But generally it just goes on blowing itself up until the person dies."

"And that's what has happened, I gather, to your Granny Lakshmi."

"And now she needs someone to help her die."

"Does your mother often help people die?"

The child nodded. "She's awfully good at it."

"Have *you* ever seen anyone die?"

"Of course," Mary Sarojini answered, evidently surprised that such a question should be asked. "Let me see." She made a mental calculation. "I've seen five people die. Six, if you count babies."

"I hadn't seen anyone die when I was your age."

"You hadn't?"

"Only a dog."

"Dogs die easier than people. They don't talk about it beforehand."

"How do you feel about . . . about people dying?"

"Well, it isn't nearly so bad as having babies. That's awful. Or at least it *looks* awful. But then you remind yourself that it doesn't hurt at all. They've turned off the pain."

"Believe it or not," said Will, "I've never seen a baby being born."

"Never?" Mary Sarojini was astonished. "Not even when you were at school?"

Will had a vision of his headmaster in full canonicals conducting three hundred black-coated boys on a tour of the Lying-In Hospital. "Not even at school," he said aloud.

"You never saw anybody dying, and you never saw anybody having a baby. How did you get to know things?"

"In the school *I* went to," he said, "we never got to know things, we only got to know words."

The child looked up at him, shook her head and, lifting a small brown hand, significantly tapped her forehead. "Crazy," she said. "Or were your teachers just stupid?"

Will laughed. "They were high-minded educators dedicated to *mens sana in corpore sano* and the maintenance of our sublime Western Tradition. But meanwhile tell me something. Weren't you ever frightened?"

"By people having babies?"

"No, by people dying. Didn't that scare you?"

"Well, yes—it did," she said after a moment of silence.

"So what did you do about it?"

"I did what they teach you to do—tried to find out which of me was frightened and why she was frightened."

"And which of you was it?"

"This one." Mary Sarojini pointed a forefinger into her open mouth. "The one that does all the talking. Little Miss Gibber—that's what Vijaya calls her. She's always talking about all the nasty things I remember, all the huge, wonderful, impossible things I imagine I can do. She's the one that gets frightened."

"Why is she so frightened?"

"I suppose it's because she gets talking about all the awful things that might happen to her. Talking out loud or talking to herself. But there's another one who doesn't get frightened."

"Which one is that?"

"The one that doesn't talk—just looks and listens and feels what's going on inside. And sometimes," Mary Sarojini added, "sometimes she suddenly sees how beautiful everything is.

No, that's wrong. *She* sees it all the time, but *I* don't—not unless she makes me notice it. That's when it suddenly happens. Beautiful, beautiful, beautiful! Even dog's messes." She pointed at a formidable specimen almost at their feet.

From the narrow street they had emerged into the market place. The last of the sunlight still touched the sculptured spire of the temple, the little pink gazebos on the roof of the town hall; but here in the square there was premonition of twilight and under the great banyan tree it was already night. On the stalls between its pillars and hanging ropes the market women had turned on their lights. In the leafy darkness there were islands of form and color, and from hardly visible nonentity brown-skinned figures stepped for a moment into brilliant existence, then back again into nothingness. The spaces between the tall buildings echoed with a confusion of English and Palanese, of talk and laughter, of street cries and whistled tunes, of dogs barking, parrots screaming. Perched on one of the pink gazebos, a pair of mynah birds called indefatigably for attention and compassion. From an open-air kitchen at the center of the square rose the appetizing smell of food on the fire. Onions, peppers, turmeric, fish frying, cakes baking, rice on the boil—and through these good gross odors, like a reminder from the Other Shore, drifted the perfume, thin and sweet and ethereally pure, of the many-colored garlands on sale beside the fountain.

Twilight deepened and suddenly, from high overhead, the arc lamps were turned on. Bright and burnished against the rosy copper of oiled skin, the women's necklaces and rings and bracelets came alive with glittering reflections. Seen in the downward-striking light, every contour became more dramatic, every form seemed to be more substantial, more solidly there. In eye sockets, under nose and chin the shadows deepened. Modeled by light and darkness young breasts grew fuller and the faces of the old were more emphatically lined and hollowed.

Hand in hand they made their way through the crowd.

A middle-aged woman greeted Mary Sarojini, then turned to Will. "Are you that man from the Outside?" she asked.

"Almost infinitely from the outside," he assured her.

She looked at him for a moment in silence, then smiled encouragingly and patted his cheek.

"We're all very sorry for you," she said.

They moved on, and now they were standing on the fringes of a group assembled at the foot of the temple steps to listen to a young man who was playing a long-necked, lute-like instrument and singing in Palanese. Rapid declamation alternated with long-drawn, almost birdlike melismata on a single vowel sound, and then a cheerful and strongly accented tune that ended in a shout. A roar of laugher went up from the crowd. A few more bars, another line or two of recitative, and the singer struck his final chord. There was applause and more laughter and a chorus of incomprehensible commentary.

"What's it all about?" Will asked.

"It's about girls and boys sleeping together," Mary Sarojini answered.

"Oh—I see." He felt a pang of guilty embarrassment; but, looking down into the child's untroubled face, he could see that his concern was uncalled for. It was evident that boys and girls sleeping together were as completely to be taken for granted as going to school or eating three meals a day—or dying.

"And the part that made them laugh," Mary Sarojini went on, "was where he said the Future Buddha won't have to leave home and sit under the Bodhi Tree. He'll have his Enlightenment while he's in bed with the princess."

"Do you think that's a good idea?" Will asked.

She nodded emphatically. "It would mean that the princess would be enlightened too."

"You're perfectly right," said Will. "Being a man, I hadn't thought of the princess."

The lute player plucked a queer unfamiliar progression of chords, followed them with a ripple of arpeggios and began to sing, this time in English.

Everyone talks of sex; take none of them seriously—
  Not whore nor hermit, neither Paul nor Freud.
Love—and your lips, her breasts will change mysteriously
  Into Themselves, the Suchness and the Void.

The door of the temple swung open. A smell of incense mingled with the ambient onions and fried fish. An old woman emerged and very cautiously lowered her unsteady weight from stair to stair.

"Who were Paul and Freud?" Mary Sarojini asked as they moved away.

Will began with a brief account of Original Sin and the Scheme of Redemption. The child heard him out with concentrated attention.

"No wonder the song says, Don't take them seriously," she concluded.

"After which," said Will, "we come to Dr. Freud and the Oedipus Complex."

"Oedipus?" Mary Sarojini repeated. "But that's the name of a marionette show. I saw it last week, and they're giving it again tonight. Would you like to see it? It's nice."

"Nice?" he repeated. "Nice? Even when the old lady turns out to be his mother and hangs herself? Even when Oedipus puts out his eyes?"

"But he doesn't put out his eyes," said Mary Sarojini.

"He does where *I* hail from."

"Not here. He only says he's going to put out his eyes, and she only tries to hang herself. They're talked out of it."

"Who by?"

"The boy and girl from Pala."

"How do *they* get into the act?" Will asked.

"I don't know. They're just there. '*Oedipus in Pala*'—that's what the play is called. So why shouldn't they be there?"

"And you say they talk Jocasta out of suicide and Oedipus out of blinding himself?"

"Just in the nick of time. She's slipped the rope round her neck and he's got hold of two huge pins. But the boy and girl from Pala tell them not to be silly. After all, it was an accident. He didn't know that the old man was his father. And anyhow the old man began it, hit him over the head, and that made Oedipus lose his temper—and nobody had ever taught him to dance the Rakshasi Hornpipe. And when they made him a king, he had to marry the old queen. She was really his mother; but neither of them knew it. And of course all they had to do when they did find out was just to stop being married. That stuff about marrying his mother being the reason why everybody had to die of a virus—all that was just nonsense, just made up by a lot of poor stupid people who didn't know any better."

"Dr. Freud thought that all little boys really want to marry their mothers and kill their fathers. And the other way round for little girls—*they* want to marry their fathers."

"Which fathers and mothers?" Mary Sarojini asked. "We have such a lot of them."

"You mean, in your Mutual Adoption Club?"

"There's twenty-two of them in our MAC."

"Safety in numbers!"

"But of course poor old Oedipus never had an MAC. And besides they'd taught him all that horrible stuff about God getting furious with people every time they made a mistake."

They had pushed their way through the crowd and now found themselves at the entrance to a small roped-off enclosure, in which a hundred or more spectators had already taken their seats. At the further end of the enclosure the gaily painted proscenium of a puppet theater glowed red and gold in the light of powerful flood lamps. Pulling out a handful of the small change with which Dr. Robert had provided him, Will paid for two tickets. They entered and sat down on a bench.

A gong sounded, the curtain of the little proscenium noiselessly rose and there, white pillars on a pea-green ground, was the façade of the royal palace of Thebes with a much-whiskered divinity sitting in a cloud above the pediment. A priest exactly like the god, except that he was somewhat smaller and less exuberantly draped, entered from the right, bowed to the audience, then turned towards the palace and shouted "Oedipus" in piping tones that seemed comically incongruous with his prophetic beard. To a flourish of trumpets the door swung open and, crowned and heroically buskined, the king appeared. The priest made obeisance, the royal puppet gave him leave to speak.

"Give ear to our afflictions," the old man piped.

The king cocked his head and listened.

"I hear the groans of dying men," he said. "I hear the shriek of widows, the sobbing of the motherless, the mutterings of prayer and supplication."

"Supplication!" said the deity in the clouds. "That's the spirit." He patted himself on the chest.

"They had some kind of a virus," Mary Sarojini explained in a whisper. "Like Asian flu, only a lot worse."

"We repeat the appropriate litanies," the old priest querulously piped, "we offer the most expensive sacrifices, we have the whole population living in chastity and flagellating itself every Monday, Wednesday and Friday. But the flood of death spreads ever more widely, rises higher and ever higher. So help us, King Oedipus, help us."

"Only a god can help."

"Hear, hear!" shouted the presiding deity.

"But by what means?"

"Only a god can say."

"Correct," said the god in his *basso profundo*, "aboslutely correct."

"Creon, my wife's brother, has gone to consult the oracle. When he returns—as very soon he must—we shall know what heaven advises."

"What heaven bloody well commands!" the *basso profundo* emended.

"Were people *really* so silly?" Mary Sarojini asked, as the audience laughed.

"Really and truly," Will assured her.

A phonograph started to play the Dead March in *Saul*. From left to right a black-robed procession of mourners carrying sheeted biers passed slowly across the front of the stage. Puppet after puppet—and as soon as the group had disappeared on the right it would be brought in again from the left. The procession seemed endless, the corpses innumerable.

"Dead," said Oedipus as he watched them pass. "And another dead. And yet another, another."

"That'll teach them!" the *basso profundo* broke in. "I'll learn you to be a toad!"

Oedipus continued:

"The soldier's bier, the whore's; the babe stone-cold
Pressed to the ache of unsucked breasts; the youth in horror
Turning away from the black swollen face
That from his moonlit pillow once looked up,
Eager for kisses. Dead, all dead,
Mourned by the soon to die and by the doomed
Borne with reluctant footing to the abhorred
Garden of cypresses where one huge pit
Yawns to receive them, stinking to the moon."

While he was speaking, two new puppets, a boy and a girl in the gayest of Palanese finery, entered from the right and, moving in the opposite direction to the black-robed mourners, took their stand, arm in arm, downstage and a little left of center.

"But we, meanwhile," said the boy when Oedipus had finished:

"Are bound for rosier gardens and the absurd
Apocalyptic rite that in the mind
Calls forth from the touched skin and melting flesh
The immanent Infinite."

"What about Me?" the *basso profundo* rumbled from the welkin. "You seem to forget that I'm Wholly Other."

Endlessly the black procession to the cemetery still shuffled on. But now the Dead March was interrupted in mid-phrase. Music gave place to a single deep note—tuba and double bass—prolonged interminably. The boy in the foreground held up his hand.

"Listen! The drone, the everlasting burden."

In unison with the unseen instruments the mourners began to chant. "Death, death, death, death . . ."

"But life knows more than one note," said the boy.

"Life," the girl chimed in, "can sing both high and low."

"And your unceasing drone of death serves only to make a richer music."

"A richer music," the girl repeated.

And with that, tenor and treble, they started to vocalize a wandering arabesque of sound wreathed, as it were, about the long rigid shaft of the ground bass.

The drone and the singing diminished gradually into silence; the last of the mourners disappeared and the boy and girl in the foreground retired to a corner where they could go on with their kissing undisturbed.

There was another flourish of trumpets and, obese in a purple tunic, in came Creon, fresh from Delphi and primed with oracles. For the next few minutes the dialogue was all in Palanese, and Mary Sarojini had to act as interpreter.

"Oedipus asks him what God said; and the other one says that what God said was that it was all because of some man having killed the old king, the one before Oedipus. Nobody had ever caught him, and the man was still living in Thebes, and this virus that was killing everybody had been sent by God—that's what Creon says he was told—as a punishment. I don't know why all these people who hadn't done anything to anybody had to be punished; but that's what he says God said. And the virus won't stop till they catch the man that killed the old king and send him away from Thebes. And of course Oedipus says he's going to do everything he can to find the man and get rid of him."

From his downstage corner the boy began to declaim, this time in English:

"God, most Himself when most sublimely vague,
  Talks, when His talk is plain, the ungodliest bosh.
Repent, He roars, for Sin has caused the plague.
  But we say 'Dirt—so wash.' "

While the audience was still laughing, another group of mourners emerged from the wings and slowly crossed the stage.

"*Karuna*," said the girl in the foreground, "compassion. The suffering of the stupid is as real as any other suffering."

Feeling a touch on his arm, Will turned and found himself looking into the beautiful sulky face of young Murugan.

"I've been hunting for you everywhere," he said angrily, as though Will had concealed himself on purpose just to annoy him. He spoke so loudly that many heads were turned and there were calls for quiet.

"You weren't at Dr. Robert's, you weren't at Susila's," the boy nagged on, regardless of the protests.

"Quiet, quiet . . ."

"Quiet!" came a tremendous shout from Basso Profundo in the clouds. "Things have come to a pretty pass," the voice added grumblingly, "when God simply can't hear Himself speak."

"Hear, hear," said Will, joining in the general laughter. He rose and, followed by Murugan and Mary Sarojini, hobbled towards the exit.

"Didn't you want to see the end?" Mary Sarojini asked, and turning to Murugan, "You really might have waited," she said in a tone of reproof.

"Mind your own business!" Murugan snapped.

Will laid a hand on the child's shoulder. "Luckily," he said, "your account of the end was so vivid that I don't have to see it with my own eyes. And of course," he added ironically, "His Highness must always come first."

Murugan pulled an envelope out of the pocket of those white silk pajamas which had so bedazzled the little nurse and handed it to Will. "From my mother." And he added, "It's urgent."

"How good it smells!" Mary Sarojini commented, sniffing at the rich arua of sandalwood that surrounded the Rani's missive.

Will unfolded three sheets of heaven-blue notepaper embossed with five golden lotuses under a princely crown. How many underlinings, what a profusion of capital letters! He started to read.

Ma Petite Voix, cher Farnaby, avait raison—AS USUAL! I had been TOLD again and again what Our Mutual Friend was predestined to do for poor little Pala and (through the financial support which Pala will permit him to contribute to the Crusade of the Spirit) for the WHOLE WORLD. So when I read his cable (which arrived a few minutes ago, by way of the faithful Bahu and his diplomatic colleague in London), it came as NO surprise to learn that Lord A. has given you *Full Powers* (and, it goes without saying, the WHEREWITHAL) to negotiate on his behalf—on *our* behalf; for his advantage is also yours, mine and (since in our different ways we are all Crusaders) the SPIRIT's!!

But the arrival of Lord A's cable is not the only piece of news I have to report. Events (as we learned this afternoon from Bahu) are *rushing* towards the Great Turning Point of Palanese History—rushing far more rapidly than I had previously thought to be possible. For reasons which are partly political (the need to offset a recent decline in Colonel D's popularity), partly Economic (the burdens of Defense are too onerous to be borne by Rendang alone) and partly Astrological (these days, say the Experts, are *uniquely* favorable for a joint venture by Rams—myself and Murugan—and that *typical* Scorpion, Colonel D.) it has been decided to precipitate an Action originally planned for the night of the lunar eclipse next November. This being so, it is essential that the three of us here should meet *without delay* to decide what must be Done, in these new and swiftly changing Circumstances, to promote our special interests, material and Spiritual. The so-called "Accident" which brought you to our shores at this most critical Moment of Time was, as you must recognize, Manifestly Providential. It remains for us to collaborate, as dedicated Crusaders, with that divine POWER which has so unequivocally espoused our Cause. So COME AT ONCE! Murugan has the motorcar and will bring you to our modest

Bungalow, where, I assure you, my dear Farnaby, you will receive a *very* warm welcome from *bein sincèrement vôtre,* Fatima R.

Will folded up the three odorous sheets of scrawled blue paper and replaced them in their envelope. His face was expressionless; but behind this mask of indifference he was violently angry. Angry with this ill-mannered boy before him, so ravishing in his white silk pajamas, so odious in his spoiled silliness. Angry, as he caught another whiff of the letter, with that grotesque monster of a woman, who had begun by ruining her son, in the name of mother love and chastity, and was now egging him on, in the name of God and an assortment of Ascended Masters, to become a bomb-dropping spiritual crusader under the oily banner of Joe Aldehyde. Angry, above all, with himself for having so wantonly become involved with this ludicrously sinister couple, in heaven only knew what kind of a vile plot against all the human decencies that his refusal to take yes for an answer had never prevented him from secretely believing in and (how passionately!) longing for.

"Well, shall we go?" said Murugan in a tone of airy confidence. He was evidently assuming as axiomatic that, when Fatima R. issued a command, obedience must necessarily be complete and unhesitating.

Feeling the need to give himself a little more time to cool off, Will made no immediate answer. Instead, he turned away to look at the now distant puppets. Jocasta, Oedipus and Creon were sitting on the palace steps, waiting, presumably, for the arrival of Tiresias. Overhead, Basso Profundo was momentarily napping. A party of black-robed mourners was crossing the stage. Near the footlights the boy from Pala had begun to declaim in blank verse:

"Light and Compassion," he was saying,
"Light and Compassion—how unutterably
Simple our Substance! But the Simple waited,
Age after age, for intricacies sufficient
To know their One in multitude, their Everything
Here, now, their Fact in fiction; waited and still
Waits on the absurd, on incommensurables
Seamlessly interwoven—oestrin with
Charity, truth with kidney function, beauty

With chyle, bile, sperm, and God with dinner, God
With dinner's absence or the sound of bells
Suddenly—one, two, three—in sleepless ears."

There was a ripple of plucked strings, then the long-drawn notes of a flute.

"Shall we go?" Murugan repeated.

But Will held up his hand for silence. The girl puppet had moved to the center of the stage and was singing:

"Thought is the brain's three milliards
Of cells from the inside out.
Billions of games of billiards
Marked up as Faith and Doubt.

"My Faith, but their collisions;
My logic, their enzymes;
Their pink epinephrin, my visions;
Their white epinephrin, my crimes.

"Since I am the felt arrangement
Of ten to the ninth times three,
Each atom in its estrangement
Must yet be prophetic of me."

Losing all patience, Murugan caught hold of Will's arm and gave him a savage pinch. "Are you coming?" he shouted.

Will turned on him angrily. "What the devil do you think you're doing, you little fool?" He jerked his arm out of the boy's grasp.

Intimidated, Murugan changed his tone. "I just wanted to know if you were ready to come to my mother's."

"I'm not ready," Will answered, "because I'm not going."

"Not going?" Murugan cried in a tone of incredulous amazement. "But she expects you, she . . ."

"Tell your mother I'm very sorry, but I have a prior engagement. With someone who's dying," Will added.

"But this is frightfully important."

"So is dying."

Murugan lowered his voice. "Something's happening," he whispered.

"I can't hear you," Will shouted through the confused noises of the crowd.

Murugan glanced about him apprehensively, then risked a somewhat louder whisper. "Something's happening, something tremendous."

"Something even more tremendous is happening at the hospital."

"We just heard . . ." Murugan began. He looked around again, then shook his head. "No, I can't tell you—not here. That's why you *must* come to the bungalow. *Now.* There's no time to lose."

Will glanced at his watch. "No time to lose," he echoed and, turning to Mary Sarojini, "We must get going," he said. "Which way?"

"I'll show you," she said, and they set off hand in hand.

"Wait," Murugan implored, "wait!" Then, as Will and Mary Sarojini held on their course, he came dodging through the crowd in pursuit. "What shall I tell her?" he wailed at their heels.

The boy's terror was comically abject. In Will's mind anger gave place to amusement. He laughed aloud. Then, halting, "What would *you* tell her, Mary Sarojini?" he asked.

"I'd tell her exactly what happened," said the child. "I mean, if it was *my* mother. But then," she added on second thought, "my mother isn't the Rani." She looked up at Murugan. "Do you belong to an MAC?" she enquired.

Of course he didn't. For the Rani the very idea of a Mutual Adoption Club was a blasphemy. Only God could make a Mother. The Spiritual Crusader wanted to be alone with her God-given victim.

"No MAC." Mary Sarojini shook her head. "That's awful! You might have gone and stayed for a few days with one of your other mothers."

Still terrified by the prospect of having to tell his only mother about the failure of his mission, Murugan began to harp almost hysterically on a new variant of the old theme. "I don't know what she'll say," he kept repeating. "I don't know what she'll say."

"There's only one way to find out what she'll say," Will told him. "Go home and listen."

"Come with me," Murugan begged. "Please." He clutched at Will's arm.

"I told you not to touch me." The clutching hand was hastily withdrawn. Will smiled again. "That's better!" He raised his staff in a farewell gesture. "*Bonne nuit, Altesse.*"

Then to Mary Sarojini, "Lead on, MacPhail," he said in high good humor.

"Were you putting it on?" Mary Sarojini asked. "Or were you really angry?"

"Really and truly," he assured her. Then he remembered what he had seen in the school gymnasium. He hummed the opening notes of the Rakshasi Hornpipe and banged the pavement with his ironshod staff.

"Ought I to have stamped it out?"

"Maybe it would have been better."

"You think so?"

"He's going to hate you as soon as he's stopped being frightened."

Will shrugged his shoulders. He couldn't care less. But as the past receded and the future approached, as they left the arc lamps of the marketplace and climbed the steep dark street that wound uphill to the hospital, his mood began to change. Lead on, MacPhail—but towards what, and away from what? Towards yet another manifestation of the Essential Horror and away from all hope of that blessed year of freedom which Joe Aldehyde had promised and that it would be so easy and (since Pala was doomed in any event) not so immoral or treacherous to earn. And not only away from the hope of freedom; away quite possibly, if the Rani complained to Joe and if Joe became sufficiently indignant, from any further prospects of well-paid slavery as a professional execution watcher. Should he turn back, should he try to find Murugan, offer apologies, do whatever that dreadful woman ordered him to do? A hundred yards up the road, the lights of the hospital could be seen shining between the trees.

"Let's rest for a moment," he said.

"Are you tired?" Mary Sarojini enquired solicitously.

"A little."

He turned and, leaning on his staff, looked down at the marketplace. In the light of the arc lamps the town hall glowed pink, like a monumental serving of raspberry sherbet. On the temple spire he could see, frieze above frieze, the exuberant chaos of Indic sculpture—elephants and Bodhisattvas, demons, supernatural girls with breasts and enormous bottoms, capering Shivas, rows of past and future Buddhas in quiet ecstasy. Below, in the space between sherbet and mythology, seethed the crowd, and somewhere in that crowd was a sulky face and a pair of white satin pajamas. Should he go back? It would be the sensible, the safe, the prudent thing to do. But an inner voice—not little, like the Rani's, but stentorian shouted, "Squalid! Squalid!" Conscience? No. Morality? Heaven forbid! But supererogatory squalor, ugliness and vulgarity beyond the call of duty—these were things which, as a man of taste, one simply couldn't be a party to.

"Well, shall we go on?" he said to Mary Sarojini.

They entered the lobby of the hospital. The nurse at the desk had a message for them from Susila. Mary Sarojini was to go directly to Mrs. Rao's, where she and Tom Krishna would spend the night. Mr. Farnaby was to be asked to come at once to Room 34.

"This way," said the nurse, and held open a swing door.

Will stepped forward. The conditioned reflex of politeness clicked automatically into action. "Thank you," he said, and smiled. But it was with a dull, sick feeling in the pit of the stomach that he went hobbling towards the apprehended future.

"The last door on the left," said the nurse. But now she had to get back to her desk in the lobby. "So I'll leave you to go on alone," she added as the door closed behind her.

Alone, he repeated to himself, alone—and the apprehended future was identical with the haunting past, the Essential Horror was timeless and ubiquitous. This long corridor with its green-painted walls was the very same corridor along which, a year ago, he had walked to the little room where Molly lay dying. The nightmare was recurrent. Foredoomed and conscious, he moved on towards its horrible consummation. Death, yet another vision of death.

Thirty-two, thirty-three, thirty-four . . . He knocked and waited, listening to the beating of his heart. The door opened and he found himself face to face with little Radha.

"Susila was expecting you," she whispered.

Will followed her into the room. Rounding a screen, he caught a glimpse of Susila's profile silhouetted against a lamp, of a high bed, of a dark emaciated face on the pillow, of arms that were no more than parchment-covered bones, of clawlike hands. Once again the Essential Horror. With a shudder he turned away. Radha motioned him to a chair near the open window. He sat down and closed his eyes—closed them physically against the present, but, by that very act, opened them inwardly upon that hateful past of which the present had reminded him. He was there in that other room, with Aunt Mary. Or rather with the person who had once been Aunt Mary, but was now this hardly recognizable somebody else—somebody who had never so much as heard of the charity and courage which had been the very essence of Aunt Mary's being; somebody who was filled with an indiscriminate hatred for all who came near her, loathing them, whoever they might be, simply because they didn't have cancer, because they weren't in pain, had not been sentenced to die before their time. And along with this malignant envy of other people's health and happiness had gone a bitterly querulous self-pity, an abject despair.

"Why to me? Why should this thing have happened to me?"

He could hear the shrill complaining voice, could see that tearstained and distorted face. The only person he had ever really loved or wholeheartedly admired. And yet, in her degradation, he had caught himself despising her—despising, positively hating.

To escape from the past, he reopened his eyes. Radha, he saw, was sitting on the floor, cross-legged and upright, in the posture of meditation. In her chair beside the bed Susila seemed to be holding the same kind of focused stillness. He looked at the face on the pillow. That too was still, still with a serenity that might almost have been the forzen calm of death. Outside, in the leafy darkness, a peacock suddenly screamed. Deepened by contrast, the ensuing silence seemed to grow pregnant with mysterious and appalling meanings.

"Lakshmi." Susila laid a hand on the old woman's wasted arm. "Lakshmi," she said again more loudly. The death-calm face remained impassive. "You mustn't go to sleep."

Not go to sleep? But for Aunt Mary, sleep—the artificial sleep that followed the injections—had been the only respite from the self-lacerations of self-pity and brooding fear.

"Lakshmi!"

The face came to life.

"I wasn't really asleep," the old woman whispered. "It's just my being so weak. I seem to float away."

"But you've got to be here," said Susila. "You've got to know you're here. All the time." She slipped an additional pillow under the sick woman's shoulders and reached for a bottle of smelling salts that stood on the bed table.

Lakshmi sniffed, opened her eyes, and looked up into Susila's face. "I'd forgotten how beautiful you were," she said. "But then Dugald always did have good taste." The ghost of a mischievous smile appeared for a moment on the fleshless face. "What do you think, Susila?" she added after a moment and in another tone. "Shall we see him again? I mean, over there?"

In silence Susila stroked the old woman's hand. Then, suddenly smiling, "How would the Old Raja have asked that question?" she said. *"Do you think 'we' (quote, unquote) shall see 'him' (quote, unquote) 'over there' (quote, unquote)?"*

"But what do *you* think?"

"I think we've all come out of the same light, and we're all going back into the same light."

Words, Will was thinking, words, words, words. With an effort, Lakshmi lifted a hand and pointed accusingly at the lamp on the bed table.

"It glares in my eyes," she whispered.

Susila untied the red silk handkerchief knotted around her throat and draped it over the lamp's parchment shade. From white and mercilessly revealing, the light became as dimly, warmly rosy as the flush, Will found himself thinking, on Babs's rumpled bed, whenever Porter's Gin proclaimed itself in crimson.

"That's much better," said Lakshmi. She shut her eyes. Then, after a long silence, "The light," she broke out, "the light. It's here again." Then after another pause, "Oh, how wonderful," she whispered at last, "how wonderful!" Suddenly she winced and bit her lip.

Susila took the old woman's hand in both of hers. "Is the pain bad?" she asked.

"It would be bad," Lakshmi explained, "if it were really *my* pain. But somehow it isn't. The pain's here; but I'm somewhere else. It's like what you discover with the *moksha*-medicine. Nothing really belongs to you. Not even your pain."

"Is the light still there?"

Lakshmi shook her head. "And looking back, I can tell you exactly when it went away. It went away when I started talking about the pain not being really mine."

"And yet what you were saying was good."

"I know—but I was *saying* it." The ghost of an old habit of irreverent mischief flitted once again across Lakshmi's face.

"What are you thinking of?" Susila asked.

"Socrates."

"Socrates?"

"Gibber, gibber, gibber—even when he'd actually swallowed the stuff. Don't let me talk, Susila. Help me to get out of my own light."

"Do you remember that time last year," Susila began after a silence, "when we all went up to the old Shiva temple above the High Altitude Station? You and Robert and Dugald and me and the two children—do you remember?"

Lakshmi smiled with pleasure at the recollection.

"I'm thinking specially of that view from the west side of the temple—the view out over the sea. Blue, green, purple—and the shadows of the clouds were like ink. And the clouds themselves—snow, lead, charcoal, satin. And while we were looking, you asked a question. Do you remember, Lakshmi?"

"You mean, about the Clear Light?"

"About the Clear Light," Susila confirmed. "Why do people speak of Mind in terms of Light? Is it because they've seen the sunshine and found it so beautiful that it seems only natural to identify the Buddha Nature with the clearest of all possible Clear Lights? Or do they find the sunshine beautiful because, consciously or unconsciously, they've been having revelations of Mind in the form of Light ever since they were born? I was the first to answer," said Susila, smiling to herself. "And as I'd just been reading something by some American behaviorist, I didn't stop to think—I just gave you the (quote, unquote) 'scientific point of view.' People equate Mind (whatever *that* may be) with hallucinations of light, because they've looked at a lot of sunsets and found them very impressive. But Robert and Dugald would have none of it. The Clear Light, they insisted, comes first. You go mad about sunsets because sunsets remind you of what's always been going on, whether you knew it or not, inside your skull and outside space and time. You agreed with them, Lakshmi—do you remember? You said, 'I'd like to be on your side, Susila, if only because it isn't good for these men of ours to be right *all* the time. But in this case—surely it's pretty obvious—in this case they *are* right.' Of course they were right, and of course I was hopelessly wrong. And, needless to say, you had known the right answer before you asked the question."

"I never *knew* anything," Lakshmi whispered. "I could only *see.*"

"I remember your telling me about seeing the Clear Light," said Susila. "Would you like me to remind you of it?"

The sick woman nodded her head.

"When you were eight years old," said Susila. "That was the first time. An orange butterfly on a leaf, opening and shutting its wings in the sunshine—and suddenly there was the Clear Light of pure Suchness blazing through it, like another sun."

"Much brighter than the sun," Lakshmi whispered.

"But much gentler. You can look into the Clear Light and not be blinded. And now remember it. A butterfly on a green leaf, opening and shutting its wings—and it's the Buddha Nature totally present, it's the Clear Light outshining the sun. And you were only eight years old."

"What had I done to deserve it?"

Will found himself remembering that evening, a week or so before her death, when Aunt Mary had talked about the wonderful times they had had together in her little Regency house near Arundel where he had spent the better part of all his holidays. Smoking out the wasps' nests with fire and brimstone, having picnics on the downs or under the beeches. And then the sausage rolls at Bognor, the gypsy fortuneteller who had prophesied that he would end up as Chancellor of the Exchequer, the black-robed, red-nosed verger who had chased them out of Chichester Cathedral because they had laughed too much. "Laughed too much," Aunt Mary had repeated bitterly. "*Laughed* too much . . ."

"And now," Susila was saying, "think of that view from the Shiva temple. Think of those lights and shadows on the sea, those blue spaces between the clouds. Think of them, and then let go of your thinking. Let go of it, so that the not-Thought can come through. Things into Emptiness. Emptiness into Suchness. Suchness into things again, into your own mind. Remember what it says in the Sutra. 'Your own consciousness shining, void, inseparable from the great Body of Radiance, is subject neither to birth nor death, but is the same as the immutable Light, Buddha Amitabha.' "

"The same as the light," Lakshmi repeated. "And yet it's all dark again."

"It's dark because you're trying too hard," said Susila. "Dark because you want it to be light. Remember what you used to tell me when I was a little girl. 'Lightly, child, lightly. You've got to learn to do everything lightly. Think lightly, act lightly, feel lightly. Yes, feel lightly, even though you're feeling deeply. Just lightly let things happen and lightly cope with them.' I was so preposterously serious in those days, such a humorless little prig. Lightly, lightly—it was the best advice ever given me. Well, now I'm going to say the same thing to you, Lakshmi . . . Lightly, my darling, lightly. Even when it comes to dying. Nothing ponderous, or portentous, or emphatic. No rhetoric, no tremolos, no self-conscious persona putting on its celebrated imitation of Christ or Goethe or Little Nell. And, of course, no theology, no metaphysics. Just the fact of dying and the fact of the Clear Light. So throw away all your baggage and go forward. There are quicksands all about you, sucking at your feet, trying to suck you down into fear and self-pity and despair. That's why you must walk so lightly. Lightly, my darling. On tiptoes; and no luggage, not even a sponge bag. Completely unencumbered."

Completely unencumbered . . . Will thought of poor Aunt Mary sinking deeper and deeper with every step into the quicksands. Deeper and deeper until, struggling and protesting to the last, she had gone down, completely and forever, into the Essential Horror. He looked again at the fleshless face on the pillow and saw that it was smiling.

"The Light," came the hoarse whisper, "the Clear Light. It's here—along with the pain, in spite of the pain."

"And where are *you?*" Susila asked.

"Over there, in the corner." Lakshmi tried to point, but the raised hand faltered and fell back, inert, on the coverlet. "I can see myself there. And she can see my body on the bed."

"Can she see the Light?"

"No. The Light's here, where my body is."

The door of the sickroom was quietly opened. Will turned his head and was in time to see Dr. Robert's small spare figure emerging from behind the screen into the rosy twilight.

Susila rose and motioned him to her place beside the bed. Dr. Robert sat down and, leaning forward, took his wife's hand in one of his and laid the other on her forehead.

"It's me," he whispered.

"At last . . ."

A tree, he explained, had fallen across the telephone line.

No communication with the High Altitude Station except by road. They had sent a messenger in a car, and the car had broken down. More than two hours had been lost. "But thank goodness," Dr. Robert concluded, "here I finally am."

The dying woman sighed profoundly, opened her eyes for a moment and looked up at him with a smile, then closed them again. "I knew you'd come."

"Lakshmi," he said very softly. "Lakshmi." He drew the tips of his fingers across the wrinkled forehead, again and again. "My little love." There were tears on his cheeks; but his voice was firm and he spoke with the tenderness not of weakness, but of power.

"I'm not over there any more," Lakshmi whispered.

"She was over there in the corner," Susila explained to her father-in-law. "Looking at her body here on the bed."

"But now I've come back. Me and the pain, me and the Light, me and you—all together."

The peacock screamed again and, through the insect noises that in this tropical night were the equivalent of silence, far off but clear came the sound of gay music, flutes and plucked strings and the steady throbbing of drums.

"Listen," said Dr. Robert. "Can you hear it? They're dancing."

"Dancing," Lakshmi repeated. "Dancing."

"Dancing so lightly," Susila whispered. "As though they had wings."

The music swelled up again into audibility.

"It's the Courting Dance," Susila went on.

"The Courting Dance. Robert, do you remember?"

"Could I ever forget?"

Yes, Will said to himself, could one ever forget? Could one ever forget that other distant music and, nearby, unnaturally quick and shallow, the sound of dying breath in a boy's ears? In the house across the street somebody was practicing one of those Brahms Waltzes that Aunt Mary had loved to play. One-two and three and One-two and three and O-o-o-ne two three, One- and One and Two-Three and One an . . . The odious stranger who had once been Aunt Mary stirred out of her artificial stupor and opened her eyes. An expression of the most intense malignity had appeared on the yellow, wasted face. "Go and tell them to stop," the harsh, unrecognizable voice had almost screamed. And then the lines of malignity had changed into the lines of despair, and the stranger, the pitiable odious stranger started to sob uncontrollably. Those Brahms Waltzes—they were the pieces, out of all her repertory, that Frank had loved best.

Another gust of cool air brought with it a louder strain of the gay, bright music.

"All those young people dancing together," said Dr. Robert. "All that laughter and desire, all that uncomplicated happiness! It's all here, like an atmosphere, like a field of force. Their joy and our love—Susila's love, my love—all working together, all reinforcing one another. Love and joy enveloping you, my darling; love and joy carrying you up into the peace of the Clear Light. Listen to the music. Can you still hear it, Lakshmi?"

"She's drifted away again," said Susila. "Try to bring her back."

Dr. Robert slipped an arm under the emaciated body and lifted it into a sitting posture. The head drooped sideways onto his shoulder.

"My little love," he kept whispering. "My little love . . ."

Her eyelids fluttered open for a moment. "Brighter," came the barely audible whisper, "brighter." And a smile of happiness intense almost to the point of elation transfigured her face.

Through his tears Dr. Robert smiled back at her. "So now you can let go, my darling." He stroked her gray hair. "Now you can let go. Let go," he insisted. "Let go of this poor old body. You don't need it any more. Let it fall away from you. Leave it lying here like a pile of worn-out clothes."

In the fleshless face the mouth had fallen carvernously open, and suddenly the breathing became stertorous.

"My love, my little love . . ." Dr. Robert held her more closely. "Let go now, let go. Leave it here, your old worn-out body, and go on. Go on, my darling, go on into the Light, into the peace, into the living peace of the Clear Light . . ."

Susila picked up one of the limp hands and kissed it, then turned to little Radha.

"Time to go," she whispered, touching the girl's shoulder.

Interrupted in her meditation, Radha opened her eyes, nodded and, scrambling to her feet, tiptoed silently towards the door. Susila beckoned to Will and, together, they followed her. In silence the three of them walked along the corridor. At the swing door Radha took her leave.

"Thank you for letting me be with you," she whispered.

Susila kissed her. "Thank *you* for helping to make it easier for Lakshmi."

Will followed Susila across the lobby and out into the warm odorous darkness. In silence they started to walk downhill towards the marketplace.

"And now," he said at last, speaking under a strange compulsion to deny his emotion in a display of the cheapest kind of cynicism, "I suppose she's trotting off to do a little *maithuna* with her boy friend."

"As a matter of fact," said Susila calmly, "she's on night duty. But if she weren't, what would be the objection her going on from the yoga of death to the yoga of love?"

Will did not answer immediately. He was thinking of what had happened between himself and Babs on the evening of Molly's funeral. The yoga of antilove, the yoga of resented addiction, of lust and the self-loathing that reinforces the self and makes it yet more loathsome.

"I'm sorry I tried to be unpleasant," he said at last.

"It's your father's ghost. We'll have to see if we can exorcise it."

They had crossed the marketplace and now, at the end of the short street that led out of the village, they had come to the open space where the jeep was parked. As Susila turned the car onto the highway, the beam of their headlamps swept across a small green car that was turning downhill into the bypass.

"Don't I recognize the royal Baby Austin?"

"You do," said Susila, and wondered where the Rani and Murugan could be going at this time of night.

"They're up to no good," Will guessed. And on a sudden impulse he told Susila of his roving commission from Joe Aldehyde, his dealings with the Queen Mother and Mr. Bahu.

"You'd be justified in deporting me tomorrow," he concluded.

"Not now that you've changed your mind," she assured him. "And anyhow nothing you did could have affected the real issue. Our enemy is oil in general. Whether we're exploited by Southeast Asia Petroleum or Standard of California makes no difference."

"Did you know that Murugan and the Rani were conspiring against you?"

"They make no secret of it."

"Then why don't you get rid of them?"

"Because they would be brought back immediately by Colonel Dipa. The Rani is a princess of Rendang. If we expelled her, it would be a *casus belli*."

"So what can you do?"

"Try to keep them in order, try to change their minds, hope for a happy outcome, and be prepared for the worst."

"And what will you do if the worst happens?"

"Try to make the best of it, I suppose. Even in the worst society an individual retains a little freedom. One perceives in private, one remembers and imagines in private, one loves in private, and one dies in private—even under Colonel Dipa." Then after a silence, "Did Dr. Robert say you could have the *moksha*-medicine?" she asked. And when Will nodded, "Would you like to try it?"

"Now?"

"Now. That is, if you don't mind being up all night with it."

"I'd like nothing better."

"You may find that you never liked anything worse," Susila warned him. "The *moksha*-medicine can take you to heaven; but it can also take you to hell. Or else to both, together or alternately. Or else (if you're lucky, or if you've made yourself ready) beyond either of them. And then beyond the beyond, back to where you started from—back to here, back to New Rothamsted, back to business as usual. Only now, of course, business as usual is completely different."

XV

ONE, TWO, THREE, FOUR . . . THE CLOCK IN THE KITCHEN struck twelve. How irrelevantly, seeing that time had ceased to exist! The absurd, importunate bell had sounded at the heart of a timelessly present Event, of a Now that changed incessantly in a dimension, not of seconds and minutes, but of beauty, of significance, of intensity, of deepening mystery.

"Luminous bliss." From the shallows of his mind the words rose like bubbles, came to the surface, and vanished into the infinite spaces of living light that now pulsed and breathed behind his closed eyelids. "Luminous bliss." That was as near as one could come to it. But *it*—this timeless and yet ever-changing Event—was something that words could only caricature and diminish, never convey. *It* was not only bliss, *it* was also understanding. Understanding of everything, but without knowledge of anything. Knowledge involved a knower and all the infinite diversity of known and knowable things. But here, behind his closed lids, there was neither spectacle nor spectator. There was only this experienced fact of being blissfully one with Oneness.

In a succession of revelations, the light grew brighter, the understanding deepened, the bliss became more impossibly, more unbearably intense. "Dear God!" he said to himself. "Oh, my dear God." Then, out of another world, he heard the sound of Susila's voice.

"Do you feel like telling me what's happening?"

It was a long time before Will answered her. Speaking was difficult. Not because there was any physical impediment. It was just that speech seemed so fatuous, so totally pointless. "Light," he whispered at last.

"And you're there, looking at the light?"

"Not looking at it," he answered, after a long reflective pause. "Being it. *Being* it," he repeated emphatically.

Its presence was his absence. William Asquith Farnaby—ultimately and essentially there was no such person. Ultimately and essentially there was only a luminous bliss, only a knowledgeless understanding, only union with unity in a limitless, undifferentiated awareness. This, self-evidently, was the mind's natural state. But no less certainly there had also been that professional execution watcher, that self-loathing Babs addict; there were also three thousand millions of insulated consciousnesses, each at the center of a nightmare world, in which it was impossible for anyone with eyes in his head or a grain of honesty to take yes for an answer. By what sinister miracle had the mind's natural state been transformed into all these Devil's Islands of wretchedness and delinquency?

In the firmament of bliss and understanding, like bats against the sunset, there was a wild crisscrossing of remembered notions and the hangovers of past feelings. Bat-thoughts of Plotinus and the Gnostics, of the One and its emanations, down, down into thickening horror. And then bat-feelings of anger and disgust as the thickening horrors became specific memories of what the essentially nonexistent William Asquith Farnaby had seen and done, inflicted and suffered.

But behind and around and somehow even within those flickering memories was the firmament of bliss and peace and understanding. There might be a few bats in the sunset sky; but the fact remained that the dreadful miracle of creation had been reversed. From a preternaturally wretched and delinquent self he had been unmade into pure mind, mind in its natural state, limitless, undifferentiated, luminously blissful, knowledgelessly understanding.

Light here, light now. And because it was infinitely here and timelessly now, there was nobody outside the light to look at the light. The fact was the awareness, the awareness the fact.

From that other world, somewhere out there to the right, came the sound once more of Susila's voice.

"Are you feeling happy?" she asked.

A surge of brighter radiance swept away all those flickering thoughts and memories. There was nothing now except a crystalline transparency of bliss.

Without speaking, without opening his eyes, he smiled and nodded.

"Eckhart called it God," she went on. "'Felicity so ravishing, so inconceivably intense that no one can describe it. And in the midst of it God glows and flames without ceasing.'"

God glows and flames . . . It was so startlingly, so comically right that Will found himself laughing aloud. "God like a house on fire," he gasped. "God-the-Fourteenth-of-July." And he exploded once more into cosmic laughter.

Behind his closed eyelids an ocean of luminous bliss poured upwards like an inverted cataract. Poured upwards from union into completer union, from impersonality into a yet more absolute transcendence of selfhood.

"God-the-Fourteenth-of-July," he repeated and, from the heart of the cataract, gave vent to a final chuckle of recognition and understanding.

"What about the fifteenth of July?" Susila questioned. "What about the morning after?"

"There isn't any morning after."

She shook her head. "It sounds suspiciously like Nirvana."

"What's wrong with that?"

"Pure Spirit, one hundred per cent proof—that's a drink that only the most hardened contemplation guzzlers indulge in. Bodhisattvas dilute their Nirvana with equal parts of love and work."

"This is better," Will insisted.

"You mean, it's more delicious. That's why it's such an enormous temptation. The only temptation that God could succumb to. The fruit of the ignorance of good and evil. What heavenly lusciousness, what a supermango! God had been stuffing Himself with it for billions of years. Then all of a sudden, up comes *Homo sapiens*, out pops the knowledge of good and evil. God had to switch to a much less palatable brand of fruit. You've just eaten a slice of the original supermango, so you can sympathize with Him."

A chair creaked, there was a rustle of skirts, then a series of small busy sounds that he was unable to interpret. What was she doing? He could have answered that question by simply opening his eyes. But who cared, after all, what she might be doing? Nothing was of any importance except this blazing uprush of bliss and understanding.

"Supermango to fruit of knowledge—I'm going to wean you," she said, "by easy stages."

There was a whirring sound. From the shallows, a bubble of recognition reached the surface of consciousness. Susila had been putting a record on the turntable of a phonograph and now the machine was in motion.

"Johann Sebastian Bach," he heard her saying. "The music that's closest to silence, closest, in spite of its being so highly organized, to pure, hundred per cent proof Spirit."

The whirring gave place to musical sounds. Another bubble of recognition came shooting up; he was listening to the Fourth Brandenburg Concerto.

It was the same, of course, as the Fourth Brandenburg he had listened to so often in the past—the same and yet completely different. This Allegro—he knew it by heart. Which meant that he was in the best possible position to realize that he had never really heard it before. To begin with, it was no longer he, William Asquith Farnaby, who was hearing it. The Allegro was revealing itself as an element in the great present Event, a manifestation at one remove of the luminous bliss. Or perhaps that was putting it too mildly. In another modality this Allegro *was* the luminous bliss; it was the knowledgeless understanding of everything apprehended through a particular piece of knowledge; it was undifferentiated awareness broken up into notes and phrases and yet still all-comprehendingly itself. And of course all this belonged to nobody. It was at once in here, out there, and nowhere. The music which, as William Asquith Farnaby, he had heard a hundred times before, he had been reborn as an unowned awareness. Which was why he was now hearing it for the first time. Unowned, the Fourth Brandenburg had an intensity of beauty, a depth of intrinsic meaning, incomparably greater than anything he had ever found in the same music when it was his private property.

"Poor idiot" came up in a bubble of ironic comment. The poor idiot hadn't wanted to take yes for an answer in any field but the aesthetic. And all the time he had been denying, by the mere fact of being himself, all the beauty and meaning he so passionately longed to say yes to. William Asquith Farnaby was nothing but a muddy filter, on the hither side of which human beings, nature, and even his beloved art had emerged bedimmed and bemired, less, other and uglier than themselves. Tonight, for the first time, his awareness of a piece of music was completely unobstructed. Between mind and sound, mind and pattern, mind and significance, there was no longer any babel of biographical irrelevances to drown the music or make a senseless discord. Tonight's Fourth Brandenburg was a pure datum—no, a blessed *donum*—uncorrupted by the personal history, the second-hand notions, the ingrained stupidities with which, like every self, the poor idiot, who wouldn't (and in art plainly couldn't) take yes for an answer, had overlaid the gifts of immediate experience.

And tonight's Fourth Brandenburg was not merely an unowned Thing in Itself; it was also, in some impossible way, a Present Event with an infinite duration. Or rather (and still more impossibly, seeing that it had three movements and was being played at its usual speed) it was without duration. The metronome presided over each of its phrases; but the sum of its phrases was not a span of seconds and minutes. There was a *tempo*, but no time. So what was there?

"Eternity," Will was forced to answer. It was one of those metaphysical dirty words which no decent-minded man would dream of pronouncing even to himself, much less in public. "Eternity, my brethren," he said aloud. "Eternity, blah-blah." The sarcasm, as he might have known it would, fell completely flat. Tonight those four syllables were no less concretely significant than the four letters of the other class of tabooed words. He began to laugh.

"What's so funny?" she asked.

"Eternity," he answered. "Believe it or not, it's as real as shit."

"Excellent!" she said approvingly.

He sat there motionlessly attentive, following with ear and inward eye the interwoven streams of sound, the interwoven streams of congruous and equivalent lights, that flowed on timelessly from one sequence to another. And every phrase of this well-worn familiar music was an unprecedented revelation of beauty that went pouring upwards, like a multitudinous fountain, into another revelation as novel and amazing as itself. Stream within stream—the stream of the solo violin, the streams of the two recorders, the manifold streams of the harpsichord and the little orchestra of assorted strings. Separate, distinct, individual—and yet each of the streams was a function of all the rest, each was itself in virtue of its relationship to the whole of which it was a component.

"Dear God!" he heard himself whispering.

In the timeless sequence of change the recorders were

holding a single long-drawn note. A note without upper partials, clear, pellucid, divinely empty. A note (the word came bubbling up) of pure contemplation. And here was another inspirational obscenity that had now acquired a concrete meaning and might be uttered without a sense of shame. Pure contemplation, unconcerned, beyond contingency, outside the context of moral judgments. Through the uprushing lights he caught a glimpse, in memory, of Radha's shining face as she talked of love as contemplation, of Radha once again, sitting cross-legged, in a focused intensity of stillness, at the foot of the bed where Lakshmi lay dying. This long pure note was the meaning of her words, the audible expression of her silence. But, always, flowing through and along with the heavenly emptiness of that contemplative fluting was the rich sound, vibration within passionate vibration, of the violin. And surrounding them both—the notes of contemplative detachment and the notes of passionate involvement—was this network of sharp dry tones plucked from the wires of the harpsichord. Spirit and instinct, action and vision—and around them the web of intellect. They were comprehended by discursive thought, but comprehended, it was obvious, only from the outside, in terms of an order of experience radically different from that which discursive thinking professes to explain.

"It's like a Logical Positivist," he said.

"What is?"

"That harpsichord."

Like a Logical Positivist, he was thinking in the shallows of his mind, while in the depths the great Event of light and sound timelessly unfolded. Like a Logical Positivist talking about Plotinus and Julie de Lespinasse.

The music changed again, and now it was the violin that sustained (how passionately!) the long-drawn note of contemplation, while the two recorders took up the theme of active involvement and repeated it—the identical form imposed upon another substance—in the mode of detachment. And here, dancing in and out between them, was the Logical Positivist, absurd but indispensable, trying to explain, in a language incommensurable with the facts, what is was all about.

In the Eternity that was as real as shit, he went on listening to these interwoven streams of sound, went on looking at these interwoven streams of light, went on actually *being* (out there, in here, and nowhere) all that he saw and heard. And now, abruptly, the character of the light underwent a change. These interwoven streams, which were the first fluid differentiations of an understanding on the further side of all particular knowledge, had ceased to be a continuum. Instead, there was, all of a sudden, this endless succession of separate forms—forms still manifestly charged with the luminous bliss of undifferentiated being, but limited now, isolated, individualized. Silver and rose, yellow and pale green and gentian blue, an endless succession of luminous spheres came swimming up from some hidden source of forms and, in time with the music, purposefully constellated themselves into arrays of unbelievable complexity and beauty. An inexhaustible fountain that sprayed out into conscious patternings, into lattices of living stars. And as he looked at them, as he lived their life and the life of this music that was their equivalent, they went on growing into other lattices that filled the three dimensions of an inner space and changed incessantly in another, timeless dimension of quality and significance.

"What are you hearing?" Susila asked.

"Hearing what I see," he answered. "And seeing what I hear."

"And how would you describe it?"

"What it looks like," Will answered, after a long silence, "what it sounds like, is the creation. Only it's not a one-shot affair. It's nonstop, perpetual creation."

"Perpetual creation out of no-what nowhere into something somewhere—is that it?"

"That's it."

"You're making progress."

If words had come more easily and, when spoken, had been a little less pointless, Will would have explained to her that knowledgeless understanding and luminous bliss were a damn sight better than even Johann Sebastian Bach.

"Making progress," Susila repeated. "But you've still got a long way to go. What about opening your eyes?"

Will shook his head emphatically.

"It's time you gave yourself a chance of discovering what's what."

"What's what is *this,*" he muttered.

"It isn't," she assured him. "All you've been seeing and hearing and being is only the first *what.* Now you must look at the second one. Look, and then bring the two together into a single inclusive *what's-what*. So open your eyes, Will. Open them wide."

"All right," he said at last and reluctantly, with an apprehensive sense of impending misfortune, he opened his eyes. The inner illumination was swallowed up in another kind of light. The fountain of forms, the colored orbs in their conscious arrays and purposefully changing lattices gave place to a static composition of uprights and diagonals, of flat planes and curving cylinders, all carved out of some material that looked like living agate, and all emerging from a matrix of living and pulsating mother-of-pearl. Like a blind man newly healed and confronted for the first time by the mystery of light and color, he stared in uncomprehending astonishment. And then, at the end of another twenty timeless bars of the Fourth Brandenburg, a bubble of explanation rose into consciousness. He was looking, Will suddenly perceived, at a small square table, and beyond the table at a rocking chair, and beyond the rocking chair at a blank wall of whitewashed plaster. The explanation was reassuring for in the eternity that he had experienced between the opening of his eyes and the emergent knowledge of what he was looking at, the mystery confronting him had deepened from inexplicable beauty to a consummation of shining alienness that filled him, as he looked, with a kind of metaphysical terror. Well, this terrifying mystery consisted of nothing but two pieces of furniture and an expanse of wall. The fear was allayed, but the wonder only increased. How was it possible that things so familiar and commonplace could be *this?* Obviously it wasn't possible; and yet there it was, there it was.

His attention shifted from the geometrical constructions in brown agate to their pearly background. Its name, he knew, was "wall"; but in experienced fact it was a living process, a continuing series of transubstantiations from plaster and whitewash into the stuff of a supernatural body—into a god-flesh that kept modulating, as he looked at it, from glory to glory. Out of what the word bubbles had tried to explain away as mere calcimine some shaping spirit was evoking an endless succession of the most delicately discriminated hues, at once faint and intense, that emerged out of latency and went flushing across the god-body's divinely radiant skin. Wonderful, wonderful! And there must be other miracles, new worlds to conquer and be conquered by. He turned his head to the left and there (appropriate words had bubbled up almost immediately) was the large marble-topped table at which they had eaten their supper. And now, thick and fast, more bubbles began to rise. This breathing apocalypse called "table" might be thought of as a picture by some mystical Cubist, some inspired Juan Gris with the soul of Traherne and a gift for painting miracles with conscious gems and the changing moods of water-lily petals.

Turning his head a little further to the left he was startled by a blaze of jewelry. And what strange jewelry! Narrow slabs of emerald and topaz, of ruby and sapphire and lapis lazuli, blazing away, row above row, like so many bricks in a wall of the New Jerusalem. Then—at the end, not in the beginning—came the word, in the beginning were the jewels, the stained-glass windows, the walls of paradise. It was only now, at long last, that the word "bookcase" presented itself for consideration.

Will raised his eyes from the book-jewels and found himself at the heart of a tropical landscape. Why? Where? Then he remembered that, when (in another life) he first entered the room, he had noticed, over the bookcase, a large, bad water color. Between sand dunes and clumps of palms a widening estuary receding towards the open sea, and above the horizon enormous mountains of cloud towered into a pale sky. "Feeble," came bubbling up from the shallows. The work, only too obviously, of a not very gifted amateur. But that was now beside the point, for the landscape had ceased to be a painting and was now the subject of the painting—a real river, real sea, real sand glaring in the sunshine, real trees against a real sky. Real to the *n*th, real to the point of absoluteness. And this real river mingling with a real sea was his own being engulfed in God. " 'God' between quotation marks?" enquired an ironical bubble. "Or God (!) in a modernist, Pickwickian sense?" Will shook his head. The answer was just plain God—the God one couldn't possibly believe in, but who was self-evidently the fact confronting him. And yet this river was still a river, this sea the Indian Ocean. Not something else in fancy dress. Unequivocally themselves. But at the same time unequivocally God.

"Where are you now?" Susila asked.

Without turning his head in her direction, Will answered, "In heaven, I suppose," and pointed at the landscape.

"In heaven—*still*? When are you going to make a landing down here?"

Another bubble of memory came up from the silted shallows. " 'Something far more deeply interfused, Whose dwelling is the light'—of something or other."

"But Wordsworth also talked about the still sad music of humanity."

"Luckily," said Will, "there are no humans in this landscape."

"Not even any animals," she added, with a little laugh. "Only clouds and the most deceptively innocent-looking vegetables. That's why you'd better look at what's on the floor."

Will dropped his eyes. The grain on the floorboards was a brown river, and the brown river was an eddying, ongoing diagram of the world's divine life. At the center of that diagram was his own right foot, bare under the straps of its sandal, and startlingly three-dimensional, like the marble foot, revealed by a searchlight, of some heroic statue. "Boards," "grain," "foot"—through the glib explanatory words the mystery stared back at him, impenetrable and yet, paradoxically, understood. Understood with that knowledgeless understanding to which, in spite of sensed objects and remembered names, he was still open.

Suddenly, out of the tail of his eye, he caught a glimpse of quick, darting movement. Openness to bliss and understanding was also, he realized, an openness to terror, to total incomprehension. Like some alien creature lodged within his chest and struggling in anguish, his heart started to beat with a violence that made him tremble. In the hideous certainty that he was about to meet the Essential Horror, Will turned his head and looked.

"It's one of Tom Krishna's pet lizards," she said reassuringly.

The light was as bright as ever; but the brightness had changed its sign. A glow of sheer evil radiated from every gray-green scale of the creature's back, from its obsidian eyes and the pulsing of its crimson throat, from the armored edges of its nostrils and its slitlike mouth. He turned away. In vain. The Essential Horror glared out of everything he looked at. Those compositions by the mystical Cubist—they had turned into intricate machines for doing nothing malevolently. That tropical landscape, in which he had experienced the union of his own being with the being of God—it was now simultaneously the most nauseating of Victorian oleographs and the actuality of hell. On their shelves, the rows of book-jewels beamed with a thousand watts of darkness visible. And how cheap these gems of the abyss had become, how indescribably vulgar! Where there had been gold and pearl and precious stones there were only Christmas-tree decorations, only the shallow glare of plastic and varnished tin. Everything still pulsed with life, but with the life of an infinitely sinister bargain basement. And that, the music now affirmed, that was what Omnipotence was perpetually creating —a cosmic Woolworth stocked with mass-produced horrors. Horrors of vulgarity and horrors of pain, of cruelty and tastelessness, of imbecility and deliberate malice.

"Not a gecko," he heard Susila saying, "not one of our nice little house lizards. A hulking stranger from outdoors, one of the bloodsuckers. Not that they suck blood, of course. They merely have red throats and go purple in the face when they get excited. Hence that stupid name. Look! There he goes!"

Will looked down again. Preternaturally real, the scaly horror with its black blank eyes, its murderer's mouth, its blood-red throat pumping away while the rest of the body lay stretched along the floor as still as death, was now within six inches of his foot.

"He's seen his dinner," said Susila. "Look over there to your left, on the edge of the matting."

He turned his head.

"*Gongylus gongyloides,*" she went on. "Do you remember?"

Yes, he remembered. The praying mantis that had settled on his bed. But that was in another existence. What he had seen then was merely a rather odd-looking insect. What he saw now was a pair of inch-long monsters, exquisitely grisly, in the act of coupling. Their bluish pallor was barred and veined with pink, and the wings that fluttered continuously, like petals in a breeze, were shaded at the edges with deepening violet. A mimicry of flowers. But the insect forms were undisguisable. And now even the flowery colors had undergone a change. Those quivering wings were the appendages of two brightly enameled gadgets in the bargain basement, two little working models of a nightmare, two miniaturized machines for copulation. And now one of the nightmare machines, the female, had turned the small flat head, all mouth and bulging eyes, at the end of its long neck—had turned it and (dear God!) had begun to devour the head of the male machine. First a purple eye was chewed out, then half the bluish face. What was left of the head fell to the ground. Unrestrained by the weight of the eyes and jaws, the severed neck waved wildly. The female machine snapped at the oozing stump, caught it and, while the headless male uninterruptedly kept up his parody of Ares in the arms of Aphrodite, methodically chewed.

Out of the corner of his eye Will glimpsed another spurt of movement, turned his head sharply, and was in time to see the lizard crawling towards his foot. Nearer, nearer. He averted his eyes in terror. Something touched his toes and went tickling across his instep. The tickling ceased; but he could sense a little weight on his foot, a dry scaly contact. He wanted to scream; but his voice was gone and, when he tried to move, his muscles refused to obey him.

Timelessly the music had turned into the final Presto. Horror briskly on the march, horror in rococo fancy dress leading the dance.

Utterly still, except for the pulse in its red throat, the scaly horror on his instep lay staring with expressionless eyes at its predestined prey. Interlocked, the two little working models of a nightmare quivered like windblown petals and were shaken spasmodically by the simultaneous agonies of death and copulation. A timeless century passed; bar after bar, the gay little dance of death went on and on. Suddenly there was a scrabbling against his skin of tiny claws. The bloodsucker had crawled down from his instep to the floor. For a long life-span it lay there absolutely still. Then, with incredible speed, it darted across the boards and onto the matting. The slitlike mouth opened and closed again. Protruding from between the champing jaws, the edge of a violet-tinted wing still fluttered, like an orchid petal in the breeze; a pair of legs waved wildly for a moment, then disappeared from view.

Will shuddered and closed his eyes; but across the frontier between things sensed and things remembered, things imagined, the horror pursued him. In the fluorescent glare of the inner light an endless column of tin-bright insects and gleaming reptiles marched up diagonally, from left to right, out of some hidden source of nightmare towards an unknown and monstrous consummation. *Gongylus gongyloides* by millions and, in the midst of them, innumerable bloodsuckers. Eating and being eaten—forever.

And all the while—fiddle, flute and harpsichord—the final Presto of the Fourth Brandenburg kept trotting timelessly forward. What a jolly little rococo death march! Left, right; left, right . . . But what was the word of command for hexapods? And suddenly they weren't hexapods any longer; they were bipeds. The endless column of insects had turned abruptly into an endless column of soldiers. Marching as he had seen the Brown Shirts marching through Berlin, a year before the war. Thousands upon thousands of them, their banners fluttering, their uniforms glowing in the infernal brightness like floodlit excrement. Numberless as insects, and each of them moving with the precision of a machine, the perfect docility of a performing dog. And the faces, the faces! He had seen the close-ups on the German newsreel, and here they were again, preternaturally real and three-dimensional and alive. The monstrous face of Hitler with his mouth open, yelling. And then the faces of assorted listeners. Huge idiot faces, blankly receptive. Faces of wide-eyed sleepwalkers. Faces of young Nordic angels rapt in the Beatific Vision. Faces of baroque saints going into ecstasy. Faces of lovers on the brink of orgasm. One Folk, One Realm, One Leader. Union with the unity of an insect swarm. Knowledgeless understanding of nonsense and diabolism. And then the newsreel camera had cut back to the serried ranks, the swastikas, the brass bands, the yelling hypnotist on the rostrum. And here once again, in the glare of his inner light, was the brown insectlike column, marching endlessly to the tunes of this rococo horror music. Onward Nazi soldiers. Onward Marxists. Onward Christian soldiers, and Moslems. Onward every chosen people, every Crusader and Holy War maker. Onward into misery, into all wickedness, into death. And suddenly Will found himself looking at what the marching column would become when it had reached its destination—thousands of corpses in the Korean mud, innumerable packets of garbage littering the African desert. And here (for the scene kept changing with bewildering rapidity and suddenness), here were the five flyblown bodies he had seen only a few months ago, faces upwards and their throats gashed, in the courtyard of an Algerian farm. Here, out of a past almost twenty years earlier, was that old woman, dead and stark naked in the rubble of a stucco house in St. John's

Wood. And here, without transition, was his own gray and yellow bedroom, with the reflection in the mirror on the wardrobe door of two pale bodies, his and Babs's, frantically coupling to the accompaniment of his memories of Molly's funeral and the strains, from Radio Stuttgart, of the Good Friday music out of *Parsifal*.

The scene changed again and, festooned with tin stars and fairy lamps, Aunt Mary's face smiled at him gaily and then was transformed before his eyes into the face of the whining, malignant stranger who had taken her place during those last dreadful weeks before the final transformation into garbage. A radiance of love and goodness, and then a blind had been drawn, a shutter closed, a key turned in the lock, and there they were—she in her cemetery and he in his private prison sentenced to solitary confinement and, one unspecified fine morning, to death. The Agony in the Bargain Basement. The Crucifixion among the Christmas-tree decorations. Outside or in, with the eyes open or with the eyes closed, there was no escape.

"No escape," he whispered, and the words confirmed the fact, transformed it into a hideous certitude that kept opening out, opening down, into depth below depth of malignant vulgarity, hell beyond hell of utterly pointless suffering.

And this suffering (it came to him with the force of a revelation)—this suffering was not merely pointless; it was also cumulative, it was also self-perpetuating. Surely enough, frightfully enough, as it had come to Molly and Aunt Mary and all the others, death would come also to him. Would come to him, but never to this fear, this sickening disgust, these lacerations of remorse and self-loathing. Immortal in its pointlessness, suffering would go on forever. In all other respects one was grotesquely, despicably finite. Not in respect to suffering. This dark little inspissated clot that one called "I" was capable of suffering to infinity and, in spite of death, the suffering would go on forever. The pains of living and the pains of dying, the routine of successive agonies in the bargain basement and the final crucifixion in a blaze of tin and plastic vulgarity—reverberating, continuously amplified, they would always be there. And the pains were incommunicable, the isolation complete. The awareness that one existed was an awareness that one was always alone. Just as much alone in Babs's musky alcove as one had been alone with one's earache or one's broken arm, as one would be alone with one's final cancer, alone, when one thought it was all over, with the immortality of suffering.

He was aware, all of a sudden, that something was happening to the music. The tempo had changed. *Rallentando*. It was the end. The end of everything for everyone. The jaunty little death dance had piped the marchers on and on to the edge of the cliff. And now here it was, and they were tottering on the brink. *Rallentando, rallentando*. The dying fall, the fall into dying. And punctually, inevitably, here were the two anticipated chords, the consummation, the expectant dominant and then, *finis*, the loud unequivocal tonic. There was a scratching, a sharp click, and then silence. Through the open window he could hear the distant frogs and the shrill monotonous rasp of insect noises. And yet in some mysterious way the silence remained unbroken. Like flies in a block of amber, the sounds were embedded in a transparent soundlessness which they were powerless to destroy or even modify, and to which they remained completely irrelevant. Timelessly, from intensity to intensity, the silence deepened. Silence in ambush, a watching, conspiratorial silence incomparably more sinister than the grisly little rococo death march which had preceded it. This was the abyss to whose brink the music had piped him. To the brink, and now over the brink into this everlasting silence.

"Infinite suffering," he whispered. "And you can't speak, you can't even cry out."

A chair creaked, silk rustled, he felt the wind of movement against his face, the nearness of a human presence. Behind his closed lids he was somehow aware that Susila was kneeling there in front of him. An instant later he felt her hands touching his face—the palms against his cheeks, the fingers on his temples.

The clock in the kitchen made a little whirring noise, then started to strike the hour. One, two, three, four. Outside in the garden a gusty breeze whispered intermittently among the leaves. A cock crowed and a moment later, from a long way off, came an answering call, and almost simultaneously another and another. Then an answer to the answers, and more answers in return. A counterpoint of challenges challenged, of defiances defied. And now a different kind of voice joined in the chorus. Articulate but inhuman. "Attention," it called through the crowing and the insect noises. "Attention. Attention. Attention."

"Attention," Susila repeated; and as she spoke, he felt her fingers starting to move over his forehead. Lightly, lightly, from the brows up to the hair, from either temple to the midpoint between the eyes. Up and down, back and forth, soothing away the mind's contractions, smoothing out the furrows of bewilderment and pain. "Attention to *this*." And she increased the pressure of her palms against his cheekbones, of her fingertips above his ears. "To *this*," she repeated. "To *now*. Your face between my two hands." The pressure was relaxed, the fingers started to move again across his forehead.

"Attention." Through a ragged counterpoint of crowing, the injunction was insistently repeated. "Attention. Attention. Atten . . ." The inhuman voice broke off in midword.

Attention to her hands on his face? Or attention to this dreadful glare of the inner light, to this uprush of tin and plastic stars and, through the barrage of vulgarity, to this packet of garbage that had once been Molly, to the whorehouse looking glass, to all those countless corpses in the mud, the dust, the rubble. And here were the lizards again and *Gongylus gongyloides* by the million, here were the marching columns, the rapt, devoutly listening faces of Nordic angels.

"Attention," the mynah bird began to call again from the other side of the house. "Attention."

Will shook his head. "Attention to what?"

"To *this*." And she dug her nails into the skin of his forehead. "*This*. Here and now. And it isn't anything so romantic as suffering and pain. It's just the feel of fingernails. And even if it were much worse, it couldn't possibly be forever or to infinity. Nothing is forever, nothing is to infinity. Except, maybe, the Buddha Nature."

She moved her hands, and the contact now was no longer with nails but with skin. The fingertips slid down over his brows and, very lightly, came to rest on his closed eyelids. For the first wincing moment he was mortally afraid. Was she preparing to put out his eyes? He sat there, ready at her first move to throw back his head and jump to his feet. But nothing happened. Little by little his fears died away; the awareness of this intimate, unexpected, potentially dangerous contact remained. An awareness so acute and, because the eyes were supremely vulnerable, so absorbing that he had nothing to spare for the inner light or the horrors and vulgarities revealed by it.

"Pay attention," she whispered.

But it was impossible *not* to pay attention. However, gently and delicately, her fingers had probed to the very quick of his consciousness. And how intensely alive, he now noticed, those fingers were! What a strange tingling warmth flowed out of them!

"It's like an electric current," he marveled.

"But luckily," she said, "the wire carries no messages. One touches and, in the act of touching, one's touched. Complete communication, but nothing communicated. Just an exchange of life, that's all." Then, after a pause, "Do you realize, Will," she went on, "that in all these hours we've been sitting here—all these centuries in your case, all these eternities—you haven't looked at me once? Not once. Are you afraid of what you might see?"

He thought over the question and finally nodded his head. "Maybe that's what it was," he said. "Afraid of seeing something I'd have to be involved with, something I might have to do something about."

"So you stuck to Bach and landscapes and the Clear Light of the Void."

"Which you wouldn't let me go on looking at," he complained.

"Because the Void won't do you much good unless you can see its light in *Gongylus gongyloides. And* in people," she added. "Which is sometimes considerably more difficult."

"Difficult?" He thought of the marching columns, of the bodies in the mirror, of all those other bodies face downwards in the mud, and shook his head. "It's impossible."

"No, not impossible," she insisted. "*Sunyata* implies *karuna.* The Void is light; but it's also compassion. Greedy contemplatives want to possess themsleves of the light without bothering about compassion. Merely good people try to be compassionate and refuse to bother about the light. As usual, it's a question of making the best of both worlds. And now," she added, "it's time for you to open your eyes and see what a human being really looks like."

The fingertips moved up from his eyelids to his forehead, moved out to the temples, moved down to the cheeks, to the corners of the jaw. An instant later he felt their touch on his own fingers, and she was holding his two hands in hers.

Will opened his eyes and, for the first time since he had taken the *moksha*-medicine, found himself looking her squarely in the face.

"Dear God," he whispered at last.

Susila laughed. "Is it as bad as the bloodsucker?" she asked.

But this was not a joking matter. Will shook his head impatiently and went on looking. The eye sockets were mysterious with shadow and, except for a little crescent of illumination on the cheekbone, so was all the right side of her face. The left side glowed with a living, golden radiance—preternaturally bright, but with a brightness that was neither the vulgar and sinister glare of darkness visible nor yet that blissful incandescence revealed, in the far-off dawn of his eternity, behind his closed lids and, when he had opened his eyes, in the book-jewels, the compositions of the mystical Cubists, the transfigured landscape. What he was seeing now was the paradox of opposites indissolubly wedded, of light shining out of darkness, of darkness at the very heart of light.

"It isn't the sun," he said at last, "and it isn't Chartres. Nor the infernal bargain basement, thank God. It's all of them together, and you're recognizably you, and I'm recognizably me—though, needless to say, we're both completely different. You and me by Rembrandt, but Rembrandt about five thousand times more so." He was silent for a moment; then, nodding his head in confirmation of what he had just said, "Yes, that's it," he went on. "Sun into Chartres, and then stained-glass windows into bargain basement. And the bargain basement is also the torture chamber, the concentration camp, the charnel house with Christmas-tree decorations. And now the bargain basement goes into reverse, picks up Chartres and a slice of the sun, and backs out into this—into you and me by Rembrandt. Does that make any sense to you?"

"All the sense in the world," she assured him.

But Will was too busy looking at her to be able to pay much attention to what she was saying. "You're so incredibly beautiful," he said at last. "But it wouldn't matter if you were incredibly ugly; you'd still be a Rembrandt-but-five-thousand-times-more-so. Beautiful, beautiful," he repeated. "And yet I don't want to sleep with you. No, that isn't true. I would like to sleep with you. Very much indeed.

But it won't make any difference if I never do. I shall go on loving you—loving you in the way one's supposed to love people if one's a Christian. Love," he repeated, "*love*. It's another of those dirty words. 'In love,' 'make love'—those are all right. But plain 'love'—that's an obscenity I couldn't pronounce. But now, now . . ." He smiled and shook his head. "Believe it or not, now I can understand what it means when they say, 'God is love.' What manifest nonsense. And yet it happens to be true. Meanwhile there's this extraordinary face of yours." He leaned forward to look into it more closely. "As though one were looking into a crystal ball," he added incredulously. "Something new all the time. You can't imagine . . ."

But she *could* imagine. "Don't forget," she said, "I've been there myself."

"Did you look at people's faces?"

She nodded. "At my own in the glass. And of course at Dugald's. Goodness, that last time we took the *moksha*-medicine together! He started by looking like a hero out of some impossible mythology—of Indians in Iceland, of Vikings in Tibet. And then, without warning, he was Maitreya Buddha. Obviously, self-evidently Maitreya Buddha. Such a radiance! I can still see . . ."

She broke off, and suddenly Will found himself looking at Incarnate Bereavement with seven swords in her heart. Reading the signs of pain in the dark eyes, about the corners of the full-lipped mouth, he knew that the wound had been very nearly mortal and, with a pang in his own heart, that it was still open, still bleeding. He pressed her hands. There was nothing, of course, that one could say, no words, no consolations of philosophy—only this shared mystery of touch, only this communication from skin to skin of a flowing infinity.

"One slips back so easily," she said at last. "Much too easily. And much too often." She drew a deep breath and squared her shoulders.

Before his eyes the face, the whole body, underwent another change. There was strength enough, he could see, in that small frame to make head against any suffering; a will that would be more than a match for all the swords that fate might stab her with. Almost menacing in her determined serenity, a dark Circean goddess had taken the place of the Mater Dolorosa. Memories of that quiet voice talking so irresistibly about the swans and the cathedral, about the clouds and the smooth water, came rushing up. And as he remembered, the face before him seemed to glow with the consciousness of triumph. Power, intrinsic power—he saw the expression of it, he sensed its formidable presence and shrank away from it.

"Who *are* you?" he whispered.

She looked at him for a moment without speaking; then, gaily smiling, "Don't be so scared," she said. "I'm *not* the female mantis."

He smiled back at her—smiled back at a laughing girl with a weakness for kisses and the frankness to invite them.

"Thank the Lord!" he said, and the love which had shrunk away in fear came flowing back in a tide of happiness.

"Thank Him for what?"

"For having given you the grace of sensuality."

She smiled again. "So *that* cat's out of the bag."

"All that power," he said, "all that admirable, terrible will! You might have been Lucifer. But fortunately, providentially . . ." He disengaged his right hand and with the tip of its stretched forefinger touched her lips. "The blessed gift of sensuality—it's been your salvation. *Half* your salvation," he qualified, remembering the gruesomely loveless frenzies in the pink alcove, "*one* of your salvations. Because, of course, there's this other thing, this knowing who in fact you are." He was silent for a moment. "Mary with swords in her heart," he went on, "and Circe, and Ninon de Lenclos and now—who? Somebody like Juliana of Norwich or Catherine of Genoa. Are you really all these people?"

"Plus an idiot," she assured him. "Plus a rather worried and not very efficient mother. Plus a bit of the little prig and daydreamer I was as a child. Plus, potentially, the old dying woman who looked out at me from the mirror the last time we took the *moksha*-medicine together. And then Dugald looked and saw what *he* would be like in another forty years. Less than a month later," she added, "he was dead."

One slips back too easily, one slips back too often . . . Half in mysterious darkness, half mysteriously glowing with golden light, her face had turned once again into a mask of suffering. Within their shadowy orbits the eyes, he could see, were closed. She had retreated into another time and was alone, somewhere else, with the swords and her open wound. Outside, the cocks were crowing again, and a second mynah bird had begun to call, half a tone higher than the first, for compassion.

"*Karuna.*"

"Attention. Attention."

"*Karuna.*"

Will raised his hand once more and touched her lips. "Do you hear what they're saying?"

It was a long time before she answered. Then, raising her hand, she took hold of his extended finger and pressed it hard against her lower lip. "Thank you," she said, and opened her eyes again.

"Why thank me? *You* taught me what to do."

"And now it's you who have to teach your teacher."

Like a pair of rival gurus each touting his own brand of spirituality, "*Karuna,* attention," shouted the mynah birds; then, as they drowned out one another's wisdom in overlapping competition, "Runattenshkarattunshon." Proclaiming that he was the never-impotent owner of all females, the invincible challenger of every spurious pretender to maleness, a cockerel in the next garden shrilly announced his divinity.

A smile broke through the mask of suffering; from her private world of swords and memory, Susila had returned to the present. "Cock-a-doodle-doo," she said. "How I love him! Just like Tom Krishna when he goes around asking people to feel his muscles. And those preposterous mynah birds, so faithfully repeating the good advice they can't understand. They're just as adorable as my little bantam."

"And what about the other kind of biped?" he asked. "The less adorable variety."

For all answer she leaned forward, caught him by the forelock and, pulling his head down, kissed him on the tip of his nose. "And now it's time you moved your legs," she said. Climbing to her feet, she held out her hand to him. He took it and she pulled him up from his chair.

"Negative crowing and parroted antiwisdom," she said. "That's what some of the other kind of bipeds go in for."

"What's to guarantee that I shan't return to my vomit?" he asked.

"You probably will," she cheerfully assured him. "But you'll also probably come back again to this."

There was a spurt of movement at their feet.

Will laughed. "There goes my poor little scrabbling incarnation of evil."

She took his arm, and together they walked over to the open window. Announcing the near approach of dawn, a little wind fitfully rattled the palm fronds. Below them, rooted invisibly in the moist, acrid-smelling earth, was a hibiscus bush—a wild profusion of bright glossy leaves and vermilion trumpets, evoked from the double darkness of night and overarching trees by a shaft of lamplight from within the room.

"It isn't possible," he said incredulously. He was back again with God-the-Fourteenth-of-July.

"It isn't possible," she agreed. "But like everything else in the universe, it happens to be a fact. And now that you've finally recognized my existence, I'll give you leave to look to your heart's content."

He stood there motionless, gazing, gazing through a timeless succession of mounting intensities and ever-profounder significances. Tears filled his eyes and overflowed at last onto his cheeks. He pulled out his handkerchief and wiped them away.

"I can't help it," he apologized.

He couldn't help it because there was no other way in which he could express his thankfulness. Thankfulness for the privilege of being alive and a witness to this miracle, of being, indeed, more than a witness—a partner in it, an aspect of it. Thankfulness for these gifts of luminous bliss and knowledgeless understanding. Thankfulness for being at once this union with the divine unity and yet this finite creature among other finite creatures.

"Why should one cry when one's grateful?" he said as he put his handkerchief away. "Goodness knows. But one does." A memory bubble popped up from the sludge of past reading. "'Gratitude is heaven itself,'" he quoted. "Pure gibberish! But now I see that Blake was just recording a simple fact. It is heaven itself."

"And all the more heavenly," she said, "for being heaven on earth and not heaven in heaven."

Startlingly, through the crowing and the croaking, through the insect noises and the duet of the rival gurus, came the sound of distant musketry.

"What on earth is that?" she wondered.

"Just the boys playing with fireworks," he answered gaily.

Susila shook her head. "We don't encourage those kinds of fireworks. We don't even possess them."

From the highway beyond the walls of the compound a roar of heavy vehicles climbing in low gear swelled up louder and louder. Over the noise, a voice at once stentorian and squeaky bellowed incomprehensibly through a loudspeaker.

In their setting of velvet shadow the leaves were like thin shavings of jade and emerald, and from the heart of their gem-bright chaos fantastically sculptured rubies flared out into five-pointed stars. Gratitude, gratitude. His eyes filled again with tears.

Snatches of the shrill bellowing resolved themselves into recognizable words. Against his will, he found himself listening.

"People of Pala," he heard; then the voice blasted into amplified inarticulateness. Squeak, roar, squeak, and then, "Your Raja speaking . . . remain calm . . . welcome your friends from across the Strait . . ."

Recognition dawned. "It's Murugan."

"And he's with Dipa's soldiers."

"Progress," the uncertain excited voice was saying. "Modern life . . ." And then, moving on from Sears, Roebuck to the Rani and Koot Hoomi, "Truth," it squeaked, "values . . . genuine spirituality . . . oil."

"Look," said Susila, "look! They're turning into the compound."

Visible in a gap between two clumps of bamboos, the beams of a procession of headlamps shone for a moment on the left cheek of the great stone Buddha by the lotus pool and passed by, hinted again at the blessed possibility of liberation and again passed by.

"The throne of my father," bawled the gigantically amplified squeak, "joined to the throne of my mother's ancestors . . . Two sister nations marching forward, hand in hand, into the future . . . To be known henceforth as the United Kingdom of Rendang and Pala . . . The United Kingdom's first prime minister, that great political and spiritual leader, Colonel Dipa . . ."

The procession of headlamps disappeared behind a long range of buildings and the shrill bellowing died down into incoherence. Then the lights re-emerged and once again the voice became articulate.

"Reactionaries," it was furiously yelling. "Traitors to the principles of the permanent revolution . . ."

In a tone of horror, "They're stopping at Dr. Robert's bungalow," Susila whispered.

The voice had said its last word, the headlamps and the roaring motors had been turned off. In the dark expectant silence the frogs and the insects kept up their mindless soliloquies, the mynah birds reiterated their good advice. "Attention, *Karuna*." Will looked down at his burning bush and saw the Suchness of the world and his own being blazing away with the clear light that was also (how obviously now!) compassion—the clear light that, like everyone else, he had always chosen to be blind to, the compassion to which he had always preferred his tortures, endured or inflicted, in a bargain basement, his squalid solitudes, with the living Babs or the dying Molly in the foreground, with Joe Aldehyde in the middle distance and, in the remoter background, the great world of impersonal forces and proliferating numbers, of collective paranoias, and organized diabolism. And always, everywhere, there would be the yelling or quietly authoritative hypnotists; and in the train of the ruling suggestion givers, always and everywhere, the tribes of buffoons and hucksters, the professional liars, the purveyors of entertaining irrelevances. Conditioned from the cradle, unceasingly distracted, mesmerized systematically, their uniformed victims would go on obediently marching and countermarching, go on, always and everywhere, killing and dying with the perfect docility of trained poodles. And yet in spite of the entirely justified refusal to take yes for an answer, the fact remained and would remain always, remain everywhere—the fact that there was this capacity even in a paranoiac for intelligence, even in a devil worshiper for love; the fact that the ground of all being could be totally manifest in a flowering shrub, a human face; the fact that there was a light and that this light was also compassion.

There was the sound of a single shot; then a burst of shots from an automatic rifle.

Susila covered her face with her hands. She was trembling uncontrollably.

He put an arm round her shoulders and held her close.

The work of a hundred years destroyed in a single night. And yet the fact remained—the fact of the ending of sorrow as well as the fact of sorrow.

The starters screeched; engine after engine roared into action. The headlamps were turned on and, after a minute of noisy maneuvering, the cars started to move slowly back along the road by which they had come.

The loudspeaker brayed out the opening bars of a martial and at the same time lascivious hymn tune, which Will recognized as the national anthem of Rendang. Then the Wurlitzer was switched off, and here once again was Murugan.

"This is your Raja speaking," the excited voice proclaimed. After which, *da capo*, there was a repetition of the speech about Progress, Values, Oil, True Spirituality. Abruptly, as before, the procession disappeared from sight and hearing. A minute later it was in view again, with its wobbly countertenor bellowing the praises of the newly united kingdom's first prime minister.

The procession crawled on and now, from the right this time, the headlamps of the first armored car lit up the serenely smiling face of enlightenment. For an instant only, and then the beam moved on. And here was the Tathagata for the second time, the third, the fourth, the fifth. The last of the cars passed by. Disregarded in the darkness, the fact of enlightenment remained. The roaring of the engines diminished, the squeaking rhetoric lapsed into an inarticulate murmur, and as the intruding noises died away, out came the frogs again, out came the uninterruptable insects, out came the mynah birds.

"Karuna. Karuna." And a semitone lower, "Attention."

ABOUT THE AUTHOR

The longer fiction of ALDOUS HUXLEY has been in the mainstream of the "Novel of Ideas" since the publication in England in 1921 (America 1922) of *Crome Yellow,* his first novel. Huxley is one of the most skillful and most successful social satirists of the twentieth century. His novels go far in defining the character of modern man, while his later work reflects an interest in mysticism and the effect of the consciousness-expanding drugs.

Born in England in 1894, Mr. Huxley took to writing when his eyesight temporarily failed. From 1934 until his death in 1963, Aldous Huxley lived in California.